JANET TRONSTAD

An Angel for Dry Creek

A Gentleman for Dry Creek

Steeple
Hill®

Published by Steeple Hill Books™

STEEPLE HILL BOOKS

Steeple
Hill®

ISBN-13: 978-0-373-65273-0
ISBN-10:   0-373-65273-9

AN ANGEL FOR DRY CREEK AND
A GENTLEMAN FOR DRY CREEK

AN ANGEL FOR DRY CREEK
Copyright © 1999 by Janet Tronstad

A GENTLEMAN FOR DRY CREEK
Copyright © 2000 by Janet Tronstad

www.SteepleHill.com

Printed in U.S.A.

Prologue
December 1992

Today millions of fans across the world celebrate the thirty-fifth birthday of cult superstar Nick Angel, and the opening of his latest movie, Killer Blue.

A statement issued by Panther Studios disclosed that Nick will not be present at the Los Angeles premiere of Killer Blue *as expected.*

A spokesperson for Angel reported that the actor will spend his birthday in New York.

U.S.A. Today
December 1992

NEW YORK, DECEMBER 15, 1992

Mornings were always a bad time for Nick Angel. He lay in bed, eyes closed, unwilling to surrender the peaceful darkness, fighting the fact that he had to get up and face another day. Especially this day. His birthday.

Thirty-five.

Nick Angel was thirty-five.

Jesus! The newspapers would have an orgasmic overdose on this one. He was no longer the boy wonder. Age was creeping up on him.

He lay very still. It was probably past noon, but the longer he delayed getting up the better, for he knew that once he stirred they'd be all over him. Honey—his live-in girlfriend. Harlan—his so-called valet. And Teresa—his faithful karate-champion assistant.

He heard a sudden movement in the room. A subtle rustle of silk and the faint aroma of White Diamonds—

Honey was a big Liz Taylor fan. In fact Honey was a fan, period.

So . . . why was he with her?

Good question. The problem was there were too many questions in his life and not enough answers.

Honey was on the prowl. Pretty blond Honey with the lethal body and vacant mind. He sensed her standing by the bed staring down at him, willing him to wake up.

Too bad, sweetheart. Get lost. Not in the mood.

As soon as he was sure she'd left, he quickly rolled out of bed and made it to the safety of his steel and glass high-tech bathroom, locking the door behind him.

Ah . . . Nick Angel in the morning. Not the man he once was, although still handsome in spite of ten pounds of excess flesh, bloodshot eyes and an altogether dissipated demeanor.

He hated the way he looked. The extra weight he'd put on disgusted him. He had to stop drinking. Had to get his life together.

Nick Angel. Longish black hair. Indian green eyes. Pale skin, stubbled chin. At five feet ten inches he was tall without being overpowering. His handsomeness was not perfect. More brooding . . . mesmerizing. And in spite of being bloodshot his green eyes were hypnotic and watchful. His nose, once broken, gave him the dangerous edge he needed.

And now he was thirty-five.

Old.

Older than he'd ever thought he'd be.

But the world still loved him. His fans would continue to worship because he was Nick Angel and he belonged to them. They'd elevated him to a rare and crazy place where nobody could expect to remain sane.

It's too much, he thought bitterly, splashing cold water on his face. *The adulation, the never-ending attention. Crushing . . . stifling . . . suffocating . . . Too fucking much.*

He smiled grimly.

Welcome to the insane asylum.

Welcome to my life.

4

CONTENTS

Books by Janet Tronstad

Love Inspired

*An Angel for Dry Creek #81
*A Gentleman for Dry Creek #110
*A Bride for Dry Creek #138
*A Rich Man for Dry Creek #176
*A Hero for Dry Creek #228
*A Baby for Dry Creek #240
*A Dry Creek Christmas #276
*Sugar Plums for Dry Creek #329
*At Home in Dry Creek #371

*Dry Creek

JANET TRONSTAD

grew up on a small farm in central Montana.
One of her favorite things to do was to visit her grandfather's bookshelves, where he had a large collection
of Zane Grey novels. Janet's always loved a good
story. Today, Janet lives in Pasadena, California,
where she is a full-time writer.

AN ANGEL FOR DRY CREEK

Be not forgetful to entertain strangers; for thereby
some have entertained angels unawares.

—*Hebrews* 13:2

This book is dedicated with love to my parents,
Richard and Fern Tronstad.
First they gave me roots and
then they gave me wings.
Who could ask for more?

Chapter One

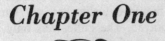

Glory Beckett peered out her car window. She'd driven all day and now, with the coming of dusk, snowflakes were beginning to swirl around her Jeep. The highway beneath her was only a faint gray line pointing northeast across the flatlands of Montana. Other than the hills and a few isolated ranches, there had been little to see in miles. Even oncoming traffic was sparse. For the first time in three days she questioned her hasty decision to leave Seattle and drive across country.

She must be a sight. For ease, she'd given up on curls and simply pushed her flaming auburn hair under a beige wool cap her mother had knitted one Christmas long ago. Her lips were shiny with lip balm and she'd forgotten most of her makeup in Seattle. She considered herself lucky to have remembered her toothbrush. She hadn't had time even to pray about the trip before the decision was made and she was on the road. She'd let the captain scare her for nothing. He'd been a cop too long. Just because a stray bullet had whizzed by her last Wednesday, it was no reason to panic and leave town.

Ever since he'd married her mother last month his worrying had grown worse. She'd reminded him she'd picked up a lot of street savvy in the six years she'd been a sketch artist for his department, but it didn't help.

And maybe he was right. She could still feel the stress that hummed inside her, not letting up even when she prayed. The bullet was only part of it. It was the shooting she'd witnessed that was the worst of it. Even though she'd seen this crime with her own eyes instead of the eyes of others, it still rocked her more than it should. Crimes happened. She knew that. Sometimes she spent a long time in prayer, asking God why something happened. God had always given her peace before.

But prayer hadn't been able to calm her this time. Her nerves still shivered. She didn't feel God was distant. No, that wasn't it. He comforted her, but He didn't remove the unease. Not this time. Since Idaho she'd been thinking maybe stress wasn't all there was to it. Her nerves didn't just shudder, they itched. Something was pushing at her consciousness. Something that she should remember, but couldn't. Something to do with what she'd seen that afternoon at Benson's Market when the butcher, Mr. Kraeman, had been killed. *Dear God, what am I overlooking?* The kid who had shot Mr. Kraeman had been arrested and taken to the county jail. The investigation was closed, awaiting nothing more than the trial. The killer had been caught at the scene. She should relax.

Maybe this cross-country trip would help. She'd always wanted to just take off and drive across the top of the United States. Idaho. Montana. North Dakota. Minnesota. Right to the Great Lakes. And now that her mother had married the captain, there was nothing holding her back. It was odd, this feeling of rootlessness.

In a small town farther east on Interstate 94, the bare branch of an oak tree rested lightly against an upstairs window. Standing inside and looking out through the window, a man could see the soft glow from the security light reflected on the snow in the crevices of the old tree. The snow sparkled like silver dust on an angel's wing.

The midnight view out this second-story window was appreciated by his young sons, but Matthew Curtis didn't get past the glass. All he saw was a window without curtains and his own guilt. If Susie were still alive, she'd have curtains on all the windows. If only Susie were alive, the Bible verses the twins memorized for Sunday school would have some meaning in his life. If only Susie were still alive, everything would be different. If only… Matthew stopped himself. He couldn't keep living in the past.

"Is so angels," Josh was saying as Matthew helped him put his arm into the correct pajama opening. Tucking his five-year-old twin sons into bed was the best part of the day for Matthew. "Miz Hargrove said so. An' they got a big light all round 'em." Josh was fascinated with lights.

Mrs. Hargrove, the twins' Sunday school teacher, was the closest thing to a mother the two had these days. She was one of the reasons Matthew had put aside his own bitterness and rented the old parsonage next to the church when they'd moved to Dry Creek,

Montana, six months ago. He wanted the twins to be able to go to church even if he didn't. In Matthew's opinion, a man who wasn't talking to God during the week had no business pretending to shake His hand on Sunday morning just to keep the neighbors quiet.

"I'm sure Mrs. Hargrove is thinking of the angel Gabriel," Matthew said as he smoothed down Josh's hair. Josh, the restless one, was in Power Rangers pajamas. Joey, the more thoughtful twin, was in Mickey Mouse pajamas even though he didn't really like them that much. Joey wasn't enthused about anything, and Matthew worried about him. "And that angel definitely exists."

"See," Josh said to no one in particular. "And my angel can have ten wings if I want and a Power Ranger gun to zap people."

"Angels don't carry guns," Matthew said as he scooped the twins into bed and tucked the quilt securely around them. The weatherman on the news had predicted a mid-December blizzard. "They bring peace."

"Peace," Josh said. "What's peace?"

"Quiet," Matthew said as he turned down the lamp between the twins' beds. "Peace and quiet." And a reminder. "No guns. Angels don't like guns."

Matthew kissed both twins and turned to leave.

"I want to see my angel," Joey whispered. The longing in his voice stopped Matthew. "When can I see her?"

Matthew turned around and sat down on the edge of one of the beds again. "Angels are in heaven. That's a long way away. Most of the time it's too far—they can't come down and see people. They just stay in heaven."

"Like Mommy," Joey said.

"Something like that, I guess." Matthew swallowed.

"Miz Hargrove said that when God took our mommy, He gave us a guardian angel to watch over us," Josh explained.

"I'm here to watch over you." Matthew pulled the covers off his sons and gathered them both to him in a hug. He blinked away the tears in his eyes so his sons would not see them. "You've got me—you don't need an angel."

"We got one anyway," Josh said matter-of-factly, his voice muffled against Matthew's shoulder. "Miz Hargrove says."

The night road was sprinkled with square green exit signs marking rural communities. Glory had pulled off at a rest stop close to Rosebud and slept for a few solitary hours, curled up in the back seat of her Jeep. Finally, around four in the morning, she decided to keep driving. It was quiet at that time of night even when she came into Miles City, where over 8,000 souls lived. Once she left Miles City behind, the only lights Glory saw were her own, reflected in the light snow on the ground. If all of this darkness didn't cure her stress, nothing would.

Glory needed this time to think. The shooting at the grocery store, and the long minutes afterward when she waited for the paramedics to arrive, reminded her of the accident that had changed her own life six years ago. Gradually, sitting there in the grocery store, all of the old feelings had surfaced. The terror, the paralyzing grief and the long-lasting guilt. Her dreams had stopped the night of the car accident that took her father's life. That night Glory stopped being a carefree college graduate and became a tired adult. She'd awakened in the hospital bed knowing her life was forever changed. Her father was dead. Her mother was shattered. And the words inside Glory's head kept repeating the accusation that it was all her fault. She'd had the wheel. She should have seen the driver coming. It didn't matter that the other driver was drunk and had run a red light. She, Glory, should have known. Somehow she should have known.

There was nothing to do. Nothing to bring her father back.

She tried to put her own pain aside and comfort her mother. Her mother had always seemed like the fragile one in the family. Glory vowed she would take care of her mother. She would do it even if it meant giving up her own dream.

Glory didn't hesitate. Her dream of being a real artist wasn't as important as her mother's happiness. She took the job as a police sketch artist and packed away her oils. Right out of art school, Glory had wanted to see if she could make it in the art world, but the accident had changed all of that. Dreams didn't pay the bills. She'd be willing to live on sandwiches while she painted, but she couldn't ask her mother to do that with her.

But now, seeing her mother happy again, Glory could start to breathe. She no longer felt so responsible. The captain would take care of her mother. Maybe, Glory thought, she could even dream again. She'd always wanted to paint faces. All she needed to do was give her notice to the police department and take out her easel full-time. She had enough in savings to last awhile. When she put it that way, it sounded so simple.

The more miles that sped beneath the wheels of Glory's Jeep, the lighter her heart felt. Maybe God was calling her to paint the faces of His people. Faces of faith. Faces of despair. All of the faces that showed man's struggle to know God. She needed to rekindle her dream. For years she'd been—

"Dry..." Glory murmured out loud as she peered into the snow at the small sign along the interstate. Even with the powerful lights of her Jeep she could barely read it. "Dry as in 'Dry Creek, Montana. Population 276. Five Miles to Food and Gas.'"

Glory turned her Jeep to the left. A throbbing headache was starting between her eyes, and her thermos of coffee had run out an hour ago. It was five-thirty in the morning and she wasn't going to count on there being another town along this highway anytime soon. There was bound to be a little café that served the ranchers in the area. She didn't have much cash left, but her MasterCard had given her a healthy advance back in Spokane and it would no doubt be welcomed here, too. She'd learned that roadside coffee was usually black and strong—just the way she liked it.

Matthew woke with the dawn and went to check on the twins. Ever since Susie had died, he'd been aware of how easy it was for someone to simply stop living. He couldn't bear to lose one of his sons. So he stood in his slippers and just looked at them sleeping in their beds. The security light from the outside of the old frame house shone through the half-frosted window and gave a muted glow to the upstairs bedroom. He pulled the blankets back up on Joey. The electric heater he'd put in the twins' bedroom kept the winter chill away. But the rest of the house was heated with a big woodstove, and he needed to light it so the kitchen would be warm when the twins came down for breakfast.

There were no windows in the hall and the dawn's light didn't come into the stairway that led down to the living room. He took one sleepy step down the stairway. Then another. He needed to add a light for the stairway. Just one more thing in the old house that needed fixing. Like the— Matthew stepped on the loose stair at the same time as he remembered it. The board's edge cracked and his foot slipped. All he could think of as he tumbled down the stairs was that the twins would have no one to fix their breakfast.

Matthew clenched his teeth and fought back the wave of black that threatened to engulf him. Thank God he was alive. "Josh, Joey," Matthew called in a loud whisper. The pain the words cost him suggested he'd broken a rib. That and maybe his leg. "Boys—"

He didn't need to call. They must have heard his fall, because almost immediately two blond heads were staring at him. "Go next door." Matthew said the words deliberately, although his tongue felt swollen. Pain continued to swim around his head. "Get help."

Glory left her Jeep lights on so she could see to make her way to the door of the house next to the church. She had stopped at the café long enough to see that the Closed sign had fly specks on it. It didn't look as if a meal had been served there in months. By then she needed some aspirin for her headache almost more than she needed her morning coffee. When she saw the lights on inside the house that must be the parsonage, she was relieved.

Matthew relaxed when he heard the knock at the door. The twins must have already gone for help. Maybe he'd blacked out. That must be it. Someone had turned the lights on.

Glory heard a rustling behind the door and then she saw it open slowly. She had to look down to see the small blond head, covered by the hood of a snowsuit, peek around the edge of the door. The boy must be going out to play before breakfast. "Is your father here?" she asked as she pulled off her cap. "Or your mother?"

"Who are you?" Another blond head joined the first one. This one had a scarf tied around his neck, even though his Mickey Mouse pajamas didn't look warm enough for outdoor playing.

"My name's Glory. But you don't know me." And then remembering all the warnings children received about strangers, she added, "Don't worry, though. And don't be afraid."

"Don't be afraid." The boy in the snowsuit echoed her words slowly. Glory watched his eyes grow big. "Where are you from?"

Glory decided they didn't get much company around here. They'd probably never heard of Seattle. She pointed west. "A long way away—over those mountains."

"Do you like guns?" the boy in the pajamas demanded.

"Guns? No, I don't approve of guns. Not at all."

"And she's got a big light behind her," the other

boy said. "Just like Miz Hargrove said. A glory
light."

"Those are my Jeep headlights. Special high
beam," Glory explained. "They'll turn off in a minute. If I could just see your father. All I want is an
aspirin and maybe a little peace and quiet...and
then—"

"Peace and quiet." The twins breathed the words
out together as their faces started to beam. "She
came."

"Boys," Matthew called weakly. Who were they
talking to? He couldn't make out the words, but
surely it didn't take that long for someone to figure
out he needed help.

"We need you," the twins said as they opened the
door wide and each reached out a hand. Glory noticed
they were both in slippers. "Our daddy's hurt."

Matthew decided he'd blacked out again, because
a woman's face was staring at him. She had hair the
color of copper, and it fanned out around her face like
a halo. He'd never seen her before. Maybe he was
hallucinating, especially because of that sprinkling of
freckles that danced across her nose. No one could
have freckles like that. So pretty. He tried to concentrate, but felt the darkness closing in on him. He wondered what the perfume was that she wore. It smelled
like cinnamon. Cinnamon and something else. That
reminded him he hadn't fixed breakfast for the twins.
And his job at the hardware store—old Henry would
be fretting mad if he called in from his vacation in
Florida and no one answered the phone at the hardware store.

Glory looked down at the man in dismay. She

could see he'd fallen down the stairs and his leg was at an awkward angle.

"Where's your phone? We've got to call 911," she said as she turned around to the twins. "We'll need an ambulance right away."

The boys just looked at her expectantly. The one had already taken off his scarf and the other was half-way out of his snowsuit. "Can't you just make daddy all better?" one of them finally asked.

"I'm not a doctor," she said quickly as her eyes scanned the living room. Old sofa, wooden rocker, plaid recliner, Christmas tree with lights but no or-naments—ah, there, on the coffee table, next to a magazine, was a phone. She dialed the numbers: 911. Nothing. Glory shook the phone. She must have di-aled wrong. She tried again: 911. Still nothing. What was the matter? There was a dial tone. Surely—then it dawned on her. There was no 911 here. Probably no ambulance, either.

"Who's your nearest neighbor?" Glory put down the phone and turned to the boys. She could already feel her hair flying loose as a result of the static from taking off her cap earlier.

"Mr. Gossett," the boy in the Power Rangers pa-jamas finally said, but then he leaned closer and con-fided, "But you won't like him. He drinks bottles and bottles of whiskey. I seen them. Miz Hargrove says he's gonna go to hell someday."

"Well, just as long as he isn't planning to go to-day," Glory said as she pulled her knit cap over her head and walked toward the door.

The next time Matthew woke up he was in the clinic in Miles City. He'd recognize the antiseptic smell of a clinic anywhere. And the gruff voice of Dr. Norris in the background.

"My boys." Matthew croaked out the words. His mouth felt as if it was filled with dry sand.

"Don't worry, your boys are fine," Dr. Norris said as he turned around. "At least for the moment."

"What?"

"Your angel is unloading the vending machine downstairs on their behalf," the doctor said with a smile as he leaned over Matthew. He picked up a small light. "Open wide. We need to check for concussions." The doctor peered into Matthew's eyes.

"What angel?" Matthew asked, and then brightened. "Oh, you mean Mrs. Hargrove. I was hoping someone would think to call her."

"That's not Mrs. Hargrove," the doctor said as he frowned slightly. "At least, not the Mrs. Hargrove I know. I assumed Angel was a family nickname."

"For who?" Matthew asked, bewildered.

"I meant I assumed you called the woman Angel and that's why your sons..." The doctor's voice trailed off and then he added suspiciously, "It's not like a five-year-old to call a woman Angel."

"What are you suggesting?" Matthew started to rise. The room tilted, but he bit his lip and kept going. "And why you would let my boys just go off with a stranger—"

"Don't worry." The doctor put his arm around him and forced him to lie down again. "I'll have the nurse go bring them here. I'm sure it's just some simple misunderstanding. The woman certainly looked harmless enough."

Harmless isn't how Matthew would have described her a few minutes later. She was too pretty to be harmless. Her copper hair was still fanning around her face. This time he saw her gray eyes more clearly. They looked like a stormy afternoon in summer when the blues and grays swirled together without quite mixing. And his sons were looking at her as if they were starstruck. "What are you doing with my boys?"

"What am I doing?" Glory said, dumbfounded. Whatever happened to thank you? Thank you for getting that grumpy Mr. Gossett up in the early-morning hours so he could get help from Mr. Daniel, who ran the volunteer fire department's medical transportation unit. Thank you for writing a fifty-dollar check so the volunteer department would respond to your request, since you were new in town and not on the "paid" list. Thank you for following along in the Jeep the forty miles into Miles City just so the twins could be with you.

"What am I doing?" she repeated, trying to keep her voice calm. "You mean when I'm not emptying my last quarters into the machine out there so that Josh can get a package with only yellow M&M's in it?"

"They don't make them with only yellows," Matthew said. She reminded him of fire. The way her hair shone in the fluorescent light.

"I know," the woman said wearily.

"You asked me what I wanted," Josh said simply. "I thought it'd be easy for you, since you're—"

Glory held up her hand to stop him.

Matthew watched as Josh closed his mouth. The woman had more powers than he did, Matthew thought to himself ruefully. He could never get Josh to close his mouth when he wanted to speak.

"That might be the wrong way to say it," Matthew said, easing back to the bed. He needed to clear his mind. "I'm grateful for all you've done, of course."

"You're welcome," Glory said politely. She needed to remember the man was disoriented. Disoriented and not nearly so naked now that the doctor had wrapped a wide white bandage around his rib cage. She wondered if he remembered that she'd been the one to gently run her fingertips over his chest to check for broken ribs before she put a blanket over him and they waited for the fire department to come. His chest was the kind that would inspire her if she were a sculptor.

"It's just—" Matthew bit his lips. "I don't know who you are. And with all the strange people around lately…"

"She's not strange people," Josh protested. "She's—"

"I'm Glory." Glory interrupted the boy and gave him a stern look. "Glory Beckett."

"She's an angel," Joey said, his eyes sparkling with excitement.

"And she's got a glory light," Josh added. The boy literally glowed with pleasure.

Glory bowed her head. She'd been through this explanation already. Four times. And that was before the requested M&M's miracle. "I've got special beams on my Jeep. That's all it is. No angel magic." She turned to look at the man in the bed. Now he'd really be worried. "I'm sorry, this isn't my idea."

"I know." Matthew smiled, and then he started to chuckle until he felt the pain in his ribs. "But you haven't tried to argue with the logic of our Mrs.—"

"Your Mrs.?" Glory interrupted stiffly. She should

have known there would be a Mrs. somewhere in this picture. "If I'd known you were married, I'd have tried to locate your wife. But the twins didn't mention—"

"Married? Me? No, I meant our Mrs. Hargrove," Matthew echoed, his smile curling around inside himself. He liked the way her lips tightened up when she talked about him being married. "Mrs. Hargrove isn't married. I mean—" he fumbled "—of course, Mrs. Hargrove *is* married, but not to me. I'm not, that is. Married."

"I see," Glory said, and drew in her breath. "Well, that explains the boys. A single father and all."

"Oh," Matthew said ruefully. The woman hadn't been thinking of his being married at all. At least, not in those terms. "Is there something wrong with the boys?"

"Of course not," Glory protested. "They're wonderful boys." She'd already grown to like them. "They're bright—and warmhearted." She stopped. Sometimes, looking at children, she'd feel the pain again from the accident that had robbed her of the chance to be a mother. She was determined to fight that pain. She refused to be one of those sentimental women who either wept or gushed over every child they saw. She cooled her enthusiasm. "And they have good bone structure."

Glory patted the twins on the head. She was safe with bone structure.

Josh scowled a minute, before Joey poked him with his elbow.

"Is that something angels have?" Joey asked hopefully. "That good bone stuff?"

"No, I'm afraid not," Glory said as she knelt so

that she was at eye level with the boys. "Angels aren't worried about bone structure. I don't even know if God created them with bones. Although I suppose with those big wings and all they'd have to have something like bones...."

"See, I told you," Josh began. "She knows—"

Glory held up her hand. "The only thing I know about angels is what I've read in the Bible. I wouldn't know an angel if I met one on the street."

"You wouldn't?" Joey asked sadly.

"Not a chance," Glory assured him. She started to reach out to ruffle his hair again, but then pulled back. Maybe little boys didn't like that any more than she'd liked it as a little girl. "But you don't need an angel. You've got a father—" She eyed Matthew a little skeptically and then continued determinedly, "A good father—and you've got Mrs. Hargrove, and each other."

"We don't have a dog," Josh said plaintively.

"Well, maybe someday you can get a dog," Glory said. She was handling this pretty well, she thought. "Wouldn't you rather have a puppy than an angel?"

Glory didn't look at Matthew. She knew she had no right to even suggest he get the boys a puppy. But it seemed like a small thing. And they really were very nice little boys. Josh was already starting to beam.

"Can it be a yellow dog?" Josh asked, looking at Glory as if she had a dozen in her purse. "I'd like a yellow dog."

"Well, I don't know if today is the day," Glory stalled.

"I don't want a puppy." Joey shook his head and

looked at Josh. "A puppy hasn't been in heaven. He can't tell us what our mommy looks like."

Joey looked expectantly at his father. "Mommy used to sing to us and make us cookies."

"Oatmeal with extra raisins," Matthew assured him. The trust in his son's eyes made him forget all about his cracked rib and his sprained knee. If he had been wearing more than this flimsy hospital robe, he would have walked over to them and hugged them no matter how his ribs felt. "And she loved you both very much."

"I don't even care about the cookies," Joey said bravely. "I just want to know what she looked like."

"Well, surely you have pictures." Glory turned to look at Matthew.

"There was a fire," Matthew said. The fire had burned down the first house they'd lived in after they moved away from Havre. At the time, it felt as if the fire was just finishing the job fate had already begun. He hadn't known the twins would miss a few pictures this much.

"Well, your father can tell you what she looked like," Glory offered softly. For the first time, she wished she was an angel. She'd give those little boys a puppy and a cookie-baking mother, too.

"But I can't *see* her," Joey said. "Telling isn't seeing."

"I can help you," Glory said without thinking.

"What?" Matthew and Dr. Norris both asked at the same time and in the same disapproving tone.

"I can help them see their mother," Glory said, turning to Matthew. She would do it, she thought excitedly.

"Look, I guess it's fair play after all they've put

you through,'' Matthew said indignantly. ''But I won't have you making fun of their make-believe.''

''I wouldn't do that,'' Glory protested. How could such a distrustful man raise two such trusting sons? ''And I can help. I've drawn hundreds of pictures from descriptions I've been given.''

''You could?'' Matthew asked, and then blinked suspiciously fast. ''You really could draw a picture of the boys' mother—of Susie?''

''Yes,'' Glory said. Why was it that the same dreamy quality in the boys' eyes irritated her when it was mirrored in the eyes of their father, the man who had been married to the woman she was going to paint? She squared her shoulders. She didn't have time to worry about a man. She was an artist now. She was going to paint a masterpiece. The face of one of God's creations. ''It'll be my pleasure.''

''Hallelujah,'' Dr. Norris said as he bent down and swabbed Matthew's arm. Then, as he stuck a needle in Matthew's arm, he added. ''Sounds like maybe she's an angel after all.''

Matthew grunted.

Glory swallowed her protest. She was the only one who saw the self-satisfied nod the twins exchanged.

The Bullet kept his eyes averted. He wore his cap pulled low over his forehead even though the musty darkness shadowed his face. The inside of the parked limo was damp and the rain slid silently over the windshield. A streetlight overhead cast a feeble glow inside the car, outlining the man next to him.

''You're sure she's a new hit?''

''Not technically,'' the man finally admitted. His words were low and clipped. ''But she's as good as…the other try was nothing…a gang shooting—slid by easy."

"I charge extra for repeats," the Bullet said, his lips drawing together. He didn't like it when clients tried to get gang kids to do their dirty work. "Extra for cops, too."

"She's no cop," the man said impatiently. "Draws pictures. That's all."

"Still, they look out for their own," the Bullet pressed further. "She got any cop training? Guns, anything?"

"Naw. She's easy."

The Bullet grimaced. "I'll settle for fifteen," the Bullet said. "Half up front."

The client nodded and held out a paper bag full of cash. "Here's seventy-five hundred, Mr. Forrest Brown."

The Bullet froze. Nobody knew him by name. He was the Bullet to all of Seattle. *If he knows who I am, he knows where I live. My God, he knows about my Millie!*

Chapter Two

"**Y**ou best behave yourself," Mrs. Hargrove whispered to Matthew as she leaned on the counter of the hardware store. Matthew was sitting on a folding chair behind the counter with his leg propped up on a trash can. He wasn't feeling too well, and Mrs. Hargrove's powdered violet perfume didn't help.

"I assure you..." Matthew started, but he didn't have a full head of steam going and it was almost impossible to stop the older woman without one. Besides, truth to tell, he didn't really mind her scolding him. Listening to her gave him time to watch Glory set up an easel with the twins' help in the front of the store.

"Humph," Mrs. Hargrove said, turning to follow the aim of his eyes before continuing, "You may be a man of the cloth—"

"What?" Matthew jerked himself back to the conversation. That was his secret. No one here was supposed to know. "What do you mean?"

Sweat broke out on Matthew's forehead. He had

hoped no one here would ever find out. How could he explain that his faith was tied in knots? He used to love the ministry, knowing he was helping people find God's mercy. He'd known he needed to leave the ministry when he no longer believed in that mercy, when he couldn't even pray in public anymore. That last morning, he'd just stood in the pulpit, unable to speak. Finally the choir director figured out something was wrong and had the choir start a hymn. But the hymn didn't help. He was still mute. All he could remember were the words of the prayers he'd prayed for Susie and the confidence he'd had. The words of those prayers rose like bile in his throat. His prayers had turned to dust when she died. How could a man with no faith be a minister? "I'm not a minister. Not anymore…"

"But a man's a man in my book," Mrs. Hargrove continued, and pointed her finger at him. "And that woman over there is a sight more tempting than a real angel would ever be. And don't think other people haven't noticed."

"What other people?" Matthew looked around. The only two other people in the store were Elmer and Jacob, two semi-retired ranchers who stopped by the hardware store every morning for their cup of coffee. They were arguing across the checkerboard Henry kept by the woodstove. When Matthew looked at them, Elmer lifted his bearded face, gave him a slow knowing wink, stood up and then started walking toward the counter.

When Elmer reached the front of the counter, he looked squarely at Matthew. "Heard you got yourself an angel."

"She's not an angel," Matthew protested automatically.

Elmer nodded solemnly. "Looks like an angel to me. You lucky dog. Got an inside track with her, since she's staying at your place."

"Staying at my place—" Matthew echoed in panic. He hadn't given any thought to where Glory would stay. The only hotel around was back in Miles City. That would be too far. But where would she stay at his place? He supposed she'd have to stay in his room. The old house had only two bedrooms, and the sofa was too lumpy for a guest. No, he'd have to take the sofa. Which was fine, but he worried about her up in his room. He couldn't remember if he'd put his socks away last night or not. Last night, nothing— try the past week. Socks everywhere.

"She can't stay at my place. I'm single," Matthew said, relieved to remember the fact. Glory would never see his dirty socks. Or the calendar on his wall that was stuck back in September even though it was December 19. "It wouldn't be proper, would it, Mrs. Hargrove?"

Matthew smiled confidently. Being single did have certain advantages.

"I would ask her to stay with me. She seems like a very nice lady," Mrs. Hargrove said earnestly, and then shrugged her shoulders. "But I can't."

The smile that was forming on Matthew's lips faded. "Why not?"

"The twins love the Christmas story," Mrs. Hargrove explained. "They'd be very disappointed if they couldn't keep the angel in their house. Besides, the doctor says there's no way you can get up those stairs, so it's perfectly proper."

As though that settled the matter, Mrs. Hargrove ran her finger over the plastic jug of wrenches standing on the counter. "Doesn't that Henry ever dust anything in here? Decent folks wouldn't shop here even if they had any extra money."

"Henry doesn't notice the dust," Matthew said. He wondered if Glory had noticed how dusty it was in the hardware store. Of course she'd noticed, he thought. He could see her frowning at the window beside her. It could use a good washing. He'd started to clean up Henry's store now that the man was gone to his daughter's in Florida for a long winter vacation, but Matthew had started in the back, in the stockroom.

"Excuse me, Mrs. Hargrove," Matthew said as he reached for his crutches. "I think I best get my bottle of window cleaner and—" Matthew nodded in the general direction of Glory.

But before Matthew could stand, Glory came over to the counter.

"I'd like to buy a brush," Glory said. The hardware store looked as if it could use some business, and she assumed they had a fine-tip brush that could serve her uses. "Make that a dozen and a can of turpentine."

"Brushes are over there," Matthew said, and started to rise. "Most of them are for real painting—I mean, not for artists, but there might be one or two small enough."

"You just sit back down," Mrs. Hargrove said as Matthew fitted the crutches under his arms. "You aren't in any shape to be fetching brushes." Mrs. Hargrove walked toward the shelf and returned with a dozen paintbrushes. Glory put her platinum plastic card on the counter. "I assume you take credit cards."

"Some days that's all we take," Matthew said as he pulled out the credit card duplicator and picked up the phone for verification.

Matthew punched in the numbers of Glory's credit card. He didn't want to admit it, but hers was the first platinum card he'd ever processed. Most people in Dry Creek thought they were rich if they qualified for the gold card. "Is there something different about a platinum card?"

"Different?"

"Your numbers aren't taking," Matthew said as he punched another number to speak to an operator. "Maybe I'm doing something wrong."

"Oh." Matthew's frown had grown deeper as the operator on the other end spoke.

Matthew hung up the phone. "Your card's been canceled."

"Canceled? How could it be canceled?"

"It seems you're, ah, dead."

"Dead! But that's ridiculous. I mean—how?"

"They didn't say how it happened," Matthew offered. He didn't want to think of the implications of Glory trying to run a fraudulent card through his system.

"There's no 'how' to it," Glory snapped. "It hasn't happened. I'm perfectly healthy, as anyone can see."

"Perfectly," Matthew agreed. She did look healthy, especially with the indignant flush on her cheeks. Maybe she'd simply missed a payment or two and that was the reason they were canceling her card.

"Can I use your phone?" Glory finally said. She'd

call the captain. He'd said he'd take in her mail while she was gone. He could solve the mystery. "Collect, of course."

Matthew handed her the phone, and Glory turned her back slightly to make the call.

"Thank God you called," the captain said when he heard her voice. "I was worried."

"I just called two days ago," Glory protested. "I'm fine, except for my credit card."

"Ah, yes. I canceled your card. Not as easy as you'd think. I had to claim official business and tell them you'd died."

"You *what?*" Glory protested and then, remembering her audience, turned to give a reassuring smile to Matthew and Mrs. Hargrove. She didn't want them to think she was broke, let alone dead. She turned her back to them.

"Someone jimmied your mailbox yesterday," the captain said. "Took your credit card bill."

"The bill—they can have it."

"With the bill, someone can trace you," the captain pointed out patiently. "Find out what hotels you're staying at. Where you're buying gas. It's not that hard. Someone real sophisticated will find a way to get your charges the same day you make them. By now, they probably know what state you're in. Remember that shot. First the shooting at the grocery store and then that shot coming the next day so close to you. I don't like it. Not with someone taking your credit card bill."

"Surely you don't think—" Glory sputtered. "Thank goodness I haven't used the card since Spokane. But I can't believe— It was probably just some kids breaking in."

"They didn't break in to the other mailboxes in your building."

"Maybe they got tired. Thought of something better to do."

The captain was silent. "Maybe. Then I keep wondering if something wasn't fishy about that shooting at Benson's. Could be more was happening than you've remembered."

"Just the butcher standing by the meat counter. Had a package of steaks in one hand and the time card of one of his assistants in the other."

"We checked the name on the time card. The clerk didn't have a dispute."

"Least, not one they're talking about," Glory added.

"No extra keys on him, either," the captain continued. "If it was a robbery, there was no reason to shoot the man. He wasn't holding anything back."

"But if it was a robbery, why wait to make the hit when the armored transport had just made the pickup to go to the bank?"

"Ignorance?"

"Yeah, and anyone that ignorant wouldn't think to trace a credit card." Glory pushed back the prickles that were teasing the base of her spine. The captain was paranoid. He had to be. She hadn't been the only one at Benson's. She'd already told the police everything she knew. Besides, the bullet that had gone whizzing by a day later was gang related. The department was sure of that.

"Yeah, you're probably right. I'll go ahead and call the credit card company."

"Good." Glory took a deep breath. "When can I use the card?"

"Ten days. Takes them that long to verify," the captain said hesitantly. "I'll wire you some money. Your mom and I are heading off for that trip we told you about, but we'll drop it on our way. Tell me where you are."

"Dry Creek, Montana," Glory said. She looked over her shoulder. Matthew and Mrs. Hargrove were trying to look inconspicuous, a sure sign they'd overheard everything.

"Trouble?" Matthew said sympathetically as Glory hung up the phone and turned around. He could see she was embarrassed. "Don't worry about the brushes. Henry runs tabs for people all the time. You can pay when you can."

"No problem. I'm expecting a money order to come here to the post office, maybe even tomorrow," she said brightly.

Matthew looked at Mrs. Hargrove. Mrs. Hargrove looked at Matthew.

"We don't have a post office," the older woman finally said.

"No post office?" Glory said as her stomach started to sink. "Can I borrow the phone again?"

The captain's phone rang seven times before the secretary came on the line to say he'd just walked out the door to leave for his vacation.

"Can you leave a message just in case he calls before he leaves?" Glory asked. She wished she'd brought the captain's new unlisted home phone number with her. She hadn't bothered, because her mother and the captain were going to be on their trip.

After she left the message, Glory turned around. She was stuck. Stuck in Dry Creek. Unless. "I'd be happy to work in exchange for the brushes. The store looks like it could use some more help.''

Matthew hesitated.

"I'm willing to work for minimum wage."

"I wish I could," Matthew said apologetically. "But we've already got a dozen job applications in the drawer. There aren't many jobs in Dry Creek this time of year. There'd be an uprising if I gave a job to an outsider when so many people here want one," Matthew finished lamely. Maybe he should chance the anger of the townspeople.

"I didn't know it was that bad." Glory said.

"We get by." Mrs. Hargrove lifted her chin. "In fact, there's talk of starting a dude ranch over on the Big Sheep Mountain place."

"That's just talk," Elmer said sharply. "The Big Sheep's been a cattle ranch for more than a hundred years. Started out as the XIT Ranch and then became the Big Sheep. We've got history. Pride. We don't need a bunch of city folks messing things up with their Jeeps and fancy boots. You know as good as me, they won't stay inside the fences. They'll scare the elk away. Not to mention the eagles. Before you know it, the Big Sheep Mountains will be empty— no animals at all, not even the cows."

"Better that than empty of people," Mrs. Hargrove replied as she tightened her lips. "It's old fools like you that can't make way for progress."

"Old fool? Me?" Elmer protested. "Why, I rode in the Jaycee Bucking Horse Sale last May. On Black Demon. Nothing old about me." He sighed. "Ah, what's the use. You're just worried about your son's family."

Mrs. Hargrove nodded slowly. "He said they'd

have to move come spring if something doesn't open up. He's worked for the Big Sheep Mountain Cattle Company for ten years, but this rustling has them in a bind. They're losing too many cattle and they're going to start laying off hands.'' Mrs. Hargrove refocused on Glory as though just remembering she was there. The older woman settled her face into a polite smile. ''I don't mean to go on about our troubles. We get by just fine. God is good to us.''

''Of course,'' Glory said carefully. She knew a wall of pride when she bumped into it, and Mrs. Hargrove had it in abundance. Matthew did, too. She hadn't given any thought to how Matthew managed on his salary, but now she remembered the frayed collars on the twins' shirts and the mended pocket on Joey's jacket. She'd have to send him some money when she got home. In fact—

''How about a check? I can pay for the brushes with a check,'' Glory offered in relief. She wasn't totally stranded, after all.

''A check is fine,'' Matthew said heartily. He'd remember to pull it out and replace it with cash from his own pocket before he took the checks to the bank. He had no doubt her check would bounce as high as her credit card had and he didn't want to embarrass her further. ''It's $12.64 for the brushes and turpentine.''

''Good.'' Glory started to write the check. ''And I'll add a little extra for you—''

''You don't need to tip someone who works in a hardware store,'' Matthew said stiffly. A red flush settled around his neck. ''The service is free.''

''Of course,'' Glory said quickly. There she'd gone

and offended him. She finished the check. "Twelve sixty-four exactly."

Glory counted the checks in her checkbook. She had ten left. That was enough to pay for meals and a hotel for a few nights.

"Where's the hotel from here?" she asked. She couldn't remember seeing one, but there must be one. Every town had a hotel.

"There's no hotel here," Mrs. Hargrove said as she nudged Matthew.

"Oh. Maybe a bed-and-breakfast place?"

There was a long pause as Mrs. Hargrove nudged Matthew again.

Matthew finally said, "I'm sure there's someone in town with an extra room who would let you—"

"Well, aren't you in luck, then," Mrs. Hargrove said with a determined enthusiasm. "Since Matthew hurt his knee, his room will be empty. The doctor says he can't climb the stairs with his sprain, so I'm sure no one will think anything of it. Besides, the twins are good chaperones."

Matthew felt trapped and then guilty. The least he could do was provide her lodging. "We'd be honored to have you stay with us for a few days."

"There's no one who does this more like a business?" Glory asked. The thought of staying in this man's room made her feel uneasy. She'd smell his aftershave on the pillows and see his shirts in the closet. "I can pay." Surely one of those families that wanted a job would take in a boarder for a few nights. "I'll even throw in a turkey for Christmas dinner."

"I'm afraid there's only Matthew and his boys," Mrs. Hargrove said.

Glory bent her head to start writing her check. "How does one hundred dollars a night sound?"

"One hundred!" Matthew protested. No wonder she had financial troubles. "We're not the Hilton. Besides, you'd be our guest."

Glory had finished the check by the time he finished. No wonder he had financial troubles. "I can be your guest and still pay a fair price."

"No, there's no need," Matthew said.

"I insist," Glory said as she ripped off the check and presented it to him.

Matthew raised his eyebrows at the amount of the check. He supposed it didn't matter what amount she wrote the check for when it was going to bounce anyway, but three hundred dollars was a lot to pay for several nights' food and lodging.

"Consider it a Christmas present," Glory said grandly. "For the twins."

"They'll appreciate it," Matthew said dryly.

Glory flipped her wallet to the plastic section. "You'll want to see my driver's license."

"Henry doesn't bother. He knows the folks here who write checks," Matthew said as he took a sidelong look at the driver's license anyway. He was pleased to see she was Glory Beckett. She might be a bad risk from the credit company's viewpoint, but she wasn't a thief. That is, unless she was so polished she had gotten a fake driver's license to go with her story.

"He doesn't know me," Glory said as she moved her driver's license so it came into Matthew's full view. "You'll want to write down the number."

"All right," Matthew said as he noted her driver's license number.

"Good," Glory said as she put her checkbook back in her purse and turned to walk back to her easel.

"You're not going to cash those checks, Matthew Curtis," Mrs. Hargrove demanded in a hushed whisper as they watched Glory sit down to her easel across the store in front of the display window.

"Of course not," Matthew agreed as he slipped the checks out of the drawer.

Carl Wall, the deputy sheriff, was running for reelection and his campaign slogan was No Crime's Too Small To Do Some Time. He'd happily jail an out-of-towner for writing a bad check and brag about it to voters later.

Ten minutes later, Glory repositioned the easel. Then she arranged her brushes twice and turned her stool to get more light. She was stalling and she knew it. She suddenly realized she'd never painted a portrait as agonizingly important as this one. The sketches she'd done of criminals, while very important, were meant only for identification and not as a symbol of love.

"Do you want your mother to be sitting or standing?" Glory asked the twins. The two identical heads were studying the bottom of a large display window. They each had a cleaning rag and were making circles in the lower portion of the window while Matthew reached for the high corners, standing awkwardly with one crutch.

"I don't know." Josh stopped rubbing the window and gave it a squirt of window cleaner. "Maybe she could be riding a dragon. I've always wanted a picture of a dragon."

"Mommie's don't ride dragons," Joey scolded his brother. "They ride brooms."

Matthew winced. Susie had been adamantly opposed to celebrating Halloween and, consequently, the twins had only a sketchy idea of the spooks that inspired other children's nightmares.

"No, sweetie, it's witches who ride brooms." Mrs. Hargrove corrected the boy with a smile as she picked up a cleaning rag and joined Matthew on the high corners. "Maybe you could have a picture painted of your mother praying."

"No," Matthew said a little more loudly than he intended. His memories of Susie praying tormented him. He knew she would be heartbroken that her death had brought a wedge between him and God, but his feelings were there anyway. If he lived to be a hundred, he'd never understand how God could have answered his prayers for so long on the small things like good crops and passing tests but when it came to the one big thing—Susie's recovery—God had let him down flat. No sense of comfort. No nothing. He'd expected his faith to carry them through always.

Matthew didn't feel like explaining himself. His arms were sore from the crutches and he hobbled over to a stool that was beside Glory. "I want the twins to remember their mother laughing. She was a happy woman."

"Well, that'd make a good picture, too," Mrs. Hargrove said, and then looked at the twins. The twins had stopped wiping their circles and were listening thoughtfully. "You'd like that, wouldn't you?"

The twins nodded.

"Okay, smiling it is," Glory said. This Susie woman sounded like a saint, always smiling and praying and baking cookies, and Glory had no reason to resent her. None whatsoever, she thought to herself. "I assume she had all her teeth."

"What?" Matthew seemed a little startled with the question.

"Her teeth," Glory repeated. "If I'm going to paint her smiling, I need to know about her teeth. Were there any missing?"

"Of course not."

"Were any of them crooked?" Glory continued. "Or chipped? Did she have a space between the front ones?"

"They were just teeth," Matthew said defensively. Why did he suddenly feel guilty because he couldn't remember what kind of teeth Susie had? He knew her image was burned onto his heart. He just couldn't pull up the details. "Her eyes were blue—a blue so deep they'd turn to black in the shadows."

"Eyes. Blue. Deep," Glory said as she wrote a note on the butcher paper she'd stretched over her easel. "And her nose, was it like this? Or like this?" Glory sketched a couple of common nose styles. "Or more like this?"

"It was sort of like that, but more scrunched at the beginning," Matthew said, pointing to one of the noses and feeling suddenly helpless. He hadn't realized until now that the picture Glory was going to paint was the picture that was inside his head. He'd spent a lot of time trying to get Susie's face out of his mind so he could keep himself going forward. What if he'd done too good a job? What if he couldn't remember her face as well as he should?

"Pugged nose," Glory muttered as she added the words to the list on the side of the paper. "Any marks? Moles? Freckles? Warts?"

"Of course not. She was a classic beauty," Matthew protested.

"I see," Glory said. She tried to remind herself that she was doing a job and shouldn't take Matthew's words personally. "I have freckles."

Glory winced. She hadn't meant to say that.

"I noticed them right off." Matthew nodded. "That's how I knew you couldn't be an angel."

"I see," Glory said icily. Couldn't be an angel, indeed. Just because Susie didn't have freckles. She'd show him who couldn't be an angel. "Any other identifying facial marks?"

"I liked the way your hair curled," Matthew offered thoughtfully as he remembered lying on his back after his fall and looking up at Glory. "It just spread all out like a sunflower—except it was brass instead of gold." He had a sudden piercing thought of what it would be like to kiss a woman with hair like that. Her hair would fall around him with the softness of the sun.

"I meant Susie. Did she have any other identifying facial marks?" Glory repeated.

"Oh," Matthew said, closing his eyes in concentration. Could Susie have had freckles after all? Even a few? No, she'd made this big production about never going out in the sun because her skin was so fair—like an English maiden, she used to say. What else did Susie always say? Oh, yes. "Peaches and cream. Her skin was a peaches-and-cream complexion."

"Well, that's a nice poetic notion," Glory said as she added the words to her list.

"What do you mean by that?" Matthew opened his eyes indignantly. Glory had gone all bristly on him, and he was trying his best to remember all the details just as she wanted.

"It's just that peaches have fuzz—and cream eventually clots. The whole phrase is a cliché. It doesn't describe anything. No one's skin looks like that. Not really."

"Well, no," Matthew admitted. "It's just hard to remember everything."

"True enough." Glory softened. She had gotten descriptions from hundreds of people in her career. She should know not to push someone. Often a victim would have a hard time recalling the features of their assailant. She imagined the same thing might be true when grief rather than fear was the problem. "Don't worry about it. We'll do it one step at a time. We'll be done by Friday."

"But Friday's not the pageant. You've got to stay until the pageant," Josh said solemnly. "They've never had a real angel before in the pageant."

"I'm not an—" Glory protested automatically as she turned to the twins. They both looked so wistful. "I'm sorry, but I can't stay. Even though I'd love to see my two favorite shepherds in their bathrobes."

"How'd you know we're wearing bathrobes?" Josh demanded.

"She's an angel, that's how," Joey said proudly. "She's just an undercover angel, so she can't tell anyone. Like a spy."

"Do you know everyone's secrets?" Josh asked in awe.

"I don't know anyone's secrets," Glory said, and then smiled teasingly. "Unless, of course, you do something naughty."

"Wow, just like Santa Claus," Josh breathed excitedly. "Can you get me a *Star Trek* laser light gun for Christmas?"

"I thought we talked about that, Josh," Matthew interjected. "You know Santa is just a story."

"I know," Josh said in a rush. His eyes were bright with confidence. "But she's an angel and she can tell God. That's even better than Santa Claus. God must have lots of toys."

"We'll talk about this later," Matthew said. He'd have to sit down with Josh and explain how the universe worked. Whether he asked God or Santa Claus for a present, it didn't matter. Neither one of them could buy Josh a gift unless it could be found in Miles City for twenty dollars or less.

"Can you tell God?" Josh ignored his father and whispered to Glory. "I've been a good boy, except for—well, you know—the bug thing."

Glory didn't think she wanted to know about the bug thing. "I'm sure you have been a good boy," she said as she knelt to look squarely at the boy. "I'll tell you what, why don't you draw a picture of this laser gun and color it. That way, if you want to send God a picture, He'll know what it looks like."

"Me, too," Joey asked. "Can I make a picture, too?"

"Why not?" Glory said, and included him in her smile. Even if her credit card wouldn't live again by Christmas she could send a check to one of her girlfriends. Her friend Sylvia ran a neighborhood youth center and would be visiting that huge toy store in Seattle anyway. Even though most of the kids Sylvia worked with were more likely to own a real pistol than a water pistol, Sylvia insisted on treating them as though they were ordinary children at the holidays. The kids loved her for it.

"But…" Matthew tried to catch Glory's eye.

"Daddy needs one, too," Joey said. The twins both looked at her with solemn eyes. It had taken her several hours to figure out how to tell them apart. Joey's eyes were always quieter. "But Daddy's old."

"No one's too old for Christmas wishes," Glory said.

"Really?" Joey smiled.

It was dusk by the time Glory finished her sketch of Susie and they all went home for dinner. Glory offered to cook, but Matthew declared she had already done her work for the day. Glory was too tired to resist. Sketching Susie had been difficult. Matthew had never wanted to look at the full face of the sketch, and so she'd pieced it together an eyebrow at a time. Even when she'd finished, he'd pleaded fatigue and asked to look at the sketch on the next day.

Matthew went to the kitchen to cook dinner, leaving Glory on the sofa with a *Good Housekeeping* magazine.

"I've learned to be a good cook," Matthew said a little bleakly as he sat down a little later and leaned his crutches against the dining-room wall. The smell of burned potatoes still hung in the air even though all the windows were now open. "Dinner doesn't usually float in milk."

"Cereal is all right," Glory assured him. She'd realized when the smoke drifted into the living room that dinner would be delayed.

"I like the pink ones," Joey said as he poured his bowl full of Froot Loops.

"I always keep cornflakes for me," Matthew said as he handed the box to Glory. "I'm afraid we don't have a wide selection."

"Cornflakes are fine," Glory said. "I often eat light."

Matthew chided himself. He should have realized. She lived on the road, likely by her wits. Of course she ate light. He should have made sure she had a decent meal.

"We'll eat better tomorrow, I promise. Something with meat in it. And if you need anything, just ask."

"I will," Glory assured him, and smiled.

Her smile kicked Matthew in the stomach. The sun shone about her when she smiled. No wonder his sons thought she was an angel.

"Daddy?" Joey was looking at Matthew.

Matthew pulled himself together. It was time for grace.

"Hands," Matthew said and offered his hand to Joey on the one side. He didn't realize until his hand was already extended that Glory was on his other side.

"I'll say grace," Josh offered as he put one hand out to Joey and the other to Glory. He looked shyly at Glory. "I washed. I'm not jammy."

"I know." Glory smiled softly as she reached easily for his hand. His small hand snuggled trustingly in her palm. She held her other hand out to Matthew. His hand didn't snuggle. Instead, it enveloped her. She swore her pulse moved from her wrist to the center of her palm. She wondered if he could feel the quickening beat in her. What was wrong with her? He'd think she'd never held a man's hand before. Not that she was holding his hand now. It was prayer hand-holding. That's all. Just because his thumb happened to caress the inside of her finger.

"Okay, Daddy?" Josh asked again, looking at his father. "It's my turn to say grace."

Matthew nodded his permission. What was wrong with him? Even Josh was looking at him funny. Matthew was beginning to think he'd never held a woman's hand before. Glory's skin was softer than fine leather. She must use some kind of lotions on her hands because of her work in paints. That must be it. Just lotions. He cleared his throat. "Sure. Go ahead."

Josh bowed his head and carefully screwed his eyes closed. "Thank you, God, for this day and for this food and for our comp—" Josh stumbled "—company. Amen."

"Thank you, Josh," Glory said when he looked up again. "I'm honored to be your company."

"If there's anything you need..." Matthew offered again.

The only thing she needed, she thought later that evening, was some more paint. The twins had been put to bed and she was sitting on the sofa reading her magazine and talking with Matthew as he sewed a button on Josh's winter coat. The light from the two lamps made round circles on the ceiling and bathed Matthew in a yellow glow. She hated to tell the twins, but it was their father who looked like the angel. His chestnut hair waved and curled all over his head and down to his collar. Forceful cheekbones sloped down to a square chin. He was the most manly-looking man she'd seen in a long time. Not that, of course, she assured herself, there was anything personal in her admiration.

"I best get the fire banked for the night," Matthew said.

"Let me do it," Glory said as she set aside the magazine. "Rest your leg. Just tell me how and it won't take a minute."

Matthew pulled himself up by holding on to the bookshelf and then put one crutch under his arm. "No need, I can do it."

"But I'd like to help," Glory protested as she rose. "You're in no condition to be banking a fire."

"I'm fine," Matthew said. "It takes more than a sprained knee to stop me."

Glory looked at him. A thin sheen of sweat was showing on his forehead and it was definitely not hot in the room. "You've got more pride than sense."

"Pride?" Matthew said as he hobbled over to the woodstove. "It's not pride. It's learning to take care of yourself. I've learned not to rely on others. I can do whatever I need to do to take care of me and my boys."

"Without help from anyone," Glory said dryly. Relying on others was the key to trust. Trust in others. Trust in God.

"We don't need any help," Matthew said as he lifted the grate on the stove. "It's best not to count on anyone else. I can do what needs doing."

"Can you?" Glory said softly as she watched Matthew reach down and pick up several pieces of wood. The fire wrapped golden shadows around his face. His frown burrowed itself farther into his forehead. She had no doubt Matthew could do everything that needed to be done in raising his sons—everything, that is, except teach them how to have faith. For how can you have faith in God if you can't trust anyone,

not even Him? No wonder the boys clung to the belief
she was an angel. It would take an angel to bring
healing to their little family.

The Bullet folded his socks and put them in an old
duffel bag that was carefully nondescript. No logos.
No fancy stripes. Just brown.

"My uncle…" the Bullet said as he added a
sweater. "He's sick. Spokane."

Millie nodded. She'd just come back from her job
at Ruby's Coffee Shop and sat on the edge of the bed
with her back straight and her eyes carefully not looking at the socks. She always looked so fragile with
her wispy blond hair and slender body.

"I—ah—I'll be back soon," the Bullet continued.
*She knows where I'm going. Oh, not the location. But
she knows the why.* "A week or so is all."

Millie nodded again and stood up. "Better take another sweater. It's cold in Spokane." She walked to
the closet.

"No, let me." The Bullet intercepted her. He didn't
want Millie to be part of any of this, not even the
packing.

"Don't go. You don't have to go." Millie turned
to him and spoke fiercely.

"I already told my uncle I was coming," the Bullet
said slowly. It was too late to change his mind.

Chapter Three

Matthew stared at the glass coffeepot in his hand. He'd come to the hardware store at eight o'clock just like any other regular working day. But never before had the coffeepot been so sparkling clean and never before had a can of gourmet hazelnut coffee stood beside it. Old Henry was fussy about his coffee, and he always made it plain and strong. "Nothing fancy," he'd often say. "My customers are ranchers, not ballet dancers."

Glory and Matthew had shared a ride to the store after dropping the twins off at the church's nursery. "I think your customers might like some of these coffee flavors," Glory said.

"Coffee flavors?" Matthew hadn't slept well last night and he wanted his coffee thick and black with no frills. It wasn't the sofa that had kept him awake or even the pain in his knee. No matter how many times he turned over on the old sofa, his mind kept wandering back to dreams of Glory. Now he needed a good kick of coffee to keep him awake.

"You know, orange, raspberry, chocolate," Glory replied as she pulled the three bottles out of her purse. She hadn't slept well last night. She assured herself it was the creaking of the old house that had kept her awake and not the picture that stayed in her mind of Matthew adding more wood to the fire last night. She had gotten up this morning determined to make good progress on her painting today. That meant coffee.

"That's nice," Matthew said as he tried to hide as much of the white doily under the sugar bowl as he could. He'd have to tell Elmer and Jacob that the doily was a Christmas decoration. He expected they'd tolerate the concept of a few holiday decorations more kindly than the idea that their domain was being citified. Citified wasn't popular here. As it was, the two old men spent half their time here arguing about the dude ranch over on the Big Sheep Mountain Ranch. Anything that smacked of change and city people was suspect. And coffee flavors. The next thing you knew she'd want a...

"Cappuccino machine—that's what we need," Elmer said a half hour later. He was sipping his orange-flavored coffee most politely and beaming at Glory as she set up her easel. "I've always had a hankering to have one of those coffees."

"I don't even know if they have a cappuccino machine in Miles City. We'd have to send to Billings to buy one," Matthew protested.

What was wrong with Elmer? Once he'd complained because Henry put a different kind of toilet paper in the bathroom. And yet, here he was, wearing a new white shirt, the kind he only wore to funerals. "And no one's complained before. You've always liked the usual."

"But sometimes it's good to have a change," Glory said from her place by the window.

"Yeah, don't be such an old stick-in-the mud," Jacob said as he peered into his coffee cup suspiciously. Apparently Jacob didn't find anything too alarming in his cup, because he took a hot, scalding gulp. "Ahh, none of us are too old to try something new."

"I thought I'd set Susie's sketch up in the display window, too," Glory said. It had occurred to her last night that most gas stations wouldn't take checks. She could use some cash. "I might get another order for a portrait."

Matthew swallowed. He'd prefer to rearrange these receipts and dust the merchandise all morning. Anything to put off looking at the picture of Susie.

"I've got the sketch ready," Glory said. She'd placed the drawing of Susie on her easel. She'd drawn Susie smiling and holding a plate of oatmeal cookies almost level with her chin.

"I see that," Matthew said as he stood and hobbled over to the sketch. He took a deep breath. He felt the rubber band squeeze his heart. He'd been unable to cry at Susie's funeral. He'd just sat there with that rubber band squeezing the life out of him. This time he'd take a quick look and be done with it. He felt as if he'd been called upon to identify someone in the morgue. It wasn't a duty he wanted to prolong.

"That's her," Matthew said in surprise. He'd expected an identification picture of Susie, something that looked like a passport photo where you see the resemblance but not the person. But Glory was good. It was Susie's eyes that smiled at him from the paper.

"I wasn't sure about the cheekbones," Glory fretted. She didn't like the stillness that surrounded Matthew. "I think they might be a little too high."

"No, it's perfect. That's Susie."

Matthew braced himself for the inevitable second wave of pain. Susie had trusted him to save her life, trusted his faith to make her well. He'd never forgiven himself for letting her down. Somehow he hadn't prayed hard enough or loud enough to make any difference.

"Did she have a pink dress?" Glory interrupted his thoughts. Matthew's face had gone white and she didn't know what else to offer but chatter. "I thought I'd paint her in a pink dress with a little lace collar of white."

"Pink is good," Matthew said as he turned to walk away on his crutches. The sweat cooled on his brow. He'd made it past the hard part. He'd seen Susie again. Seen the look of trust on her face. He'd promised he'd take care of her and he had failed. He had told her God would come through for them. But he'd been wrong. In the end, Matthew had bargained bitterly with God to let him die. But God had not granted him even that small mercy. Matthew kept his face turned away from everyone. He'd fight his own demons alone.

"You like pink, do you?" Elmer said as he walked over to Glory.

"Who, me? No, I'm more of a beige-and-gray type of person," Glory said. She didn't like the closed look on Matthew's face or the ramrod straightness of his back when he'd turned around. But he'd made it clear he didn't want to talk.

"Beige—gray—that's good," Elmer murmured as he leaned closer to Glory.

Matthew hobbled stiffly back to the counter and sat back down on his chair. The air cooled the remaining sweat off his face as he watched Elmer make his moves. The old fox. Matthew took a deep breath. Today he'd rather watch the nonsense with Elmer than hold on to his own pain. He wanted to live in today and not yesterday. It made him feel better to know he wasn't the only one being charmed by Glory. No wonder the old man drank his orange coffee as if he enjoyed it. ''No checker game this morning, Elmer?''

''Checkers—ah, n-no.'' Elmer stammered a little. ''I thought I'd sit and talk a bit with the ang—with Miss Glory.'' Elmer gave a curt nod in Glory's direction. ''Get acquainted, so to speak.''

''That's very friendly of you,'' Glory said. She'd watched Matthew make his way to the counter and had relaxed when he turned to face them. When he started watching them, she turned her attention to Elmer. The old man was safer. She didn't mind company while she painted and almost welcomed it while she set out her brushes as she did now. Since Matthew had approved the sketch, she'd move on to the first stages of the oil painting.

''My pleasure,'' Elmer said, and then took another dainty sip of his orange coffee. ''It isn't often we have a young woman visiting—at least, not one your age.''

''Hmm,'' Glory murmured pleasantly. She'd need to mix some blue with that mauve to get the eye color right.

''Your age,'' Elmer repeated. ''And what might that be?''

''Twenty-eight.''

''Ah,'' Elmer said.

Matthew watched as the older man marked down a figure in a little notepad he pulled out of his pocket.

"And your birthday?"

"March 15."

"Good month," Elmer said as he nodded and marked another figure in his notepad. "That means you were born in oh three, fifteen, ah, 19…ah…?"

"Say, what are you doing?" Matthew demanded in surprise as he hobbled over to Elmer and stared at the older man.

"What?" Elmer bristled as he slid the notepad into his jacket pocket. "Just making conversation."

"You're planning to buy a lottery ticket from your daughter in L.A., aren't you?" Matthew said in amazement. "And you're getting some lucky numbers."

"It's all right." Glory looked up at the two of them and smiled. "At least that way, he'll have to call her."

"Yeah," Elmer said smugly as he patted the notebook in his pocket. "It'll be our family time. Nothing better than talking to your family."

Matthew grunted. "You've got better things to talk about than numbers and lottery tickets. Besides, her numbers aren't magic. She's not an angel."

"And how do you know that?" Elmer lifted his chin. "She could be. The Bible says we sometimes entertain angels unaware. Right in Hebrews 13:2. I looked it up."

"But the angels aren't unaware." Glory didn't like the direction this discussion was going. She was as earthbound as anyone. "And an angel? I assure you, I'm not one." She was just finishing up the right eyebrow on Susie's picture. Eyebrows were important

character pieces. They could make a face look innocent, bewildered, sad. Glory had settled on innocent
for Susie.

"You could be," Elmer stubbornly insisted. "You
just might not want us to know."

Matthew snorted. "An angel wouldn't lie." He
didn't know why he cared, but it gave him a funny
feeling to have people talk about Glory as though she
was an angel.

Not that the people of Dry Creek didn't need an
angel. Fact is, they needed a whole troupe of angels
and a basket of miracles, too. He didn't begrudge
them their hope. It's just that he, of all people, knew
the disappointment that came when expected miracles
didn't happen.

The bell over the door rang as the door swung open
and a half dozen little children in snowsuits walked
in. A huge gust of wind and Mrs. Hargrove came in
behind them.

"Josh! Joey!" Matthew recognized his sons, or, at
least, he recognized their snowsuits. There was much
flapping about before the hoods were down and the
young faces looked around the hardware store.

"There she is!" Josh shouted to his friends, and
pointed at Glory.

Matthew tensed.

"Hi, there." Glory looked up at the children and
smiled. Their bright snowsuits made a lovely study in
color. Blue. Red. Pink. Even a purple one. "I should
paint you all sometime. Just like this."

"I see you do have everything set up," Mrs. Hargrove said in satisfaction as she stepped out in front
of her charges. "I was hoping you did. The children

have never seen a real artist at work. If you don't mind them watching. I thought it'd be educational."

Matthew relaxed. That's why they were here.

"And she's an angel, too," Joey boasted quietly.

Matthew bit back his tongue. If Josh had done the boasting, he'd have corrected him in an instant. But it had been so long since he'd seen Joey care enough to speak up about anything, he didn't have the heart to correct him.

"Well, maybe not quite an angel," Matthew did offer softly. "Sometimes a good person can seem like an angel to others without really being one."

"Josh said she'd take our pictures to God," said another little boy, Greg, glancing sideways at Glory. "For Christmas."

Glory put down her brushes and turned to face the expectant faces looking at her. She noticed that most of the pockets had a piece of paper peeking out of them.

"I'd be happy to take your pictures," Glory said as she stepped forward. It had been a long time since she'd done this much Christmas shopping, but it'd be fun. Sylvia, she knew, would enjoy being her go-between and Glory had enough in her checking account to cover it. "Just be sure you put your full names on the pictures—first and last."

"Last, too?" one of the boys asked, his forehead puckering in a quick frown. "I can't write my last."

"Maybe Mrs. Hargrove can help you," Glory said. "But I do need first name and last name so the right present gets to the right child."

"I thought God knew our names," a little girl in a pink snowsuit said suspiciously as she stepped out of the leg of her suit. "If you're his angel you should know, too."

"I'm not an angel," Glory said.

"Then why do you want our pictures?" the little girl demanded.

"She'll give your pictures to your parents." Mrs. Hargrove stepped in front of the children. "It's your parents that—" She stumbled. Glory could see why. Those shining little faces looked up with such trust.

"My parents already said I won't get no Betsy Tall doll," the girl said. "They said it's too ex—cen—sive."

"Expensive, dear." Mrs. Hargrove corrected the pronunciation automatically. "Too expensive. And I'm sure there are other dolls."

The hope was beginning to fade on the young faces.

"I'd be happy to take your pictures," Glory said again softly. She held out her hands and the children quickly stuffed their pictures into them.

"Mrs. Hargrove will help me figure out who's who," Glory assured the children.

Glory was watching the children and didn't hear Matthew coming up next to her.

"I'll help with the pictures," Matthew whispered in her ear.

Glory jumped. Matthew startled her. He was so…well, just so close. He unnerved her. She pulled away slightly. "I don't need help. I'm fine. I can take care of it."

"How? You're not an angel."

"Just because I'm not an angel doesn't mean I can't buy a few gifts."

"For children you don't even know?"

"I know them now." Glory shrugged. What was it with this man? Didn't he believe anyone could do something for someone else just because?

The bell over the door rang again, and this time a teenage girl slipped inside. She had a tiny gold ring in her nose and a streak of red dye going through her hair. Fashion, it appeared, hadn't neglected southeastern Montana.

"Linda." Matthew greeted the girl carefully. "What can we help you with?"

"What do you think, big guy?" Linda cooed softly. The girl lifted her eyes to Matthew. She was holding a five-dollar bill in her hand and she waved it around.

Glory winced. The girl was playing at something she obviously didn't even understand. And she was looking at Matthew as if she was starving and he was a supersized hamburger. Which was ridiculous, Glory thought. Sure, he was good-looking in a rugged kind of a way. And sure he smelled like the outdoors and sure he had biceps that would get second looks at the beach and— Glory stopped herself. Okay, so the girl wasn't so far wrong. He was worth staring at. But that didn't mean the girl had any right to do it.

"Hey, Linda," called the little boy, Greg. "Come meet the angel. She's gonna get us presents."

Linda flicked an annoyed glance down that then softened at the enthusiasm on Greg's face. "That's nice. But I need to talk to the angel myself."

"I'm not—" Glory began.

"I need some advice," Linda interrupted impatiently. The teenager looked assessingly at Glory and held out the five-dollar bill. "Some love advice."

"From me?" Glory squeaked.

"I need to know if I should marry the Jazz Man."

"The Jazz Man?" Matthew asked as he leaned his crutches against a wall and sat down on a chair. "You don't mean Arnold's boy, Duane?"

"Yeah." Linda looked at him and snapped her gum. "He's forming a band. Calling himself the Jazz Man." She stood a little straighter. "Wants me to be his lead singer."

"And he's proposed?" Glory asked in studied surprise. She might not know a lot about love, but she did know about business.

"Yeah, why?" Linda looked at her cautiously.

"Mixing business and pleasure." Glory shook her head in what she hoped was a convincingly somber fashion. "He won't have to pay you if he marries you."

"Yeah, I never thought of that," Linda said slowly, and put the five dollars on Glory's easel. "Thanks."

"What's the money for—" Glory began, but was interrupted by the bell ringing over the door again.

This time the ringing was incessant and loud. A stocky man in a tan sheriff's uniform stepped into the store and looked around quickly. His eyes fastened on Glory.

"There you are," he said as he walked toward Glory and put his hand on the end of the gun that stuck out of his holster. "You're under arrest for impersonating an angel. You have the right to—"

"You can't arrest her." The protest erupted from all across the store.

"Oh, yes, I can," the deputy said as he clicked the handcuffs from behind his back and picked up the five dollars Linda had left on her easel. "I won't have no con woman plucking my pigeons. Not in my town she won't."

Plucking his pigeons, Glory thought in dismay. *Dear Lord, what have I done now?*

The Bullet leaned against the cold glass of the phone booth. The credit card company records showed the woman had stopped at a gas station in Spokane and then at a bank for a cash advance. He'd followed the usual procedure to find her. He knew loners in a new town found a bar.

"You'll never find her that way," the voice on the other end of the phone snorted.

"Why not? She's a cop."

"A Christian cop," the voice clarified. "Religious as they come. Doesn't drink. Try looking in the churches."

The Bullet swallowed hard. "Churches? Me?"

Chapter Four

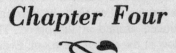

"Easy now," Deputy Sheriff Carl Wall warned Glory when she stood up. He'd forbidden the others to follow them when he escorted her up the church steps and into a small office off the church's kitchen. She'd been sitting on the edge of the desk for ten minutes now while he argued on the phone. The cuffs he'd put on her hands hung open at her wrists. The key to unlock them was in his patrol car and so he did not lock them shut. They were more for show than because he thought the woman would bolt.

"Well, there's got to be a law against it, Bert," Carl was saying for the second time into the phone. He twisted the cord around his chubby ginger. "We just can't have folks going around claiming to be angels and things."

"I never claimed to be an angel," Glory said, even though she doubted he heard her. He hadn't paid any attention to her the past two times she'd said it. It wasn't because he hadn't heard her, she figured; it was because he wasn't listening. In her experience, hearing and listening were two different things.

"But an angel's different from Santa Claus," Carl argued into the phone's mouthpiece, ignoring Glory. He'd already twisted part of the cord around his finger, so now he looped another section around his hand. "Everyone knows Santa Claus isn't real, but folks and angels, well, that's a different story. She's more like a fortune-teller. Gotta be laws against that."

Glory looked around at the office. There was a boxy window at the end of the room. Everything else was long and skinny. The whole thing wasn't much wider than the desk. She guessed the room had been a pantry at one time, running as it did side by side the whole width of the kitchen. A bookcase lined one long wall and a chair stood to the side of the desk. A filing cabinet was tucked behind the door.

"Of course she hasn't got wings on," Carl sputtered in exasperation as he eyed Glory suspiciously. He untwisted the cord around his hand and rubbed the red mark he'd created. Glory pulled a book off the shelf and tried to ignore him. "But a person doesn't need a costume to con people. Crooks don't wear signs, for Pete's sake."

Glory opened the book she held. She loved the smell of old books. They were like old friends. Just holding the book steadied her. If she had to, she could call the police station in Seattle and have them vouch for her honesty. She doubted there were any laws against claiming to be an angel anyway, not even if she sprouted wings and flew off the Empire State Building.

"Well, I can't just let her go," Carl Wall whined into the phone. Then he looked at Glory again and turned his back to her as though that would muffle his voice. "I've already taken her in. I'll look bad saying there's no law against it now. I'm going to write her up for impersonating even if the judge says no later."

A movement through the window caught her eye. Something was happening in the street. Glory looked at the deputy sheriff's back and slid closer to the window. She saw Matthew, standing in the middle of the dirt street and waving a crutch around. The people from the hardware store were gathered around him and Matthew wasn't the only one waving something. Mrs. Hargrove had a broom. Elmer had a yardstick. It looked as if Matthew was giving a speech, but she couldn't hear it through the closed window. She braced her fingers against the frame of the window-panes and pushed up. A puff of cold air came inside, a puff of dirty cold air, Glory decided as the dust beneath the window blew onto her coat. But she could finally hear the voices outside.

"He'll listen to voters. That's all he wants," Matthew was saying. A trail of white breath rose from Matthew's mouth. It was cold. Matthew wore a wool jacket over his shirt. It wasn't nearly enough to keep him warm, in Glory's opinion. "There's no need to threaten him with any more than that."

"But he's got our angel," Elmer protested.

"We don't know she's an angel," Matthew said. Glory noticed he had only a slipper on his injured foot. He needed to be inside. She was pretty sure the doctor had told him to stay inside.

"But we don't know she's not, either," Elmer persisted as he dipped his yardstick for emphasis. "The Bible talks about angels. It could be. We don't know.

And who wants to take a chance! Do you?'' Elmer took a breath. "Do you want to be responsible for turning an angel out of Dry Creek?''

The question hung in the air like brittle frost.

Glory pushed the window higher. This was getting interesting.

"Shut that window,'' Carl yelled. He was putting down the telephone and had finally noticed where she was. "You aren't going to get far, jumping out that window and evading arrest.''

"I wasn't going to jump,'' Glory said in astonishment. "I was just listening to the people in the street out front. I think they're campaigning against you.''

Carl Wall scowled at her. "Mighty lippy for an angel, aren't you?''

Glory grinned. "I'm not an angel.''

"Oh, I know that, but do they know it?'' Carl pointed out the window to the people on the street. Glory looked at them. They were gesturing as they talked, and periodically someone would wave a broom. They looked like a mob of janitors. Carl cleared his throat and continued. "These people are my responsibility. As I said, I won't have anyone plucking my flock—not while I'm on duty.''

"I've not asked for a dime from anyone,'' Glory protested indignantly. "Linda put that five-dollar bill on my easel. I didn't ask for it. I would have given it back if you hadn't stepped in. I don't want anyone's money.''

"Maybe not yet. But you'll want it sooner or later, won't you?'' Carl said as a sly smile slid over his face. "What else can you do? You don't have a job—''

"I have a job,'' Glory interrupted firmly. "Not

here, of course, but I do have a job with the Seattle Police Department.''

Carl snorted. "Expect me to believe that. You—a police officer. Where's your badge?"

"Well, I don't have a badge...."

"I didn't think so," Carl said with satisfaction.

"I work for them as a sketch artist. You know, drawing pictures of criminals from the descriptions given by the witnesses."

"Hmph." The deputy appeared to consider her words and then shook his head. "Naw, I don't think so. What I think is you're a slick customer trying to make a buck off the poor folks of Dry Creek. Taking advantage of their good holiday spirits. And I aim to catch you at it. The minute you ask for a dime, you're mine."

"It looks like I'm yours anyway," Glory said dryly. She wondered why she wasn't fighting harder to leave this little town. But she felt as if she'd begun a story, and she wanted to stay around a couple of days to see what the characters did next. "Sounds like you're all set to make a false arrest."

Carl scowled. "Don't be telling me how to do my job."

Glory didn't answer, because there was a loud knock at the door. Well, it wasn't so much of a knock as it was a pounding. A very loud pounding. The sort of sound a crutch would make in the swinging arm of an impatient man.

"Open up!" The command came with the crutch pounding.

Carl Wall walked back to the door and swung it open.

There he stood. Her avenging angel. Glory swallowed. It must be a trick of light. Maybe the reflection of the snow outside. She'd read in her Bible about angels last night and her imagination was being overactive. But Matthew sure looked like Daniel's vision, even down to the halo of golden light surrounding his head. She mouthed the words silently. *"There stood a certain man—his face like the appearance of lightning, his eyes like torches of fire."*

Glory swallowed again. Definitely torches of fire.

"Your game's over," Matthew said, and stepped inside the room.

Glory started to breathe again. The halo of light didn't follow Matthew. It stayed just where it was and, when her eyes followed the beam downward, she saw the flashlight in Josh's mittened hands. The boy loved lights even in the day. She smiled. She wasn't crazy. It was artificial light. That's all. She was perfectly able to tell the difference between an angel of God and an ordinary man.

"You can't arrest her," Matthew said as he looked squarely at Carl Well. "She hasn't done anything illegal."

"Loitering," the deputy said smoothly. "There's always loitering."

"She wasn't loitering." Matthew took a deep breath.

"Then what was she doing in the hardware store?" the deputy pressed.

"Painting." Matthew paused.

"For pay?"

"No, not for pay, but—"

"Then it's loitering," the deputy said in satisfaction. "Next thing to panhandling. Street artists. If she's got no job, she's loitering."

"Well, if she needs a job, she's got a job," Matthew said in exasperation. "She's working for me."

Carl looked from Matthew to Glory and then back to Matthew. The satisfied look on the deputy's face grew. "Told me she worked for the Seattle Police Department."

"Well, she doesn't. She's working for me," Matthew said forcefully, as though he could convince the deputy of his statement by the sheer pressure of his words. "As of today."

"But I—" Glory started to protest. Why was it these people were so willing to believe she was an angel and so reluctant to believe she worked for a police department? Which was more likely? Then she saw the look on Matthew's face. Pain was drawing his skin tight. He shouldn't be on his feet. She looked back at the deputy. "What difference does it make where I work—if you're going to arrest me, do it. If not, let me go."

"Arrest you? He can't arrest you!" Mrs. Hargrove pushed her way into the room and stood there looking solid and indignant.

"Don't be telling me how to do my job."

"I'm a voter and I can jolly well tell you how to do your job!" Mrs. Hargrove jabbed her finger in the deputy's face. "Besides, I've known you since you were in diapers. That ought to count for something."

Glory watched the muscles slowly coil in the deputy's face.

"Hmph!" Mrs. Hargrove crossed her arms and said smugly, "Can't lock her up anyway. We don't even have a jail."

"Well, I won't have to lock her up. I'll settle for a ticket if I can find an upstanding citizen to take

responsibility for watching her—maybe see she does
some community service.'' The deputy looked
pleased with himself. ''Yes, an upstanding citizen is
just what I need. Maybe someone like a minister.''

''But we don't have a minister, Carl Wall, and you
know it,'' Mrs. Hargrove said indignantly.

''We would have if you'd given the nod to my
cousin Fred,'' the deputy said smoothly.

''Your Fred isn't trained to be a pastor.'' Mrs. Hargrove put her hands on her hips. ''Besides, he isn't
even a believer.''

''Well, he needs a job. He sent in his résumé. You
didn't have any other applicants. In my book, that
makes the job his.''

''Being a pastor isn't just a job. It's a calling. Besides, it's a good thing for you we don't have a minister around.'' She drew in her breath sharply and
looked at Matthew.

''If there's no minister, that leaves jail. I can always send her to the jail in Miles City.''

''But that's an awful place,'' Mrs. Hargrove protested. ''They're talking about closing it down. It's
not even heated, just a big old cement block. You
can't put someone in there in winter!''

''Well, it's not my first choice. But since you're
too good to have the likes of Fred as a minister, I
guess I don't have any other options now, do I?''

''The voters won't like this.''

The deputy shrugged. ''I tried to be reasonable. I'm
sure Fred mentioned he was willing to read the Bible
and get an idea of what the thing was all about. On-
the-job training, so to speak. But no, you need to have
someone who believes the whole thing. It's not too
late. Fred's probably at home right now. We can call

him and make the deal," he added smugly. "Remember, no minister means the angel goes to jail."

"But…" Mrs. Hargrove struggled to speak. "This is outrageous!"

"No minister means the angel goes to jail," the deputy repeated stubbornly.

"I'm a minister," Matthew said softly. It was freezing outside and still a thin sheen of sweat covered his forehead. "At least, according to the state. Marrying, burying—I can do all those. I expect I can keep my eye on an angel."

"You're a what?" The deputy looked skeptical.

"A minister." Matthew had a sinking feeling. He shouldn't have said anything. But he couldn't stand the thought of Glory spending time in that jail.

"You had a church?"

"Yes, in Havre."

"Well, why aren't you preaching here? We could use a minister at the church," the deputy persisted. "Even Fred would give way to a real preacher."

"I don't preach anymore," Matthew said evenly. His breath was shallow, but he was plowing his way through. He couldn't let his annoyance flare. Not if he wanted the deputy to cooperate.

"What? You retired from it?"

"In a way."

"Mighty young to be retired."

"Most people change jobs over a lifetime."

"But ministers?" the deputy asked, puzzled. "I've never known a minister to just quit his job before."

"Well, now you do," Matthew snapped. "Just let me know what I need to do to supervise the ang—I mean, Glory, and I'll do it."

"See, we do have a minister," Mrs. Hargrove said triumphantly. "God provides."

"Well, God isn't providing much," the deputy said as he nodded toward Matthew. "But I suppose it'll be all right." The deputy admitted defeat grudgingly. "I'll just write that ticket and you can set her up with some worthwhile community service. She works off the fine. If she messes up, she pays the fine. Simple. I'll check in later this week."

"Community service?" Matthew asked in surprise. "Doing what? All our roads are snowpacked. We don't have a jail. Or a library. Not even a post office. We don't need anything done."

"Except," Mrs. Hargrove interrupted hesitantly, "we do need an angel for the Christmas pageant."

"Ah, yes, the pageant." Matthew sighed. Odd how this pageant had grown so big in the minds of everyone this year. Several of the churches in Miles City had decided to send a few visitors to Dry Creek for the annual Christmas Eve pageant. It all sounded very friendly. But Matthew knew enough about churches to know what was happening. A few do-gooders in Miles City had asked a handful of single people, likely mostly widows, to visit Dry Creek on Christmas Eve and they'd accepted, feeling righteous. No doubt it was a gracious way for the churches to deliver food baskets to some of the poorer families in Dry Creek. But even after they hosted their pageant, Matthew doubted the people of Dry Creek would accept charity. The people of Dry Creek were proud and they'd get by on their own or not at all. Food baskets from outsiders would not be welcome.

"We've got the costume—wings, robe, everything," Mrs. Hargrove continued, "All we need is the angel."

"That's settled, then," the deputy said as he pulled out his ticket book.

It wasn't settled at all in Glory's mind, but she decided to take the hastily scrawled ticket so the deputy would leave. There'd be no fine. She knew any judge would dismiss the charges when he saw the ticket. She'd save her objections for later.

The only reason Glory let Mrs. Hargrove talk her into looking at the costumes was so Matthew would sit down. He was being gallant and standing with his shoulder leaning on his crutch. At least if they moved to the costumes, he'd take a seat.

The costumes were stored in a small room on the other side of the church kitchen. Mrs. Hargrove pointed it out and then left with the children. The room had one small square window, high on the wall, and a single light bulb hanging from the ceiling. Glory stood on a small stool to pull down the angel wings. Matthew sat on a hard-backed chair in the corner of the room.

"Watch the dust," Matthew warned as Glory pulled the wings off the high shelf. Waves of dust floated down over her.

Glory sneezed. "Too late."

Yes, it is too late, Matthew thought to himself glumly. He'd vowed to keep his secret, and now it would be all over Dry Creek in minutes. And the irony was it wasn't true anymore. He was no more a minister than Glory was an angel. Less, in fact, because when she stood with her head in front of that single bulb, she at least looked like an angel. Flying copper hair with flecks of gold. Milky skin. A voice that melted over him like warm honey. He found himself wishing he were still a minister, that his life had been uncomplicated by searing grief and confused pain. He already knew Glory well enough to know she'd never settle for less than a godly man. A man of faith. A man he, Matthew, couldn't be anymore.

"I expect the halo's up there, too," Matthew added as Glory dusted off the white cardboard wings. He could see the strand of gold Christmas garland hanging over the top shelf.

"You know, I'd be happy to do something else for community service," Glory said as she pulled the old garland off the shelf. It had lost most of its glitter and all of its fluff. "I could give painting lessons or something."

Matthew didn't voice his protest. He'd developed a longing almost as intense as his sons to see Glory dressed up in an angel costume. "I think Henry has some gold garland at the store. You could use that if you want."

"I don't know." Glory sat down on the stool. A faint cloud of dust still fell down around her. "I just don't feel like an angel this year."

"Oh." Matthew didn't want to press. He hoped the one word was enough.

"Well, look at me," Glory said. "Here I am— broke, in a strange town, almost arrested, uncertain what to do next with my life."

"Yeah, I suppose angels never wonder what to do," Matthew agreed. For a minute he thought Glory was reading his mind and heart. Then he saw the confusion on her face. He shifted on his chair so he could see her better. "They just get their marching orders and they march. Piece of cake. But none of the excitement of being human.''

"I guess the grass is always greener. We look at them. They look at us,'' Glory agreed quietly and then asked, "Do you believe angels are really jealous of us?''

"I'm not a minister anymore.'' Matthew began his standard disclaimer. He was no longer qualified to give spiritual advice. "I mean, I'm licensed still. But that's all. Just for the state.''

"I figured that out,'' Glory said. When she'd heard Matthew admit to being a minister, she'd felt the pieces click in her heart. Matthew as a minister made sense. "But that's not why I'm asking. I just want to know what you think.''

Matthew leaned back. He tried to separate what he believed from what he'd trained himself to believe. When he was a minister, he'd chased away any question, any doubt. He believed in confidence. Now he was just Matthew.

"Yes,'' Matthew finally said. "Yes, I think they must envy us. We can have babies.''

Glory smiled. "I never thought of that.''

Matthew caught his breath. He was grateful for the shadows that hid him in the small room. She was beautiful when she smiled. Like a Botticelli goddess.

"What's it like?'' Glory asked quietly, and startled Matthew. For a second he thought she was reading his mind; then he realized she was talking about babies. "When you had the twins,'' she continued. "What was it like?''

"Like winning the World Series.''

"I thought it might be something like that,'' she said. "I envy you.''

"Someday you'll know what I mean," Matthew said. The picture of Glory with a baby glowed warm inside of him. He bet the little thing would have milk-white skin and red hair. "It's like no other feeling. I can't even describe it. You'll just have to wait and see for yourself."

"I guess so," Glory agreed. She didn't want to tell him that there was no point in waiting—she knew she'd never have a baby. The accident had snatched that dream away from her. It wasn't that she didn't think he'd understand. He'd obviously known pain in his life. Maybe he'd understand too well. She just didn't want to see pity fill his eyes when he looked at her. And what else could he feel but pity? That's one of the reasons she'd avoided becoming close to men. She didn't want to see that look in the eyes of someone she loved.

"Will you have more babies?" Glory asked, and then hurried on at the surprised look on Matthew face. "I mean, if you remarried, would you want to have more children?"

"Children are the trump card in life. I'd have as many as I could."

Glory nodded. That was good. It was as it should be. He was a good father. His sons were good. It was all very good. It just didn't include anyone like her. "I'd like to go look for that garland now."

Matthew watched the light leave Glory's face. She put the cardboard wings under her arm and headed for the door. He had no choice but to follow.

The cold air hit Glory in the face and pinched the color out of her cheeks. It was only a hundred feet between the door to the hardware store and the door to the church, but it felt as if the few steps iced her to the soul. She needed to stop thinking about babies that would never be born. Her guilt was over. Her mother had forgiven her. God had forgiven her. Some days she'd even managed to forgive herself. It was over. She needed to stop grieving.

The smell of coffee greeted her when she stepped back into the warmth of the hardware store. Elmer and Jacob were still arguing.

"Heard them federal boys are going to close in on the rustlers now that they figured it isn't just happening here," Jacob insisted.

Elmer waved the words away. "They aren't even close. They don't know how. Why or when. What've they got? Nothing."

"They'll find them at the inspection plants, now that they're requiring papers before they grade the meat," Jacob said almost fiercely. "They'll find them. They've got to."

Elmer opened his mouth and then saw Glory. His mouth hung open for a full minute before it formed into an excited oval. He turned to Jacob and gummed his mouth several times before he got the words out. "Blazes, why didn't we think of it before?"

"Huh?"

"Look at her." Elmer pointed to Glory.

Glory's heard sank. She had a feeling she was falling deeper.

"She's a government agent," Elmer said triumphantly. "I heard rumors they were hiring a civilian to look into the cattle problem. She's a spy."

Glory shook her head. First angels and then spies. "You boys need to get out more."

"Don't worry, we understand," Elmer said with a wink. "You don't want to blow your cover."

"I don't have a cover," Glory said patiently as she heard the door open behind her. A gust of wind blew against her back and then stopped as the door closed.

"Why would you need a cover?" Matthew said as he used his crutch to hobble over to the counter. The dreams of Glory in his bed had stayed with him all day. "Didn't the twins get you an extra blanket last night?"

Glory blushed. "It's not that kind of cover." Glory pulled herself together. Maybe she'd sleep on the floor tonight. It didn't seem quite right to sleep in Matthew's bed. "They mean cover like spy cover. They think I'm a spy for the government. Looking into some cattle business."

Matthew leaned his crutch against the counter. So that was it. Maybe it was business that brought a woman like her to a small town on the backside of Montana.

"You never did say why you were driving through," he said, keeping his voice light and casual. She'd be a good spy. That innocent look of hers hid a quick mind. He wondered if she worked for the FBI or the Department of Agriculture. "Or where you were headed."

"I wasn't headed anywhere. I was just driving," Glory said.

"It's winter. Most folks don't go driving through Montana for pleasure this time of year," Matthew countered. The passes were slippery over the Rockies and even the flatlands had their share of ice and snow. No, Montana wasn't a pleasant drive in the winter.

Glory shrugged. "I'm not most folks."

She had him there, Matthew thought. There was

nothing ordinary or plain about her. She was the exotic orchid of the flower kingdom. The red-hot pepper of the spice family. The flaming gold of the color spectrum. He had a fleeting desire to tell her so. But then a thought came from left field and slugged him in the stomach. If she was undercover, she was someone else in another life. She could be someone's mother. She could be someone's daughter. Worse yet, she could be someone's wife.

"I could talk to the deputy if you've got somewhere else to be on Christmas," Matthew said. His stomach muscles tensed. She'd want to be with her husband on Christmas if she had one. "He can't hold you here."

"I'd thought about spending Christmas with my mother."

Matthew's stomach knotted. The mother could be a husband as easily as he stood here. "In Seattle?"

Glory nodded.

"You won't have a white Christmas there," Matthew offered. It was none of his business if she had another life that had nothing to do with Dry Creek, but he couldn't stop himself. "The twins would love to have you stay."

Glory stopped her head from nodding. She'd love to spend Christmas with the twins as much as they wanted her to spend it with them. But she had more wisdom than the twins. She knew that sometimes a day's happiness came with a price tag attached. If she stayed for Christmas, she'd regret it later when she had to leave. And leave she would. Because as much as she might dream about a life with someone like Matthew, she wasn't the woman for him.

*   *   *

No one could accuse the churches in Spokane of being quiet. It was prayer meeting night, and the Bullet sat first on the outside steps of one church and then another. He heard it all. John 3:16. ''Amazing Grace.'' The Lord's Prayer. He'd felt a little self-conscious just sitting outside, but he did anyway. He wasn't fit to go inside, and he knew it. Besides, he needed to be at the door before anyone came out so he could be sure to see the woman if she left.

His plan earned him a few curious looks, but he congratulated himself on doing fine until he reached a church on the east side.

''Give me a hand,'' the old man asked as he started to climb the stairs.

The Bullet looked around, but everyone else was already inside the church. There was no one to help the man but him.

Chapter Five

Matthew was true to his word, Glory thought. Dinner her second night not only didn't float in milk, it didn't come from a cardboard box, either. He made a salmon loaf, baked potatoes and green beans. There were fresh chives for the baked potatoes and mushrooms in the green beans. Betty Crocker couldn't have done better.

"I could help," Glory said for the tenth time since Matthew had shooed her out of the kitchen. She listened to pans rattle as she sat on the sofa and Matthew did dishes. Glory tried to remember if she'd ever had a man make her dinner before—and then insist on doing the dishes even though he was on crutches. Not that Matthew had made the dinner especially for her, she reminded herself. The twins had needed dinner, too.

"Please, let me help. I'm not used to being waited on." She started to get up from the sofa.

Matthew grunted from the kitchen. "Stay put. Do you good to take it easy."

Two pairs of twin arms reached up to pull her back to the sofa.

"Don't angels have daddies to cook for them?" Joey asked quietly as she settled back down. He pressed so close to her she could feel his worry. "I told my daddy he needed to make angel food cake. Maybe then you'd stay."

Glory smoothed back the hair on Joey's forehead. "You don't need to feed me angel cake."

"We had to give our fish some fish food. That's all they ate," Josh added solemnly as though she hadn't spoken. He was on her other side. "They ate and ate, but they died anyway."

"Do fish go to heaven when they die?" Joey looked up at her quizzically.

"No, silly," Josh answered for her. "There's no water in heaven. Only clouds. Isn't that right?" He looked to Glory for reinforcement and then added scornfully, "Besides, fish can't be angels. They can't fly."

"You know, we should learn about angels," Glory said decisively. She remembered her father always took this tactic when she was a child. Everything led to a lesson. Once the twins learned about real angels, maybe they'd let her be human. The truth did set people free, even if those people were only five years old. "Let me go get a Bible."

"We got one." Josh ran to a shelf and pulled down an old black Bible. The gold lettering on the front said "Family Bible," and the back of the leather cover looked as if it had been scorched. Josh carried the Bible to her as if it was a basket of precious jewels. Glory put her fingers to the burned mark around the edge just to be sure. So, she thought, smiling,

something had been snatched from that fire after all.
There was hope for Matthew yet.

"Are you going to tell us about an angel?" Joey
asked, his voice low and excited.

Glory flipped through the Bible. She knew just the
angel for the boys. "Not only an angel, but some big
cats, too."

Glory saw their eyes grow big.

"The king made a rule…" Glory said, beginning
to paraphrase chapter six of Daniel. She knew the
story well. She didn't need to read it from the Bible
that lay on her lap.

The twins listened to the king's dilemma and the
story of his evil advisors.

"Finally the king had no choice. He'd been tricked.
He needed to put Daniel in a den with big cats called
lions."

"Mrs. Hargrove told us about the lions," Joey
whispered as he moved closer to Glory. "They eat
people."

Josh shivered and snuggled closer to her other side.
"I want a dog. No cats."

"These are special cats." Glory put an arm around
each boy. They both shifted closer. "Not like the cats
you know. Much, much bigger than the cats around
here."

"A trillion times bigger?" Josh asked. He was
clearly relishing the story.

"Almost. And there's no need to be afraid. There
aren't any lions around here."

The twins looked momentarily disappointed and
then Josh said. "But there's cats. Mr. Gossett next
door has cats. They'll get you."

"Cats might scratch you, but they won't eat you."

"But they're *Mr. Gossett's* cats," Josh said as though that explained everything. "He doesn't eat. He drinks his meals. Mrs. Hargrove says."

"Maybe his cats don't eat, either." Joey took up the thought excitedly. "Maybe they lick you instead. Like an ice cream cone. Maybe that's how they eat. Lick, lick, lick—then you're gone. I've seen them lick people." He shivered. "I don't want them to lick me."

"You can't get licked away." Glory had forgotten how much young boys liked to flirt with danger. "Or get drunk away. Or bitten away. You're completely safe with cats."

Glory showed the twins the picture in the Bible. The reds and blues of the scene had faded, but the lions looked scary. And the angel still looked majestic with his flowing white robes and golden hair.

"That's an angel," Joey said in awe as he traced the picture. "With real wings."

Glory felt a pair of little hands reach up and lightly touch her shoulder blades as though checking.

"No wings," she assured them.

Matthew turned the light off in the kitchen and leaned against the doorway leading to the living room. He'd built a fire earlier, and the light made Glory and his sons look golden. Their heads were bent together over a book, two little blond heads with a bronze one in the middle. He had heard the excited whispers as he washed the dishes in the kitchen. He felt a swell of contentment fill him. He'd do more than wash a few dishes to give his sons time with a woman like Glory.

Then the shadows shifted, and Matthew saw what

the three were reading. He tensed. The Bible. He'd bought that Bible when the twins were born. Susie had used it to record the twins' births—their weight, height and first gestures. They'd planned to be a family around that Bible. He and Susie had read from it for family devotions when the twins were in their strollers. They'd planned to record their anniversaries in the book and the births of more babies.

"It's time for bed," Matthew said abruptly. He supposed he shouldn't be surprised the twins had found the Bible. It wasn't hidden. He just hadn't expected to deal with their claim on it so soon.

"Aah," Josh groaned. "We were just at the good part."

"We can finish it tomorrow night," Glory said as she hugged each of the boys and then took her arm away so they could scoot off the sofa.

"Can we get a den?" Josh turned to Matthew. "Ricky's family has a den."

"Different kind of den." Glory tried to pluck the thought from him before he got going in that direction. "This kind of den is a cave. It's made from rock. All dark inside."

"Oh." Josh seemed to be thinking.

Matthew smiled. He didn't tell Glory, but he already knew a den would be made from blankets tomorrow. Josh loved acting. "Get washed up and I'll tuck you in." The boys ran out of the room.

"You can't!" Alarms went off in Glory's stomach. All thoughts of cats and dens vanished. *Tuck them in! Tucking in meant Matthew upstairs in the twins' room!* Matthew wasn't supposed to be able to climb stairs. She wasn't sure she wanted him to see the cocoon she'd built in his bed last night. She'd wrapped blankets around herself snugly, but she'd lined up one of his pillows to lie beside her in the night. She'd told the twins the pillow was her teddy bear, but a grown man would…well, he might see it differently.

"Figure of speech," Matthew said as he watched Glory's face. The gold from the fire and the blush fanning out over her face made her look like rare porcelain. "I meant I'd give them a kiss good-night. Down here, of course."

"Of course." Glory smoothed down her skirt. "I should go up, too."

"It's only seven-thirty," Matthew protested as he lowered himself onto the sofa and propped his crutches against the wall. His shoulders ached and the palms of his hands burned where he leaned on the crossbar of the crutch. He should be thinking of sleep himself, but he was wide-awake. It occurred to him that his twins weren't the only ones who missed having some quiet time with a woman. "Sit with me for a while and talk."

Glory hesitated. The sofa that had seemed so large when she and the twins were sitting on it seemed to have shrunk now that Matthew was on the other end. She didn't want to be skittish and scoot over to the edge of the sofa, but she wasn't sure it felt safe to be within reaching distance of Matthew. Not that she expected him to reach for her, she told herself. Be reasonable. He only wants some light conversation after a day's work.

Matthew watched the reluctance streak across her face, and he remembered Elmer's words about her being an undercover agent. He wondered if she was remembering a husband or boyfriend who laid claim to her real life. He sure wished he knew if she was undercover.

"We don't usually have salmon, not even canned—not this close to the Big Sheep Mountains," he began. His mouth was dry. He wasn't used to entrapping a federal agent. "These mountains are cattle country through and through. Folks here pride themselves on beefsteaks, even now with all the…" He deliberately let his voice trail off to see if she'd pick up the scent like a federal agent would.

"Yes, the rustling." Glory latched on to the topic with relief. Nothing could be more impersonal than beefsteaks, she thought to herself with satisfaction. "How long has that been going on? Tell me everything you know."

Matthew's heart sank. She'd taken the bait with gusto. Maybe she was an agent, after all. Why else would a woman from out of town care about the rustling? "Cattle have been missing for the past year, I suppose. Probably started last winter. They free range most of the cattle around here in the winter, and so they don't do a complete count until the snow thaws and it comes close to calving time."

"Surely they don't leave those cows out all winter?" Glory asked in alarm.

Matthew smiled. That narrowed the field some. Unless she was a very good actress, she didn't work for the Department of Agriculture. "They have windbreaks set up, sometimes sheds, and the cows grow a thick coat. If it's real cold they can always wander down to the fences and someone will let them into the barn area. And they drop bales of hay to them, by pickup mostly. In bad winters they've dropped hay from small planes or helicopters."

"Well, maybe there's no rustling at all," Glory offered. She was having a hard time concentrating now that Matthew had started rubbing his shoulder. The crutches must be giving him trouble. His hands were what were giving her trouble. They were large and muscled, lightly haired and lightly tanned. "Maybe the cows are still out there."

"That's why it's so hard to know for sure when it all started," Matthew admitted. His hands found the knot in his shoulder and he sighed as he rubbed it. "A few cows here and there—who knows? Maybe they're holed up in a gully somewhere. But the Big Sheep Mountain Ranch has had their hands riding all over the range—covered it with a fine-tooth comb and didn't find the cattle or any carcasses. There needs to be one or the other. Even the buzzards can't carry off a whole cow."

"Sounds just like the Old West," Glory said. She'd never given too much thought to the life of a cow. Or a buzzard. Or a cowboy. "Is it the Big Sheep Mountain Ranch that's thinking of becoming a dude ranch?"

Matthew winced. His fingers had hit a nerve on his shoulder. "They don't call it dude ranch around here. I think the politically correct term is guest ranch. Doesn't offend the 'guests' as much. And, yes, it is the Big Sheep. If they follow through. They've had some tourism consultant down from Helena. It appears the scenery around the Big Sheep Mountains is as valuable as the cows. Maybe more so when you throw in the fact that we've got the Tongue River and the Yellowstone River close by and we're not far from Medicine Rock State Park. Some say we're the not-so-bad part of the Badlands, too."

"Well, at least the town will survive, then." Glory bit her lip. She shouldn't say anything, but Matthew was going to be even more sore after he finished trying to massage his one shoulder. His angle was all wrong.

"There's survival and there's survival. Some folks think the dudes will change the town so much we might as well lie down and die in the first place. Go with dignity. Elmer keeps going on about how he doesn't want to have to look the part of a rancher when he's face-to-face with some fancy lawyer who's only coming here for two weeks to pretend he does something real with his life. Says the old ghosts of all those cowhands that used to ride for the XIT Ranch in its glory will rise up and protest if we sell out like that."

"What do the women think?" Glory shifted on the sofa. Now Matthew was both massaging at the wrong angle and twisting his shoulder the wrong way, too. He'd throw his back out if he wasn't careful.

Matthew chuckled. "Mrs. Hargrove is all set to evangelize the dudes."

Glory couldn't stand it any longer. "Here. Let me massage that for you. You're going to end up back in the clinic."

Glory stood behind the sofa and put her hands on Matthew's shoulder. She'd kneaded the shoulders of a fair number of tired cops in her day down at the station. This shouldn't be any different. It shouldn't matter that firelight instead of fluorescent light streamed into the room or that her heart beat a little too fast when she touched one particular man's shoulders.

Matthew sighed. Maybe Glory was an angel, after all. Her touch certainly put him in mind of heaven.

"Well, Mrs. Hargrove might do some good that way." Glory refocused on the conversation. She needed to concentrate. "With her evangelistic zeal."

"I don't know about that. You know as well as I do they'll only see her as 'local scenery.' A person has a right to be taken more seriously than that. I'd rather folks openly disagreed with her rather than see her as scenery."

"What was it Paul said? 'I am all things to all men whereby I might win some.'" Glory located the knot on Matthew's neck and rubbed it gently.

"He didn't mention anything about being scenery."

Glory felt the knot on Matthew's neck tighten beneath her fingers. He was even more tense now than when she'd started.

Glory had a flash of insight. "Was that what it was like for you?"

"Huh?" Matthew looked up at her too quickly.

"Being a minister," Glory said softly, and stopped massaging him. "Was that what it seemed like when you were a minister?"

Matthew took a deep breath and exhaled. How did she know? "Only at the end."

"After Susie died?"

Matthew nodded. "I was standing up there in front of the congregation and I felt so empty inside. Like I was only the picture of a minister standing in a pulpit. Like none of it was real."

"Grief will do that to you."

Matthew shook his head. He'd thought about this every day since he'd made the decision to walk away from that pulpit. "A real minister would have been able to cope. Oh, maybe not easily, but somehow. If I'm not able to be a minister in the bad times, what kind of a minister am I in the good times?"

"A human minister," Glory reassured him emphatically. She saw the defeat on his face. And the sorrow.

The sound of little feet padding swiftly down the steps distracted them both.

"I'm first," claimed Josh as he flung himself into his father's arms.

There goes one good massage wasted, Glory thought wryly. Pain didn't stop Matthew. He opened his arms wide enough to gather both boys to him. No matter what Matthew thought about his role as a minister, it was clear that his role as a father came naturally to him. Love between Matthew and his sons was a given. It was the bedrock of the twins' lives.

"Kiss?" Josh had left his father's arms and now stood before Glory.

Glory smiled. "Of course." She leaned down and hugged Josh. Then she gave him an exaggerated kiss, the kind she'd loved as a child. She "smacked" Josh so hard on the cheek that he started to giggle. Then she offered her own cheek. "Now me."

Josh puckered up and put his lips on her cheek for a big smack.

"Now Joey." Glory saw Joey was hanging back shyly. When she opened her arms to him he smiled and ran up to her. She repeated the ritual with him.

Then both twins went to the edge of the sofa and knelt down as if it was the expected thing to do. This was obviously their habit.

"God bless…" Josh ran down his list first and then

Joey followed. They both blessed classmates, Mrs. Hargrove, their father, the angel and even Mr. Gossett's cats.

Glory had to admit she was surprised. The night before she'd been upstairs putting clean sheets on her bed when the twins had made their trip down for a kiss. She'd had no idea Matthew prayed with them. Correction, she thought to herself, Matthew didn't pray with them, he watched over them while they prayed. Rather fiercely at that, as though challenging God to refuse their simple requests.

"Susie would have my hide if I didn't raise them to pray," Matthew said when the twins had gone upstairs.

"But don't they wonder why you don't pray?"

"We haven't really come to that bridge yet." Matthew picked up the family Bible, intending to stand up and put it back on the shelf. But then he realized he couldn't stand, not holding the crutches and the Bible. So he set the Bible back down on the coffee table. "So far they just assume I pray beside my bed when it's my bedtime. Since I have a later bedtime, they don't see me."

"Before too long, they're going to realize—"

"I know. I'm a coward. I keep hoping that maybe by the time they're old enough to ask the question they'll be old enough to understand." Matthew shifted his shoulder. He wished Glory would massage his neck again.

"I hope you're right." Glory watched fatigue and pain sketch lines on Matthew's face as he sat there. "Your shoulder still hurt?"

"Yes."

Glory stood up and walked behind the sofa. She

reached down and began to knead Matthew's neck muscles again. This time she felt him relax. He leaned his head back and closed his eyes. The light from the fireplace gave a golden cast to his face. She had a swift urge to lift her hands from his neck and trace the line of his jaw. The suddenness and the strength of the feeling surprised her. Abruptly she pulled her hands away from him. "You need your sleep. I should be going upstairs."

Matthew's eyes opened. "You're really good at giving neck massages."

"Experienced, anyway," Glory said. She was glad she was standing behind him and he couldn't see that her face was flushed. "I give them all the time to the men in the department."

"The police department?" Matthew asked warily. He remembered that's where she said she worked. He supposed it was possible. The FBI might borrow someone like her to do a little preliminary research on cattle rustling. She would find out things a regular agent wouldn't. Just look how the folks in Dry Creek had already taken to her. She inspired confidences. He certainly found it easy to talk to her. Too easy.

Glory nodded. "The captain taught me. He used to give them, too. Said it was one thing a policeman always needed." Glory was chattering and she knew it. But it helped her collect her composure. She'd never had these feelings while giving a neck massage to anyone else. "From all the time in the patrol cars. And then the stress."

Matthew listened. Okay, so the police department angle was true. He didn't think Glory would lie. Not even if she was undercover.

Glory didn't stop. "Some of the worst stress. The

captain used to say being on patrol was like being squeezed into a little box for hours and then stepping out for a few seconds to get shot at.''

Shot at! Matthew stiffened. ''You don't work where you get shot at, do you?'' The thought of anyone shooting anywhere near Glory made him want to lock her in the house and never let her out. He hadn't thought about the undercover job in that regard. Surely no one would shoot at Glory.

''Well, not often—''

''*Not often!* What's not often?''

''Well...usually not really,'' Glory said, stumbling.

Matthew relaxed. ''That's good. But just for my peace of mind, tell me, when was the last time someone shot at you?''

''Last Wednesday.''

''*Last Wednesday!*'' Matthew turned around and looked at her. She was already making her way to the stairs. ''That's not often? *Last Wednesday!*''

''But it was nothing. Just some gang kids.''

''Nothing! I don't care if it was kids, their bullets are just as real!''

Matthew stood up. He forgot he needed the crutch. He didn't even feel the pain in his knee. He knew he didn't have the right to order Glory to quit her job. But last Wednesday! She made it sound as if getting shot at was an everyday thing.

''Well, their bullets are not as straight as some,'' Glory said softly. She had one foot on the first stair and she smiled. She could tell Matthew that last Wednesday was the only time a bullet had come anywhere near her, that her job was as safe as being a plumber—but she found she liked the fierce look of protection that covered his face. In the firelight, with his chestnut hair mussed from the massage, he looked like a Highland warrior.

Matthew stopped himself from demanding that she quit her job. It was not his place. He knew that. But surely someone should stop her. "What does your mother think about that?"

"My mother thinks I'm a grown woman," Glory said. It was true. Her mother had been shocked that a bullet had hit the building close to where Glory was standing. But she hadn't worried about Glory's ability to take care of herself. Only the captain ever worried about her.

"Well, there's no doubt about you being grown." Matthew ran his hand over his hair. He was beginning to feel the pain in his knee, and he sank back down to the sofa. "It's just, well, bullets. That's not good."

"I'll be fine," Glory said softly. She was touched he would worry about her. "I really don't get shot at often."

Matthew snorted and shook his head. "Not often. Last Wednesday."

"Not often," Glory repeated firmly as her feet climbed the second stair. She felt a smile curling around inside her. He cared about her. Matthew cared. Well, she thought as she tried to rein in her happiness, he cared that someone didn't shoot at her. It might not be so much after all. Even a stranger might care that she not be shot and killed. Or run over by a truck. Or fall off a building.

"Say, who fixed the step?" Thinking of tragic accidents reminded her of the loose board that had tripped Matthew the day before. Only it wasn't loose any longer. She saw the bright heads of the new nails that held the board firmly in place.

"I did."

"But you can't get up these stairs?" Glory measured the distance. The loose board had been near the top of the stairs. She looked down at Matthew sitting on the sofa in the firelight.

"I can if I do a kind of backward crawl—push, sit, push." Matthew looked up at her and grinned. "Mrs. Hargrove didn't think about crawling."

"No, I guess she didn't."

Mrs. Hargrove might not have thought about it, but Glory couldn't think of anything else. She thought about it when she brushed her teeth and slipped on her pajamas. She thought about it when she turned down the sheets on Matthew's bed. She even thought about it as she lay slipping into dreamland. And every time she thought about it she smiled. Matthew's virtue, not his knee, kept him downstairs. That was as it should be. She didn't want to start getting attached to a man she couldn't trust— What? The thought pulled her away from sleep and made her sit up straight in bed. Attached? Was she getting attached to Matthew? She knew she was a little attracted to him. Okay, a lot attracted to him. But attached and attracted were two different things. She couldn't afford to be attached. They had no future together. No future at all. And she'd best remember that. She couldn't afford to get attached. No, there must be no attachment. Absolutely none.

The Bullet carefully cut into his piece of lemon meringue pie.

His plans hadn't worked out. He hadn't counted on the floor inside the church being wet from all the rain. But when they reached the doorway, the Bullet saw the slickness. The old man didn't walk very well and the Bullet worried he might slip. *I can see him to his pew. Then I'll leave. Just a quick dive in and then I'll be gone.*

But the hymn started before he got the old man settled, and a woman pressed a hymnal into his hands.

After the service the old man, Douglas was his name, insisted on buying him a piece of pie. The Bullet gave up. What would it hurt to sit with the man a bit and have a piece of pie?

Chapter Six

The hoofbeats in Glory's dream turned to pounding. She woke uncertain if the pounding was real or in her head. It took a minute to remember where she was, but in the half-light of morning the room was beginning to look familiar. Matthew's room. She was safe in Matthew's room. But something had startled her, she decided. There, she heard it again. A pounding from downstairs.

Matthew was in the kitchen starting the fire when he heard the first pound on the door. He hadn't brought his crutches with him, but had hobbled from sofa to wall to doorway to chair so that he wouldn't need to prop them up when he lit the stove. It was a good plan, but it didn't get him to the front door any too soon.

"What's wrong?" Matthew yelled when he finally pulled the door open.

There stood Duane Edison, a slender teenager with dark hair that needed cutting and a scowl on his lean face that needed tending. The boy paused for a moment before demanding. "I need to talk to the angel."

Matthew didn't open the door any farther. "Can't it wait for morning?"

"It is morning," Duane said in surprise. "It's past six. The sun's even coming up."

"Not everyone lives on Montana farm time. She doesn't get up at five."

"I'm up." Glory could hear them as she walked down the stairs. She'd thrown a woolly robe on over her pajamas and put a pair of heavy socks on her feet. Her hair wasn't combed and her teeth weren't brushed, but she was up. "What's wrong?"

"You the angel?" Duane asked as he peered past Matthew's shoulder.

"Around here I guess I am." Glory sat down on the sofa. She was too tired to debate the fact before she'd even had any coffee. "What do you need?"

"You the one that got Linda all funny on me?" Duane entered the house.

"Aah, you're the Music man." Glory remembered.

"Jazz Man," Duane said, tight-lipped. The cold had pinched his face and left it colorless. He wore a black leather jacket and had his hands jammed far down into his pockets. "I'm the Jazz Man."

"Of course, I remember." Glory pulled her robe closer. It was cold in the house. "You're her boyfriend."

"Was her boyfriend," he corrected her sourly as he joined her on the other end of the sofa. He took his hands out of his pockets and rubbed them together. He looked up at Matthew. "Want me to start a fire for you?"

"Just got one started. It takes a few minutes to warm up. But thanks for the offer."

"Heard about your leg," Duane mumbled. "Need any help, let me know."

"Thanks. I appreciate that."

"It's not like I have lots to do now, anyway." The boy looked sideways at Glory. "Not since Linda gave me her ultimatum."

"Well, it's not like it needs to be forever. You kids are awfully young to get married." Glory stuck by her decision. Neither one of them looked a day over sixteen. It might not even be legal for them to marry without parental consent. "Way too young."

"Oh, we're still getting married." Duane looked up at her in determination. "It's just that now she wants a prenuptial agreement, says she won't even—" He stopped himself and looked at Matthew. "Well, you know, she won't—unless I sign an agreement." He looked at Matthew again, measuring him. "Is it true you're a preacher?"

"Was a preacher." Matthew nodded. Dry Creek didn't need a newspaper to get the news around. "Not anymore."

"Still, you probably don't…" Duane hesitated and then he hurried on. "I mean, you don't know what it's like."

Matthew squelched his chuckle. "I was a minister. I wasn't a eunuch. I know about sex and the trouble it can cause."

"It can get you into trouble, all right," Duane agreed with a sigh.

Glory decided the room was definitely getting warmer, even without the fire. "What kind of trouble are you and Linda in?"

"Oh, not that kind." Duane blushed. "We're careful."

"You wouldn't need to be careful if you didn't—" Glory stopped herself. If she knew anything about teenagers it was that one didn't inspire confidences by scolding them for the obvious. "What trouble is it, then?"

"It's money."

"Money?" Glory was surprised.

"Yeah, we need money if we're going to get married. Five thousand dollars."

"Why five thousand?"

"If we had five thousand we could put a down payment on the old Morgan place, not John's place, but his father's old place. It's not much, but it's good dry land and it's got a small house. Needs a new roof, but I could fix that. Already talked to the bank in Billings. They said we'd need five thousand at least. But neither of our folks have that to spare—couldn't ask them, anyway. So that's why I thought of music. I play a fair guitar and Linda sings real good. My friend Bob is good on the drums. Thought maybe we'd pick up some money at small county fairs and rodeos. Nothing big." Duane's face glowed proudly while he talked about their dream. "We'd have done it, too, except, well, you talked to Linda and…"

Glory's heart sank. "I didn't mean she should never marry you. Why, you both must still be in high school."

"Graduated last fall. Both of us."

"That'd make you how old?" Glory wasn't feeling any better. Giving love advice wasn't her calling in life. She should have sent the girl back to her mother.

"I'm nineteen. Linda's eighteen. We hadn't

planned on going to college, so I've been helping my folks and Linda's working at a doughnut place in Miles City. We've both been saving our money, but so far all we have is twelve hundred dollars. That's why I thought of forming the band. Thought we'd maybe even get some Christmas gigs.''

''I know some retirement homes up near Havre that might be willing to pay for a music program,'' Matthew said. His minister friends would be so happy to hear from him they'd probably pay the kids twice the usual rate. ''That's if you know any church music.''

''We grew up in Sunday school,'' Duane said indignantly. ''We know them all from 'The Old Rugged Cross' to 'This Little Light of Mine.'''

''Well, that sounds like a good plan,'' Glory said. ''Tell Linda to invite me to the wedding.''

''Oh, she'll have to be the one inviting, all right,'' Duane said with a bitter edge to his voice. ''After the prenuptial agreement, she'll make all the decisions.''

''What?''

''The prenuptial,'' he repeated as though she must know. ''She said you told her not to let me take advantage of her talent, so the prenup puts her in charge of everything. She's the lead singer. The money person. First on the deed to the Morgan place when we sign the paper. First in everything.'' Duane slumped down on the sofa. ''She's even the one calling the shots about, well, you know.... Even kissing,'' he wailed indignantly. ''Everything. She's in charge.''

''Oh, dear,'' Glory murmured as her eyes met Matthew's over the slumped figure of Duane. Matthew's eyes had a sympathetic twinkle in them.

Matthew leaned over and whispered to Glory, ''Not as easy as a person would think to be an angel. Lot like being a preacher. Everyone expects you to always know everything and always be right.''

"Well, they picked the wrong person for always being right.''

"No one's ever always right.''

"How do I fix things now?''

Matthew straightened. "Duane, why don't you bring Linda here for supper tonight? Glory and I will talk to her.''

"I hope you'll set her straight,'' Duane muttered as he stood. "A man can't have his wife wearing the pants in the family.''

"There's nothing wrong with a woman making decisions,'' Glory began indignantly. "Most women have good heads on their shoulders.''

"She going to be talking to Linda?'' Duane looked at Matthew skeptically and cocked his thumb at Glory.

"You don't have a clue, do you, son?'' Matthew put his arm around Duane's slender shoulders. "Being married isn't about one person making all the decisions. Being married is about teamwork. And a good team takes the best from both parties.''

"Yes, sir,'' Duane agreed glumly as he walked toward the door.

"See you and Linda tonight at five-thirty,'' Matthew said as he opened the door for the young man. "And remember, think teamwork.''

"Yes, sir.''

Matthew waited for the door to completely close before he grinned and announced, "How about we start out with you talking to Duane? Then we switch.''

"Sort of like good cop, bad cop?''

"Just giving them two perspectives."

"I don't think Duane wants two perspectives."

"That's why he needs them," Matthew said as he hobbled back to the kitchen door, whistling all the way.

Glory studied his face. It wasn't just the whistling. He was excited. "You like this, don't you? This people stuff. Giving advice. Solving problems. Helping out."

Matthew turned around as he reached the kitchen. "Yeah, I guess I do."

Glory fretted about Linda and Duane until she turned the key in the hardware-store door. Matthew was late taking the twins to school, so he'd asked her to open up for him so that Elmer and Jacob could get their coffee.

"Brrr." Glory watched her breath turn white. The hardware store was as cold inside as it was outside. "It'll take more than coffee to take the edge off this morning."

"It's a cold snap, all right," Elmer agreed. "Almost didn't get the pickup started to come down."

Yesterday Glory had set up her easel close to the front window of the hardware store. The night cold had frosted over the edges of the large window, but the middle was clear. She could look out and see the whole main street of Dry Creek.

Coffee could wait a minute, she decided. The view from this window was postcard perfect.

The Big Sheep Mountains stood solid and round in the distance, their low peaks wearing blankets of fresh velvety snow. About halfway down, the thick snow changed to thin gray patches mingled with muddy-green shrubs. On the frozen ground right outside in Dry Creek, old snow lined the asphalt street and bunched up against the buildings.

"How long has this town been here?" Glory asked as she turned to Elmer and Jacob. The two men were putting wood in the fire.

"Since the days of the Enlarged Homestead Act of 1909," Elmer said as he put a match to the kindling. "Folks—a lot of them from Scandinavia—came here. Trainloads of them—a body could lay claim to 320 acres of Montana and all they had to do was live on it for three years. Sounded like a dream come true."

Elmer paused to put his hands out to the warming fire. "Course, they couldn't predict the drought. And the hard times. Wasn't long before people all over these parts were leaving. They couldn't scrape together enough to plant crops, to eat, to live. But old man Gossett—father to the Gossett who lives next to the parsonage—owned the land here and he told folks we'd make it if we worked together. That's when they founded the town—called it Dry Creek after a little creek that used to flow into the Yellowstone. Folks thought the creek would come back after the drought ended and we could change the name of the town. The creek didn't return, but we kept the name. Kinda liked it after a while. Reminded us things have been worse. Gave us hope. We've always scraped by in Dry Creek before and we'll do it again."

"Hmph," Jacob added as he shut the door to the old woodstove.

Glory didn't know if he was agreeing or disagreeing "What do the young people do?" She was still thinking of Duane and Linda. "Do they stay or move away?"

"Most leave," Elmer said with a touch of scorn as he reached behind him for the electric coffeemaker. "There's not much work here and what work there is is hard work. Kids nowadays want it easy."

"Can't blame the kids for wanting to eat." Jacob defended them as he measured coffee into the filter.

"Maybe you need to start some kind of business here," Glory offered as she walked closer to the fire and rubbed her hands "I've read about Midwestern towns that brought in businesses so there'd be jobs for people. Maybe you could try that."

Elmer gave a bitter chuckle. "You see the window there. Look out it. Do you see anything that would make a big corporation move here?"

"I didn't say it needed to be a big corporation," Glory persisted as she spread her hands out to catch the heat that was already coming from the small cast-iron stove. "All you need is a few small businesses. Maybe an outfit that makes something."

"The women at the church made up a batch of jams one year that were good—I always thought they could sell them," Jacob said thoughtfully as he put his wooden chair in front of the fire.

"Well, that would be a start," Glory said as the bell over the door rang. A gust of cold air followed Matthew into the store. "Maybe they could hook up with a catalog. Do special orders. It'd definitely be a start."

The crutches kept Matthew from swiveling to close the door quickly, so another gust of cold came in before he got the door shut. "Sorry." Matthew wiped some fresh snowflakes off his wool coat. "Start of what?"

"Glory was thinking of new business ideas for Dry

Creek,'' Elmer informed him as the coffee started to perk.

"What kind of businesses?" Matthew asked as he took off his jacket and hung it on a nail behind the counter.

Glory tried not to look, but the snowflakes made Matthew's hair shine. He had flakes on his eyelashes and eyebrows. The cold drew the skin tight against his cheeks and forehead. Lean a pair of skis against his shoulder and he could be an advertisement for sweaters or skis or some resort. He could be a model.

"Any kind of business." Glory shrugged. "Jams. Woodworking. Modeling."

"Modeling? You mean sitting for a painting?" Matthew asked thoughtfully. "Would anyone pay for that?"

"I've heard they do if you're nude." Jacob poured himself a cup of coffee.

"I wasn't thinking of nude modeling." Glory blushed.

"Kind of artistic for the folks around here," Elmer said as he joined Jacob at the coffeepot. "But I suppose folks would do it to make a buck." He looked at Glory. His face was suspiciously deadpan. "What do you art people pay for nude modeling, anyway?"

"I've never paid anything," Glory protested.

"Well, you can't expect someone to do it for free," Jacob chided her, and then paused. "Well, maybe they would for you. What do you think, Reverend, would you model for free for the little angel here?"

Matthew choked on his laughter. He didn't know if it was possible for Glory's face to turn pinker. He kind of liked it that way. "Maybe if she did one of those abstract paintings so no one would recognize me. I wouldn't want to embarrass the boys.''

''I don't paint nude pictures. I wasn't even thinking of nude pictures. I meant modeling for catalogs and things.''

Elmer nodded wisely. ''Ah, underwear.''

''No, not underwear.'' Glory forced her voice to stay calm. ''I meant sweaters. Jackets. Clothes. That kind of thing. But that's only one idea. The jam idea is better. Why doesn't one of you mention that to the women?''

''Guess we could,'' Jacob conceded.

''There could be a big market for it if the dude ranch—I mean, the guest ranch goes into operation.''

''Don't remind me,'' Elmer said.

But reminding him was exactly what Glory intended to do. It allowed her to sit back while the two older men lamented what the dudes would do to Dry Creek. She felt like fanning her face, but she knew the men would notice her behavior and remark on it, since it was still chilly inside the store. So she resolutely began to mix some oils on her palate. Blue and green. She'd use blue and green for something. She never should have thought about modeling—any kind of modeling. Even sweaters made her think of broad shoulders. And hats made her think of masculine chin lines. And belts of trim waists. No, she should wipe out any thoughts of modeling from her mind. She'd focus on the blue and green. She had the colors mixed before she realized she'd mixed the exact color of Matthew's eyes.

Matthew watched Glory bristle and pretend to ignore the older men. He wondered if he should remind her that she'd neglected to put on the smock that she'd worn yesterday when she was working with oils. It'd be a shame if she got paint on the sweater she was wearing, a light pink that emphasized the color in her cheeks. He rather liked that pink sweater—it made her look cuddly. Maybe instead of saying something he should just take her smock over to her.

It was hard to be gallant on crutches, Matthew thought, grimacing as he held out the smock to Glory. His hand had pressed wrinkles in it where he'd clutched it close to the bar of his crutch handle.

"Thank you."

The day passed slowly for Matthew. Glory spelled him at the counter so he could go home and bake the cupcakes he'd forgotten to make. The church day-care staff was having a bake sale to help pay for the set design for the Christmas pageant.

"They need any bales of hay?" Elmer asked when Matthew got back. "Tell them I can donate all they need."

"And if the manger needs fixing, I can see to it," Jacob offered.

"I don't know if hay and a manger is going to be enough this year," Matthew said as he hobbled behind the counter and sat down on his stool. "Everyone's got it in their head that this year the pageant needs to be special."

"I could spray-paint the manger gold," Jacob suggested. "Maybe put some bells on it or something. Tack on some holly, even."

"I'll pass the word along to Mrs. Hargrove." Matthew chuckled. "Don't know how else to jazz things up."

"Jazz," Glory muttered as her brush slipped. She'd been so engrossed in painting she'd completely forgotten about the Jazz Man and Linda.

"Saltshaker's on the stove." Matthew called directions to Glory from his place by the sink. Tonight he was letting everyone help with the dinner. The twins were in the living room making sure the magazines were set straight. Glory had an apron on and was boiling water for pasta. They were having chicken parmigiana.

"So you're going to go with the 'just a team' theme?" Glory asked as she bent down to locate a strainer to drain the pasta once it cooked. "Horses in harness, that sort of thing?"

"Well, I suppose."

"So what do you want me to say?"

"Whatever you want," Matthew said as he grinned over at her. "You're half of the team. You decide."

"Well, this half of the team isn't so good at giving advice." Glory found the strainer. "Look at what my advice has already done."

"Now, that wasn't your fault." Matthew defended her staunchly. "Linda came to you and asked for your opinion. Besides, all couples have this discussion— best to do it before the wedding."

"Let's just hope there'll still be a wedding after I'm through with them."

Matthew laughed.

"More garlic bread?" Glory offered the plate to Duane. He was wearing a suit and tie and Linda was wearing a long gray dress. The couple were obviously nervous and on their best behavior. Even the twins were sitting at the table politely eating.

Duane nodded and took a piece.

"You'll have to give me your recipe," Linda said, smiling slightly at Glory.

"Not my recipe. Matthew made the garlic bread."

"Oh, really?" Linda appeared interested and gave Duane a meaningful look. "So Matthew helped with the meal."

Glory choked on the sip of water she'd taken. "No, *I* helped. Matthew cooked the dinner—garlic bread to chicken parmigiana. I helped by boiling water for the pasta."

"He did it all!" Linda's face lost its politeness. She was delighted. She nudged Duane. "He cooked the dinner!"

Duane groaned and looked at Matthew in disgust. "Now see what you've done."

Matthew nodded. "I'd guess the guys tell you cooking is women's work?"

Duane nodded.

"Ever think how helpless that makes you?" Matthew helped himself to another piece of garlic bread.

"Helpless?" Duane growled. "What do you mean?"

"Well, look at me," Matthew said. "I've had to learn how to cook the hard way. Every man needs to know how to cook and clean. The chores should be split."

"But I thought you said being married was teamwork," Duane protested. "I do half, she does half. Nothing that says my half needs to be meals. Besides, getting married better be about more than who's going to do the cooking!"

Matthew laughed. "It is. But I've got to warn you. Being married has its surprises!"

"Like what?"

Matthew sobered. He didn't want his failures to dampen the enthusiasm of the young couple before him. "I never knew what it would feel like to be so responsible for someone. I'd sworn to take care of that other person with all of my heart and all of my might. To do anything to keep her safe."

Matthew stopped himself. When the dull pain of loss at Susie's death had begun to ease, the guilt had started. He hadn't kept Susie safe. His faith had not been enough. But that was his failure. It was between him and God. No one else needed to suffer it with him. He should have sidestepped that question.

"Anyway, back to cooking." Matthew forced himself to smile. "The twins have paid the price of my learning to cook."

Duane cleared his throat. "Guess I could learn to cook some things. Maybe breakfast. Or spaghetti. Or something."

"My daddy can even cook angel cake," Josh boasted.

Glory groaned. "I'm not an angel."

"Not even a little?" Linda asked hesitantly.

Glory shook her head. Something was going on here. She didn't like the guilty look on the girl's face.

"Well, Debra Guthert asked me about you. I think she's writing you up as an angel for the paper in Billings."

Matthew had a sinking sensation. Debra Guthert lived in Miles City and wrote the "Southeastern" column for the *Billings Gazette*. Her column covered the ranches and small towns along the Yellowstone River, northeast of Billings past Terry and Glendive to the North Dakota border and the area south of Interstate 94 from Hardin to the Chalk Buttes. Except for a few colorful announcements from the Crow Indian Reservation, it was usually mundane things like family reunions and rattlesnake sightings. "Why didn't someone stop her?"

Matthew didn't need an answer to the question. An angel would make the Dry Creek Christmas pageant the social event of the winter. Which would mean— suddenly Matthew felt much better.

"You have to stay now." Matthew turned to Glory. Even Glory couldn't refuse the power of the press. "It's in print."

Glory looked around her. Five pairs of hopeful eyes. She groaned. How could she leave Dry Creek now?

Matthew stared into the embers of the fire. He'd wrapped so many blankets around himself he felt like a mummy. He was warm enough. The sofa was soft enough. The house was quiet enough. But he couldn't sleep. The frozen pain he'd lived in for the past four years was shifting. He could hear the cracking inside him as surely as he could hear the cracking of the Yellowstone River when the spring thaw came. And that cracking scared him. If his pain left him, he knew he'd want to love again. And how could he love again? He couldn't take another chance on love. He'd failed one woman. He didn't need to fail another one, especially not Glory.

"Go ahead and call her," Douglas urged the Bullet. The sadness in the old man's eyes was steady.

"You don't know what I'd give for one last phone call with my Emily."

Douglas was standing in the guest bedroom of his house with the receiver of a black phone stretched out to the Bullet.

What have I gotten myself into? The Bullet didn't know what to do. He was sailing in uncharted water. He knew how to act around other hit men. He knew how to act around clients. But a friend? A new friend? He didn't know the rules.

Chapter Seven

Glory wished she had a pair of sunglasses to hide behind. Two people had already stopped by the hardware store to ask her to sign their copy of the "Southeastern" column in this morning's *Billings Gazette*. Linda had not exaggerated. The column talked in glowing terms of the two little boys who believed an angel had come to Dry Creek for Christmas.

Mrs. Hargrove predicted that attendance at the Christmas pageant would soar now that everyone from Billings knew about the angel. In fact, it appeared that attendance might be too high. No one knew what to do with all the people they were expecting.

"We could open the windows to the church and people could stand outside and watch the pageant through them," Jacob said. Earlier he'd noted that the "Southeastern" column might have spread farther than Billings. "They might not hear the shepherds singing, but they could at least see them come down the aisle."

Jacob, Elmer and Mrs. Hargrove were gathered around the potbellied stove, drinking coffee and planning the Christmas pageant. Mrs. Hargrove had called a substitute to take over for her in the day-care program so that she could devote herself to planning for the pageant now that it looked as if it would be such a big affair. It was already December 22. They didn't have much time to plan for all the extra people coming. Glory decided that if you didn't listen too closely to the words, you would almost think the three were planning a war. Or at least a Southern ball.

"We'll need a place for coats." Mrs. Hargrove had a clipboard on her lap and a pencil in her hand.

"It'll be too cold. People won't give up their coats," Matthew said from his stool behind the counter.

Matthew was, Glory would almost swear to it, sorting nuts and bolts. What else could he be doing? He had a long piece of twine and he kept attaching first one nut and then a bolt to it. She was the only one who was sane this morning, she assured herself as she added the Madonna look to her sketch. She'd found out that Lori, the little girl who wanted the Betsy Tall doll, was going to be Mary in the pageant. Glory had decided to do a rough ink sketch of the girl from memory. It might come in useful for a program for the pageant. Now that she'd decided to stay for the event, she found herself getting excited.

"There's not going to be enough room." Mrs. Hargrove repeated her worry as she wrote a number on her notepad. "The church won't hold more than a hundred people. And that's if we put folding chairs in the aisles, open the doors to the kitchen and move the tract rack into the office."

"The young'uns are smaller, they'll squeeze in, sit on a parent's lap—maybe even on the floor," Elmer suggested. He rested his elbows on the table that usually held a checkerboard. Today the game board was missing and a pot of coffee stood in its place.

"Maybe we could get in a hundred and fifty." Mrs. Hargrove frowned as she added some numbers on her notepad.

"Wonder if we should charge?" Jacob asked from the sidelines. He'd stood up to get a new mug and was walking back toward the stove.

"Charge!" Mrs. Hargrove puffed up indignantly. "Why, we can't charge! It's a holy moment. Christ coming to earth. Shouldn't be any money changing hands."

"I just thought it'd make things easier for Christmas." Jacob spread his hands and sat back down on a straight-backed chair. "Raise a little money for the children and all."

"Well." The puff went out of Mrs. Hargrove, and she glanced sideways at Glory. "It would help. Don't suppose God would mind if it was for the children. Maybe we could just ask for a donation. We could get some of the things they wished for. Awful hard to see children go without at Christmas."

Glory stopped her sketching. She'd spent some time last night sorting the pictures she'd received from the children of Dry Creek. "I'm going to place the order. I've already called my friend Sylvia. She's going to help me. I'm just waiting to find out if there are other children who want to bring me a Christmas wish. Josh and Joey said they'd spread the word."

Matthew looked up from the ornament he was making, but kept silent. Josh had told him Glory had asked them to invite all of the children of Dry Creek to bring her a drawing. He knew Glory couldn't possibly be buying presents for all of the children in Dry Creek. Why, there must be forty children under twelve in the area. And there'd be another fifteen or so who hoped they were young enough for an angel present. And if all the children were like his two, that'd mean the presents were at least twenty dollars apiece. It'd add up to a thousand dollars minimum.

Matthew knew he should speak out. But he couldn't. If it was anyone but Glory making such ridiculous claims, he'd have no trouble. But this was Glory. He wanted to believe in her as much as the children of Dry Creek did.

"Well, we need to have faith this Christmas," Mrs. Hargrove said. "We might not have all of the money in the world. Fact is, we may not have much of it. But money isn't everything with God. The Lord fed the five thousand with a few loaves and fishes." Mrs. Hargrove had a determined look on her face that said if He could do it, they could do it. "We should be able to get the children something. Christmas isn't about big gifts, anyway."

Glory gave up. It was clear the adults in Dry Creek did not believe her. But she knew the children did, and that's what counted. "If you want, you could give out sacks of peanuts and candy."

"Jacob and I could make popcorn balls," Elmer said, his eyes lighting up in anticipation.

"And the angel could give out sacks of candy," Jacob suggested.

"The children would love that." Mrs. Hargrove spoke authoritatively as though that settled the matter.

"And it would make a good picture for the *Gazette* if they send a photographer."

Glory looked around the hardware store. The shelves had been recently dusted, but it was obvious the merchandise took a long time to sell. There were some hammers. An assortment of screwdrivers. A row of small household goods like toasters and irons. Even a row of doorknobs and plumbing fixtures. The people inside the store were so convinced she was penniless that she didn't know how to convince them otherwise. All they knew of her was what they'd seen in this store and Matthew's house. She had money in neither of those places. Therefore, in the eyes of the adults of Dry Creek, her resources were limited. They liked reading in the newspaper that she might be an angel, but they didn't believe she had the power to buy even a few gifts.

Matthew watched the thoughts chase themselves through Glory's mind. He wondered if she knew how expressive her face was. When she was happy, she glowed. When she was mad, she steamed. When she was embarrassed, she blushed. Right now she was feeling frustrated. Her face was a clear road map. He liked that.

"If we're going to do candy for the children, I can also get the Ladies' Fellowship to make cookies and coffee for the adults," Mrs. Hargrove offered. "Doris June can make her lemon bars."

"You might even set up a table and sell some of that jam I hear about," Glory suggested. She wondered what was making Matthew frown like that. She'd been watching him out of the corner of her eye all morning.

"The ladies would love that." Mrs. Hargrove

beamed. "We could raise money for the church. Maybe we'll raise enough to get a substitute pastor for a few services next year. I do so miss having a preacher on Sunday mornings."

Matthew kept his eyes on his ornament. He was stepping close to quicksand. First Susie and now this. "Sounds like you do pretty good, though. I hear hymn singing every Sunday morning."

"We take turns reading from the Bible, too," Mrs. Hargrove agreed, and then sighed. "But it's not the same. And I've been thinking for the pageant it'd be nice to have a real preacher to at least give a small devotional. Especially with all the people coming. They'll expect—"

The bell above the door rang, announcing the entrance of Tavis, the son of the Big Sheep Mountain Ranch owner.

Matthew breathed more easily. He was saved by the bell. He didn't like the direction Mrs. Hargrove's thoughts were taking. He would rather wear angel wings than preach.

The cowboy was a distraction. In his early twenties, Tavis was lean and wiry. Since it was December, he wore his winter Stetson, the one with wool flaps that could be pulled down over his ears if needed.

"Hi." Tavis nodded to Matthew and then to the group around the stove. His gaze slid over to Glory, and he tipped his hat. "Ma'am."

Glory looked up from her sketch. She supposed the man in the hat was another autograph seeker. He certainly was walking toward her as if he had a mission in mind. He didn't get more than two strides toward her before Matthew spoke up.

"Can I help you?" It didn't take Matthew more

than a minute to remember that Tavis was single and the reputed ladies' man of the Big Sheep Mountain Ranch. Matthew had not dated anyone in Dry Creek, so he assumed the few other single men in the area didn't even count him as competition when someone like Glory landed in town. He supposed word of the angel had gotten to the bunkhouse at the Big Sheep just as soon as this morning's *Gazette* was delivered, and Tavis had come to investigate.

"Ah, just picking up some nails." Tavis turned to Matthew with a wink.

Matthew grunted. It was the angel, all right. The Big Sheep Mountain Ranch bought their nails by the double case a couple of times a year. Henry had the boxes shipped directly to the ranch from his supplier in Chicago. They'd just processed an order last month. "Ran out, did you?"

"Ah, no—just wanted a handful of those little ones." Tavis twisted his hat. He stood in the middle of the floor, not moving closer to Glory, but obviously not retreating, either. "Thought I'd, you know, hang a few pictures in the bunkhouse."

"Oh." Elmer busied himself with his coffee cup. "Since when do you hang pictures in the bunkhouse?"

"Aunt Francis has been trying to get us cultured, and now that the *Gazette* said there's an artist in town—well, we thought we should get a picture for the wall."

Glory measured the cowboy with her eyes. He'd gained a few points with her by calling her an artist instead of an angel, but she hadn't worked with the guys in the police department for nothing. She knew a man on the prowl when she saw one. And this one was not just on the prowl. He was out to prove a point. She'd wager Tavis was duded up for her benefit. His Stetson was midnight black with no smudges or unplanned dents. His jeans were so new they still had the package crease down the leg. His face was freshly shaven and his hair neatly trimmed. She wondered if he'd be nearly as interested in her artwork if she hadn't been written up in the newspaper or recommended by his aunt.

"I could paint you a scene around the Big Sheep Mountains," Glory offered. The snowcapped mountains took her breath away each morning. The sky was pale blue today and the sun shone off the snow as if it was freshly polished silver. "But I won't have time until the pageant is all taken care of."

"The Christmas pageant? I haven't been to that for years."

"It's going to be special this year," Mrs. Hargrove said, determination giving an edge to the words. "Tell everyone at the Big Sheep—this year will be special."

"If you need any help, let us know. The boys and I are always glad to help." Tavis managed to face Mrs. Hargrove and smile at Glory at the same time. "Lifting things—that kind of thing."

Tavis held up his arm and flexed his muscle. "Comes from lifting hay bales."

"We might need to have you hoist some of the visitors up on your shoulder," Matthew suggested from the counter. He supposed Tavis was harmless. Glory didn't seem to be taking the bait. The cowboy kept flashing his smiles in Glory's direction, but she didn't beam back at him. She was polite, but that was it. "Trying to figure out how to get everyone inside the church to see it. Now that it's been mentioned in the *Gazette,* more people will be coming.''

''Well, who says you need to have it in the church?''

Matthew almost chuckled at the look of horror that spread across Mrs. Hargrove's face as she spoke. ''Not have it in the church? Where else would we have it? We can't have it here. The café's closed, the school's too small and we can't have it in the street!''

Tavis twirled his black hat around in his hands. He'd gone full circle. ''You could use our storage barn.''

''Your barn!''

Matthew was the first to see the possibilities. ''Why not? The Big Sheep barn is huge. We could build some bleachers. There's lots of space for parking. It's right on the edge of town. Everyone knows where it is.''

''But a barn?'' Mrs. Hargrove wailed.

''Jesus was born in a stable,'' Glory reminded them all. She liked the idea. ''That's about as close to a barn as you can get.''

''But a barn? I think you still have cows there. What'll you do with them?''

''We can move them out,'' Tavis said.

''Or not,'' Matthew said. ''A few cows around might add atmosphere.''

''Cows in the pageant!'' Mrs. Hargrove was horrified. ''What will people think of us?''

''They'll think we're high society,'' Elmer said as he leaned over and put another piece of wood in the stove.

''And the carol does say 'The cattle are lowing,''' Glory offered.

"That's true." Mrs. Hargrove perked up. "It just might work. Think your dad will go for it? He hasn't been in church for years."

Tavis grimaced. "I know. But he'll do it for the town. Work is slow this time of year and the boys and I could do most of the setup."

"It just might work," Mrs. Hargrove repeated as she ripped off her old page in the notebook and started a fresh page. "We'll need ten, no, fifteen bleachers and…"

Glory half listened throughout the afternoon to the plans for the pageant. Her attention was primarily on the front window of the hardware store, however, or rather, what was happening outside the window. The children did not care about the article in the *Gazette*. They had other thoughts on their minds. Every few minutes she would see a timid wave from a child, and Glory would go to the door. First a pink mitten. Then a blue mitten. Then a gray mitten. All of the children wore warm coats, but she noticed that some of the coat sleeves were too short, as though the coats were several years old and too small. Still, each mittened hand held the same thing: a painstakingly drawn picture of a toy.

Glory made sure each child told her what the toy was called and his or her full name. She was careful to write both on the slip of paper before she went back into the store. She wanted to be sure that each child had their individual present. She knew that any present would be appreciated, but she also knew that the feeling of having a present given especially to you was one that helped children develop self-esteem and the ability to trust.

Matthew knew what Glory was doing. She was making too many quick trips outside for him not to notice. Especially because each time she came back in her cheeks and nose were rosy from the cold. He couldn't decide which he liked better—Glory with the cream-colored skin and freckles or Glory with the roses. She would make a beautiful angel. He was glad she'd been coaxed into staying. He and the twins hadn't had a really happy Christmas since Susie died. He'd barely had the energy to put a tree up this year, and it still wasn't fully decorated. But now this Christmas promised to be one they would never forget. He'd have to get the rest of the Christmas bulbs down from the upstairs closet so the tree could sparkle the way it should.

"You're welcome to listen," Glory said after she'd asked Matthew for the use of his phone again that evening. Her phone card guaranteed she could call from his phone with no charge to him, but she wanted him to know she was making arrangements for the presents. She accepted the fact that Mrs. Hargrove and the two older men didn't believe she could bring the children the presents they wanted, but she had hoped Matthew would believe her. He'd become important to her, and she wanted to know he trusted her.

"I have to set the things out for the twins' lunch tomorrow," Matthew said as he pulled himself up from the sofa. He had no reason to keep sitting there, anyway. Glory had read the twins another Bible story, and they had had their good-night prayers. This time he'd listened from the doorway with a dish towel on his shoulder. He'd been tempted to give up all pretense of not listening and just go in and sit down with

his sons. But he hadn't. Glory's voice reading from
the Bible lulled him into thinking everything was all
right with his soul, and he knew it wasn't. He didn't
want a Band-Aid slapped on his relationship with
God. He wanted to feel the pain of it until it healed
from the inside out.

"Joey said he wants peanut butter," Glory reminded him as she reached for the phone sitting on
the coffee table.

"Joey always wants peanut butter," Matthew said
as he slipped the crutches under his arms and began
to hobble toward the kitchen. "He likes the way it
sticks to his mouth."

Matthew limped into the kitchen and then turned
and closed the door between the kitchen and the living room. He wanted to give Glory privacy in his
home. He particularly did not want to make her feel
as if she had to lie to make him think she was really
ordering presents. A gift, after all, came from the
heart, and Glory's heart had opened wide to his sons.
That was a more important gift than a laser light gun
and a Lego machine set.

Glory dialed the number and said hello.

"Glory?" Sylvia's voice came through sounding
breathless. "I'm so glad you called."

"Why?" Prickles were running down Glory's
spine again. Her friend's voice didn't sound relaxed.

"I've heard some disturbing news." Sylvia paused.
"I don't know if it's true—you know how kids are.
I wasn't sure if I should say anything yet. I told the
police, but I don't know for sure."

"What is it, Sylvia?"

"Two of my kids—they're good kids, but they
hang with a bad crowd."

Glory started to breathe more easily. There were always kids in trouble at the youth center where Sylvia worked in Tacoma. Most of the teens were part of tough criminal gangs. "You'll help them go straight—remember the judge will work with you."

"Oh, they didn't do anything—at least, it didn't turn out the way they planned." Sylvia took a deep breath. "They told me there's a hit out on you. Two of the older boys in the gang had been contracted to do it. But then, last night, something happened. My two boys got scared and ended up at the mission. Even went forward for an altar call. I had mentioned your name with the presents you were buying and this morning they came back and told me. Said the hit hadn't gone through, that the guy doing the shooting had missed you and hadn't found you again. No one seems to know who the contact was or if the hit's still on. My boys feel so bad about it they want to go find you and stand in front of you so no bullets can get through."

A sliver of fear raced down Glory's back.

"Thank God you're in Montana," Sylvia continued in a rush.

"Yes, I should be safe here," Glory repeated in a daze. She slowly twisted the phone card around her finger. "These boys don't know where I am, do they?"

"No. Thank God I didn't mention where you were when I talked about the presents."

"Good."

Sylvia paused. "They did seem genuinely worried. I think they'd protect you if they could."

"Yeah, well, if I stay out of sight I won't need any protection."

Glory kept calm. She went over the list of presents with Sylvia. Glory was used to stress. She knew about shootings and crime. She would be fine. She kept repeating that phrase to herself. But when she hung up the phone she started to shake.

Matthew waited for the lull of voices to stop before he came back into the living room. He knew something was wrong. Glory's face was ashen. Even in the firelight, all warmth had left her face. No smile remained. Her hair still picked up the fire flecks and reflected them back, but all else about her was still.

"It's all right." Matthew hobbled over and sat down on the edge of the sofa. He wanted to reach over and put his arm around her, but she looked too fragile. As though even that movement would snap her control. "No one really expects them."

Glory looked up at him. "What do you mean?"

"The presents," Matthew continued patiently. "No one really expected you to be able to deliver on the presents. It's enough that you wanted to."

Glory started to laugh, even though she knew nothing was funny. Hysteria started this way. She knew that. But she couldn't stop. Matthew thought she couldn't deliver the presents. But the presents were all settled. Her problem was worse than that. She didn't know if she'd ever be able to walk the streets of Seattle again. Someone had been shooting at her. It wasn't a stray bullet. It was meant to hit her. She was the target. *Dear Lord, she was the target!*

Matthew watched Glory's teeth start to chatter, and her laughter calm down to hiccups. Suddenly he didn't care if she pulled away from him. He moved closer and put his arm around her shoulder. She whimpered. He wrapped his arm more fully around her and gathered her to his shoulder. He stroked her head and hummed a lullaby in her ear. He hoped to calm her. But it didn't work. She started to cry in earnest.

"What's wrong?" Matthew had to know. He felt a vise squeezing his heart. Something was wrong.

"They're shooting at me," Glory wailed.

"Who?"

"I don't know."

It was the bullet. Matthew knew the bullet on Wednesday had been too close. "You'll stay in your room. You're not leaving this house unless I'm along. No, you're not leaving even then. You'll just stay here. I can bring you what you need."

The determination in Matthew's voice quieted her. "Forever?"

"If necessary." Matthew nodded grimly. "I'll lock you in."

Glory smiled. She felt much better. "But that's kidnapping."

"Whatever it takes to keep you safe."

Strangely enough, Glory decided, she did feel safe. She'd just learned that there might be a contract out on her life, and yet, she felt safe here in this house. She'd like to pretend that had nothing to do with the man sitting beside her on the sofa worrying about her. But it wasn't true. His fierce protection made her feel as if nothing could harm her, not while he still drew breath.

The Bullet set down his coffee cup.

He shouldn't have stayed, but his phone call last night with Millie had unnerved him. She'd heard

Douglas's voice in the background and assumed Douglas was the uncle he visited.

"Yes, I'll invite him to visit," the Bullet had told Millie last night after she kept insisting. "But he doesn't travel much. He won't come. No, not even for Christmas."

If the Bullet had known Millie was making Christmas plans, he would have stalled her. He'd never thought about Christmas coming. Santa stockings and roasting chestnuts were not for a man like him. He usually celebrated Christmas at an all-night bar with a bottle of tequila. That's where a man like him spent Christmas.

Chapter Eight

"You're going to call?" Matthew was making pancakes for breakfast. He had been up early worrying and had decided to stir up some batter. Glory was in trouble and he needed to find a way to keep her safe. "They must know more at the precinct than they've told you. And they have the photos. They might offer a clue."

"It's not even morning there," Glory said. The small Franklin stove had a fire going in it, but the air inside the house was still cold enough to make foggy breath. She rubbed her hands together. She had pulled on her jeans and a heavy sweater when she heard Matthew moving around the kitchen. They had spent time last night talking about the shooting she'd seen inside Benson's Market. "I don't know for sure if they'll send me copies of the photos—it's not exactly regulation."

"Forget regulation," Matthew demanded as he poured more batter on the griddle and automatically made the batter into a snowman. ''Someone's out to get you.''

''Only in Seattle.''

''That's bad enough.'' Matthew reached up into the cupboard and found a small canister of raisins. He put eye, nose and button raisins on the snowman.

Glory nodded. Matthew wasn't even aware of what he was doing—making cute pancakes while talking about violence. He did everything a mother would do for his sons. ''I'll ask them to send copies of the photos—but I don't know what good they'll do.''

''Henry's got a fax at the store. Fax copies of them there,'' Matthew said as he poured another pancake snowman. He didn't know what good the photos would do, either. He just knew he needed to do something. ''And don't talk to anyone but that guy Frank you say you can trust.''

''Nobody on the force would sell me out,'' Glory said, and then thought a minute. She took some silverware from the drawer. The metal was cold to her touch. Maybe Matthew was right. How did she know for sure none of them would tell a hit man where she was if the price was right?

''And you'll work on those drawings? You must have seen something,'' Matthew said.

Glory had agreed to draw the crime scene again. The captain and she had been over this already. But Matthew sounded a lot like the captain. Both men believed she must be a target because of her trained eyes.

''Someone's worried you're going to remember something.'' Matthew repeated what he had said last night. ''Our job is to find out what that is.''

''I've been over it hundreds of times in my mind.''

"Have you drawn out the sketches of everything?"

"Just the face of the guy doing the shooting." Glory had thought about that, too. Surely there wouldn't be something in the grocery store itself. Who would leave evidence of a crime in plain sight for dozens of shoppers to see?

"And he's in jail?"

Glory nodded. "And nothing to gain by killing me at this point. I did sketches, but it wasn't necessary. He was arrested at the scene. And there were ten witnesses."

"Now, why would a guy shoot someone in front of ten witnesses?"

"Poor planning," Glory joked as she gathered four cups from the cupboard.

"Or something was happening that required immediate action," Matthew said as he flipped the first snowman pancake. "Something important enough to risk jail time."

"But that's just it—nothing was happening. The butcher was just walking out of the meat department with a package of steak in his hands."

"What kind of steaks?"

Glory looked at Matthew as if he was crazy. "What kind of steaks?"

"Yeah, T-bone, porterhouse, cube…"

"What difference does that make?"

Matthew flipped the other snowman pancake. "Who knows? My guess is it's that kind of little detail that we're looking for, something all of the other ten people have long forgotten. But with your eye, it's still in your head. If you draw it out, who knows? That's what someone is worried about."

"Makes sense." Glory walked toward the kitchen

table and set down the cups. Matthew did make sense.
If someone was out gunning for her, it was time to
empty her mind of all the crime details and put them
out front on paper. Maybe then they'd know who—
or what—they were up against.

Matthew looked up. He heard the sound of the
twins coming down the stairs before Glory did.
"Juice in the refrigerator. Apricot syrup, too. Maybe
some maple, as well."

Glory nodded and went back to the cupboard to
collect plates.

"And butter," Matthew said. "Joey won't eat pancakes without butter."

Once the plates were on the table, Glory went to
the refrigerator.

Glory turned when she heard the twins enter the
kitchen. They were in slippers and pajamas with
sweatshirts pulled over them. Their hair was mussed
and their eyes were still sleepy. Joey, in particular,
looked as if he was still dreaming.

"Hi, sport," Glory said softly as she put the juice
on the table and walked over to Joey, lifting him up.
He looked as if he needed a little bit more time to
wake up.

Joey snuggled into her shoulder with a sigh.

"Mommy." Joey whispered the word so softly
Glory wasn't sure she'd heard it right. But she knew
by the look of pain on Matthew's face that he had.

"He's still dreaming," she whispered to Matthew.
"He doesn't know what he's saying."

"I know," Matthew said quietly. Some days he
could convince himself he could give his sons everything they needed. Today, apparently, was not going
to be one of those days.

"It's Glory, honey," she whispered in Joey's ear.

His eyes opened, and he smiled contentedly. "You're still here. You didn't go back to heaven. I dreamed you were still here."

"I wouldn't go anywhere without saying goodbye."

Joey nodded. "Not even to heaven?"

Glory shook her head. "Not even there."

Joey put his head back on her shoulder and put his thin arms around her neck in a tight hug.

Glory wondered how she was ever going to say goodbye to the twins.

It was midmorning before Glory relaxed her fingers. She was holding her sketch pencil too tight, as though she could force some memory out through her fingers. At first her fingers had been too cold to sketch, but Matthew had taken a pair of women's knit gloves off the shelf and cut the fingers out of them. That kept her hands warm while letting her fingers be free.

"You remember the clock?" Elmer had walked over to where she sat with her sketch pad.

"I remember everything," Glory said as she set her fifth sketch aside. Matthew had fixed up a table for her to work at. By now it was covered with sketches.

"Not quite everything," Elmer said as he looked closely at the sketch she had made of the manager lying on the floor, a bullet through his stomach and the things in his hands scattered. The time card was halfway out of the dead man's pocket. The package of steaks was near his left shoulder.

"What do you mean?"

"That." Elmer pointed at the sketch. "On that

package of steaks. That isn't packed right. A T-bone and a cube together. Who'd do that?''

Glory looked at the sketch. She must have made a mistake. Odd, though.

A harsh scraping sound from the storeroom distracted them.

"Matthew." Glory had told Matthew she would help him move any stock he needed to relocate. Elmer had told him the same thing. Even Jacob had appeared eager to pitch in and help. "Stubborn man."

"Found the garland," Matthew announced triumphantly as he hobbled into the main part of the store. A trail of gold-and-white garland followed him and he had a cape of garland wrapped around his shoulders.

"You risked falling to get some garland?"

Matthew grinned. "I didn't know you cared if I fell."

"Of course I care if you fall," Glory said softly. The fool man. "I'm the one that has to pick you up and get you to the clinic."

Matthew's grin disappeared. "Did I ever thank you for that?"

The bell over the door rang. Glory looked up in time to see the deputy sheriff, Carl Wall, walk into the store.

Glory bit back her groan.

"Expected everyone to be out working on the pageant," the deputy said. He looked slowly around the store and his eyes rested on Glory's worktable. He walked over and picked up one of her sketches of the victim after the shooting. "Hmm, not exactly scenery." He looked at Glory.

Glory was leaning against the counter. "I told you I worked for the police."

The deputy grunted. "Maybe you do, at that."

"Want some coffee?" Matthew offered. "You public officials never seem to take time for breaks."

"Some folks say all we do is sit around drinking coffee and eating doughnuts."

"Well, I'm not one of them," Matthew said staunchly. "You have a lot to do making sure there are no undesirables coming into town."

Carl Wall looked puzzled. "I thought you were on the side of the angel."

"The angel—no, no, I don't mean her. I mean any undesirables asking about her."

"Who'd be asking about her?"

"I don't know. Just keep an eye out, all right?"

The deputy shrugged. "Most folks have accepted her. They kind of like someone who might be an angel. Makes them think the Man upstairs cares."

"God can care about Dry Creek without sending an angel," Glory said as she walked back toward her worktable. "Maybe God sent you to Dry Creek instead."

The deputy grunted and rolled his eyes. "Now don't go getting funny on me. I wasn't thinking of me. But at least I'd remember the Price boy."

"Billy Price?" Elmer looked up from the checker game.

"Yeah, I got to thinking. No one would remember him, and he'd like a visit from the angel—maybe a sack of the candy I hear is coming."

"Well, I'll add him to the list."

Glory could hear the silence in Matthew's house. A clock ticked in the kitchen and the water heater gurgled in the distance. She was making her Christmas list and checking it twice. She'd decided to order six extra basketballs and ten extra painting sets plus a couple of additional teddy bears. She wanted to be sure there were enough presents to go around.

With her list in hand, Glory called Sylvia.

The phone rang five times before Sylvia's breathless voice came over the line. "Tacoma-Seattle Youth Center, Sylvia Bannister speaking."

Glory could hear muffled laughter and cheers in the background. "Sounds like someone's happy there."

"We should be. We just got a grant to set up that summer camp you've heard me talk about for two years now. The money's not much, but it's a big start."

"Congratulations! I wish I could be there!"

"The volunteers are going wild. Pat Dawson is even dancing a jig on the table."

"I'm surprised you're not up there with him."

"I had to get down to answer the phone. Besides, I'm too old for that sort of thing."

"Forty! That's not old!"

"Well, I do feel younger since I got the news." Sylvia laughed. "If we can get some of these kids away from the gangs for a summer, I believe we can turn their lives around. Take them someplace where they don't need to worry about being jumped or shot."

"Even with the gangs, you make a difference," Glory reminded her. She herself had volunteered many weekends at the youth center, tutoring or just talking with teenage girls. "I've seen you change the most unlikely ones."

"Ah, the power of prayer. It surprises me at times, too. I always remind myself that I never know what heart God is going to open up next."

"If you have a few extra prayers, you could send them this way." Glory knew of no heart that needed softening more than Matthew's.

"I've been worried about that, too."

"What?" Glory was startled. How had Sylvia known about Matthew?

"I don't want you to worry about that contract, though," Sylvia continued. "The two boys who told me about it are being very responsible today. I think they have made a sincere decision to follow Christ."

"Oh, of course." Glory relaxed. Sylvia was talking about the shooting.

Silence.

"Is there something else bothering you?" Sylvia asked. "Something else I should pray about?"

How did Sylvia always know? Glory wondered. It must be her years of talking with teenagers.

"Just a stubborn man who hasn't forgiven himself and holds it against God."

"Ah, this would be the man you mentioned, the one you're staying with." Sylvia's voice was rich with unspoken speculation. "The minister."

"I'm not staying with him," Glory clarified. "I'm really staying with his five-year-old sons. That's all."

"If you say so."

"I know so."

Sylvia let the subject be changed to the gifts for the children of Dry Creek. Sylvia assured her there were thirty days to pay on the account, and Glory told her she would mail a check tomorrow to cover the presents and the overnight shipping. The total came to twelve hundred dollars.

"I called the shipping place and they said they can only guarantee next-day service to Miles City. They're short-staffed, since it's Christmas, and aren't taking next-day service to places like Dry Creek."

"If they can deliver it to the clinic in Miles City that'll be fine," Glory said. "I thought this might happen, and I called one of the nurses I met there. She said I can pick the boxes up anytime before five." She wanted to go to Miles City, anyway. She had some Christmas shopping to do that she didn't want to do in the toy store.

"You'll need a pickup truck." Tavis from the Big Sheep Mountain Ranch smiled at Glory. He, unlike Jacob and Elmer, was not sitting in a chair. Instead he crouched, cowboy-style, in front of the stove. "I'd be happy to drive you in. I've got a half-ton pickup, a three-quarter ton or a cattle truck. Your choice."

"I can take her." Matthew bristled. He was sitting on his stool by the counter.

"Your old car won't hold a load," Tavis challenged.

"I can take her anyway." Matthew didn't want to spell out the obvious. By now he figured Glory was honest about placing the order. But he knew her credit was no good. He figured she believed the order was coming. He wanted to be the one with her when she found out it wasn't there. She'd need a friend and not a fancy cowboy at her side to help her with her disappointment. Besides, he had some money set aside for a rainy day. He figured they could buy enough little presents in Miles City to make the children of Dry Creek happy.

Glory looked from one man to the other. "I might be able to fit everything in my Jeep."

"Matthew will take you," Mrs. Hargrove calmly announced with a silencing glance at Tavis. "I need Tavis's help with the bleachers."

It was only a trip to town, Glory chided herself that evening as she looked through her suitcase. So far she'd pulled out her gray sweatshirt with Seattle Seahawks written on the back and an ivory turtleneck with a tan vest. Neither one was exactly right. She couldn't remember the last time she'd given this much thought to the question of what to wear. Jeans were an obvious choice because of the cold weather, but she suddenly wished for a sweater with bright colors to go with them. Of course, she had the pink sweater. It was paler than she'd like, but maybe it would do.

She sat on the edge of Matthew's bed, with her suitcase and clothes scattered all around, and shook her head at herself. She was acting as if this was a date. Worse yet, she wanted it to be a date. And that was a fantasy that would be short-lived. She could sit and count the reasons she shouldn't become involved with Matthew. He was a good father; he would want more children. Children she couldn't give him. Even more important, Matthew wasn't following God at this point in his life. She believed he was still a Christian in his heart, but he wasn't willing to let go of his grief and admit it. And then there was his grief. Glory felt her breath catch in her throat at this one. What if Matthew had loved Susie so much he could never

love anyone else? Would every other woman seem
pale in comparison?

Maybe, she thought as she shook her head again at
her clothes, that's why she wanted something bright
to wear. She wanted to get Matthew's attention tomorrow. But she'd need more than a bright sweater
to do that.

The Bullet watched the inside glass of the telephone booth fog up as he breathed. He was outside a
drugstore in Spokane, calling his contact to tell him
the search was off. He hadn't picked up the scent of
the hit and he was ready to go home.

"You're looking in the wrong place." The clipped
voice came through the phone lines. "She's in Montana. Wonders of modern technology. Do a word
search on the AP wire—a name search—and there it
is. Glory Beckett in Dry Creek, Montana."

Chapter Nine

Snow, turned grayish-brown by the exhaust of passing cars, lined the isolated highway as Matthew drove down the road. After breakfast he had quickly washed his car, almost freezing his hands in the process. He was a fool to wash anything outside when he was on crutches and the weather gauge read ten below. But he wanted Glory's first impression of his car to be good even if the cleanliness she'd see would be fleeting. Cars might mean something to her. He stole a glance over at her as she sat in the passenger seat.

"The radio doesn't work, but I fixed the cassette player." Matthew fumbled in the storage compartment next to the driver's seat. He couldn't remember what was in there, but he thought he had a Mozart tape. He pulled out three tapes. All three were made by Disney. "I'm afraid I have mostly sing-along music for the twins. But I'll keep looking. I've got one classical and I've been meaning to get some instrumentals, too—maybe a flute tape."

"That's okay. I like the silence."

What does she mean by that, Matthew thought in desperation. Should he be talking more? Should he be talking less? Ever since this morning when he'd decided this trip to town was the closest thing he'd had to a date in years, he'd been tongue-tied. Worse than when he had been a teenager and had been dating. At least back then he'd known when he was on a date and when he wasn't.

"That's one thing we have in Montana. Silence—it goes with the snow."

Montana was known for her open spaces and big blue skies. Both could be seen through the car's windshield. Matthew felt as if they were driving along in a warm cocoon. The car's heater kept the air cozy, and the hum of the engine was soothing.

"In Seattle we have noise and rain."

"You like it there?" Matthew tried to keep the question light, tried to pretend he hadn't wondered if there was any chance she'd move to a small town in Montana if asked.

"I've got my family there."

Matthew held his breath.

"My mother and the captain."

Matthew took a deep breath. So far so good, but he had to know. "Any—you know—boyfriends?"

A butterfly took flight in Glory's stomach. "Not really."

Matthew frowned. What did that mean?

"Well, of course, you date...." Matthew stumbled along.

"Of course." Glory's hands went up to finger her dangling silver earrings. Maybe the jewelry had been a mistake. The zipper of her black ski jacket was open to show her pale pink sweater. Even with denim jeans the silver jewelry might be too dressy for a shopping trip. But it was the only thing in her suitcase that seemed the least bit festive. When she had looked in the mirror this morning, she'd looked colorless, so she'd put on what little makeup she had. Usually red hair clashed with pink, but the pink in her sweater was more pearl than pink. She wore a natural lipstick and barely-pink blush. She'd brushed her hair until it settled around her face in waves. She'd even put a tortoise clip in her hair. She wanted to look good, but now she wondered if she had overdone it. She didn't want to make Matthew feel uncomfortable, as if she had expectations for this trip. Date expectations. Maybe that was why he was asking about boyfriends. Maybe he wanted to be sure she had one and wasn't expecting anything from him. Maybe she should have worn the Seattle Seahawks sweatshirt, after all. There was no mistaking the nondate look of that.

"But is there someone you date regularly?" Matthew persisted with the question. "Someone you are involved with?" Even if she was undercover, she would answer this honestly to tell him there was no chance. Even a government agent would give him that courtesy.

Glory glanced at him. He had his eyes straight ahead, his chin straight forward, his hands squarely on the steering wheel. He was a study in browns. Deep brown leather jacket, open all the way down to show a pressed white shirt. Chestnut-brown hair with blond highlights. Tanned face. Fierce dark eyebrows. It was the small nervous twitch at the edge of his mouth that gave her courage.

"No," Glory said softly. "There's no one special."

"Good." Matthew breathed again. "Good."

The morning suddenly looked brighter to Matthew. The slush at the side of the road didn't look just gray anymore; it looked more like pure silver with the sun shining on it the way it was. And his car might be old, but the seat cushions were made of leather. And the trim looked like wood. He was cruising.

"I was wondering if I could buy you lunch when we're in town." Matthew tapped the steering wheel lightly and turned to smile at Glory. He came from the era when a date meant someone did the inviting, even if it was only for lunch. "There's a steakhouse if you want to play it safe. Or we can go to Billy's—never know what you'll get, but it's good."

"I'd like that—Billy's sounds good." Glory tilted her head so her earrings could sparkle. And she lifted the collar of her sweater and flipped her silver chain outside. The more jewelry the better. She, Glory Beckett, was on a date. Granted, it was a date with the wrong man, but for today she didn't care. She was going to forget he was a grieving widower who'd had a perfect wife. She was going to forget he was not following God because of that wife. She was going to forget she couldn't give him children as that wife had. She was even going to forget that wife had ever existed. She would let her jewelry sparkle like laughter. Just for today she'd forget about his past and their lack of a future. They were definitely on a date.

"We'll have lots of time to shop." Matthew slowed down some. There were likely to be patches of white ice along this strip of road, and he couldn't count on his leg with the sprained knee. Besides, they had plenty of time. "There's a department store—and Buffy's Drug. Buffy's usually carries some toys this time of year, just in case your order doesn't get here in time.''

''The boxes should be at Dr. Norris's office already.''

''Well, just in case they're held up,'' Matthew persisted. He didn't want anything to ruin their day. ''We can pick up what we need at Buffy's.''

''Buffy's won't have a Betsy Tall doll,'' Glory protested. She'd gone over the children's wish pictures. No small store in Miles City could carry all of the different things the children wanted.

''Maybe not, but they'll have another doll.''

''But that's the problem.'' Glory had seen the hope on the children's faces. ''They each have a special request for a present. Something they especially want. Not expensive things, either, just particular things. This Christmas I want them each to have the exact thing they asked for.''

''Sometimes we don't get the exact thing we want in life.''

''I know, but—'' Glory stopped. How could she explain the need children have to be unique in the eyes of God? To be known individually? ''They're expecting their angel to make arrangements to see that they get their special gift. It won't be the same if it's just any old gift. It has to be the one.''

''They'll be fine.'' Matthew's face settled into grim lines. ''They'll make do.''

''Will they?'' Glory watched the shutters go down over Matthew's face. She knew they weren't talking about the children. They were talking about Matthew. ''Or will they be like you and decide God doesn't care about them?''

A muscle flexed across Matthew's cheek, but he didn't answer.

* * *

Miles City was dressed up for Christmas. Matthew told her the town had grown up around Fort Keogh, an outpost built in 1877 to force the Crow to stay on the nearby reservation.

"We have always been half-decent and half not around here," he continued. "Starting out it was divided—brothels and beer halls to the south, banks and pawnshops to the north."

Glory imagined she could still see the old town in its heyday. The sidewalks were scraped clean of snow and many of the store windows had been decorated with winter scenes and outlined with tiny white lights. Most of the buildings along the main street were solid old buildings, which fit in well with her fantasy. The place, Glory decided, had charm. Some of the stores had Christmas carols playing, and the sounds carried out into the street. Even the other shoppers looked festive in their snow boots and knit scarves.

Matthew drove down the main street and then turned around. "I'm checking the cars."

Glory looked at him.

"Making sure they're all locals," he said.

"Surely you don't think a hit man would be looking for me in Miles City?"

"No, but I'm not taking any chances." Matthew finally pulled into a parking space. "Let's try Buffy's first. I want to get something for the boys."

"Me, too."

Glory wanted to get a gift for the boys that was from her and not from the angel. Some little thing they could have to remember her visit.

The door into Buffy's opened with the ringing of

a bell. Buffy's smelled of the perfume and scented soaps she could see in front of the long mirror at the end of the store. Racks of merchandise ran sideways down the length of the store and a checkout counter was located near the front door.

"Can I help you find anything?" An older woman wearing a lilac-flowered dress spoke from behind the counter. The woman smelled of dusting powder. "We've got a special on gloves this week. Men's. Women's. Children's. The lot."

"You must be Buffy?" Glory said, even though she knew the woman couldn't be.

"No, she's my daughter." The woman smiled indulgently and patted the braided bun loosely knotted at the back of her neck. "She's home baking cookies for her two boys for Christmas. Boys need cookies at Christmas."

Cookies and Christmas! Glory had forgotten. She'd decided earlier to buy some chocolate chips before they left Miles City. She wouldn't compete with their mother's oatmeal raisin cookies, but she was sure the twins would love the Beckett family chocolate chip cookies.

"Do you have any children's books?" Glory asked. Buffy must stock good books if she had children of her own. Both Josh and Joey loved having a book read to them. She'd already seen their favorites—*Curious George, The Runaway Rabbit* and a couple of Dr. Seuss books. She knew they loved adventure, and she might even find a book with lions and tigers in it.

The saleswoman nodded to the right. "Over there, behind the lunch boxes."

Matthew watched Glory out of the corner of his eye. He also kept his eye on the door to the store. He'd already studied the three other customers inside Buffy's and decided they were harmless. But he wasn't going to be careless. Not about Glory's safety.

He watched as she looked over the book rack. He knew she was buying presents for his sons, and he'd had a whispered conference with them before he came this morning. Josh had pressed a few nickels into his hand, asking him to buy Glory a golden crown that would light up like the one he'd seen on a Christmas card at school. Matthew suggested a shiny necklace instead. Joey, with his pennies, wanted him to buy her a mirror because he'd seen her use one when she brushed her hair at night. They both advised him that he should buy her a present, too. Matthew knew his sons were worried. They didn't want Glory to leave. He was worried, too. He hadn't known his sons would get so attached to her in just a few days. But then, why shouldn't they? He'd gotten attached himself.

"The other store is just next door." Matthew walked over to Glory. "I don't want to rush you. Why don't I go over there now, and you can come when you're done?" The department store would take longer to check out and he didn't want Glory to know what he was doing.

Glory nodded. She had been wondering how to get Matthew out of the store so she could buy his present. She'd seen a selection of music cassettes near the counter and she'd decided to get him one. It was a gift with the right balance. It showed she didn't expect him to get her anything. It was just a friendly gift.

She waited for Matthew to walk out of the store

before she headed for the cassette display. She put two books on the counter. Josh's was about a red dragon. Joey's was about a lost kitten that found his way home. "I'll take these, and do you have any James Galway tapes?"

"I don't think so." The salesclerk scanned the titles.

"Any instrumentalists?"

"Let me see, we've got *Piano Selections for...*" The salesclerk started to read the title as she pulled the cassette from the display. Black and white piano keys ran the length of the tape cover and there was a red rose lying across them. It looked slow moving, if nothing else.

"I'll take it," Glory said quickly. She thought she saw Matthew's outline in the window. He was doubling back. "Just put it in the bag quick. Christmas present."

The older woman smiled and slipped it into the bag under the two larger books.

"I thought you might want that twenty dollars I owe you," Matthew said quietly as he came inside and held out a twenty-dollar bill.

"What twenty?" Glory looked up from her purse. She opened her wallet. There was her own twenty dollars. "It's not mine."

"Take it anyway," Matthew said, his voice even. "I'm sure I owe it to you for something."

"But—"

"Go ahead and take it, sweetheart," the clerk advised with a shrug of her shoulders. "It isn't every day your husband gives you an extra twenty for Christmas shopping."

"He's not my husband." Glory felt the blush creep up her neck.

Matthew smiled.

"Even more reason to take it, then." The clerk straightened herself and glared at Matthew. "It's the least he can do if he isn't willing to make an honest woman out of you."

"I'm an honest woman already." Glory lifted her chin indignantly.

"Already married?" The older woman smoothed down the skirt of her flowered dress and shook her head. "In my day—well, you don't want to hear that. It's none of my business whose bed you're sleeping in."

"She's got you there," Matthew whispered. "You *are* sleeping in my bed."

"Well, you're right in there with me." Glory spit out the words and then stumbled when she realized what she'd said. "And if either one of us should care about their reputation it's you—you live here. Besides, you've got the boys."

"My boys couldn't care less about my reputation. They'd love it if I slept with an angel." Matthew chuckled. The one thing he didn't miss about the ministry was worrying about what people thought about him.

"Well." The salesclerk softened as she looked at Matthew. "If he thinks you're an angel…"

"The whole town of Dry Creek thinks I'm an angel."

"Oh, you're the angel at Dry Creek!" The older woman brightened. "Wait'll I tell Buffy. We were reading about you in the 'Southeastern' column."

"I'm not. Look. I've got no wings. No miracles. No divine message."

"Yeah, but you're sweet," the woman said, measuring her with friendly eyes. "And sweetness never hurt anyone. Right?" The clerk looked at Matthew.

Matthew nodded. The clerk was absolutely right. That's why people were drawn to Glory. She was a kind, sweet woman. She didn't need to be an angel.

"Let's eat lunch and then we'll hit the department store." Matthew put his hand under Glory's elbow. They were on the sidewalk outside Buffy's. He looked both ways for suspicious-looking cars and didn't see any. Mostly there were farm pickups parked on the street, since it was winter. "Slippery out here."

"Let's stop by Dr. Norris's first. The clinic might close early, since it's so close to Christmas."

"Okay." Matthew felt helpless. His worry shifted. He could protect Glory from suspicious-looking cars, but he didn't know how to protect her from disappointment. "You're sure you don't want to eat first?"

"Come on. Let's get the boxes."

Forty-five. Forty-six. Glory was sitting across the restaurant table from Matthew and counting to one hundred. She'd taken her ski jacket off and draped it over the back of her chair.

Glory barely noticed the knotty pine paneling in the room or the ferns that hung from the ceiling. Everything was clean, but old. The air smelled of cooking meat and she faintly heard the rattle of silverware coming from the kitchen as well as the murmured talk of the other customers sitting at nearby tables.

Glory hadn't realized it until now—Matthew didn't believe her. He fussed all over her in his worry about a hit man, but when it came to believing in her integrity, he didn't. She knew he hadn't believed her at first. But she'd thought that somewhere during the past days he would have decided she wasn't crazy. The boxes were coming. Sylvia had called to tell her the order had been processed. Just because the nurse at the clinic said the boxes hadn't come with the shipment today didn't mean they wouldn't come tomorrow. The nurse had promised she'd bring them with her when she came out to see the pageant tomorrow. The nurse—a stranger, really—seemed to believe her. Matthew didn't.

"We can go back to Buffy's." Matthew wasn't looking her in the eyes. Instead, his gaze kept focused on the wall behind her. "I can buy some things. You know, backup presents. Some puzzles. Some books. Maybe some coloring books."

Glory shook her head. "These kids have asked for specific things. The boxes will be here." The right presents simply needed to come. She'd call Sylvia when she got home.

Glory was at a loss. She didn't know how to manufacture faith or trust in Matthew. He didn't believe her, and there wasn't anything she could do about it. No one ever forced another one to have faith. Faith and trust came from the heart. Maybe that's why it was so upsetting to her that Matthew did not trust her. She had thought they were friends. And friends should stand beside each other.

"So what is it—crazy or lying?" Glory finally asked.

Matthew was startled. He stopped staring over her shoulder and looked her in the eye. "What?"

"Me and the boxes. Do you figure I am crazy or lying?"

"Well, n-neither…" Matthew stammered.

Glory noticed with satisfaction that he looked uncomfortable. "It's got to be one or the other. Which is it? Am I lying about the boxes coming or am I crazy to say they are coming?"

Silence. "I know you *want* the boxes to come." His blue-green eyes looked bone weary and his shoulders slumped

Glory nodded sadly. So that was as far as he could get. "Overly optimistic, huh?"

Matthew nodded. His eyes moved to a spot on the table. Glory wondered what was so fascinating about a red-checked plastic tablecloth with silverware wrapped in a paper napkin.

"Hi, folks." A bearded man set down two menus in front of them. "Welcome to Billy's, home of the best food west of the Dakotas."

Matthew looked up at the waiter in pure relief. "What've you got?"

"The special today is meat loaf with mushroom sauce and garlic mashed potatoes." The man smiled fondly. He wore blue jeans, a red-checked logger's shirt, work boots and—over it all and spotless—a white BBQ apron. "Wife's in the kitchen today and she likes to make things fancy. When I'm cooking, it's plain meat loaf and plain potatoes. No chives. No parsley. No garlic."

"Which is better?" Glory liked the way the man's eyes lit up when he talked about his wife. He couldn't be over forty, but he looked as if he'd worked long and hard in this life. The only softness on his face was the love that showed when he talked about his wife.

"Hers are," the man leaned down and whispered. "But don't tell her I said so. I like to keep the rivalry going. Keeps the marriage interesting."

"In that case, I'll have the meat loaf." She'd have to remember this man and his wife for her next talk with Linda. Apparently even meat loaf recipes could be part of what kept a couple happy. "See how your wife makes it."

"You know, my wife is really something." The man had a scar on his cheek and a faint trace of whiskers on his face, but he looked like an old-fashioned knight. "When I started this place, no one believed I could stick with it. I'd been a drifter—cattle hand mostly—until I met her three years ago. But when they said I couldn't do it, she stood by me. We weren't even married then, so she didn't have to take my side. She believed in me when no one else did. I'll never forget that."

"Good for her," Glory said softly. She envied the couple their devotion. "She must be special."

"She is." The man cleared his throat. His neck grew flushed and he had a suspicious moistness in his eyes. "Didn't mean to go on like that."

"I'm glad you did." Glory handed back her menu. "It'll make the meat loaf more memorable."

"You want extra mushroom sauce with that? Her sauce is sure good."

"I'd like that."

"And you? What'll you have?" The man looked at Matthew.

"I don't suppose you have any crow on the menu, do you?" Matthew asked sheepishly.

"Well, no…" The man looked momentarily puzzled and then he grinned. "Too close to home, huh?"

Matthew nodded.

Glory watched the shadows lift from Matthew's face. His weariness shifted, and it was as if a load was lifted off him. He looked directly at Glory. "I know I should trust you. Please forgive me."

"Should?"

"I want to do better. I just don't trust easy."

Glory nodded. She saw the sincerity in his eyes. "I guess wanting to trust someone is a step in the right direction."

"And the answer is neither crazy or lying," Matthew said firmly as he handed his menu back to the man.

Glory grinned.

"And I'll have the meat loaf, too." Matthew looked up at the man. "With extra sauce."

"I'll be back in a jiffy," the man said, then carried their menus to the back counter and took their order slip into the kitchen.

It was one o'clock, and they had just eaten the last bite of meat loaf. Matthew had to admit he'd been loitering. He checked the door for suspicious-looking people periodically, but the people who came into Billy's were humble. Besides, Mrs. Hargrove was watching the twins, and he wanted this date to last as long as it could. He loved to watch Glory's eyes when she laughed. He'd told her some of the twins' favorite jokes just to get her started. Josh had a whole series of chicken-crossing-the-road jokes that were pure corn. Her blue-gray eyes crinkled with gold when she laughed. Her bronze hair sparkled in the sunlight coming in the side window. She threw her head back and the delicate curve of her neck made him think of a swan.

"You're beautiful." The words came out before Matthew thought about whether he should say them.

Glory stopped laughing and blushed.

He cleared his throat and added, "Very beautiful." He'd never seen anything prettier than Glory blushing. She didn't blush red like some people—she just pinked. She was a pearl. He smiled. "You truly do look like an angel."

"Oh—" Glory looked flustered. Then she glanced down at her watch. "Speaking of angels, I better get back and make sure the costume fits."

Matthew nodded. All dates did come to an end. Then he brightened up. The date didn't end until he pulled in to the driveway. They still had the drive home left.

The afternoon sun reflected off the snow as Matthew drove his car back to Dry Creek. The back seat was filled with groceries and lumpy bags. The heater made the inside of the car a little stuffy.

"Mind if I turn it down?"

Glory nodded. She'd been thinking about Matthew's reluctance to trust her or anyone else, up to and including God. He couldn't have been born that distrustful. Her experience with young children was that trust came easily. "Did you grow up around here?"

"Here and a million other places."

"Father in the service?"

"Maybe." Glory noticed Matthew's fingers tighten on the wheel of the car until his knuckles were white.

"Maybe?"

"My father left us when I was six. We never heard from him regularly. But shortly after he left one of his old friends called one day—drunk—asking for Sergeant Curtis. Mom thought maybe Dad had enlisted. He'd always wanted to be in the military. Least, according to her."

"I'm sorry." Glory wanted to reach over and put her hand over Matthew's fingers, but she wasn't sure he'd welcome her touch. He looked brittle.

"Don't be." Matthew took his eyes off the road briefly to look over at her. "He wasn't much of a father when he was around."

"Your poor mother. Where is she now?"

"Died when I was eighteen. I'd just barely graduated from high school. It was like she was waiting to finish her job with me so she could leave."

"Oh, dear, no wonder you have a hard time trusting God."

Matthew grimaced and looked back at her. His eyes were deep with pain. "What makes you think it's God I don't trust?"

"Why, who else?"

"It's myself I don't trust." Matthew spit the words out. He tried to stop them, but they seemed to come of their own power. "It's me I don't trust. It's me that messes up. It's me that can't get it right."

"And was it you that let Susie die?" Glory felt as if they were lancing a boil. Was this the poison that Matthew kept inside his heart?

"Yes," Matthew whispered. "It was me that let

her die. Me that let my mother die. Me that let my father leave. It was all me.''

''No, oh, no.'' Glory reached over to touch Matthew's hand. ''It wasn't you at all.''

Matthew grimaced and then turned coldly polite. ''Then who was it? God?''

''No. No.'' Glory was at a loss. How could she convince Matthew he did not carry the fate of the whole world on his shoulders? That the choice was not just between him and God. Life threw curves. She'd had her own battles with guilt over her father's accident, but it was nothing like the burden Matthew carried.

Dear Lord, help Matthew. Help me help Matthew. Show me how to help him.

Glory wished Socrates were sitting in this car next to Matthew instead of her. Or Solomon. Even Dear Abby would do. Glory felt so inadequate. She'd tried to talk to Matthew about his feelings three times already as they drove back to Dry Creek, but each time he'd put her off with a joke or a shrug. The snow-covered tops of the Big Sheep Mountains in the distance were more likely to thaw out and talk to her than Matthew was.

''If you don't want to talk to me about it, that's fine.'' Glory gathered her ski jacket closer to her. It was still only midafternoon, but the outside cold seemed more of a threat than it had earlier. ''Not talking isn't good. It's not healthy. But it's fine.''

''I just don't want to talk about it now,'' Matthew said patiently. Some charming date he'd turned out to be. She probably thought he was a basket case. In his mind they were supposed to be talking about amusing things, light things—date things. At least, that was the way it was back when he was dating. Things couldn't have changed that much. "You never have told me about your artwork. What your favorite medium is, who your favorite artist is, your favorite art museum…"

"Refusing to talk about these things won't make them go away," Glory persisted. They'd turned the heater off to let the car cool down somewhat and Glory's ears were beginning to be chilly. She rubbed her left ear.

"Talking about them won't make them go away, either." Matthew shrugged as he slowed down so that a car behind him could pass. He switched the heater back on. "And I thought you were going to let me know when you felt chilly. I have this leather jacket on—I'd be warm in a snowdrift. But you've only got that light ski jacket."

"My jacket's warm enough. Nothing wrong with it."

Matthew sighed. He couldn't seem to say anything right. "Of course there's nothing wrong with it. You look beautiful in it. Black's a good color for you. And that shade of pink of your sweater is good, too."

Out of the corner of his eye, Matthew could see Glory smile. Now, this was the way a date was supposed to be. "I noticed you've done your hair different, too. Sort of softlike. It's good. And your earrings. I've watched them all day. They put me in mind of dolphins, with the graceful shape they have to them."

"Okay, you win," Glory said. "We won't talk about your issues now, but we will later."

Matthew nodded. He hoped he and Glory would have lots of laters to talk about all of their issues. If he was lucky, he could keep her talking to him all winter. Maybe by then she'd be charmed by eastern Montana and decide to stay. He chided himself. He shouldn't think long-term with Glory. He knew he wasn't good enough for her. He wasn't the Christian man she deserved to marry. But even if they didn't marry, he'd like to have her in his life somewhere. *Who am I fooling? Could I bear to have her in my life and not have her belong to me as my wife?*

"Mail it for me, will you?" The Bullet was back at Douglas's. He pulled two twenties from his pocket and handed them to Douglas along with an addressed box that he'd had wrapped at the store. "Overnight it. It's Millie's Christmas present and I can't wait for the post office to open."

"You're not going to be there for Christmas? Not with Millie?"

"No."

Chapter Ten

The afternoon sun was starting its slide down by the time Matthew pulled the car into Dry Creek. He'd primed Glory with a question or two, and she'd spent the rest of the drive back telling him about her desire to paint faces. He told her about the Custer County Art Center back in Miles City. He knew Glory loved art, and he wanted her to know art had a place around Dry Creek. They were, in fact, close to Charles M. Russell country, and they had his museum in Great Falls. Not that far to drive if she stayed a while.

Matthew loved to watch Glory. Her whole face lit up when she talked about art. She was a woman who noticed color and shadow and— Matthew looked down the street of Dry Creek. Over half of the houses needed painting. The whole town definitely needed tending. He hadn't noticed that it was run-down when he moved here. But now, driving up with Glory in his car, he wondered if a city woman, an artistic city woman, could ever live in a place like this. And it wasn't just the lack of a coat of paint. He could get a brush out himself and do most of the houses if needed. There were so many other things. Dry Creek wasn't Seattle. Why, there wouldn't be movies in town if it wasn't for the rack of family videos they carried for rent at the hardware store. And there wasn't a hair salon, unless you counted the back room at Marcy Enger's. She'd never had any formal training, but the people around agreed she had a knack for cutting hair. An art center and an art museum wouldn't make up for all that. Not to a woman who liked flavored coffee.

"Look at that!" Glory said as she pointed to the old café.

Matthew groaned. And the old café—it was an eyesore. He didn't need that called to his attention. "Sorry about that. Businesses don't always make it in Dry Creek."

"Well, this one just might," Glory said as she pointed again. "Look at that sign."

Matthew looked again. He was so used to seeing the old café, he hadn't really looked before. He'd missed the banner. And the clean windows. And the open door.

"Christmas Jazz and Italian Pasta—$5.00." Matthew read the words of the foot-high banner that had been strung across the door. "What in the world is that?"

The trim around the big window had been painted a bright red, and someone was pasting a frosted star inside the window's left corner. The person's head was bent, but Glory thought the hair and angle of the neck looked familiar. She was right. Matthew hadn't even parked his car before the woman in the window looked up and waved.

Linda called to them before they even got the car parked. "Come and see."

The first thing Glory noticed when she stepped into the old café was that Linda's black lipstick was gone. The young woman's face was bare of any makeup— which was a good thing, since that left room for the traces of dust that trailed over her cheek. But, while there was dirt on Linda, there didn't look as if there was a speck of dirt hiding anywhere else in the large room. Wooden tables had been righted and scrubbed. The floor had been freshly mopped. The pine smell of disinfectant came from the kitchen.

"Jazz, honey," Linda called into the kitchen. "The rev and the angel are here."

Matthew winced. Glory laughed.

Duane came out of the kitchen. He didn't look like the Jazz Man now. Instead of a black leather jacket he wore an old flannel shirt that had holes in the sleeves and grease spots on the front. He was even more thoroughly dirty than Linda. He waved his arm in the direction of the back room. "Been getting the heater set up back there. Can't open up without heat."

"Open up? You're going to open up?"

"Just for Christmas Eve, at least so far," Linda said. Her eyes shone with excitement. "And word is spreading. We have a ton of cousins that are helping. The Alfsons and the Bymasters had to go home for supper, but they'll be back. So will the Lucas kids. It was Jazz's idea, really." Linda stopped to look at her boyfriend adoringly. "He got to thinking that all those people coming to the pageant might like to have a spaghetti dinner."

"Actually, Mrs. Hargrove gave me the nudge. Told me God answered prayers. It's just that sometimes He answered with our hard work. Then she gave me the keys and suggested Linda and I take a step of faith, as she called it. I wasn't so sure at first, but then I figured if the reverend can cook so can I. And then Linda said that music makes any meal better.'' Duane pointed to a raised area at the side of the room. ''The band'll set up there.''

''What a great idea!'' Glory said, and turned to Matthew. ''We could help them get ready, can't we?''

''I don't see why not. At least, until I have to get the twins.''

Matthew disappeared into the back to help the Jazz Man with the furnace and Glory rolled up her sleeves to help Linda explore the cabinets under the counter next to the kitchen. Glory could smell that the cabinets had been cleaned. Everything that could be done in a short period of time had been done.

Linda pulled on one of the cabinet doors. She had to tug to open it. ''Those two ladies who used to own this place had good taste, all right—and they didn't mind spending some money. This café was some kind of a hobby with them. I think they were planning to bring tea and civilization to the wild West.''

''They seem to have left it soon enough.''

''Dry Creek didn't match their dreams.'' Linda held out a large apron for Glory. ''Here, wrap this around you. You don't want to get dirty like I did.''

''Not match their dreams? Why not?'' Glory said indignantly as she slipped the apron over her neck and tied the strings around her. ''Everything I've seen is charming, quaint, full of real people and their lives.''

Linda laughed as she opened a bottom cupboard door. ''Not everyone wants real.''

Glory leaned down with Linda to look into the cupboard. Inside the cupboard were stacks of old-fashioned restaurant dinner plates, the white plates with a thin green band around the rim. "Well, well, look at this. There must be a hundred plates there." Glory quickly counted the stacks of plates. She'd estimate there might be 120.

"This'll be great!" Linda lifted out a small stack of the plates. "We thought we'd have to spring for paper plates—but this, this has more style."

Glory pulled open a drawer and found it full of stainless steel spoons.

"And forks!" Linda pulled open another drawer.

"They must not have even packed when they left," Glory said as she reached up and opened a top cupboard. There in thick plastic bags were linen table-cloths and napkins.

Dust filtered down as Glory and Linda pulled the bags off the shelf. Neither one of them saw the glass pitcher leaning against the bags. When Glory pulled out the last bag, the glass pitcher rolled off the shelf, fell to the floor and shattered.

Surprised, both Linda and Glory screamed.

"No!" Matthew's roar could be heard before he burst from the kitchen and into the dining area. He didn't stop in the doorway of the room to look around. Instead, wielding a piece of pipe, he simply threw himself in front of Glory and gently but quickly pushed her to the floor. He stood, half-crouched, over her.

Only then did he look around. "Where is he?"

Matthew's face had gone pale, and he looked fierce. He had a streak of black soot on his cheek and his hair had a film of white ash covering it. His eyes were pink from some irritant in the kitchen. He even wore a dish towel slung around his hips like a holster. He looked more like a back-alley bum than a hero. But all Glory saw was a warrior ready to do battle to defend his friend.

Glory was humbled. She'd never had anyone leap to her defense. She lay on the linoleum catching her breath. "It was a pitcher."

"A water pitcher?" Matthew was puzzled until Glory gestured to her left. His face went even whiter when he saw the pieces of glass. "Well—why—thank God I didn't push you in that direction. I could have hurt you myself."

"But you didn't," Glory quickly offered. She felt nothing but smooth linoleum beneath her arms and legs. "You thought it was a bullet, and you rushed to my defense."

Glory had forgotten she and Matthew were not alone.

"A bullet?" Linda whispered. Her voice cracked. "A real bullet? Here?"

Glory pushed herself up until she was sitting. The Jazz Man was standing in the doorway from the kitchen, and Linda was still standing beside the counter with the bag of table linens in her hand.

"There's no need to worry." Glory stood and brushed her jeans off even though she knew there was no dirt left on the floor. "It's nothing."

"But why would you think there'd be a bullet?" Linda persisted. Her eyes had grown round, and she looked even younger than the first day Glory had met her.

"You some kind of crook or something?" the Jazz

Man questioned Glory. He measured her and still appeared unconvinced. ''The police after you?''

''No, the crooks are after her.'' Matthew laid his piece of pipe down on the counter and took two steps over to Glory.

Matthew willed his panic to still itself. His pulse was pounding. His hands had been too scared to sweat until now. He knew he wasn't the man for Glory. Not really. But none of that mattered to him when he thought the bullets were flying. He felt a primitive need to protect her, as an animal needs to protect his mate. It was unthinking and unquestioned. If Glory needed protection, he needed to protect her.

And that wasn't all. Matthew stepped closer to Glory and tucked her into his arms. He could smell her spice perfume and feel stray strands of her hair as they brushed his chin. But for all that, he held her loosely. It was her, not him, that he was most aware of. He didn't kiss her. Didn't dream of doing more than hold her. For now, holding her within the circle of his arms was enough. Just to simply stand together with his arms wrapped around her. Matthew slowed his breathing until his pace matched hers, and they breathed as one.

The Jazz Man cleared his throat, but neither Matthew nor Glory responded. They just stood together. Finally Linda tugged at the Jazz Man's sleeve, and they both walked into the kitchen.

Glory didn't even notice they had gone. She was wrapped in a safe, safe cocoon. She felt as if she was underwater. As if everything that was noisy or demanding was distant. Nothing could reach her. Nothing could touch her. She had never felt as safe as she did now.

"We need to check back with the department," Matthew finally said. He uncurled himself from around her. "They might know more about this hit."

"Yeah," Glory agreed as she fought her sense of loss. Reality was intruding, demanding her attention. She missed the sense of being detached with Matthew. If all that ever happened with a scare like this was that Matthew hugged her because he was worried about her, she wouldn't mind a bullet drill every half hour.

"I see," Glory said fifteen minutes later as she stood beside the counter in the hardware store and talked to her friend Frank back at the department. The fire from the potbellied stove warmed the inside of the hardware store. The air smelled faintly of this morning's coffee and fresh popcorn. The hardware store was much too homey to be a backdrop for the hesitant words she heard over the telephone from Frank's mouth.

"What'd he say?" Matthew asked, tight-lipped, when she hung up the phone.

"Sylvia called him." Glory kept her voice even. She wondered if this was how a person in shock felt. The sense that she was not inside her own body. "Those two boys she told me about—the ones that said there was a hit out on me—didn't show at the center today. Not even for basketball. Another kid said they had flown out on business last night. Frank checked the airport. They bought tickets for Billings, Montana."

Matthew felt the breath leave his body. It just whooshed away. *Dear God, we are in trouble. Help us.* He didn't even notice he had uttered his first prayer in two years.

"Can they ID them? Has the flight landed in Billings yet? Maybe we could contact the authorities there."

Glory smiled. Matthew thought like a cop. "Yes, Sylvia gave pictures to the Seattle police. Frank will fax them to us with the ones of the crime scene, said he'd fax them all right away. And yes, they contacted the Billings authorities. And yes, the boys were on the plane. But they were too late. The plane had landed, and they'd picked up their luggage forty minutes before Sylvia knew they were gone. They'd already left the airport terminal."

"So they're here."

Glory nodded. She felt like a guppy in a fishbowl. No matter which way she turned she was too visible. Where would she be safe now?

"Car rental agencies? Did they check with car rental agencies?"

"The Billings police have the whole airport under surveillance. But Sylvia didn't think they would rent a car. They don't have a credit card, don't even have legitimate driver's licenses." Sylvia had added that they probably had fake licenses, since they'd gotten on the airplane, but Matthew didn't need to know that.

Matthew raised an eyebrow. "How old are these kids?"

"One's fourteen. The other's fifteen. They probably look older."

"Great. We're doing battle with babies," Matthew muttered as he ran his hand through his hair.

"These babies have been in a gang for the past five

or six years.'' Glory bit her lip. She needed to think. ''They can probably kill someone with a knife quicker than they can cut up an apple—and with less mess.''

Matthew smiled wearily and started to pace. Even on his crutches, he seemed to need to move. ''I know. I'm just not used to how tough children are these days. Makes me worry about the twins.''

''The twins have you. They'll be okay.''

Matthew nodded, then suddenly turned. ''Kids like that—how'd they get the money for airplane tickets?''

''I don't know.'' Glory hadn't wanted to tell him this. The tickets were a problem.

''Did they pay cash?''

Glory nodded. She bit her lip again. She desperately needed to think.

Matthew stopped pacing and sat down in a straight-backed chair beside the counter. ''Somebody gave them the money, then?''

Glory nodded. She didn't need to say what was obvious. The boys were on a job. How else could they afford to fly to Montana?

Matthew ran his hands through his hair again. He stood up as though he couldn't bear to sit and, once he was up, sat down again as though he couldn't bear to stand, either.

''Where are those drawings you've made?'' Matthew demanded. ''If we can figure out why someone wants to shoot you, they won't have just one target. They'll have to kill us both.''

''What! That'd be crazy!''

''We could let Frank in on the theory, too,'' Matthew continued. "Once the authorities know why you're a target, you won't be a target."

Glory nodded. It made sense. Besides, work sounded good. If nothing else, it would stop the slow scream she felt working its way up from her belly. She'd never been hunted before. And to have the hunters be two of Sylvia's kids... Something was wrong with the world.

The drawings she'd made yesterday were still on the table near the front window of the store. She'd drawn the murdered butcher from several different angles and at several different times, ranging from when he'd just been shot to a final picture of the chalk outline just after the police came and were ready to take the body away.

"You have a photographic memory?" Matthew asked as he looked at the set of drawings for the fifth time.

Glory nodded. "For pictures, when I see something I remember it."

"Do you think it through or just close your eyes and remember?"

"Mostly, close my eyes and remember. Why?"

"Then maybe somebody switched that package of meat on you," Matthew suggested. He pointed at the only two drawings that included the fallen package of meat. Each drawing had the meat in the corner where it had flown out of the butcher's hand when he was shot. At first glance, the packages looked alike. But then Glory saw the differences. The sticker was on the right for one package and on the left for the other. There were three small steaks in one package and two medium-size ones in the other.

"I must have remembered it wrong."

"Have you ever remembered something wrong before—a picture you were drawing?"

Glory thought of the hundreds of photos she'd drawn as a student and as a sketch artist. She'd gone from bowls of fruit to crowd scenes. In school she'd learned to be quick with details and at the police station she'd learned to be accurate. Even now she could close her eyes and see the scenes from the murder scene. "No, I've never gotten it wrong before. At least, not that I know of, and I would have known."

Matthew nodded as though that's what he'd expected. "Then we have our first clue."

"But why in the world would anyone switch the packages of meat?"

"And who would do it?"

"And when," Glory added. Matthew was right. They just might have their first clue. "They had to do it while we were sitting there waiting for the police to arrive."

"Was the gunman still loose?"

"No, he was tied up with some guy's belt. A customer tied him to the end of a display case. The gunman didn't even try to escape. He just lay there on the floor and waited."

"So whoever changed the meat was just hanging around, then."

"I suppose, but there was hardly anyone near us. The store manager had some of that 'Caution—Wet Surface' tape on his counter and he taped us in."

"Us?"

"Myself, the gunman and two other customers. But the other customers were holding the gunman down. Even when he was tied up, they didn't leave his side."

"Was the meat package close enough to the tape that a customer outside the taped area could switch it?"

"Not unless he had arms the size of King Kong's."

"Then that leaves the manager."

"The manager?"

Matthew nodded. "Wasn't it Sherlock Holmes who said once you've eliminated the impossible, whatever remains, however improbable, is the truth?"

"I suppose the manager could have done it. He was walking around swinging that tape here and there. He had big pockets in his butcher's apron, too."

"Now all we need to do is figure out why."

"That's the hard one."

"We don't have time for hard." Matthew picked up the telephone. "What did you say was the name of that market?"

"You're going to call Benson's Market?"

"How else am I going to talk to this manager?"

It took Matthew five minutes to be connected to the manager at Benson's Market. It took him only two minutes and four questions to have the man swearing at him and threatening to turn state's evidence and tell the feds.

"Who'd he think you were?"

Matthew shrugged. "I told him I was Matthew. He must have heard there was a Matthew somewhere."

"Or he's so eager to squeal, he doesn't care who knows what."

Matthew nodded. "He told me there wasn't supposed to be any hassle. That the meat deal was supposed to be low risk. The money isn't that much, not when there's the murder, and he swears he didn't know about the murder. And then someone's calling asking pointed questions sounding like they know something…''

''Not that you know anything.''

Matthew grinned. ''He didn't know that.''

''We'll have Frank call him and lean on him, too.''

Matthew nodded. ''I'm beginning to think the road between here and Seattle is probably sprinkled with stolen meat.''

''The rustling!'' Glory put the two together.

''What better way to make a profit on stolen cattle than to have them butchered and sold in independent stores?''

''But why change the package of meat?''

''Something about the codes. The manager was actually pocketing a good sum of money by buying the stolen meat. When the butcher started talking about the computer red-flagging super sales based on the price the meat was logged into the system, the manager panicked. The manager was shadowing the real prices behind the invented prices to keep track of his windfall and something was going wrong.''

Pieces of the puzzle clicked together in Glory's mind. ''And the butcher figured this out. That's why they killed him.'' They'd solved the mystery. That's what had been itching at her mind. The fact that her visual pictures were different when she recalled the scene. Someone must have found out about her memory. She was noted in the police department for never forgetting a crime picture.

''I'm safe. Now that the pictures are out, there's no reason to kill me.''

''All we need to do is find those boys and convince them of that.''

Glory nodded. That was the problem, all right. Finding those boys before they found her.

Matthew spent the afternoon making and waiting for phone calls to Seattle. He talked to Frank. He tried to talk to Sylvia, but he finally found out that she had left shortly after warning Glory about the boys and was flying into Montana herself.

"Billings airport is going to be busy."

"Billings can't possibly be busier than this place," Glory grumbled. Mrs. Hargrove came into the store carrying a bent shepherd's staff.

"What's this I hear about bullets flying and hit men coming to town?" Mrs. Hargrove demanded as she walked toward the counter. She was wearing a black wool coat over a green gingham dress.

"I know now's not a good time, with the pageant and all." Glory said. "I didn't plan this."

"Well, of course you didn't, dear. And don't worry about the pageant. A few bullets won't stop us."

"Speaking of the pageant, I might not be able to be your angel."

"Well, surely you don't think they'd try anything at the pageant." Mrs. Hargrove was shocked. "That's a holy moment!"

"That didn't stop Herod in the original pageant." Matthew was worried. With everyone in costume, two teenagers could sneak up before he could pick them out. A bathrobe and a loose turban was all the disguise they'd need. He wasn't sure he'd be able to pick them out fast enough to protect Glory.

"Well, if need be I'll fly from those rafters myself," Mrs. Hargrove said starchily. "I won't fit into the costume, but I can wear a big white apron and some of my husband's winter long johns."

Glory blinked. Had she heard right? Long johns and... *"Fly from the rafters?"*

Mrs. Hargrove gulped. "I guess we haven't told you yet. Tavis had this great idea." Her face beamed. "A flying angel. Now, won't that make the pageant special?"

Glory blinked again. "A flying angel? Me?"

"Well, it won't all be flying. First you'll start out standing on the rafters, singing a carol."

"Singing? Me? I haven't even practiced." Glory didn't know what was more alarming, the singing or the flying.

"Don't worry about it, dear. I'm sure whatever you sing will be just fine."

By nine o'clock that night Glory had practiced "Silent Night" exactly three times. Each time Matthew and the twins sang it beautifully. She wasn't so sure herself.

"Hang this one on that low branch," Glory directed from her place on the chair. She, Matthew and the twins were finishing decorating the five-foot pine tree at Matthew's house. She held out a golden ornament to Matthew.

"And don't bunch all the red ones together."

"Are you really going to fly?" Joey asked for the fourth time that evening.

"It's more like a swing." Glory had gotten very specific descriptions from Mrs. Hargrove and Tavis. The ropes were heavy and the rafters strong enough to hoist machinery. The angel's long robe would hide the seat of the swing, and the ropes, Tavis had assured her, would be scarcely visible in the darkened barn.

"Nobody's going to fly or swing anywhere unless

we find those two boys,'' Matthew said sternly. After closing the hardware store, he'd looked both ways down the street before he'd rushed Glory to the car. They'd stopped at the café so Matthew could show the faxed photos to Duane and Linda and ask them to keep an eye out for the boys.

"Don't stop them," Matthew had directed the two. "You've got the number. Call the police. Those two are armed and dangerous."

"I'll show them dangerous." Duane scowled and pushed up the sleeves on the flannel shirt he was wearing.

"No heroics," Matthew ordered. "We just need an ID. I've already put Carl Wall on alert. We just call him—he'll come running. Let the other kids know."

Duane nodded. "I'll pass the word around. If they come, we'll pick them out."

"Thanks."

When Matthew had got Glory and the twins inside the house, he'd rummaged through a kitchen drawer until he'd found the keys to his house. For the first time since he'd moved to Dry Creek, he'd locked both doors. The windows were all frosted shut, but he'd checked the latches on them anyway. Then he'd pulled the shades down. Halfway through locking up, he'd started to pray—actually, it wasn't praying exactly. It was more like cursing at God for allowing Glory to be in danger. But as the words spent themselves, his anger had dried up and left him feeling empty. Glory would not appreciate him cursing at God on her behalf. Still, his anger was there anyway, ready to defend her against anyone, even God himself.

* * *

The Bullet was in the airport in Billings, Montana. He wasn't two feet inside the place before he started spotting the cops. A dozen of them, at least. He never checked his luggage, so he went to the first car rental booth he found.

The clerk seemed nervous and excited, but not about the Bullet.

The Bullet smiled. "Busy day?"

"The police have been here for hours looking for two boys," the clerk leaned over and whispered confidentially.

"Runaways?" the Bullet asked, careful to keep his voice only mildly interested.

The clerk pulled his credit card toward her and shook her head . "Much worse than runaways. The woman at the snack counter dates one of those officers, and he told her these kids are contract killers. Think of that! Hit men! In Billings!"

The Bullet clucked sympathetically. His blood went cold but he didn't let it show. There couldn't be two contracts so close to Christmas in this part of Montana. No, these kids were trouble. His trouble. They needed to be taken out of the game.

Chapter Eleven

December 24. Glory repeated the date to herself while she lay in bed the next morning, feeling lazy. It had snowed last night, and a thick layer of frost covered the window to her room. She hadn't had a white Christmas for years. It made her feel as if she was wrapped inside a Norman Rockwell sketch. Surely, contracts and hit men had no place in her life. Especially not on the day of the pageant. Not the day before the birth of Christ was celebrated.

Glory turned over and looked at the luminous hands on the alarm clock sitting on the bedside table. Almost six. Matthew would be up. She could hear him stirring around already, his crutch making an irregular thump on the floor in the kitchen. She breathed deeply. And she could smell the coffee. A gourmet orange flavor if she wasn't mistaken.

The floor was cold enough to make her dance from foot to foot when she stepped out of bed and looked in her suitcase for a pair of socks. There she found some gray woollies. Perfect. Glory sat back on the bed and pulled the socks over her tingling toes. She had a busy day today. She needed to check with the nurse in Miles City to make sure her boxes had arrived. She'd spoken last night with Mrs. Hargrove about the bags of candy the angel was to distribute. She decided she'd count on the twins to spread the word that the children's Christmas gifts would be given out after the pageant was over and the children had all taken off their costumes.

Glory pulled out a hunter-green turtleneck to wear with her jeans. Ideally, she should have red, but she hadn't packed anything with Christmas in mind. Green would have to do. Maybe she could snag a sprig of holly somewhere to pin on her collar. Lacking that, she might tie a string of Christmas ribbon around her neck. Matthew had assured her he had wrapping paper for Christmas. He must have ribbon, too. She glanced over at the presents she'd purchased yesterday. They were still in the bag; she'd need to wrap them this afternoon. Maybe while she made cookies.

Glory had promised the twins they would sit together and read the Christmas story before they got ready for the pageant. She wanted both boys to have a cookie in their hands while she read to them. Christmas, after all, was the birth of hope. Every child deserved to have Christmas memories of abundance.

Once Glory was dressed and ready to go downstairs, she picked up her Bible. She always had her morning devotions before breakfast. She'd read a psalm and then pray. Since she'd been in Dry Creek, she'd had these devotions alone in Matthew's bedroom. But today was the day before Christmas. A miracle could happen. She was going to march downstairs and ask Matthew to have devotions with her.

Miracles didn't always happen on Christmas Eve day, Glory thought. Matthew had made a blueberry coffee cake and gourmet coffee for her, but he wouldn't have devotions with her.

"It wouldn't be right," he mumbled vaguely as he opened a can of frozen orange juice.

Wouldn't be right, Glory fumed. "And why not?"

"Sometimes devotions are just a habit. That would be all it would be for me. Just words."

"Well, sometimes lack of faith is just a habit, too." Glory didn't add that bullheaded stubbornness could be a habit, too. And refusing to take another risk once you've been burned could be a habit, too.

"I suppose," Matthew said mildly as he gave her the plate of coffee cake to put on the table. "But I have other things to worry about today instead of habits."

Glory wasn't finished with him. "Well, then I guess I'll just go off by myself and have a few minutes of Bible reading and prayer..." She paused to be sure she had his attention. "Maybe on the front porch."

Matthew almost dropped the pot of coffee. "You can't sit on the front porch! There are hit men out there."

Glory shrugged and started to walk away. "I've got other things to worry about today besides hit men."

Matthew growled and set the pot of coffee back on its stand. "This is blackmail, you know." He walked over to the table and sat down.

"I know." Glory grinned and sat down at the table, too.

*   *   *

Matthew decided it wasn't so bad. He loved watching Glory's lips move while she read, and it was cozy here in the kitchen. The sun was beginning to flirt with the idea of rising, making the light outside soft. He never got over the morning light in Montana. It was as if the day just snapped into focus.

Matthew smiled. Glory had given him a reprieve so he could bring them both a cup of steaming coffee, and he sipped his now. He could get accustomed to flavored coffee. He even half listened to the words Glory was reading—Psalm 61. A psalm full of faith from its "Hear my cry" to its "vows day after day." He'd preached a sermon on that psalm once—a rather compelling one. He'd used the old-fashioned illustration of a tapestry that was beautiful on the top even though a person looking at the back might not see the pattern. He hadn't realized at the time that a single snag could pull the whole tapestry apart. The threads were so connected. He'd never seen the backside of faith, the side he was on now. He wished he had the words to tell Glory about the confusion in his heart. Sometimes he thought the problem wasn't that he had too little faith now, but that he'd once had too much faith. If he had not expected so much of God, he wouldn't have fallen flat on his face when God let him down. But he hadn't thought it was too much to ask for Susie to live. Not from his God. He'd gripped God with all his might and refused to let go, never once thinking that God might let go of him.

"'Lead thou me to the rock that is higher than I.'" Glory reread the words aloud. "'For thou art my refuge, a strong tower against the enemy. Let me dwell in thy tent for ever! Oh, to be safe under the shelter of thy wings!'''

Nothing but the sound of the oven timer ticking could be heard when Glory finished. Glory stole a glance at Matthew. His face was stoic. Only the white knuckles on his hand gripping the coffee cup gave away his feelings.

Glory opened her mouth to speak, but Matthew stirred instead.

"Yeah, well," Matthew muttered as he drained the last of his coffee.

"Isn't it inspiring?" Glory ignored Matthew's indifference and continued. "It's one of my favorite psalms."

"I'm glad it means so much to you."

Glory held her breath. She usually didn't push. She knew no one was ever forced into faith. But she had to try. "It could mean as much to you."

Matthew grimaced. "It did once."

"It could again." Glory looked directly at Matthew. She thought she'd see annoyance in his eyes, but she saw only sadness. "Just ask Him to help you."

Matthew didn't answer for a long minute. Then he took a final gulp of coffee and rose from his chair. "I need to finish getting breakfast ready for the twins."

"With me it was guilt," Glory said, talking to Matthew's back as he reached into the cupboard for the cereal boxes.

"Hmm?"

"Guilt. That's what stopped me from accepting God's love. I didn't see how I could take in His love when I was alive and my father was dead. I was driving the car. I should have died. Not him. I didn't deserve God's love.''

"Oh, no." Matthew turned around and balanced on his one crutch. "You must never think that. Accidents happen. It wasn't your fault. God wouldn't hold that against you."

"What does it matter to you? You don't accept His love, why should I?"

Matthew frowned. "You're not me, that's why."

"You're not the only one who can be a martyr."

"I'm not a martyr—"

The phone rang, interrupting Matthew.

"I can get it." Glory stood.

"Sit down," Matthew commanded as he began to hobble across the kitchen. "And watch the windows. No one's supposed to know you're here."

Glory snorted. "The whole town of Dry Creek knows I'm here."

"It's not the people of Dry Creek I'm worried about," Matthew said from the living room as he grabbed the telephone. "It's who else that might be snooping around."

"Hello." Matthew twisted the telephone cord as he sat down on the sofa.

Glory went to the door to the living room and listened. In Seattle, a 6:00 a.m. phone call was unusual and likely to be bad news, but here six o'clock was almost prime time.

"It's your friend Sylvia." Matthew held the phone out to her.

"From the airport?" Glory walked to the sofa and sat down next to Matthew.

The telephone connection was filled with static. "Sylvia?"

"Glory, thank God it's you. Are you all right?"

Glory gripped the phone. Sylvia sounded a million miles away. "I'm fine. Where are you? Can I come get you?"

"No." There was noise in the background. It sounded like the grinding of metal objects. Sylvia herself sounded breathless and shaken. "I can get a ride into Dry Creek."

"Where are you? You're not thinking of hitching a ride, are you? It's not safe."

"No, Mr. Elkton is going to give me a ride."

Glory strained to hear Sylvia's voice. Something was definitely not right. Usually cheer spilled out of Sylvia's lips. Even when she was worried, Sylvia always sounded confident. But her voice now reminded Glory of a little girl, a little orphaned girl with no friends.

"Are you all right?" Glory pressed. "Mr. Elkton, who's that?" Glory searched her mind. The name was familiar. Then she saw Matthew mouth some words. "You don't mean Tavis Elkton's father? The owner of the Big Sheep Mountain Ranch?"

"Yes," Sylvia said at the same time as Matthew nodded.

"But how did you meet him?"

"I took a wrong exit off the interstate. Someone moved the exit sign to Dry Creek. Instead of leading to Dry Creek the sign led to a dirt road on Mr. Elkton's property. I took the exit and ended up with my car in the ditch."

"You weren't hurt?"

"No, I'm fine," Sylvia said. "Mr. Elkton found me."

"Well, thank God for that. Who would do a fool thing like move the exit sign?"

"That's what Garth—I mean Mr. Elkton—would like to know."

Glory listened. She had heard Sylvia talk about pregnant teenagers, arrested teenagers, addicted teenagers, but she'd never heard this particular tone in her voice before. Then it dawned on her. Glory grinned. Sylvia was flustered. That's what she was hearing through the telephone lines.

"I haven't met Mr. Elkton," Glory said calmly. "About how old is he?"

"Old? I don't know. Maybe in his forties."

"Hmm, a man of forty is in his prime here in Montana. Lots of outdoor exercise. Sunshine. Nature. I suppose he's attractive."

Glory looked at Matthew sitting on the sofa. He was eyeing her as if she'd lost her senses.

"He probably thinks so," Sylvia fumed.

"It's awfully nice of him to drive you into Dry Creek."

"He said he needed to drive in anyway. Something about getting some nails from the hardware store."

"Nails from the hardware store," Glory repeated for Matthew's benefit. "Mr. Elkton needs nails." Glory smiled as Matthew raised his eyebrows. It was as she thought. "Well, then, I'll see you when you get here."

"You're not going outside, are you?" Sylvia asked, sounding worried. "They didn't pick up K.J. and John at the airport. They're around here somewhere. You should just stay put."

"There's no point in hiding. They could shoot me inside as well as outside. Besides, it's probably safer at the hardware store than here. It's inside, too, and I stay away from the windows."

"Well, be sure to have the police check the place out before you go in. And tell them to give you an escort across the street."

"That'll be the day," Glory muttered. She could just see Carl Wall escorting her anywhere

"I'll get to Dry Creek as soon as I can. If they're hiding, they might come out if they see me."

"It'll be good to see you. And to meet Mr. Elkton. Just have him bring you to the hardware store."

"I'll be there soon. See you then."

"Yeah, see you then." Glory hung up the telephone.

Glory couldn't stop smiling. It was definitely Christmas.

"You look like the cat that swallowed the cream," Matthew observed.

"I think Sylvia's got a boyfriend."

"Garth Elkton?" Matthew asked dubiously. "I doubt that. He's a confirmed bachelor these days if I've seen one. His last marriage soured him on women. Not that he might not have an affair. But marriage? No."

Glory shrugged. "Well, Sylvia isn't the kind of woman a man has an affair with, so maybe you're right."

"But he is coming in for nails," Matthew muttered as he shook his head. "The last thing the Big Sheep Ranch needs is more nails."

Matthew thought Sylvia's idea of an armed escort was a good one. "Carl Wall doesn't have anything better to do. Besides, he likes to stop at the store for coffee.''

Glory was sitting on the sofa with the twins, looking at the Christmas tree. The boys sat huddled in quilts, one on each side of her. They were still drowsy with sleep. Glory smoothed back Josh's hair. ''Call him if you want to, but let's not talk about it now.''

''They know about it anyway,'' Matthew said quietly with a pointed look at the twins. ''I'm sure the whole town knows. News like this doesn't keep quiet.''

''But we still don't have to talk about it before breakfast.''

''No.'' Matthew smiled. ''We don't.''

''We have enough to talk about, anyway,'' Glory said as she squeezed each twin. ''This afternoon we make cookies and then we celebrate just a little before the pageant.''

''I need a new scarf for my costume,'' Joey said. ''To tie me in with. Judy Eslick got gum on my old one.''

''Well, we'll see to that before cookies. Maybe we can get the gum out. And I'll want to hear your lines for the pageant.''

''I say, 'Look yonder,''' Josh announced.

''And I point at the angel,'' Joey added. ''That's you.''

Matthew cleared his throat and sat down on the sofa next to the twins. ''I know how much you're looking forward to having Glory be the angel, but she might not be able to, not tonight.''

The twins nodded. ''That's what Mrs. Hargrove said.''

"But I can watch you," Glory offered.

Matthew frowned. "I don't know if that's a good idea."

"Well, the whole town is going to be there," Glory said. "It's probably safer there than anywhere else."

Glory was surprised that Carl Wall agreed to escort her and Matthew over to the hardware store. She gathered from his comments that she was now one of his pigeons and, as such, would be defended from outsiders like every other citizen of Dry Creek.

"I've cleared the street," the deputy said as he stood on Matthew's porch. "We best move while everything's empty."

"But it's only seven-thirty," Glory protested. Mrs. Hargrove had stopped by to pick up the twins already. "Matthew doesn't open the hardware store until eight."

"I can open early," Matthew said as he balanced on one crutch so he could put on his leather jacket.

"That's right. You don't want to go by your usual schedules," the deputy warned them. "Do the unexpected. Change your routine. That way no one can set an ambush."

"Makes sense." Glory put her arms into an old army jacket the deputy had brought with him. It was his version of a disguise.

"And put your hair under this." The deputy held out a gray scarf and then a baseball cap. "Then put this on."

"Sorry for the trouble I caused you earlier," Glory said.

"Ah, that was just a little misunderstanding. No hard feelings, I hope." The deputy had done an about-face with her. Glory suspected he might have run a check on her and found out that she did work for the Seattle Police Department.

Glory smiled. "No. No hard feelings."

"Matthew?" the deputy asked.

"All's forgotten and forgiven." Matthew held the door open for Glory, then, before she could go through it, put a hand out to delay her and went through the door himself instead. "Need to change the order. Keep it unexpected."

"But if—" Glory gulped. If someone was planning to shoot her while she was going through a door, she wouldn't want them to shoot Matthew instead. For the first time, the bullets seemed all too real. It wasn't just her life that was in danger; it was the lives of those she cared about, too.

The few steps to the deputy's patrol car were cold and slippery. A fine sheen of frost was still on the ground from the night's low temperatures. Glory almost slipped twice hurrying down the sidewalk to the patrol car. Matthew struggled to keep up with her on his crutches, but she deliberately kept ahead of him. If she was a target, she didn't want him near her.

"Keep low in the seat," Carl said when Glory slid into the back seat of the car. He already had the heater going and the ice scraped off all the windows. Except for the sound of the car's engine, the day was silent. No traffic. No children outside walking anywhere. Not even any dogs barking.

It was only three blocks to the hardware store, but the deputy kept his eyes darting about the whole time. He studied the porch of each house that lined the street, starting with Mr. Gossett's. Nothing was unusual.

The deputy pulled up as close to the hardware store as possible, even though he had to park in a crust of old snow that had been shoveled up next to the store. Car exhaust had turned the top of the snow gray.

Glory had her hand on the door handle when Matthew reached over from the seat beside her to stop her.

"Not now," Matthew commanded, and jerked his head toward the store. "We got company inside."

"What?" The deputy rolled down his window and lifted his nose in the air as if he could smell something. "Smoke."

"There's a fire going in the stove."

Glory looked up. The sky was a washed-out morning blue, but she still saw the thin trail of vapor. It was so small it was almost invisible. "I don't suppose Elmer or Jacob would have gone inside and built a fire?"

Matthew shook his head.

The deputy reached for the radio in his car. "I'm calling for backup."

"Backup won't do us any good if they're inside watching us. It'll take the guys from Miles City twenty minutes to get here." Matthew ran his hands through his hair and looked over at Glory. "And stay down on the seat, for pity's sake."

"I won't stay down unless we all stay down."

"What?"

"I know about decoys," Glory said stubbornly. She refused to be the only one who wasn't a target. "Making them think they have a target just to draw a reaction."

Matthew grinned. "Now you're thinking."

Glory gasped. "I meant I don't want anyone to be

a decoy. You're not to take any chances." Glory looked at the deputy, who was speaking into the radio. "Either of you!"

"But what about him?" Matthew pointed to his crutch that was lying sideways on the floor of the back seat. "We could put the deputy's hat on my crutch and wave it in front of the window. Those windows are so frosted up all anyone will see is a shadow."

"It's worth a try." The deputy hung up the radio. "Especially since everyone's out on a call already. I'd guess it'll be forty-five minutes before anyone gets here to help us."

Matthew pulled a handkerchief out of his pocket and wrapped it around the handle of his crutch to make the shape of a face. The deputy took off his cap and handed it back to Matthew.

"I'll walk it along," the deputy said to Matthew. "You stay with Glory."

"No, you stay with her." Matthew touched the door handle.

"But…" the deputy started.

"You have the gun," Matthew answered simply. "Even if you left it with me, I'm not sure what my aim would be. If something happens, I want the gun with you."

"You can't do this," Glory protested. No one had ever risked their life before for her, and now Matthew seemed to be doing it all morning. "You could be hurt." *Or worse.*

The windows on the car were still iced, even though the heater in the patrol car was spitting out coughs of heat. Glory herself was shivering. But Matthew's forehead had a thin sheen of sweat covering it.

"Don't worry." Matthew tied his jacket around the crutch, too. His crutch now looked like a skinny scarecrow.

"Of course I'll worry," Glory fretted.

"Well, pray instead, then," Matthew offered mildly as he unlatched the door.

"Pray," Glory squeaked. She tried, but the words spun in her throat. Matthew stepped out of the car. His boots crunched on the snow. She wanted to close her eyes. But she couldn't. *Dear Lord*—the words finally came— *Oh, dear Lord. Help this man, this exasperating man, the one I don't want to see hurt, the one I care about....*

The car windows were beginning to fog over, so Glory saw Matthew as if he was in a grainy out-of-focus film. He crouched low, keeping his crutch held high. With every step he took Glory expected an explosion of gunfire. But the silence held. Finally Matthew was in front of the side window to the store. His jacket waved in front of the window. Whoever was inside wouldn't resist a target like that.

Glory felt she didn't breathe for the next two minutes. It seemed like hours, but she knew it was only two minutes because she watched the minutes change on the digital clock in the patrol car. One minute. Two minutes.

"I better go in the front door," the deputy finally said, pushing open his car door. "Maybe someone just forgot to put the fire out yesterday."

Glory began to breathe again. That must be it. So much had been happening yesterday that everyone's nerves were stretched. Matthew had just forgotten to see that the fire was completely out. Maybe Jacob or Mrs. Hargrove had put in a large chunk of wood at the day's end and it had lain smoldering all night. That must be it.

The car door handle was cool to Glory's touch. "I'll go tell Matthew."

Matthew had already turned toward them, and gave a relieved thumbs-up sign.

Glory pushed the store door open first. Matthew had twisted the key in the lock. The deputy took his hand off the butt of his gun to put his cap back on his own head. All three of them were standing in the doorway unraveling Matthew's crutch decoy.

Glory looked into the dim store first. It was too early for the morning sun to come in through the display window, and the inside was poorly lit. Matthew had left three salt blocks and a small box of bolts close to the counter for Timothy Stemm to pick up this morning. Glory reached for the switch to the overhead lights.

The overhead lights came on.

"What the—?" Glory blinked. It looked as if there was a big bundle of blankets tied to the large center post. Gray blankets. Khaki blankets. Then she saw a foot.

Matthew slammed the door shut and looked at Glory. "Back into the car."

"But—"

"This time he's right," the deputy said as he drew his gun.

Glory stepped back to the side of the store. "That's as far away as I can go."

Matthew frowned, but the deputy was already slowly opening the door.

"Deputy Sheriff Wall here. Don't try anything. We're coming in."

"We ain't done nothing." The muffled wail came from inside the store.

When Glory got to the door, Matthew was holding two thin teenage boys by the scruff of their necks as if they were puppies. When she got closer, she saw that their hands were tied behind their backs and they were both anchored with another rope to the center post.

"You've got it all wrong," one of the boys protested. "We're the good guys. We was here to stop the hit man. He's the one that tied us up."

"Contract killers aren't known for using rope to do their business," the deputy said wryly as he patted the blankets in a weapons search.

"Or building fires to keep their victims warm," Matthew added. He'd sat down on the floor next to the boys so he could keep them still while the deputy searched.

"But he did!" the boy with a Seahawks cap insisted. "We was trying to help. We tried to keep him away. Even moved the road sign off the interstate so he'd get lost."

"You know it's illegal to tamper with road signs?" Matthew scolded.

One of the boys shrugged. Glory figured they had done worse than move a road sign or two in their short lives.

"No wonder Sylvia got lost," Matthew half muttered.

"Sylvia?" The jaws of both boys dropped. They were clearly worried more about her than they were about the law. "*Sylvia's* here!"

"You'll have some explaining to do." Glory looked at her watch. "In about one hour, I'd say."

"What's Sylvia doing here?"

"She came to keep you out of trouble," Glory scolded.

"Ahh, man."

"No guns," the deputy reported after a thorough search of the blankets.

Glory watched the boys exchange worried looks. It was clear they didn't want to disappoint Sylvia. Glory wondered how long they had been gang members. They each had a small gold earring in each ear, but that was more fashion than rebellion these days. The one with a Seahawks cap had a recent haircut and a bruise on his chin. The other boy had a tattoo that ran the length of his arm. Both wore white T-shirts and jeans.

"Where are your coats?" Matthew asked.

Glory noticed for the first time that both boys had goose bumps on their arms and the tips of their ears were red.

"Don't need none," one of the boys declared defiantly. "It's not cold."

Matthew looked at the two boys a moment and then nodded. "I'll see what we have in back. I think we have a jacket or two. That'll keep you until we rebuild the fire."

The deputy shook his head as he laid one of the wool blankets over each boy's shoulders. "You boys would have frozen out there last night without even a coat. This is Montana. You need to thank whoever brought you here."

The boy with the tattoo scowled. "Ain't going to thank no killer."

"Wonder who it was who put them here." The deputy looked up as Matthew hobbled back into the main room of the store. Matthew had his crutch under one arm and two worn jackets under the other.

Matthew tossed the jackets to the deputy. "I figure the whole county saw that picture I gave to Duane and Linda. Most likely one or two of the hands at the Big Sheep Mountain Ranch caught them asking questions. They wouldn't have wanted to wait for morning to come—chores awaiting—so they left them here for us to find this morning."

The deputy nodded. "Makes sense."

Glory was glad something made sense. She hadn't caught her breath all morning. Something was chewing its way into her consciousness, but she couldn't grasp it. Maybe it was because she was still reeling from the way Matthew had risked taking a bullet from these two boys and then noticed so quickly that they needed coats. If she hadn't already decided Matthew was a natural minister, she would have known it after this morning. Matthew was someone who was off course with his life. He'd given up his calling because his wife had died.

That must be it, Glory decided with relief. She was only worried about Matthew. Worried that he wasn't doing what he wanted with his life. Worried that he was so wrapped up in remembered love that he couldn't live.

That must be it, Glory tried to convince herself. She was only worried for Matthew. She let her breath escape—and that's when it hit her.

She remembered the moment. The stab of knowing. She'd sat in the back seat of the patrol car, watching Matthew wave his crutch around to tempt a bullet out of the boys inside the store, and fear had emptied her mind. And then her mind had filled in a flash with one thought and one thought only. She'd sat there motionless and realized that if a bullet hit Matthew it would hit her, too. Square in the middle of her heart. She'd seen the truth and then she'd pushed it away until now. Cautiously she let the thought come back. She worried over her revelation, afraid to even say the words to herself. But she couldn't stop them. It was true.

She was in love with Matthew.

Yes, she, Glory Beckett, was in love.

She knew it was foolish to love him. She knew he did not love her now and probably would not love her in the future. She knew they would never marry. They would probably not even see each other after Christmas. But she knew when she left Dry Creek she'd leave her heart behind. This wasn't at all how she'd planned to fall in love.

The Bullet pulled the brim on the Stetson down lower. He wondered if the farmer would notice that his hat and overalls had been stolen out of his pickup last night.

It had snowed last night—frigid, stingy flakes with more wind than moisture—and the porch where the Bullet chose to hide was cold.

The sun had barely risen when the Bullet heard the patrol car drive up to the house where he knew Glory was staying. He didn't even raise his head to look over the porch railing at her. No, it was too soon in the game. A patient cat waited for the mice to weary themselves before he stretched out his claws.

Chapter Twelve

Glory watched Sylvia question the two boys. Sylvia was petite, only four-eleven in the short stacked heels she wore. But Sylvia didn't need height. She was second-generation Italian and waved her arms around fearlessly while she spoke. Her gold rings flashed and her long fingernails pointed. She towered over the teenagers, who still huddled by the stove. Sylvia alternated between sympathy and scolding. The love she had for the teens was so obvious she had them talking in minutes. They told her everything.

"But what about the plane tickets?" Matthew was sitting on a stool behind the counter watching Sylvia's drama.

"I told you, man. I earned that money," insisted K.J., the teenager with the tattoo. "Busted my butt all last summer sweeping up in my uncle's restaurant."

"You told me before you worked for him for nothing," Sylvia challenged. Her blue eyes snapped and her lips drew together reprovingly.

K.J. grimaced. "Yeah, well…"

Sylvia looked at the two teenagers for a moment. Her face relaxed.

Glory saw that Sylvia was tired. Faint lines gathered around her usually laughing eyes. Her black hair, shiny and full, was bunched up and tied back with a scarf. *A scarf?* Glory looked more closely. It wasn't a scarf. The material tying Sylvia's hair back was a red bandanna, the kind the ranchers here used. And unless Glory was mistaken, the thick knot holding the bandanna in place could only have been tied by the expert fingers of a rancher.

Glory slid her gaze over to the only rancher in the store. Garth Elkton. He didn't look any too fresh, either, now that she looked at him closely. He needed a shave and his scowl seemed to fasten on Sylvia with some regularity.

"What's your uncle's name?" Matthew asked K.J. "I'm sure the police can find out if you worked for him."

"Ah, don't call the police," K.J. whined. "My uncle'll freak. Besides, you shouldn't keep worrying about us when there's a killer out there."

"A killer?" The deputy paused. "Describe him."

"Well, he's sort of average looking."

"What color's his hair?"

"Brown. No, black." The boy looked miserable. "Just hair. No particular color."

"Can't you describe him any more than that?"

K.J. frowned. "He's hard to remember. The kind of guy that hangs out in the shadows at school. You'd hardly know he was around except for the gun."

"I thought so," the deputy said smugly. "You never saw anybody."

"Hey, I ain't lying. We're innocent. All we did was move the road sign."

"Son, you're lucky you're dealing with Sylvia and not me." Garth Elkton spoke for the first time. His voice was low and gravelly. "I'd turn you over my knee and show you the consequence of moving road signs. This is snow country. People could die if they take the wrong turn in a blizzard. Someone could have died last night because of you."

"Nobody did, did they?" K.J. asked in alarm.

"Hey, we didn't mean to kill nobody," protested John, the other boy. "We've been trying to do good to show—"

John bit back his words to a mumble.

"To show what?" Sylvia persisted.

"That we meant it." John looked down at the floor and whispered, "The other day in church, we meant it."

Glory looked at their faces. They looked honest. Besides, it was almost Christmas, and they were so young. She turned to Sylvia. "Maybe it has all been one of those misunderstandings."

"Maybe." Sylvia looked thoughtful.

"I guess no harm's been done," Glory offered.

"You don't want to press charges, then?" the deputy asked.

Glory looked at Matthew. He answered, "If they leave today with no funny business, we'll let it go."

"I already called the airport in Billings and got two tickets back to Seattle for this afternoon. If no one minds, I'll put them on the plane myself," the deputy said eagerly. He clearly wanted the boys out of there.

Sylvia nodded. "I'll go with them."

"Can't. I had to pressure the agents to get these

two tickets. There's a waiting list a mile long. Seems everyone wants to go someplace the day before Christmas.''

Sylvia bit her lip. "I see. Well, I guess I'll need to stay, then."

"Good." Garth Elkton rocked back on his boot heels. He'd already removed his Stetson and laid it on the store counter. His sheepskin coat was open, showing off a green flannel shirt. He looked down and smiled politely at Sylvia. "You can go to dinner with me, then."

Sylvia looked up at him as if he'd just grown two heads. "Us? Dinner?"

The polite smile ended. A muscle tensed in the rancher's cheek. "It's a custom."

"I—I can't," Sylvia stammered, frantically looking around until she latched on to Glory. "I have to—to help Glory with the pageant."

"We can eat before the pageant." The rancher's eyes grew flint hard.

Sylvia flushed, and she looked at the floor. "Before the pageant I, ah, I need to help Glory get dressed up in her angel costume."

The rancher looked around coldly. "Matthew here can help her. It's only wings and a halo."

"It might only be wings and a halo to you, but Glory here cares how she looks in that costume," Sylvia protested as she walked over and put her arm around Glory.

"I do?" Glory squeaked. Sylvia pinched her. Glory corrected herself. "I mean, yes, of course, I do care."

The rancher looked exasperated. "Look, we eat and talk or we just talk. Take your pick. We've got business to finish. And we might as well eat while we do it. If you want to stay in Dry Creek, we'll eat the spaghetti dinner those kids are fixing up. After all their hard work, they deserve some support."

"Kids?" Sylvia looked up.

Glory smiled. Whether the rancher knew it or not, he had hooked Sylvia. Nothing got to her like kids.

"They're going to have music," Glory offered mildly. "You have to eat anyway."

"I suppose we could eat a short meal together."

"We'll call it a snack." The rancher smiled.

Sylvia took her eyes off the rancher and returned them to the boys. "I'm going to call Pat Dawson and have him meet your plane. I'm also going to call the police. And don't even think of ditching this flight along the way. If I hear you're not in Seattle by tonight I'll have the police in fifty states looking for you."

"Yes, ma'am," both boys said.

"Well, we best get going into Billings," the deputy said. "I want to make it back and see this pageant myself. Especially now that the angel is going to be in it."

Matthew pondered. "I guess there's no reason why she can't be the angel now."

Glory grunted. She could think of a reason or two not to be the angel. But she doubted anyone would listen. "In that case, I better see about my halo."

The midday sun shone in the display window of the hardware store. Jacob and Elmer were sitting beside the wood-burning stove with their legs stretched out in front of them. Matthew was moving around in the back storage room. He'd already brought out the gold garland and cut off a length for a halo. He was back there now looking for glitter to sprinkle on the cardboard wings they'd brought over from the church.

Glory was putting the last of the oils on the portrait of the twins' mother. She added a smudge of light gray paint to the woman's cheek. Glory patted it to make it look like a dusting of flour. She was going to give the painting to the twins to be opened after the pageant. That reminded her she would need to go back to the house soon and make cookies for the twins.

The bell above the door rang, and Glory looked up to see Linda come in. The young woman was all dressed up for the holidays. She'd dyed one streak of hair Christmas red and another hunter green. A jingling bell earring dangled from each ear and she had a sprig of holly behind one ear. She wore red leotards and a white sweater.

"Figure I'll get more tips if I look Christmassy," Linda whispered as she came over to where Glory painted. "Least, that's what my friend Sara Enger said. She even took a picture of me with Gus in his Santa suit."

"Gus?"

Linda shrugged. "This old cowboy that's been helping us. Used to work for one of the ranchers up north that sold out. Jazz told him he could bunk down in the kitchen for a while if he helped us tonight by being Santa. He don't talk much, but he sure can look jolly."

"How's the sauce coming?" Glory asked. Matthew had already reported that there were several gallons of spaghetti sauce simmering away at the old café. Young people and apparently some older ones had been coming and going from the place all day. The smell of Italian herbs was settling over Dry Creek, and when a person walked down the street they could hear the faint sounds of a band practicing inside the café.

"We're almost ready for everyone. You and Matthew are coming, aren't you?"

"Wouldn't miss it," Glory assured her.

"Hey, you should wear your costume for dinner." Linda snapped her gum.

"This angel would need a bib as big as a sheet if I had to eat with my wings on."

"Yeah, I suppose it wouldn't work too well with the wings."

The door to the hardware store opened again, and Sylvia came in.

"Cold out there." Sylvia blew on her hands to warm them.

"It's not too bad, really." Glory felt like a Montana native. "Not cold enough to crack the vinyl on car seats or to freeze your nose hairs or to—"

"I get the picture," Sylvia interrupted.

Glory grinned. "I thought maybe a certain rancher would keep you warm—give you his jacket, that kind of thing."

Sylvia snorted. "The only thing Garth Elkton is going to give me is high blood pressure. That man is impossible."

"If you say so," Glory assured her friend with another grin.

Just then Matthew hobbled out from the back storeroom. Glory's grin faded. It was all she could do to keep her mouth from dropping open. His chestnut hair was rumpled and shot through with gold. In fact, he was golden all over from his forehead to his big toe.

His face was sprinkled with gold. His clothes were sprinkled with gold. It appeared Matthew had found the glitter.

"Speaking of keeping warm," Sylvia leaned over and muttered to Glory. "You never did tell me how you ended up catching a man like him."

"Catching? Matthew?" Glory's voice squeaked. She continued in a whisper. "I didn't catch anyone. Matthew is just a friend. He's not caught at all."

"If you say so." Sylvia righted herself and patted her hair. "I better get back to the barn. Mrs. Hargrove needs help with some pine cones she's arranging."

"She still at it?" Elmer groaned and stood up. He slapped Jacob on the knee. "Guess we better go give her a hand."

Matthew shook his head. Glitter spun off him. "Give me a minute to get this stuff off me and I'll go give everyone a hand, too. I'll just put a note on the door so anyone who wants to buy something knows where to find me."

They all stood in the door to the barn. It was high noon and the air was cold enough so that they all looked like smokers when they breathed. Each word brought a puff of gray-white air. The barn itself was rough-hewn. Unvarnished pine boards lined the walls and the thirty-foot-high ceiling. A hayloft hung down from the front of the barn and Glory could see the angel's swing that the ranch hands had built. Two thick ropes hung from a hoist and met at the swing's bottom with a wide plank to stand on. The swing looked like every child's fantasy. Glory was beginning to anticipate soaring over the heads of everyone as she swung from side to side in the barn.

"You'll have to wear some ruffled petticoats," Sylvia offered. "They'd swish and sway when you swing. It'll look very feminine. Southern belle-like."

"Petticoats?" Matthew frowned. Suddenly he wasn't so sure about Glory and this swing. There were too many single men out at the Big Sheep Mountain Ranch. They'd love to get a glimpse of Glory's petticoats. "Long johns," Matthew said decisively. "You'll wear a pair of my long johns. I won't have anyone ogling your legs."

"Long johns?" Glory frowned. "I don't think an angel would wear long johns."

"In Montana they do. We've got cold winters here," Matthew insisted.

"It is cold, isn't it?" Mrs. Hargrove said as she walked over to them. She rubbed her hands even though they were in knit mittens. "We've been trying to think of a way to warm up this barn for tonight."

"Henry has some secondhand camp stoves," Matthew suggested. "They'd at least take the edge off the cold."

"I'll buy them from you," Tavis offered.

"I'm sure Henry won't mind if we use them on loan. They're already used."

"I'd like to buy them anyway. I've been thinking we might use this barn for other things, too. Plays, maybe concerts."

"We could have rock concerts," Linda gushed. "Wait'll I tell the Jazz Man. We could set up right here!"

"Not a bad idea," Mrs. Hargrove agreed, and turned to Tavis. "But what will your dad say? I'm surprised he even agreed to the pageant."

"Me, too." Tavis grinned. "That's why I thought

I'd ask about the rest—he's not himself lately. Aunt Francis has him rattled. She's cleaning everything in sight. Even threw away his favorite coffee mug because it was stained. He probably doesn't even know what he's agreeing to, but he's a man of his word. Once he's said yes, he won't back down. Besides, we've built all these bleachers and we don't need the barn anyway. Only use it for trucking, and that was before we built the good road to the main corrals.''

Glory looked around her. The barn had been transformed. Six rows of sturdy bleachers lined both sides of the barn. The floor of the barn had been hosed down and polished until it shone. At the front of the barn, a fake building front stood with the words *Bethlehem Inn* painted across it. Nearby an open stable was fashioned with bales of hay strewn around. A metallic gold star hung down from the hayloft above the manger. As she looked more closely, she noticed that the gold star was on a pulley so that it could travel on a wire from one end of the barn to the other.

"Amazing," Glory complimented Tavis and Mrs. Hargrove.

The older woman beamed. "Tavis and the other ranch hands did most of it.''

Tavis shrugged. "Just some sawing and hammering.''

"It's perfect." Sylvia added her praise.

Mrs. Hargrove nodded proudly. "We've got it all set to go. The only thing we're missing is a minister to say a prayer before we begin." Mrs. Hargrove looked at Matthew. "It could be an already printed prayer. Maybe from a book or something.''

"Then anybody can say it." Matthew leaned on his crutch.

"Not everybody has the voice," Mrs. Hargrove explained wistfully. "There's something about the voice of a minister. It would add the right touch." She added quickly, "Don't say no yet. Think about it. If you don't do it, Elmer will stand in."

"I'll think about it," Matthew agreed as he turned around to leave.

Glory watched Matthew walk slowly out of the barn. The floor was smooth and he had to place his crutches with care. She wished she knew what he was thinking.

"He won't do it." Glory spoke aloud.

"I'm thinking he will," Mrs. Hargrove contradicted confidently. "He's been walled in long enough. It's time for him to take back his faith."

"I'm not even sure he's planning to read the Christmas story to the twins," Glory said, worrying aloud. "If he won't do that, he surely won't pray."

"Wait and see," Mrs. Hargrove advised. "That man may surprise you."

The smell of chocolate chip cookies carried all through the house. Glory had added a few more ornaments to the tree so that it shone and sparkled from every angle. The nurse from Dr. Norris's clinic had called and told her the boxes had arrived and she would bring them with her to the pageant. Knowing that the children's presents were taken care of, Glory carefully wrapped her own gifts and placed them beneath the tree. The books for the twins were easy to tie up in red tissue paper. She had more trouble with Matthew's gift. She hadn't looked closely enough at the cassette when she bought it. It was *Piano Selections for Lovers. Lovers!* Since she didn't have anything else for him, she'd put it in her purse. If he gave her a present, she'd give it to him.

The big present for the twins was still upstairs in Matthew's room—the picture she had painted of their mother. Glory imagined the look on the twins' faces when they saw their mother for the first time. She wondered if they would ever realize that half of the love that shone out at them from the picture belonged to her, Glory. In the last brush strokes of the painting, Glory had begun to cry herself. She felt the love of the twins' mother as surely as though the woman were standing in the room with her. And Glory felt her own love pour out of her heart onto the canvas.

"Are you all right?" Matthew pushed open the front door and hobbled into the house. Snowflakes covered his hair and the shoulders of his wool jacket. He wasn't using his crutches properly. He'd obviously been using his own feet and carrying the crutches.

"Yeah, why wouldn't I be?"

Matthew frowned. "I told you to keep the door locked."

"Oh, there's no need now," Glory said. "The boys are on a plane back to Seattle."

"Still, we can't be too careful." Matthew turned around and twisted the lock.

"Well, nobody around here is going to hurt me," Glory protested. "At least, not with a bullet. I'm more likely to fall off that angel swing than anything."

"We're going to tie you in. I've already thought of that and fixed it so you can't fall. And I thought of a way to tie your skirts down while we're at it."

"A straitlaced angel?"

"Angels are supposed to be straitlaced. Besides—" Matthew caught himself and stopped.

"Besides what?"

Matthew smiled slightly. "Besides, you're so beautiful nobody's going to care about sneaking a look at your legs. They'll just be looking at your face."

Glory blushed. "You're just saying that so I'll weaken and give you one of the cookies I made for the twins."

"I thought I smelled chocolate."

It was almost five o'clock, but it was already dark outside. The winter sky was sprinkled with stars. Matthew had added a large log to the fireplace in the living room and made spiced cider for everyone. Glory had plugged in the lights to the Christmas tree, and the twins had taken their baths early in honor of the evening.

The twins sat on the sofa with a cookie in each hand, waiting impatiently for Matthew to finish pouring the cups of cider.

"Before we open the presents we need to read the Christmas story." Glory twisted two new bulbs onto the strand of lights. All of the lights shone now.

"We could read it real fast," Josh suggested as he took another bite of cookie.

"Not too fast. You'll want to know about the presents they gave to the little baby Jesus before we open ours," Glory said, trying to make the story relevant to the boys.

"What'd He get? Lego?" Josh asked.

"Not exactly. He got gold, myrrh and frankincense."

"We know about frankin—whatever," Josh explained. "We got a book about him at preschool."

"Him?" Glory was bewildered.

"Yeah. Frankin—frankin—sense." Josh laid his cookies down and stood up from the sofa. "He walks like this." Josh held his arms out stiffly and clumped along.

"Oh, Frankenstein." Glory deciphered his meaning. "But that's not—"

"I'll bet he's a Terminator," Joey said excitedly. "And God sent him to be a bodyguard for the baby Jesus."

"That's a cool gift." Josh sat back down on the sofa. "And I bet this Frank guy has a laser gun that zaps people." Josh held out a pretend gun and took aim at the fireplace. "Rat-tat-tat-tat!"

"Nobody is zapping anyone around here," Matthew said firmly as he set down four mugs of cider on the coffee table. "And no guns."

"I was pointing at the fireplace," Josh explained. "That's okay. It's not people."

"Frankincense wasn't a person or a machine," Glory said as she moved one of Josh's cookies and sat down beside the twins.

"Oh." Josh picked up the cookie and thought a moment. "Was it a car?"

"They didn't have cars when Jesus was born."

"No cars!" Joey squirmed closer to Glory. "What was it, then?"

"It's a...well, a...perfume."

"Like in soap?" Josh asked skeptically.

Glory nodded. "Something like that."

"Who'd give a baby soap for Christmas?" Josh was getting indignant.

"Had Jesus been a bad boy?" Joey asked in awe.

"Well, no, not at all. Jesus was only a baby. A very good baby."

Josh snorted. "Good boys don't get soap in their stocking."

Glory looked at the two boys and then looked at Matthew. "It wasn't like that at all," she protested weakly.

"Maybe I better read the story from the Bible," Matthew said, and grinned at Glory. "We can't have them thinking Jesus was a bad boy or that He needed a Terminator to protect Him. Of course—" Matthew eyed his two sons thoughtfully "—He did have that trouble with the bad guys coming to get Him."

"Bad guys?"

Matthew hobbled over to the bookshelf and pulled the family Bible down. He held it in his hands briefly before he turned around and came back to the sofa. "It all started two thousand years ago halfway around the world in a town called Bethlehem."

"Is that farther away than Billings?" Joey asked.

"It's a lot farther away than Billings," Matthew assured his sons, and then looked at Glory. "Remind me to get a globe for these boys. They have no idea."

Glory smiled. She thought it was rather sweet for five-year-old boys to think the whole world was in their backyard.

Glory leaned back. She couldn't believe it. Matthew was reading the Bible to his sons as if he did it every day.

She watched his face in the firelight. She smiled as he made donkey noises to make his sons giggle when he told of Mary and Joseph's trip to Bethlehem. The two boys looked up at their father with rapt attention.

Glory felt the happiness squeeze into her heart. She'd never thought she'd love someone like Matthew. Someone strong and good and kind. Someone who took in a stranger like her just because his sons thought she was an angel. *How many ways do I love you, Matthew Curtis?* she asked herself. *How many ways?*

"No," she heard Matthew say to Josh. "The wise men couldn't just call the cops. Besides, they weren't lost. They were following the star."

The Bullet patted his very red stomach and hitched up his very black belt. He circulated through the little café and gave out candy canes to everyone. He even posed for pictures with some of the diners. He hoped all of the jolliness would pay off.

The Bullet had spent the day planning. The more he thought about when to shoot the woman, the closer he came to realizing he couldn't do it. He just wasn't up to pulling another trigger. He'd be a marked man, of course. But he was so tired of killing people.

He was going to march outside to the pay phone and call Millie. He'd spend Christmas with her and then head down to Mexico. She might even come with him.

The air was brittle, and the Bullet needed to take his gloves off to punch the numbers on the telephone. He'd expected Millie to pick up on the first ring. But the phone rang right through to the message.

He heard Millie's breathless voice. "Forrest, if that's you, your uncle stopped by. We're out to dinner." A giggle. "He said to tell you he's taking real good care of me."

The Bullet's mouth went dry. This client that knew

Forrest's name would know he used an old uncle as a screen for his trips. Since the Bullet had no uncle, that left only one conclusion. The client had Millie. The Bullet let the knowledge slice through him.

Chapter Thirteen

The early-evening light filtered into the church. Glory could hear the women outside in the church kitchen as they put the coffee on to brew. Through the open door she saw the kitchen counter piled high with cookies. Lemon bars. Gingersnaps. Sugar cookies. Plus trays and trays of date bars. Glory wished she was out there chatting with the ranchers' wives she'd just met—Margaret Ann and Doris June. But instead she was the angel, so she was inside the costume room listening to Matthew's quiet breathing as he helped her adjust her wings. The bare overhead light was bright and, once Matthew had pushed some choir robes out of the way, she could see herself in the old full-length mirror.

Glory wrinkled her nose at her reflection as she circled her head with garland. She'd loosely pulled her hair up on top of her head to help keep the garland in place. Tiny flecks of gold fluttered down on her nose. Not that it mattered. She was already covered with specks of glitter from when Matthew had hooked her wings onto the harness she wore under her white angel gown. The wings had been recently dipped in glitter.

Glory blew a strand of hair off her forehead, knowing she had to be careful what she touched. Mrs. Hargrove had unearthed a pair of long white gloves so that Glory could point with a white finger when she said, "Behold…"

"Not many angels look like they're ready to swear," Matthew observed mildly as he bent the flap on Glory's left wing to attach it more firmly. "Well, I expect the Archangel did a time or two—all that wrath and destruction."

"They all would look that way if they had to fly around in wings like this." Glory cautiously flexed a shoulder. She had a tiny little itch under the harness.

Matthew chuckled. "I doubt they could even get off the ground with those wings."

"Now you tell me."

"They'll do fine in the swing, though." Matthew cleared his throat. He thought he was doing pretty well with the chitchat. No one would know his hands trembled from adjusting Glory's wings. She wasn't an angel; she was a goddess. Her flaming red hair, more copper than gold, was gathered on top of her head. But it was so fine, wisps of hair circled her head. She scarcely needed a halo. Her hair floating around her sparkled as much as the glitter. Matthew leaned just a little closer to her hair and breathed deeply.

"Peaches?"

"My shampoo," Glory answered. She had forgotten her lipstick and rouge, but she had remembered her favorite matching shampoo and lotion.

Matthew nodded. "I'd better pin your garland on better. Wouldn't want the halo to slip when you're out there."

Matthew stood behind Glory, positioning her halo and noticing once again the graceful line of her neck. Swanlike didn't begin to cover it. Glory looked so much like an angelic bride as she stood there that Matthew couldn't help himself. He leaned closer and pressed his lips very lightly to the back of her neck. His kiss was more of a breath than an act.

"My hair's falling down." Glory tried to reach her arm up to her neck. That's all she needed. "I just felt it fall."

"You're fine."

"Yeah, men always say that, even when we have broccoli in our teeth."

"You don't have broccoli in your teeth."

"I know. It's my hair."

Matthew decided he was a rat all the way. He put his hands up to Glory's hair and did what wasn't necessary. He pretended to smooth it back up. Her hair was silky soft. He smoothed it again. "There." His voice was little more than a whisper. "Your hair's fine."

"Thank you."

"It's time we got you to the barn." Matthew's voice was thick. He knew they still had a half hour before the performance started, but he also knew that he'd better get Glory over to the barn and away from this small room before he gave in to the urge to kiss more than her neck. Not even that growing stack of cookies on the counter would distract the church women if they happened to look over into the small room and see him kissing the Christmas angel the way he wanted to right now.

Glory stood in the door of the barn. Matthew had walked over with her, refusing to use his crutch so that he could hold a blanket around her shoulders even though it was almost impossible to do so with her wings jutting out behind them. The night was cold and starless. Fluffy snowflakes were beginning to fall. When they got to the door of the barn, Glory had had to enter sideways so that her wings would not be bent.

"I don't know what I'd do without you," Glory said to Matthew as he bent to unhook the hem of her white gown that had caught on a nail by the door.

"I'll get a hammer and come back and smooth that over," Matthew muttered as he stood. "Yours won't be the only hem it catches."

Matthew was right. Glory looked around. There was an abundance of long, flowing robes. She'd never seen such a colorful array of little boys in bathrobes, most of them dragging along the barn floor. Some had pastel-striped robes; some had white cotton robes; some had plain colored robes. All of them had a striped dish towel wrapped around their heads with a band of red material holding it in place. Several boys had a wooden staff in their hands. Two of the boys even had leashes. Leashes? Glory looked again. If there were leashes, there must be— Yes, there they were. The animals.

"Come see," Josh called excitedly to Matthew and Glory. "We've got sheep!"

"I'll believe this when I see it," Matthew whispered to Glory as they walked over to where a group of boys stood.

"Don't knock it. The sheep are as real as the angel."

Glory had never realized that a dog wrapped in a fluffy white towel could look so much like a sheep in the shadows.

"Hey, Glory," a woman called to her from the front of the bleachers.

Glory turned and recognized Debra Hanson, the nurse from Dr. Norris's office, who had promised to bring the boxes of toys Glory had ordered.

"I got them, honey," Debra said in a stage whisper as Glory walked closer. Debra snapped her gum and spoke with a Southern accent. She wore a red scarf wrapped around her head like a turban and a long black coat. Christmas bell earrings shimmered as she spoke. "Where do you want me to put them?"

Glory looked around. She'd like to surprise the children. "Behind the stable."

"I'll tell the boys." Debra turned and smiled at a couple of the hands from the Big Sheep Mountain Ranch. She raised her hand to wave and used one of her red-tipped fingers to summon the men over to her. They came eagerly.

Glory decided her boxes were in good hands, so she could mingle. Since this was a barn, there was no backstage area. The six-foot-high, ten-foot-wide stable was the only structure. The actors were in plain sight doing last-minute errands. One little choir angel had a nosebleed, and one of the older shepherds took him outside to get some snow to put on his nose. One of the boys was teasing Mary about the makeup someone had put on her. Mrs. Hargrove was muttering to herself.

Glory decided Mrs. Hargrove was the one who needed rescuing the most. "Everything looks ready," Glory said reassuringly when she came near the older woman. Glory had noticed the musicians from the café setting up their small sound system at the side of the stable.

Mrs. Hargrove had abandoned her usual gingham dresses and wore a green wool suit with a hat. She was rubbing her hands so fiercely Glory feared for the woman's skin.

"It'll go all right," Glory added. "The pageant will be just fine."

"Well, not with *him* here," Mrs. Hargrove seethed. "It's practically blasphemy!"

"Who?"

"Him." Mrs. Hargrove jerked her head in the direction of the Santa Claus who had entertained diners at the café earlier.

"Oh, he's all right," Glory said. Linda had told her the man was an old cowboy who was down on his luck. He certainly looked down on his luck with his fake white beard and red stocking hat. His shoulders slumped as if he carried the weight of the world.

Even at that, though, he was handing out candy canes. "He's just cheering folks up."

"Folks don't need cheering up! This is Christmas." Mrs. Hargrove pursed her lips.

Just then the girl who was playing Mary tugged on Mrs. Hargrove's arm.

"Yes, dear?" the older woman said as she leaned over.

Mrs. Hargrove's voice softened when she talked to the girl and Glory could see why. Lori was all pink and blue in her costume. She looked sugar sweet, except for her eyes.

"Johnny Ellis stole the dish towels!" The girl's eyes snapped with anger.

"Dish towels?" Mrs. Hargrove seemed disoriented.

"The swaddlin' clothes!" the girl wailed, and burst into tears. "For my baby!"

Mrs. Hargrove soothed the girl and then straightened herself for battle. "Just wait until I get my hands on Johnny Ellis."

The girl stopped crying and perked up significantly when Mrs. Hargrove left.

Matthew came over and stood slightly behind Glory. She would have known he was there by the smell of his aftershave even if she hadn't heard the quiet thumping of his crutches. She'd noticed the pleasing scent at dinner and wondered if he was meeting someone special at the pageant. Not that it was any of her business, she reminded herself.

"Boys can be so annoying, can't they, Lori?" Matthew said sympathetically.

Glory was inclined to agree, but she didn't expect the girl to nod her head so vigorously.

"Thinks he's so smart—ordering me around saying he's my husband," Lori said.

"Well, he won't be your husband for long," Glory consoled her. "After the pageant he goes back to being plain Johnny Ellis." Glory couldn't resist a little consciousness-raising. "Besides, just because he's your husband doesn't mean he gets to order you around."

"Yeah." The girl brightened. "I could order him, too."

"That's not what I meant," Glory said, but it was too late. Lori had gone off to find Johnny Ellis.

Glory looked at Matthew. He was a constant surprise to her. Just when she thought his head was filled with hammering loose nails she found out that he'd had time to watch over the little children.

She fought the impulse to adjust Matthew's tie. It didn't need adjusting, not really. But he wouldn't know that and it would give her a good cover as she leaned closer to smell his aftershave.

Fortunately, she was saved from her own foolishness by Mrs. Hargrove, who fluttered by gathering up children like a mother hen circling her chicks. "It'll be time to start soon. I'm having the children go to the back of the barn, by the far bleachers, so we can file in when we start the Scripture reading."

"I better get up in the hayloft, then." Glory picked up her long skirts.

"Let me go with you," Matthew said. "Make sure your skirt doesn't get caught on those narrow stairs."

"Oh, I asked Tavis to help her." Mrs. Hargrove looked down at a clipboard that she had picked up from somewhere. "Someone needs to go up with her and help her with the swing. You're on crutches."

"I'll help her," Matthew muttered as he positioned the crutches under his shoulders. A look of stubborn determination settled on his face. "I'm the one that knows how to add the extra train to the outfit so that people won't be looking at the angel's legs. Besides, I don't trust Tavis alone with the angel around all that hay."

"Well." Mrs. Hargrove studied Matthew with a bright, pleased look in her eyes. Then she took the pen off the clipboard and made a couple of check marks on her list.

There was a rail instead of a wall on the inside of the stairs leading to the overhead hayloft, and it was just as well. Glory could never have squeezed between two walls with her seven-foot wingspan.

"Ever wonder why angels just appear?" Glory muttered as she twisted her shoulders so her wings wouldn't be dented. "They can't get around in these things, so they have to—puff—appear out of nowhere. Puffing is a lot easier than flying."

Matthew looked down at her. He had half hobbled, half crawled to the top of the stairs and stood waiting for her. He leaned his crutches against the wall of the hayloft and reached down a hand to Glory. "Here, let me help you."

The smell of dry hay greeted Glory when she stood on the floor of the hayloft. The decorators for the pageant had not come up here. It was still ready for cattle. Several bales of hay were broken and strewn around. A pitchfork stood upright, embedded in one bale. Straw and wisps of hay lay all over the rough wood floor.

The hayloft was dim. The bright light from downstairs filtered through the end of the hayloft and gave everything a warm cast. Glory looked around. While she and Matthew could see the people down below, no one from down there could see the two of them. It was a perfect place for— Glory pushed the thought aside. She knew this ex-minister would never kiss an angel. Best not to even think about it.

Ten minutes later Glory was sitting on a bale of hay watching Matthew. Men! He had spent the entire past ten minutes going over every inch of the swing that she was going to use. "You're making me nervous. Besides, Tavis has already checked everything."

Matthew scowled up at her from where he was crouched by the ropes.

"It's even got a safety rope. See?" Glory pointed to her backup rope.

Glory sighed. Mention of the safety rope only gave Matthew another thing to check out.

People were filling up the bleachers down below them. Glory saw just the tops of everyone, but she could tell people had dressed up for the occasion. She saw black Stetson hats and gray Stetson hats. The men who didn't have Stetson hats wore hunter-green caps. And the women's hair—from gray to towheaded—was shiny and curled.

The only one who stood out was Santa in his bright

red cap. He'd stopped giving out candy canes and sat at the end of one of the far bleachers. The old man must be tired. Glory could think of no other reason why he seemed to be staring up at the hayloft where she was.

Just then a crackle of static sounded through the barn.

"It's—" Elmer's voice came out over the loud-speaker "—time."

The rustle of the audience stilled. Elmer stood beside the manger. Someone turned off a few of the lights.

Elmer cleared his throat. "I want to thank all you friends and neighbors for coming to celebrate the birth of our Lord. The children of Dry Creek have worked hard to prepare for this pageant, and so have the adults." Elmer paused. "We may as well get to it." He bent his head over a Bible and began to read. "'And it came to pass in those days, that there went out a decree from Caesar Augustus, that all the world should be taxed....'"

Glory smiled. Elmer's grandfatherly voice was perfect for the reading.

The band's sound system must have been more than a microphone, because the sound of a symphony filled the barn as Joseph started to walk the length of the barn leading a young heifer that was carrying a very pregnant Mary. The girl's long robe fell against the heifer's side and the heifer kept swishing its tail trying to get rid of the annoyance.

"'And Joseph also went up from Galilee, out of

the city of Nazareth, into Judea, unto the city of David, which is called Bethlehem.'''

The heifer stopped in front of the wooden storefront that said Bethlehem Inn. A boy wearing a white butcher's apron came out of a door in the storefront. He was carrying a chicken under one arm and a No Vacancy sign under the other. The chicken was squawking indignantly at being carried, and when the boy went to hang the No Vacancy sign on the larger sign, the chicken escaped and flew to a perch on the very top of the stable. The boy stood watching the chicken with his mouth open.

There was silence. Mrs. Hargrove cleared her throat loudly. There was more silence.

Finally Mary spoke from her position on top of the heifer. "Does that—" she pointed to the sign the boy still held "—mean there's no room in the inn?"

"No…" The boy regained his lines. He repeated loudly, "No room in the inn."

Mary nodded, satisfied. "I thought so. We'll stay in the stable." And then she slid to the floor, took the heifer's rope and said with an unmistakable tone of command, "Joseph, you bring the bags. And don't forget the baby things."

Slack jawed with surprise, Joseph watched her leave and then hurried to catch up.

A choir of children's voices started singing "Away in the Manger."

In the hayloft Matthew had finally stopped checking equipment and sat down on the hay bale across from Glory. Glory smiled up at him and moved some of the yards of material so Matthew could move closer. "Mrs. Hargrove must have decided to use animals after all."

"Goes with the barn theme," Matthew whispered.

The carol ended and Elmer's voice continued with his reading. "'And so it was, that, while they were there, the days were accomplished that she should be delivered....'"

"We'd better get you in that swing," Matthew whispered. "The angel's coming up pretty soon."

Glory nodded, stood, and then it happened. A hiccup.

"I—can't—" Glory hiccuped again. She looked at Matthew. "I've got—the—" She hiccuped again.

Some miracles happen, Matthew decided. Others are snatched out of the possibilities of the moment, like this one. He did what he'd wanted to do ever since they climbed into the loft. He dipped his head and kissed Glory.

Matthew felt surprise ripple through Glory, so he deepened the kiss. His own surprise slugged him in the belly a second later. Who would know it would be like this? Her lips tasted like molten honey. Hot and sweet. He decided he might as well hang for the real thing as for a polite peck, so he deepened it even further. He could be dead and kissing a real angel for all he knew—or cared.

Glory stopped breathing. She half thought she might have stopped living. Everything stopped except Matthew's kiss.

Matthew pulled his lips away.

"You—k-kissed—" Glory stuttered. "Me."

"Yes." Matthew tried to stop the lightness inside

him. If he wasn't careful, he'd be able to float along-side Glory even without a swing.

"The hiccups. They stopped." Glory put her hand to her cheek. She needed to stop staring. He'd think she'd never been kissed before. And she had. Not like that, of course, but she had. Only, why had he kissed her now? Of course. The hiccups. That must be it. "Is that an old remedy?"

"Remedy?"

"For the hiccups. A grandmother's remedy? Like a slap on the back?"

Matthew winced. Granted, he'd thought the hiccups were a good cover for a kiss before he began the kiss, but now… Surely she knew it meant more now. And even at that, his kisses surely weren't grandmotherly.

The microphone below crackled as Elmer read. Glory stepped onto the swing. She hooked on the ma-terial that Matthew had rigged to trail beneath her. She hoped Matthew was satisfied. No one could see her feet, let alone her legs, with all that material. She watched as Matthew fastened the safety ropes.

"'And there were in the same country shepherds abiding in the field, keeping watch over their flock by night.'" Elmer's voice continued.

The boys in bathrobes and their "sheep" walked to the center of the barn and sat down. Two of the boys even lay down.

"'And, lo,'" Elmer read. "'An angel of the lord came upon them…'"

"I'm off," Glory whispered to Matthew before she took a deep breath.

Matthew helped her push off. The swing slid off

its mooring and she was free. She felt the rush of air as she swooped over the shepherds below. Maybe, she thought, it wouldn't be so bad being an angel, after all. She'd talked Mrs. Hargrove into letting the children sing instead of the angel, so she concentrated on flying.

Glory's ecstasy was short-lived. The chicken, perched on top of the stable, had not been there earlier in Glory's practice run. And when Glory had practiced, she hadn't had a long white train of angel gown following her in flight. It was Matthew's modesty veil. When the chicken saw the thick cloud of material coming straight at it, it panicked and took flight again. Unfortunately, by taking flight, the chicken only rose up higher until it was swept along in the train of angel gown as Glory swung low over the stable.

"Oh, oh," Glory whispered to herself, and then added for the benefit of the passenger she carried beneath her, "Good chickie, good chickie. Just stay calm."

The chicken didn't stay calm. It screeched indignantly as it clung with its claws and beak to the train of angel gown.

Glory reached the arc of her swing just as the dogs decided they'd rather be dogs than sheep. They started to howl at Glory as if she was the moon. She comforted herself with the thought that maybe they were baying at the chicken.

Elmer kept reading. "'And the glory of the Lord shone round about them: and they were sore afraid.'"

Glory was sore afraid herself. The weight of the

chicken began to pull even harder on the gown she wore, and she heard a slow tearing sound. She'd be lucky if the bird didn't pull the gown right off her and leave her swinging in the white long johns Matthew had insisted she wear. She could just see the headlines in the *Billings Gazette:* Chicken Strips Angel At Church Pageant. She'd probably make the tabloids with that one.

Not even looking up, Elmer kept reading. "'And the angel said unto them...'"

Glory took a deep breath. She pointed out with her white-gloved finger and shouted loudly, "'Fear not, for behold, I bring you good tidings of great joy.'"

Amazingly, Glory's words calmed the chicken. Unless— *I wonder if the poor bird finally had too much and went into shock?*

With the chicken silent, the dogs quit howling and lay down like the sheep they were meant to be. Even the shepherds looked reverent as they watched the angel swing back toward the hayloft.

Elmer took up the angel's pronouncement for her. "'For unto you is born this day in the city of David a Savior, which is Christ the Lord.'"

Glory swung back and straight into Matthew's arms. Unfortunately, she'd built up so much speed she knocked them both to the floor of the hayloft.

"Oh." Glory blinked.

Elmer's voice continued. "'And suddenly there was with the angel a multitude of the heavenly host praising God and saying...'"

The children's choir began to sing "Glory to God."

"Oh." Glory blinked again. She was lying on top of Matthew and she couldn't seem to move. She could hear Matthew breathing beneath her. Fact is, she could feel him breathing as his chest rose and fell. He hadn't screamed, so her wings must not have jabbed him. He was all right. It was her. She couldn't move. It must be the excitement of the swing, she consoled herself. After all, look what the swing had done to that chicken—

"The chicken!" Glory exclaimed, remembering.

Matthew felt Glory lift herself up. He wanted to pull her back and try another home remedy. As far as he was concerned, he could lie right there until he died. He was singing the Hallelujah chorus and it had nothing to do with Christmas. But she was right, there was the chicken to consider.

"It looks all right," Glory whispered as she studied the chicken. They had unhooked the train to Glory's gown and unfolded the material until they freed the bird. The chicken fluffed itself up and then started hopping around looking for something to eat.

"Why don't you unhook my wings, too?" Glory asked. She was already kneeling. "I want to get them off before I do major damage."

The wise men were ready to make their entrance by the time Glory and Matthew got back to the pageant. The shepherds were surrounding the manger and the children's choir was standing in front of the inn. The dogs had decided the excitement was over for the day and were lying half-asleep at their masters' feet.

Elmer's voice continued his reading, "'When they

saw the star, they rejoiced with exceeding great joy.'"

Matthew stood up to slowly pull the metal star on the pulley toward the stable. It was rigged like an old-fashioned laundry line. In fact, as Glory looked at the brackets more closely, she saw that it *was* an old-fashioned laundry line.

Solemnly the wise men followed the star until it reached the stable.

"We brought you some presents," one of the wise men announced proudly as he pulled out three prettily wrapped packages. The wise men turned to Mary. "We got receipts so you can return them if you want."

Mary nodded her thanks.

The children's choir and the shepherds began to sing "Silent Night." The pageant was drawing to a close.

Christmas truly was a time of goodwill, Glory thought as she shook the hand of another well-wisher. Everyone along the Yellowstone River was out and thanking her for being their angel. Why, there was almost a crowd in this barn, Glory decided as she looked over the people. She recognized a few of them. Linda, of course, and a couple of the hands from the Big Sheep Mountain Ranch. And then there was Sylvia and the rancher, talking animatedly in the corner of the barn. Glory decided now wasn't the time to go and say hello to her friend.

Mrs. Hargrove invited everyone over to the church for refreshments, and people began adjusting scarves

for the walk over to the other building. Matthew stood
talking with Deputy Wall.

Glory decided it was time to slip behind the stable
and get her presents ready for the children. She'd seen
Josh look her way several times, so she knew he was
hopeful. Glory walked over to him and bent down to
whisper in his ear, "Tell everyone the angel's giving
out presents behind the stable in five minutes."

Josh's eyes lit up and he nodded.

The Bullet had let the people of Dry Creek have
their pageant. But now he watched the angel make
her way to the rear of the barn.

The light was dim behind the stable, but the space
was completely out of sight of the other people. And
there was the angel, kneeling down and sorting
through one of several huge boxes of toys.

The Bullet unbuttoned his red shirt and drew out
his gun.

He'd hoped the angel would not even look up, but
she did. Her eyes widened as he put his arm out and
aimed the gun.

Then the Bullet heard a sound behind him.

"Santa?" a small voice asked. The Bullet turned
his head slightly and saw the twin boys staring at him.

Chapter Fourteen

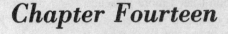

Glory felt all the blood drain from her head when she saw the gun. She thought she'd faint. When she saw the twins, she knew she didn't have the luxury of fainting.

"Oh, boys," she called out, hoping her voice was bright and normal. "You caught us. Santa was trying out some of the toys."

Please, Lord, Glory prayed. *Have the man go along with me. Let him have a heart. If I need to die, don't take the twins, too.*

"He's not supposed to point guns at people," Josh said righteously.

"That's right," Glory agreed. "But Santa and I need a few more minutes. Go back to your dad now. And keep the other kids away, too."

Glory kept her eyes on the killer. She begged him silently to let the twins go. "No one knows what Santa looks like," she reminded him. "Not with a beard and the suit."

"Yeah, get out of here, kids," the killer finally said.

Josh turned to go, but Glory watched the indecision on Joey's face.

"Run along, Joey." Glory tried not to let her voice plead as loudly as her heart. "Go to your dad."

"I want us to go home, now," Joey said softly. "We don't need more presents."

Glory wished she were a better actress. "Please, just do what I ask, sweetheart."

Joey waited a minute before finally turning to go. Glory watched him reluctantly step around the corner of the stable.

"Thank you," Glory whispered softly as she looked up at the killer.

Santa nodded as he reaimed his gun.

Glory closed her eyes.

"You going to pray, too?" the man asked incredulously.

Glory opened her eyes. "If I may." She wouldn't tell him she'd closed her eyes not to pray but so she wouldn't have to watch him pull the trigger. "Sort of my last request."

"Hit men don't do last requests. That's the feds." But he lowered his gun.

"Dear Lord," Glory whispered aloud. She wanted the hit man to know she was still praying. "I've had a good life. So much to be thankful for. My mother. The captain. Sylvia. The twins—and their father—"

"Hurry it up, lady. This isn't the Oscars," the killer interrupted. "I haven't got all day to wait while you thank the little people. Wrap it up."

"The Oscars?" Glory forced herself to laugh. "Very clever. Did you see them?"

Santa glowered at her. "No."

"Oh." Glory folded her hands together just as the twins did when they prayed. She couldn't think of what to pray when it looked as if she would see God in a few seconds anyway. Then she thought of the comforting prayer and closed her eyes to begin. "Now I lay me down to sleep. I pray the Lord my soul to keep. If I should—"

Glory heard the loud sound of a gun cocking. Odd, she thought Santa had already pulled the hammer back. Then she heard the voice.

"Hold it right there, Santa!"

Glory opened her eyes. Deputy Wall was standing with his gun aimed at Santa's belly. The only problem was that Santa still had his gun aimed at Glory. Both men seemed to realize the difficulties of that arrangement as quickly as she did.

"You shoot her, I'll get you," Deputy Wall threatened as he steadied his aim.

Santa shrugged without lowering his gun. "She'll still be dead."

"They'll put you away for murder if you kill her," the deputy promised.

"They'll put me away for murder if I give up, too," Santa countered.

Glory decided now was as good a time as any to faint. She willed herself to faint. She held her breath. In the end, she had to half fake her slide down to the barn floor.

She'd no sooner started her slide than a shot was fired. Glory's last conscious thought was that Santa swore like a sailor.

Matthew blamed himself all the way to the stable. Why had he let Mrs. Hargrove lead him off with some story about the wise men so that Josh took longer to find him? Josh had gotten only the words *Santa* and *gun* out of his mouth before Matthew was frantically looking around the barn. Where was Glory?

"I told the deputy, too," Josh was saying proudly. "He knows you shouldn't point guns at people."

Matthew saw the deputy slip behind the stable.

"Stay here, son," Matthew called down as he started toward the stable. His crutches were only slowing him down, so he tossed them away and started to lope along.

"Glory!" Matthew whispered when he rounded the corner and saw what was behind the stable wall. The air smelled like burned gunpowder. And Glory lay there so still.

"You shot her!" Matthew started to lunge toward Santa.

Deputy Wall dropped his gun and grabbed Matthew. Deputy Wall was 250 pounds of muscle, but he didn't stop Matthew easily. "I've wrestled bulls tamer than you." The deputy spit the words out after he'd steadied Matthew. "That man has a gun, for Pete's sake. Keep still."

"Don't worry. I didn't even hit her," Santa said disgustedly. He turned so the gun was now aimed at the two men. "She slid right out of my range. The bullet hit the wall."

Matthew took a deep breath. He looked at Glory carefully. In all of that white, blood would show up readily and so would the scorched mark a bullet would make in passing. There was no sign of either and she appeared to be breathing normally. Besides, there was a bullet hole in the back of the stable.

"You don't need to kill her, anyway." Matthew began to pray. *Help me, God.* "Glory already told the police about the tie-in with the rustling. The manager at the grocery store is going to turn state's evidence."

Santa grunted. "None of my concern. Not my side of the business."

It must have been twenty degrees in the barn, and Matthew's hands were sweating. *Lord, I need you. I won't ask for anything else. Just keep Glory alive.*

"If you want to shoot someone, shoot me instead," Matthew offered.

Matthew heard the surprised protest from Deputy Wall, but he didn't turn to look at the officer. Matthew kept his eyes trained on Santa.

"Nobody's paying me to shoot you," Santa snorted indignantly. "I don't just go around shooting people. I'm a professional."

"I see." Matthew did some quick arithmetic in his head. "If you're a professional, how much would it cost to unshoot someone?"

Santa just laughed. "Money won't do me any good if I don't shoot her."

"Ah, they'd come and get you?" Matthew asked to keep the killer talking. The longer Santa kept talking the longer Matthew had to think of something.

"That isn't the half of it," Santa muttered into his

fake beard. "It's who else they'd get that worries me."

Matthew knew from his ministerial counseling that sometimes it was these half-muttered, throwaway lines that no one expected anyone else to listen to that were the most important in understanding a person's troubles.

"A child?" Matthew probed.

Santa shook his head and mumbled, "Girlfriend."

"Girlfriend?" the deputy wailed. "How can you get a girl when I can't?"

"Charm," Santa said without looking at the deputy.

"Aah, a girlfriend." Matthew nodded as if he understood. He kept his eyes focused on Santa's brown eyes. *Lord, Lord, be with me.*

"They've already got Millie," Santa continued, as if the worry couldn't stay trapped inside him any longer. "If I don't shoot this Beckett woman, they'll shoot my Millie."

"Aah." Matthew nodded this time because he did understand. "So we're just two men trying to protect our women."

Santa eyed Matthew skeptically. "Yeah, I suppose so."

Matthew started to breathe again. He'd made the first rung in negotiations. He'd found a common ground from which they could work. "Now all we need to do is figure out a way to keep both of them alive."

"Like what?" Santa asked.

Matthew began to pray even more earnestly. The

bait was being nibbled. "Well, what happens if you couldn't kill Glory?"

"What do you mean 'couldn't' kill her?"

"What if there was a storm and Montana was cut off from the rest of the country for a month? No one in or out?"

"Well…" Santa began to think. "I suppose in unusual circumstances they wouldn't hold me to the contract. But they read the papers. They'd know about a storm."

"What about if you were arrested before you got to Glory? Like on a speeding ticket?"

"Well, I suppose if I was arrested and put in jail they couldn't complain too much," Santa agreed, and then pointed out, "But I haven't got a speeding ticket."

"The deputy here could give you one," Matthew offered.

"You want me to give him a *ticket?* A cold-blooded killer? A *speeding ticket?*"

"What do you think, Santa? We could give you a speeding ticket and fingerprint you and then find out about some past crimes."

Santa was thinking. "I work clean. You wouldn't find much. Besides, what if they found out it didn't happen that way? These guys have moles everywhere."

"They don't have any moles in Dry Creek, Montana," Deputy Wall said proudly.

"Well, that's probably true," Santa said as he lowered his gun. "Might not be a better place anywhere to cut a deal."

Matthew left the two men and went over to kneel beside Glory. He picked up her arm to feel her pulse. Her heart was certainly beating strongly.

"Now, about that ticket, what speed were you driving when you came into Dry Creek?" Deputy Wall said as he took Santa's gun.

"Hey, I thought there's no speed limit in Montana."

"There is in towns. We're posted for forty-five. We'll say you were doing eighty." The deputy unclasped his handcuffs and snapped them around Santa's hands.

"She okay?" asked Deputy Wall, turning toward Matthew.

"Seems fine. Just give her a minute."

"Aah…" Santa squirmed as the deputy started to leave. "Mind if we go out the back way? There's a lot of kids out there who don't need to see Santa in handcuffs."

"I'll settle him in my car," the deputy said as he passed Matthew. "Then I'll be back for Glory."

"Back for Glory?"

"She can't stay here now," Deputy Wall patiently explained. "There's a contract out. He—" he nodded at Santa "—he might not be the only one. We'll need to take Glory into protective custody. For her own good."

Glory wondered how long she could feign unconsciousness before someone called a doctor. She supposed she needed to open her eyes, but her world was already here. She knew Matthew held her. She smelled the aftershave and heard the soft murmur of his prayers. She would lie in his arms forever if it kept Matthew praying.

But she supposed it wasn't fair.

"Glory—" The voice that finally pulled her out of her daze was Mrs. Hargrove's. The older woman's voice was determined enough to call back the dead. Glory didn't feel as if she should resist it for something as minor as a slipping spell. Glory refused to accept that she might have fainted, just for a minute. She preferred to think she'd purposely slipped into a daze.

"Are you all right, dear?" Mrs. Hargrove was pressing something wet against Glory's forehead.

Glory opened her eyes. She supposed it was time.

"You'll need to come with me," Deputy Wall ordered Glory. "I've radioed ahead. They'll have a couple of cells ready."

"You can't put her in jail. Not on Christmas Eve." Mrs. Hargrove was horrified.

"I'm not putting her in jail," the deputy explained impatiently. "Protective custody."

"It's for the best," Glory assured the older woman.

Glory looked up at the circle of concerned people looking down at her. All of these people would be in danger if she stayed in Dry Creek before everything was settled. If one contract killer could get through, another one might not be far behind. And bullets didn't always just hit the one for whom they were intended.

"I'll go with her to jail," Matthew offered decisively. "That is, if you'll take the twins home with you tonight, Mrs. Hargrove?"

Mrs. Hargrove nodded. "They're so excited they'll probably fall right to sleep on my sofa."

Matthew didn't correct her, although he was pretty sure the reverse would be true. The boys would be up all night talking about the gunman.

"And hand out the presents," Glory added.

For the first time everyone looked at the boxes.

"That's them?" Matthew asked, and then corrected himself. "I mean, of course that's them. Glad to see they got delivered in time."

"W-well, I'll be..." Mrs. Hargrove stammered. "I'll be."

"The names are already on them," Glory said. "Sylvia saw to that in the ordering."

"Well, the children will be very pleased," Mrs. Hargrove finally managed.

Deputy Wall cleared his throat. "We better be going."

"I can't go like this." Glory looked down at herself. "Let me stop and put on some jeans."

"If you're quick about it," the deputy agreed as Glory started to stand.

The jail clanked. Metal scraped every time anyone moved. And it smelled like a closed-up basement. But, Glory thought to herself, it was safe. And Matthew was here, sitting on the cot on the other side of the cell. They were both safe. No one could shoot a bullet through those thick cement walls, and no one

would even try to get in the door past the four deputies called out for special duty tonight.

"Sorry you're missing Christmas Eve with your
family," Glory called out to one of the young deputies as he walked past their opened cell.

"It's okay." The deputy ducked his head. "We've
never had a hit man in these cells."

"You know, he didn't seem bad for a hit man,"
Glory mused as she wrapped herself in the blankets
she and Matthew had picked up from his house.

From the outside office the strains of the hymn "O
Holy Night" reached them in the cells.

"Somebody thought to bring a CD player," Matthew noted.

"And spiced cider." The sweet apple smell began
to cut through the basement smell in their cell.

Just then Sylvia stepped through the door from the
deputy's office. She was wearing a red Santa's hat
and carrying a big box tied up with a silver bow.
Behind her came the rancher Garth Elkton, carrying
a CD player and a large cup of cider.

"Merry Christmas," Sylvia shouted, and suddenly
it was.

An hour later Glory folded up the metallic paper.
Sylvia and the rancher had set up a coffeepot of
spiced cider outside. There was unmistakable tension
between the two of them, but they'd done their job
of delivering Christmas cheer very well. They'd even
brought a large plate of cookies, compliments of the
ladies at the church. There was more than enough for
all the deputies and inmates. Of course, the only in-

mates were Glory, Matthew and the Bullet, as he called himself. Glory shuddered at the name.

Sylvia had sat with Glory while she opened the silver box. It contained a dozen jars of homemade jam from the booth the women of Dry Creek had set up outside the barn tonight. Chokecherry jam. Rhubarb jam. It couldn't be a more perfect gift. Every time Glory opened a jar she'd think of the people of Dry Creek. She looked across the cell at Matthew. There was one person she couldn't bear to remember only with jam.

"The twins will be sleeping now," she said.

Matthew grunted. He'd been waiting for a romantic moment and it wasn't easy to find one in a cramped cement cell in the middle of winter. When they'd stopped by his house for Glory to change to jeans and a sweatshirt, he'd picked up the gift he'd bought for her. He was waiting for the right time to give it to her, but maybe that moment wouldn't come tonight. He might as well do it now. At least they were alone—something that rarely happened, as one or the other of the deputies was always walking back to chat.

"I have a present for you." Matthew reached into the pocket of his black leather jacket and pulled out a small box wrapped in white tissue paper. "It's not much, but—"

Glory's face lit up. "I got a present for you, too, but it's at your house."

"You've already given me the best Christmas gift." Matthew handed her the box. "Being an angel in this pageant was important to my boys."

Glory opened the little box and pulled out a silver necklace charm in the shape of an angel. "It's beautiful."

"I'll always remember what you've done for me and my boys," Matthew began. He was a man accustomed to words, so he had no excuse for not being able to just spit out the words that would tell Glory what he was feeling. But those words were hard. He wished he were a better man. He knew Glory deserved someone better. Someone whose faith had not been shipwrecked. He wasn't going to ask her to settle for less than she deserved and he wasn't going to ask her to wait for him to become the man she deserved. He just wanted her to know he wished it were different.

Before Matthew could speak again, a burly barrel of a man stomped through the door.

"Captain!" Glory whispered in surprise. "What are you doing here?"

It took the captain only an hour to get Glory and Matthew out of the cell. "There's feds all over Dry Creek by now. Frank talked to that grocery-store manager and we found out the hit had been ordered by the men selling the stolen meat. They were afraid you'd put the pieces together and talk to that store manager. He cracked just like they suspected. They located you through the AP wire—that silly angel story." The captain shook his head. "You were lucky. That hit man—" The captain shook his head again. "When they ran his fingerprints, they didn't find anything. But then they checked with an informant and half the bureau headed to Dry Creek. Funny, you folks catching him here on a speeding ticket.''

Glory shrugged. The best story of her police career, and she'd never be able to tell it around the water-cooler.

Glory took her time repacking her suitcase. She was upstairs at Matthew's house and the early-morning sun was just beginning to warm up the sky. The captain had insisted she return with him, and he was right. Until the business of the contract on her was settled, she didn't want to jeopardize Matthew or the boys. So, instead of thinking of excuses to stay another day, she folded her socks and laid them in the suitcase one pair at a time.

Even inside the house, Glory could feel the activity in Dry Creek. The captain was outside now talking with the federal agents who were combing through Dry Creek looking for clues. They were mildly puzzled that a pro like the Bullet would trip up on a traffic ticket, but they were so relieved to have him in custody they didn't press their questions.

Finally, Glory snapped the lid shut on her suitcase. It was time.

Glory started down the stairs for the last time, smiling slightly when she came to the step where Matthew had fallen. That one step had changed her whole life. They should put a plaque there, she mused.

Matthew was sitting on the sofa waiting for her. Glory had half expected him to be outside checking with the feds to make sure they kept her safe, but he appeared willing to let them do their jobs now that they were here in such numbers.

With each step down Glory took, she tried to think of something suitable to say to Matthew. But her mind was as empty as her heart was full. None of the words seemed right.

It wasn't until Glory reached the last step on the stairs that she realized what Matthew was doing. He was staring at the portrait of his late wife, Susie. Glory had put all of the twins' presents down under the tree so that they'd see them when they came over later this morning. She hadn't wrapped the portrait, so they could see their mother the first thing. She hadn't counted on Matthew sitting on the sofa silently weeping in front of the woman's picture.

All of the hopeful words that Glory had been trying to form died unspoken. What could she say to a man who was still so in love with his late wife that he sat there weeping?

"Take care of the twins." Glory managed the words. She focused on Matthew's back. "I'll stop at Mrs. Hargrove's to tell them goodbye."

"Goodbye?" The word seemed dragged from Matthew.

He turned to look at her. Glory meant to look away, but she couldn't. The pain and despair in Matthew's eyes struck deep inside her. His cheeks were wet with new tears and his eyes were red with unshed ones. He must still love his wife very much.

"You're not going?"

"I'll call," Glory said as she stumbled to the door. It was time for her to leave.

"But—?" Matthew protested, and then mumbled in defeat, "Maybe it is best for now. You'll call?"

Glory nodded as she opened the door. She didn't trust her voice to speak.

The Bullet waited impatiently for morning. He had one call coming, and he didn't want to waste it on the answering machine.

The Bullet punched in the numbers and held his breath. One ring. Two rings—

"Hello, Millie's place." A man's voice answered.

The Bullet almost hung up, but he needed to know. "Is Millie there?"

"Forrest, is that you?" The man's voice warmed. "It's me. Douglas from Spokane."

"Douglas?"

"Yeah, I got Millie's number off the shipping label you left and called to wish her a Merry Christmas. We got to talking and she invited me out to spend the holiday with the two of you. Only you never showed. You all right?"

"Not exactly." Relief poured through the Bullet. Douglas would take care of Millie. He'd ask him to take her back to Spokane. No one would find her there.

Chapter Fifteen

Almost two months later, Glory was sitting at her drawing board in the Seattle police station. She was spending as much time as possible at work. The captain had insisted she stay with him and her mother until the federal agents arrested the distributors in the cattle-rustling ring. Glory had given in to the captain rather than argue. Besides, she hadn't wanted to be alone. For weeks she kept expecting to hear the twins giggle, and then she'd look up from her sketching or her reading and realize she'd probably never see them again—or their father.

Being with her family helped her feel better, but she couldn't stay with them forever. The feds had arrested the distributors last week, and she had moved back into her own apartment. The distributors had squealed loud and clear, but they didn't know enough to help the feds find the actual rustlers. Still, Glory was safe.

She had thought that when she moved back into

her apartment she'd feel more like her old self, but she didn't. Her life stretched forward with nothing but gray in it.

Glory laid down the black pencil she held in her hand and sighed. The face of crime never changed. All of the perpetrators were beginning to look alike. Actually, in her moments of acute honesty, she realized they all had a tendency to look like Matthew. It didn't help that today was Valentine's Day and that was the deadline she'd set for him. When she first returned to Seattle, she'd had a message on her answering machine telling her he'd call later when he had things worked out. Later was stretching into never as far as she could tell. If he hadn't called her by today, she decided that someplace deep and cold she'd bury her hopes of being with him. Like the North Pole. Or maybe Siberia.

"Anyone home?" Sylvia stood in the door of Glory's small office with her hands behind her back and a secretive smile spreading across her face.

"Come in." Glory welcomed her friend, grateful for the distraction. "What brings you here on a work day?"

"Roses," Sylvia replied as she stepped into the office. "Or should I say one rose?"

Sylvia held a vase with a yellow rose. "For you— from some of the kids."

"John and K.J.?"

Sylvia nodded as she set the vase on the corner of Glory's table. "They still feel bad about that contract business."

Glory chuckled. "Tell them thanks for the rose and for not fulfilling the contract."

Sylvia nodded as she settled into a chair. "Don't suppose you heard from anyone else on Valentine's Day? Say someone from Dry Creek?"

Glory snorted. "Of course not. It would appear the phone lines don't work between here and Dry Creek, even though Garth Elkton seems to do fine."

Sylvia blushed. "Garth only called once—and that was to ask about the kids. And you," Sylvia continued. "He asked about you. Said something about Matthew being depressed. Speaking of whom, I thought Matthew asked you to call?"

"But that was months ago. He should call. I wouldn't know what to say."

"Well, maybe he doesn't, either."

"He could send a postcard."

Sylvia winced. "Ever try to put your heart on a postcard?"

"Even that man—the Bullet—sent me a postcard from prison. To apologize. And let me know he's in a Bible study there. He managed to write."

"Well, don't be too hard on Matthew. After all—" Sylvia stood up and flung her arms wide "—he came all the way to Seattle to see you."

Glory shook her ears. She wasn't hearing right. "What?"

"He came all the way to Seattle to see you," Sylvia repeated with satisfaction in her voice. "Garth brought him."

"Oh." The pieces clicked into place now. "Garth brought him?"

Sylvia nodded. "Garth thought the two of you needed to talk."

"You don't suppose it's the other way around, do you? That Garth wanted to talk to you and Matthew is his excuse?"

"Don't be silly. Garth didn't even know where to find me. He had to hunt on foot for the center. Almost got into trouble until John rescued him. By the way, Matthew's taking you out to dinner tonight."

"I'm busy."

"I already told him you were free." Sylvia winked. "Give the guy a break. It's Valentine's Day. And he's taking you to dinner at the top of the space needle."

"He won't be able to do that," Glory protested in relief. "People had to make reservations weeks ago for Valentine's night there."

Sylvia smiled. "I know. Matthew says he made them weeks ago." She turned to leave and then said over her shoulder, "Wear your black dress—with the pearls."

"It's too short."

"No, it's not."

The dress was too short. Glory frowned at herself in the mirror. Especially to be with Matthew. She didn't want him to think she was trying to get his attention. If he wasn't interested in her in blue jeans, he wouldn't be interested in her in a black dress that showed more leg than it should.

The doorbell of her apartment rang. That must be him. She'd told Sylvia she'd meet Matthew at the foot of the needle. But Matthew was a stubborn man. He'd told Sylvia he had hired a limo to take them to dinner, and she would be picked up at six-thirty.

Glory almost walked away from the door instead of toward it. She wasn't looking forward to tonight. She expected Matthew did want to talk to her, to explain how sorry he was that he was unable to be more to her than a distant friend because of his feelings for his late wife. But Glory would just as soon skip the speech.

The doorbell rang again.

When Glory answered the door, Matthew stood there in a black tux holding a dozen red roses. She'd never realized how good he would look in a tux. His chestnut hair was brushed back in soft waves. His freshly shaven chin was set in a determined smile. His blue-green eyes looked hopeful.

It was too much. Glory almost shut the door in his face.

Matthew watched the emotions chase themselves across Glory's face. He'd held his breath until she opened the door, fearful she wouldn't come, and when he saw her he almost couldn't get his breath anyway. Glory was dazzling. Her golden-bronze hair was pulled up in the Grecian-goddess style he well remembered. She could be Venus with arms. Her eyes went from molten to icy in the space of a heartbeat. Quicksilver. That was Glory. She wore a black dress that was too sophisticated and sexy for him. He wondered if he'd even get the nerve to talk to her when she looked so polished. And then he saw it. Around her neck she wore a little silver angel charm on a chain.

Glory saw the direction Matthew's eyes were taking and stifled the impulse to hide the charm with her hand. She'd forgotten to take it off. She was so used to wearing it under everything she wore and not having it show that she'd forgotten about it. She hadn't realized the low-cut black dress would reveal that much about her.

Matthew smiled. "I'm glad you're wearing my angel."

Glory gritted her teeth and nodded. "I like silver."

Sitting in the restaurant at the top of the space needle was like sitting on top of the world. The tables were arranged in a circle on the inside rim of the revolving restaurant. Each table had a big window to view the city below. At night, the lights below sparkled clear to the ocean.

"How are the boys?" Glory asked politely as she folded the linen napkin on her lap.

"Fine. Thanks for calling them at Mrs. Hargrove's. They get so excited."

Glory nodded. "I'm fond of them."

"They like you, too," Matthew replied.

"They have really good bread here," Glory said as she took another piece of fresh sourdough from the basket.

Matthew despaired. Were they going to small-talk the night away?

"My boys aren't the only ones who like you." Matthew took a deep breath and plunged. There, he'd started it.

Glory looked at him skeptically.

Maybe, Matthew thought, he needed to be more specific. "I like you, too."

Glory smiled woodenly. "Thank you."

Silence stretched between them.

"When you went away, I felt like Job," Matthew finally said. Glory looked at him quizzically. He had her attention. "The day Job said, 'He hath taken me by my neck, and shaken me to pieces.' That was me with God. He needed to get my attention and turn me around before I could be any good to Him or anyone else. Fortunately, He did...."

Matthew had his hand lying on the table and Glory reached over to cover it with her own. "I'm so glad," she said.

"I've never prayed so much in my life. Not even in seminary. Now I know what it means to wrestle with God. You lose and win all at the same time."

Glory looked into Matthew's eyes. If she hadn't been so distracted by her own emotions earlier, she would have noticed the peace she now saw there.

"I went up to Havre for a couple of weeks and stayed with an old minister friend of mine," Matthew continued. "I never listened before when he said other ministers have gone through what I did." Matthew smiled. "I thought I was the only one who'd ever been deeply disappointed. He told me I needed to learn I wasn't in control of the world. God is. As believers, we can pray to Him, but our job isn't to carry the world on our shoulders. Our job is to trust."

"You're going back to the ministry, aren't you?" Glory asked softly. Joy rose within her.

Matthew nodded. "In Dry Creek for now. I don't

want to move the twins again, and this way I can keep working at the hardware store, too.''

''Mrs. Hargrove got her wish, after all.''

''Mrs. Hargrove is so pleased with me she's even watching the twins for me while I'm here.''

Glory smiled. ''So this is what you wanted to tell me. Sort of like the steps in Alcoholics Anonymous where you go and speak to the people you've met and tell them you've changed.''

Glory gave a sigh of relief. She didn't know what she'd expected of the evening, but it wasn't this. She was happy about Matthew, though, and glad she'd come to dinner.

''No,'' Matthew said in alarm. ''That's not it. I mean—that's part of it. But I can't stop with that.''

''Oh. I haven't done something, have I? Something I need to apologize for?''

''What could you have done?'' Matthew asked in astonishment.

''Then it must be you. Did you do something you need to apologize to me for?''

Matthew finally realized what she was talking about—the AA practice of asking for forgiveness. ''No! This has nothing to do with AA.'' Matthew was starting to sweat now and it was February in Seattle. ''I guess the subtle way isn't working. I'm trying to work up to asking you to marry me.''

''Marry you?'' Glory was dumbfounded.

Matthew grimaced. He hadn't meant to blurt it out quite that way. ''Well, now that I'm back in the ministry and...''

Glory's heart went from hot to cold. ''That's why you want to marry me,'' she said flatly. ''Because you're in the ministry and every minister needs a wife.''

Just then the waiter appeared with their dinners. "Blackened chicken for the lady and grilled mahi-mahi for the gentleman. Will there be anything else?'' The waiter beamed.

Glory found her teeth were beginning to ache from the effort to keep her jaw from clenching. "If you'll excuse me for a moment, I need to go, ah, powder my nose.''

Glory stood and walked to the ladies' rest room.

Matthew stared after her in dismay. How had everything gone so wrong? He knew he wasn't a Don Juan, but he hadn't expected to chase a woman away from her dinner with his proposal.

Glory stood in front of the full-length mirror in the rest room and counted to ten. She supposed she shouldn't be so angry. At least Matthew had been honest about what he wanted. He hadn't pretended to have a feeling that he was apparently reserving for the memory of his late wife. Glory sighed. It was so hard to compete with a dead woman. But still, the marriage offer did come from Matthew.

Matthew watched Glory walk back to the table. She held her head high with pride, and he scrambled around in his mind for words to apologize with....

"All right,'' Glory said quite calmly as she picked up her fork. "I'll marry you.''

"What?'' Matthew's roar was so loud the other people in the restaurant looked at him. He didn't care.

Apparently Glory did care. "Eat your fish. It'll get cold."

Matthew was speechless.

"Well, you did ask me," Glory reminded him after a moment of silence.

"But—" Matthew looked at her. "You don't seem very happy about the idea. I don't want you to marry me out of pity." Matthew had a sudden insight. "It's the boys, isn't it? You're marrying me for the sake of the twins. You think they need a mother."

Glory's heart broke. She'd forgotten. She couldn't marry Matthew. "I can't be a mother."

"But you like the twins."

"I love the twins. But I can't have children myself. I'm sorry, I should have told you before I accepted your proposal. I, of course, withdraw my acceptance." Glory speared another bite with her fork. "Delicious chicken."

"Hang the chicken," Matthew said. The muscle along his cheek started to twitch. "Look at me. We're not going to get married for the boys or for the ministry."

Glory laid down her fork, but she couldn't look at him. Not square in the eye. She didn't want him to see the tears that waited for a moment's privacy to fall.

"You may not be able to marry me because you love me," Matthew said softly. "But please, at least, marry me because I love you."

"You?" Glory lifted her eyes. "You do?"

"Of course. That's what I've been trying to tell you."

"Well, it wasn't very clear."

Matthew held her eyes steady with his. She'd never seen him look so serious. "Then let me make it clear. I love you, Glory Beckett. I love you so much it takes my breath away. It has, in fact, taken my breath away a time or two. I can't even begin to count the ways in which I love you. You own my heart."

"But what about the children I can't have?"

"We have the twins. If we want more children, we can adopt."

"And what about Susie?" Glory couldn't help asking. "On Christmas Day I saw you looking at her picture and crying."

Matthew smiled. "I was crying for all the anger toward God I've carried inside me because of Susie. Seeing that gun pointed at you that night—with me being unable to save you—brought everything back. Feeling so helpless. But it was you I was crying for. Susie doesn't make me cry anymore."

"Really?"

Matthew nodded. "Really."

They looked into each other's eyes for a minute. The restaurant was filled with candlelight and the sound of soft music.

"You're sure?" Glory asked again.

Matthew nodded. "I'm sure."

Glory studied him some more. "Really?"

Matthew grinned. "Finish your chicken so I can take you someplace and convince you I'm seriously in love with you."

Glory smiled and rose from the table. "I'm not really that hungry, after all."

"Me neither."

* * *

The waiter insisted on boxing up their dinners to go. He didn't seem surprised about their decision to leave early. He said it happened quite often on Valentine's Day.

The limousine chauffeur didn't find it odd that they returned after just twenty minutes, either. He merely suggested a drive around to look at the lights of Seattle. Matthew told him to make it a very long drive—maybe over to Puget Sound—and Glory couldn't have agreed more. After all, Matthew had promised to tell her, in detail, why he really, really loved her. And she was going to do the same.

* * * * *

Dear Reader,

Thank you for visiting Dry Creek with me. Although Dry Creek is a fictitious place, it is inspired by dozens of small communities in rural Montana. In many of these areas there is a church that adds strength to the whole community. I was privileged to grow up in one of these churches, the Fort Shaw Community Church in Fort Shaw, Montana. If you have a chance, stop in and visit the good people there. (Sunday services at 11:00, but you'll want to go for Sunday school, too, at 9:45.) You will find a group of people who are faithful to God and each other.

When God asks us to "gather together in His name," I believe he does so more for our good than for His. Old-Fashioned fellowship—with friendships and commitments that have spanned years and even decades—strengthens our faith and enriches us deeply. Troubles shared are troubles made lighter with prayer and comfort. Joys shared are joys made brighter with common rejoicing—especially during the Christmas season when we all have reason to celebrate.

So if you're currently part of a church family, cherish those ties. If you are not, my hope and prayer for you is that you find one soon so that you can rejoice in the Christmas season with them.

Janet Tronstad

A GENTLEMAN FOR
DRY CREEK

And it shall come to pass in the day
that the Lord shall give thee rest from thy sorrow,
and from thy fear, and from the hard bondage
in which thou wast made to serve.
—*Isaiah* 14:3

Dedicated with love to my two sisters,
Margaret Enger and Doris Tronstad. How fortunate
I am to have both of you in my life.

Chapter One

Sylvia Bannister checked the rearview mirror, not because there was likely to be any traffic on this one-lane road outside of Miles City, Montana, but because she had anxiously checked the mirror every few minutes all the way here from the airport in Billings. Between checking the mirror and praying, she didn't notice that the snowflakes were falling thicker and the temperature was dropping.

She was worried. She kept expecting a pulsing red light to fill the back window of her rental car. She'd asked the police to flag her down if they found out anything new about K.J. and John—anything at all.

But the window stayed dark except for the snow that gathered around the edges. The two boys could be anywhere between here and Dry Creek, Montana. And they probably didn't have warm jackets with them. Or anything more substantial than a candy bar to eat. And certainly not a map—

Sylvia stopped herself. The two boys would be fine. They'd faced tougher odds on the streets of Seattle.

The teenagers were two of the gang members her center was pledged to help. She'd had such hopes for these two boys. She knew their background—in one of the deadliest gangs in the area—but she knew kids and she'd pinned some hopes on these two.

That's why, when she'd found out they had been offered money to kill someone in Dry Creek, Montana—and then had bought plane tickets to Billings— she barely had time to activate the center's prayer chain before she rushed to the airport, flew to Billings and then rented this car to drive the rest of the way.

She'd chase those two boys to the ends of the earth if that's what it took to snatch them back from a life of crime.

She looked in her rearview mirror again. She wondered just how far away Dry Creek, Montana, could possibly be. She'd driven down Interstate 94 and turned off at the exit that said Dry Creek. It was dark outside, but her headlights had shown the sign clearly. She couldn't have made a mistake. Still, she'd expected to be in Dry Creek by now. So far, she hadn't seen any buildings, and the road she was driving on was little more than a path over a washboard of foothills.

Sylvia opened the window and a fine flurry of snow blew in her face. She loved the soft touch of snow. Besides, the wet coldness of the flakes kept her awake. She was sleepy. She didn't realize she didn't have a firm grip on the car's wheel until she was jarred by a bump in the road and automatically swerved. With all the snow it was hard to tell, but she felt like she hit something. She was on the bank of an old creek bed and she needed to pull the car back on the path. She twisted the wheel, but the car spun to the right. Something was wrong. Then she realized the something she hit must have had a sharp point to it. She had a flat tire.

She pulled harder, but the red Buick was already tilting. She couldn't control it. She was going down the bank. She barely had time to whisper a prayer as she tipped. She felt a stabbing pain as her head hit the windshield.

Her last thought was that she'd freeze to death if no one found her soon.

And who would find her? It was four o'clock in the morning and she hadn't seen another car for twenty long miles.

Dear Lord, what have I done?

Garth Elkton sat crouched down in the cab of his ranch pickup and peered out his window at the Buick Skylark. Someone had driven the car right down the side of the creek bed and lodged it into a snowdrift.

Looked like a fool's mistake.

Trouble is, there weren't that many fools around Miles City. Not with the tourists all down in California at this time of year. Even drunks had better sense than to venture out in the middle of winter—and if they did, they didn't end up in his cow pasture half-buried in a snowdrift.

No, something wasn't right.

The early-morning light was still hazy, so he carefully checked the snow-covered ground in all directions. He was looking for boot marks or hoof prints. Rustlers had been hitting this part of Montana, and he'd even heard rumors of contract killers coming into the Billings airport yesterday.

But there were no prints around the car. He didn't

see anything but frostbitten sage and, in the distance, the low rolling hills of the Big Sheep Mountain range. He could make out the smoke coming from the fire in one of the bunkhouses on his ranch and he sighed. He should be home with his feet propped up in front of the fire having a second cup of coffee.

Instead he'd come out to be sure all the cows made it to the storm shelter last night, and here he was. Trying to decide what kind of trouble that red car was going to be.

He studied the car. Most likely it was empty. Failing that, however, it was a trap set by the rustlers. Whoever drove that car into the creek bed knew someone passing by couldn't resist walking over and taking a look inside. Not after a brittle winter night like last night. Because—if the car wasn't empty—it meant some poor fool needed help desperately.

Well, he might as well get it over with. He reached under the seat. He'd feel a lot more comfortable with a weapon of some sort. He usually had more tools there, but all he found was one old hammer. He'd picked up the hammer in a ditch a month or so ago when he was out mending fences.

Garth eyed the hammer doubtfully. He'd heard of men who could kill someone with a dinner fork, but he doubted even they could do much with this hammer. The wooden handle was splintered and the metal was rusty. It looked like it'd crumble with the first blow. Not that he needed to worry about giving a second blow anyway if the men inside the car were packing guns. He'd be finished before he began.

Garth opened his cab door cautiously. A light filter of snow was falling and the weather was so cold, Garth's breath hung around him like smoke. He hefted the hammer in his bare hand as he walked low, gliding from sagebrush to sagebrush.

Garth half slid along the ground when he got closer to the car. The snow was cold on his stomach, but he hardly noticed.

The window of the Skylark was steamed up but Garth could see a shape. It could be a bundle of blankets. Or it could be a man.

A soft moan came from inside the car.

This is it, Garth said to himself. He took a deep breath, rose to his full height, hefted the hammer and opened the car door all in one swift movement. Garth was braced for the blast of a rifle, but not for the shrill scream that shook his earlobes.

He dropped the hammer on his toes.

''What the—'' He swore until the small face in front of him blinked and then opened up a pair of eyes so blue, he couldn't believe they were real.

How in the world had she gotten eyes the color of polished turquoise? Garth shook himself. Forget her eyes, old man. Remember where you are. She could be a criminal. Rustlers wouldn't hesitate to use a pretty woman as bait. ''What are you doing here?''

Sylvia looked up at the man. He was standing with his back to the rising winter sun. Flecks of snow clung to the gray Stetson that kept his face in shadows even though it was early morning. The hat was worn and dipped to shield his eyes like it had been trained for the task. He was tall, six foot two or three she'd judge, and sturdy.

She shivered a little from the sheer size of him. Big men made her nervous, not that she ever let them see it. With dogs and big men, she needed to keep her nerve up.

He was angry—she could see that. His face was red with anger even in the cold. But then she saw that his eyes didn't squint the way a mean man's eyes would. She had become expert at reading anger on a man's face. At least her ex-husband had done that much for her.

"What?" Sylvia tried to listen to the man. She felt like she was coming out of a sleep. Something important had happened and she couldn't remember what it was. Maybe this man knew. She'd driven so far and so fast, she felt as if she was still moving. Then she felt the pain in her head and she remembered—the accident, the twisting of her shoulder, the impact on her head and then the blackness.

"What are you doing here?" the man repeated, and then paused. "Are you working with the rustlers?"

"No," Sylvia whispered. Her head was pounding. "I'm working with the—"

"The what?"

"The gang." Sylvia didn't know why her tongue was so thick. "The boys in the gang."

The pain in Sylvia's head twisted and she saw white...

Sylvia woke later to the sound of voices. There was a man's voice. The big man. She remembered him. His voice sounded like a low rumble. Then there was an old man's voice, raspy and quiet. Over it all, a woman's voice soothed them.

"She's coming round," the old voice said with assurance.

Sylvia opened her eyes. She was in a Norman Rockwell painting. A white-haired man with a stethoscope around his neck was beaming down at her. A sweet-faced woman with her hair pulled back was looking around his shoulder and beaming, too.

Behind her she saw the big man. He must not have heard of Norman Rockwell. Instead of a smile he wore a scowl. "Give her room to breathe."

"I'm fine," Sylvia mouthed the words. They squeaked out softer than she wanted so she took a breath and tried again. "I'm fine."

"You're sure she doesn't need to be in the clinic?" The big man kept talking about her like she wasn't there. She noticed his gray jacket was still damp from melted snow. "I can take her to Miles City easy enough—the roads aren't that bad."

Mention of the roads reminded Sylvia. "I've got to go." She started to sit up.

"You're not going anywhere," the woman said firmly, turning to the big man. "Is she, Garth?"

"Garth." Sylvia rolled the name around on her tongue. She liked it. Even if he had a wife. "Thank you—all of you—but I need to leave."

Sylvia slowly raised herself completely. She'd been lying on a plaid sofa in a high-ceiling living room. Huge windows opened onto a snow-dusted outdoor deck.

"What do I owe you?" Sylvia looked at the doctor. Doctors in Seattle didn't make house calls, but if one did it'd be expensive. She wondered how much cash she had with her.

"No need for that." The old man waved away her offer. "I was out here anyway—the boys had a horse that needed a look-see."

"A horse?"

"I tend to all of God's creatures," the old man said with a smile. "Don't worry. I went to medical school.

Only took up vetting in my later years. Not that you're complicated. A vet could tell you what you need to know. Take it easy, don't doze off, someone to watch you—that sort of thing. But don't worry. Francis will look out for you."

"Thanks, but—" Sylvia took a ragged breath and swung her legs around so she'd be sitting normally. The room started to spin.

"What the—" Garth stepped to the other side of the sofa where Sylvia was sitting, and grabbed her shoulders. "Fool woman. Don't you listen to the doctor?"

Sylvia felt the man's hands on her shoulders. She wanted to shrug them off, to show she didn't need help. But even she could tell that without his support she'd fall over like a rag doll.

"I need to get to Dry Creek." Sylvia said the words distinctly. Carefully.

"Whatever it is, it can wait," Garth said, eyeing her. What he saw stopped him. Pain stretched the pale skin of her face and her startling blue eyes half closed with the effort of breathing. He could feel every breath she took through his hands as they held her shoulders.

When she'd passed out in the car he'd been alarmed at her stillness. He'd put his cheek close to her lips to feel the warmth of her breath. He wanted to do the same again. Even though Dr. Norris said there were no broken ribs, he was sure there were some bruised ones. She wasn't breathing right.

"No, it can't. Life and death—"

"Death! Oh, surely not," the doctor sputtered as he patted her knee. "That much of a doctor I've always been. No, you're not going to die—a concussion maybe, but that's it.''

Sylvia wondered why the doctor's hands felt merely comforting while Garth's hands on her shoulders felt like an anchor. Her muscles settled into the palms of his hands and she leaned slightly. She'd rest a minute before she stood. "It's not me—it's Glory Beckett.''

"You're with her?'' Garth demanded. "She's the one who's mixed up with those contract killers I've heard about.''

"I—I can explain,'' Sylvia said as she took another partial breath.

"Explanations can wait,'' Garth said. He didn't like the whiteness in the woman's face now that she was sitting. And he could feel the effort her body spent in drawing each breath. He'd taken off her coat when he'd first laid her on the sofa. Nothing separated him from her skin but the white silk blouse she was wearing. The material was cool and sleek, but he could feel her warmth beneath the material. Yes, explanations could wait. He'd just as soon hold this butterfly of a woman a minute or two longer before he found out what was making her so worried.

Chapter Two

Six weeks later, on a side street in Seattle

Garth Elkton figured he was the sorriest excuse for a man alive. He'd let his butterfly woman fly right out of his life and he'd been too tongue-tied to stop her. The fact that she was avoiding him at the time— and had avoided him most of the two days that she spent in Dry Creek—should not have stopped him.

You'd have thought it was his fault she hadn't known those two boys had come to Dry Creek to save Glory Beckett instead of shoot her and that Glory Beckett had ended up helping the Feds cut off the distribution network for the stolen beef that was being rustled out of Montana. He had not known those things himself. He couldn't have told Sylvia.

But that didn't ease her coldness to him. As near as he could figure, Sylvia had been annoyed with him just for breathing the same air as everyone else. A sane man would give up on a woman so set against him. At first he'd thought it'd been the confusion about Francis. But he'd told her Francis was his sister. It hadn't seemed to make a difference.

He told himself a dozen times he should forget her.

Still, he tapped his shirt pocket. Sylvia had lost a butterfly-shaped, gold earring when she rode in his pickup the morning he'd found her. He hadn't noticed it until after she left Dry Creek. He'd meant to mail it to her in Seattle, but he'd found he was reluctant to part with it. He kept hoping she'd write and ask about it. But she didn't.

He glanced down at the faded Polaroid picture that he'd taped to the dash of his pickup—he'd given Santa five bucks to take that picture of Sylvia on Christmas Eve and it was the best five bucks he'd ever spent. She'd been talking to the kids serving the spaghetti dinner that night in Dry Creek and her face was alive with laughter. Her smile had haunted him ever since she climbed into Glory Beckett's Jeep and headed back to Seattle.

At the time, he'd thought his yearning for her would fade. He didn't know her. He knew that. The shadows of emotions that had chased themselves across her face when he talked to her could be misread. But he had an itch inside his gut to know Sylvia Bannister, and he figured the only way to get rid of it was to do something about it.

He didn't have a plan past returning the earring. A man needed hope to have a plan and he didn't have any of that. Sylvia Bannister had made it clear she was a church woman and he figured a church woman would never take up with the likes of him. But plan or no plan, hope or no hope, it seemed the best way to start was to go to Seattle.

And here he was. Lost as a stray sheep on some wet Seattle street. Or maybe he was even in Tacoma. He'd dropped Matthew Curtis off so the man could do his own courting of Glory Beckett. Garth had thought he'd find Sylvia's youth center with no problem. He'd flown missions in the army with a flashlight held to a map the size of a baseball card.

But the streets here were confusing. Too many hills and detours. Too many gang markings covering street signs. Too many empty, shelled buildings with the street numbers erased off their sides. He knew he wasn't in the safe part of town and he didn't like the thought of Sylvia's center being here.

And then he saw a familiar face. One of the kids. John. The kid was half walking, half running down the street beside an abandoned building. Gray metal sheets were nailed over the windows of the building and rust outlined the doorway. Garth guessed the building used to be a factory of some kind.

Then he noticed that John's face was as gray as the weathered sheet metal. The kid was afraid, looking over his shoulder and trotting along like some lop-sided chicken.

Garth pulled over and parked his pickup. He was going to call out to John when he saw what was happening. Kids—thugs, Garth thought—were coming toward John from all directions. Instead of running faster, John slowed down like it was hopeless.

Garth reached over and opened the passenger door of his pickup truck. John could make it to the pickup if he gave one good burst of speed. Garth honked the horn and John looked up but didn't move. Garth had seen this before. Someone so scared they couldn't move even to save themselves.

Garth half swore. He'd have to do this the hard way. He opened his door and reached behind the seat for an old bullwhip he'd bought at an auction last week. The Gebharts were selling out and he'd paid as much for the whip as their pride would allow. At the time he wasn't sure it'd stay together long enough for him to nail it to his barn wall.

Now he hoped the whip would hold together a bit longer than that.

Sylvia stopped her fingers from twisting together nervously. She was sitting behind her desk in the small office at the center. The other staff—Melissa Hanson and Pat Dawson—were conspicuously absent. Cowards. They were no more prepared to chat with Mrs. Buckwalter than she was.

At first she'd felt like Alice in Wonderland when Mrs. Buckwalter had called, asking to see the center. Sylvia knew of the Buckwalters. True, she never traveled in those financial—or social—circles, but she knew they existed. Just like she knew the queen of England existed. She'd just never expected to have the queen—or Mrs. Buckwalter—for tea.

The Buckwalter Foundation was not the kind of donor that usually supported the center—in fact, they were more likely to donate millions to a Seattle museum than ten dollars to a small, church-funded youth center that needed a camp.

Of course, she'd be happy to show Mrs. Buckwalter around. She'd smiled into the phone in frozen shock. Today? Yes, four o'clock would be fine.

Sylvia wasn't off the phone for two seconds before she realized something was very wrong. She had assumed somehow in those magical minutes that someone from the staff had approached the Buckwalters about their ideas for a youth camp. The funding they had counted on had fallen through at the last minute and her first wild hope was that somehow word had gotten to the Buckwalters and they were coming to their rescue.

She realized how naive that sounded the moment she thought about it. A lion in the jungle didn't worry about whether or not an ant had funding. She didn't even know anyone who knew the Buckwalters well enough to get past the army of secretaries that fielded their calls. They were notorious for being difficult to contact.

Her fears were confirmed when she questioned the staff. No one had called Mrs. Buckwalter. No one even knew how to reach Mrs. Buckwalter.

That's when Sylvia panicked. The phone call had not been a miracle—it had been a mistake. Mrs. Buckwalter must have thought she was calling someplace else. She must have looked in the phone book under Tacoma-Seattle Youth Center and dialed the wrong place.

Sylvia took a deep breath. So it wasn't perfect. It was still a slim hope and that was better than anything else she had. After all, Jesus was an old hand at drawing a rabbit out of a hat. He had fed five—or was it ten—thousand with a few biscuits and a couple of fish fillets. If he could do that, he could help her with Mrs. Buckwalter.

Sylvia braced herself. Yes, she'd do her best pitch. She had the grant proposal. She needed to make some changes and it would be ready. Then all that remained was—

Oh, no, the office! Or more like the nonoffice. Sylvia used the room that had once been a janitor's storage room. The room met her needs but it still smelled of floor wax. She'd always kept lots of green plants around, but surely a woman like Mrs. Buckwalter would expect more to sit on than a gray folding chair.

And her clothes! Sylvia looked down at herself. Usually she wore a suit when meeting with prospective donors. But today she had on a bulky navy sweater and acid-washed jeans. There wasn't time to drive back to her apartment and change.

Sylvia took a deep breath and reminded herself what Jesus could do with a biscuit. That reminded her—yes, tea. She needed a pot of tea and some English biscuits.

By four o'clock the tea was cooling in the cups and Sylvia's glow was fading by the second. Mrs. Buckwalter certainly wasn't interested in the proposal Sylvia had managed to get ready.

"—we'd pair each teen with a mentor." Sylvia pressed forward with her proposal because she didn't know what else to do. Mrs. Buckwalter still held her purse in her lap. The purse was genuine leather and the lap was ample. Sylvia had seen Mrs. Buckwalter at a distance in several local charity events and thought she looked imposing. Up close she looked downright intimidating. English tweed suit, hand-tailored for her. Starched blouse. Iron hair, severely pulled back. Intelligent green eyes that seemed impatient.

Mrs. Buckwalter looked at the diamond watch on her wrist.

Sylvia gave up. Mrs. Buckwalter must have realized the mistake early on and was just waiting for enough minutes to pass so she could politely leave. She obviously wasn't used to this part of town. There must be thirty carats of diamonds on that watchband alone. "You shouldn't wear your good watch down here."

Mrs. Buckwalter looked up blankly. "I didn't."

"Well, it would be the watch of a lifetime for any of the kids down here," Sylvia said dryly. "We try not to wave temptation in front of them."

Mrs. Buckwalter nodded and slowly unhooked her watch. Then she laid the watch out beside the teapot. "It's yours."

"But I didn't mean for you to—"

"I know." Mrs. Buckwalter waved aside her protest. "I'm an old woman and I don't have time to be subtle. Don't know what made me think I might be able to pull this off slowly. Let me put it to you straight. I'll fund this camp of yours but I have one condition—I pick the campsite, no questions asked. If you have a problem with that—"

"No, no—" Sylvia was speechless. She started to rise out of her chair. Could it really be that simple?

"We'll need at least a hundred and fifty thousand dollars," Sylvia clarified. She wasn't sure Mrs. Buckwalter had been paying attention.

Mrs. Buckwalter nodded complacently. "We'll probably want to make it two hundred thousand dollars, plus whatever the watch brings. I never liked it anyway. I want to be sure they have the best of everything. Not that it's necessary for learning good manners, but it helps."

Sylvia half choked as she sank lower into the folding chair. "Manners?" She was right. Mrs. Buckwalter hadn't been listening. She had them confused with some other youth center. Maybe one of those upscale places that prepares girls to be debutantes.

"We work with young people who have been in gangs," Sylvia offered quietly as she got up and walked over to a locked cabinet and turned a key. She pulled the drawer open to reveal a jumble of knives, cans of spray paint and bullets. Each item had a tag. "These are only from the past month. Kids give them to us for a month at a time. We hope that at the end of the month they're ready to give up the stuff forever. Usually they do. Sometimes they don't. Either way, they know fear every day of their lives. They see other kids killed. They've all robbed someone. They need more than manners."

Mrs. Buckwalter looked at the drawer and raised an eyebrow. "Well, if you're set on it, you're welcome to add the prayer and Bible stuff I hear you're famous for—I don't believe it will harm anyone. But you're to include a proper amount of old-fashioned manners, too. I don't care how violent these children have been—we are a civilized nation and manners will do them good."

"You don't mean table manners? Salad forks—that kind of thing?" Now that Sylvia concluded Mrs. Buckwalter knew where she was and what she was saying, she tried to sort the thing out. Was "manners" a code name for some new therapy she hadn't read about yet? Some kind of new EST thing—or maybe Zen something. Mrs. Buckwalter didn't look the type to go in for psychological fads, but she must be.

"And everyday etiquette, too," Mrs. Buckwalter added complacently. "Respect for elders. Ladies first, boys opening the door for girls—that kind of thing.

Maybe even wrap it up with a formal dance." Mrs. Buckwalter's face softened. "I've always thought there's nothing like a formal dance to bring out the manners in everyone."

Sylvia felt as if her head was buzzing. Most of the kids she worked with had probably never seen a dance more formal than the funky chicken. And if a boy opened the door for a girl, she wouldn't go through it, suspecting he was using her as a body shield to stop bullets from someone on the other side of it.

"But—" Sylvia started to explain when she noticed that Mrs. Buckwalter was no longer listening to her. Instead, the older woman had her head tilted to the outer room. Things were getting a little noisy, even for the center.

"Excuse me," Sylvia said. She'd worry about manners later. "I'd better check and see what's happening."

The thud of a basketball sounded as it hit the wire hoop in the main, gymlike room of the center, but no one even looked as the ball circled the hoop before slowly dropping through the basket. The two teenage boys, who had been shooting baskets, had their backs to the hoop. They stood frozen, half-crouched, undecided about whether to run or to hit the floor as the front door slammed open.

Sylvia scanned the big room in a glance. The air was humid; it'd been raining off and on all day. Sometimes the weather made everyone short-tempered. But it wasn't the weather today. She saw the two boys in the middle of the floor and three or four girls sitting on the edge of the floor where they'd been gossiping.

All of the kids were staring at the front door. And she couldn't blame them. A large figure was shouldering its way inside. If they were anywhere else, Sylvia would say it was a bear. Or Bigfoot. But then she saw that the figure had two parts. John was slung over the shoulder of a man as big as a mountain. She could already hear the squeal of rubber as a car screeched to a stop outside.

The man turned to face the room and Sylvia drew in her breath. That gray Stetson. It couldn't be anyone but— No, she wasn't mistaken. She'd know that arrogant masculinity anywhere. The question was— "What are you doing here?"

Sylvia meant to have the question come out strong, but it must have been little more than a whisper. In any event, Garth didn't seem to hear her. Instead he bowed down in a graceful arc to let John roll off his back and, at the same time, uncoiled a massive bullwhip from his shoulder.

Sylvia cleared her throat and tried again. "What are—"

This time she had his attention. She knew it with the first word out of her mouth. His eyes swung to her and he took a step toward her. He dipped his hat and his eyes were in the shadows again. If she didn't know better, she would have sworn he was feeling shy. "I—ah—"

He never finished his sentence. The first bullet shattered the glass in the window beside the door. Garth didn't wait to see what the second bullet would hit.

"Everybody down," he bellowed as he dropped the whip and took another step toward her.

Sylvia looked around to be sure everyone was obeying. She was going to slide down when she knew the kids were all right. But that wasn't soon enough for Garth.

He sprinted to her side and in one fluid movement wrapped his body around her before rolling with her to the floor. Sylvia braced herself to hit the floor, but Garth twisted his body so that he took the impact. He landed on his back with Sylvia resting on his chest. Then he quickly somersaulted so that Sylvia was enclosed inside his arms.

Sylvia froze. She forgot all about the bullets that might be flying overhead. She hadn't been this close to a man since that day her ex-husband had threatened her—she pushed the very suggestion from her mind. She couldn't afford to think of that now. She had to concentrate on breathing. If she could only keep breathing.

Garth felt Sylvia stiffen. *Good Lord, she's been shot!*

Garth turned to his side. He ran his hands quickly down Sylvia's back. What was she doing wearing a sweater? Blood would soak into a sweater. Her breathing seemed fainter and fainter. And he didn't like the fluttering heartbeat. She felt like a frightened bird. He wondered if shock was setting in. He needed to find the bullet hole.

He slipped his hand under her sweater. If she was limb shot, they could deal with that later. But if the bullet had hit her internal organs he needed to act fast. His hand slid over the smoothness of her back. Her muscles tensed and her breathing stopped. He'd run his hand up and down her back twice before he convinced himself there was no blood.

"Where does it hurt?" he demanded.

A warm ember settled in his stomach. Her skin was

softer than sunshine on a spring day. The faint scent
of peaches was reaching his nostrils, too, and he noticed her hair. Luxurious strands of midnight-black
hair were nestled near his neck. For a moment, he
forgot why she lay curled inside his arms. It was
enough that she was there.

"Ummmph." A muffled noise came from near
Garth's heart and he realized Sylvia was trying to
talk.

"Oh, excuse me—I didn't—" Garth pulled away
from Sylvia. Her skin was white. He felt a sudden
surge of anger at the thugs outside that had frightened
Sylvia. "I shouldn't have led them here. They frightened you."

"No, you did," Sylvia answered automatically.
One of the things she'd been taught in her battered-
wife course ten years ago was to be honest. "You
frightened me."

Sylvia took a deep breath and looked up at Garth
Elkton, at least as nearly up as she could. He still had
her half-encased in his arms and she saw more of his
chin than his eyes. She took another breath. Calmness
was the key. "You need to let me go now."

Give a directive, Sylvia reminded herself. Be calm.
Expect them to obey. Keep your mind focused. Count
to ten. One. Sylvia stared at Garth's neck. Two. She
saw his Adam's apple move up and down as he swallowed. She saw faint strands of hair curled around his
shirt collar. Three. Remember to breathe.

The skin around his collar was a little lighter than
the tan on his face. He obviously got his tan the hard
way instead of in a tanning booth. Another breath.
Then she smelled him. He smelled of wet wool from
his jacket, and forest pine. She breathed in again for

the sheer pleasure of it. He smelled like Christmas and reminded her of Dry Creek. She'd thought about him often since she'd left that little town in Montana. More accurately, she hadn't thought about him as much as she'd dreamed about him. Little secret segments of sleep that left her restless when she woke in the morning.

His arms loosened around her. "I was only—" Garth protested as he moved away from her. He untwined his leg from around hers.

"I know," Sylvia said quickly. She didn't need to be so prickly. He couldn't know about her problems with men. Or those unwanted dreams. "You meant well."

Garth wasn't sure what he had meant. But he sure hadn't meant to frighten her.

"I was only—" Garth had rehearsed this line in his head and he had to spit it out. "I mean since I was in the neighborhood, I thought I'd return your earring."

"Earring?"

"In Dry Creek. You lost an earring," Garth patted his shirt pocket until he found the little bit of metal. He fumbled inside his pocket and brought out the earring.

"Would you look at that!" The voice came from the far side of the room and bounced off all of the walls. Even the kids instinctively turned toward Mrs. Buckwalter. "He not only saved your life, he returned your jewelry. What a gentleman—and a hero!"

"Well, no, I," Garth protested as he handed the earring to Sylvia, "I wouldn't say that...."

Mrs. Buckwalter walked toward Garth and Sylvia like a general chasing away a retreating foe. Her tweed suit bristled with command. "You certainly are, young man, and I'll hear no more about it." Mrs. Buckwalter stood in the center of the room and looked down at Garth's Stetson. A small smile softened her mouth as she picked up the hat. "Quite the gentleman. A fine example of chivalry if I've ever seen one, Mr...?"

"Elkton. Garth Elkton," he supplied. Something about the way that woman was smiling made him uneasy.

"I rather thought so," Mrs. Buckwalter said smugly as she walked over to Garth and offered him the hat.

Sylvia decided Mrs. Buckwalter was going senile. The older woman couldn't know who Garth Elkton was. She had him confused with someone else. "He's not from around here," Sylvia offered gently.

"I know that, dear," Mrs. Buckwalter said smoothly.

Sylvia wondered if another member of the Buckwalter family would be showing up soon to escort their mother home. The older woman was sweet but obviously not all she used to be mentally. That must explain her bizarre fixation on manners.

"I ranch in Montana, just outside of Miles City," Garth said to Mrs. Buckwalter. He brushed off the Stetson and sat it squarely on his head.

"A large place, is it?" the older woman asked conversationally as she smoothed back her hair.

"A good piece," Garth agreed as he looked around him. Two of the windows—the only two windows in the room—were shattered. "Don't anyone go near all that glass until I get it cleaned up."

"I'll get it cleaned up," John said as he rose from his crouch on the floor.

Garth nodded his thanks.

"I'd like to buy some of it," Mrs. Buckwalter said as though it were a settled agreement.

"Huh?" Garth was looking at the glass. There were little pieces everywhere. "You want to buy what?"

"The land. Your land," Mrs. Buckwalter repeated. "I'd like to buy some."

"I'm not planning to sell any of it," Garth said politely as he noted a broom in the corner. What would a city woman like her do around Miles City?

"I can pay well."

Garth thought a moment. He wasn't interested, but some of his neighbors might be. Still, he had to be fair. Sometimes there were items in the news that were misleading. "There's no oil around there—least none that's not buried too deep for drilling."

"I'm not looking for oil."

"No dinosaur bones, either." Garth added the other disclaimer. Ever since those dinosaur bones had been discovered up by Choteau, tourists thought they could stop beside the road and dig for bones.

"I'm not interested in bones. I'm looking for a campsite."

Sylvia stifled a groan. If they set up the camp there, she'd never be able to sleep again. "Montana would never do. These kids are all used to the urban situation."

"I thought you wanted to get them out of the city." Mrs. Buckwalter waved her arm to indicate the windows. "They don't have drive-bys in Montana."

Garth had already started to join John, but he

turned back. "You're talking about a camp for these kids?"

Mrs. Buckwalter nodded emphatically. "Sylvia and I were just talking about it."

Some opportunities in life came from sweat and hard work. Others drop from the sky like summer rain. When Garth figured out what was happening—he'd heard Sylvia talk about her camp when she was in Dry Creek—he knew he wasn't about to let this opportunity get away. "I could rent some space to you for the camp—fact is, I'll give you some space for the camp. No charge."

"But it's not that easy—" Sylvia was feeling cornered. She didn't like the glow on Mrs. Buckwalter's face. Granted the woman was senile, but one never knew whether or not the rest of her family would indulge the woman and let her play out her fantasy of teaching inner-city kids to use salad forks. Not that Sylvia was fussy. She'd thought more along the lines of rock climbing than etiquette, but she'd welcome a camp no matter what classes she needed to offer the kids. But not Montana. Not close to Garth. "We'd need to have dormitories—and classrooms—it's not just the land, it's the facilities."

"I've got two bunkhouses I never use and a couple of grain sheds that could be cleared out and heated," Garth persisted. He tried not to press too hard. He didn't want to make Sylvia bolt and run. He knew from riding untamed horses that it was best not to press the unwary too hard. "And it would only be temporary, of course, until you can locate another place that you like."

"We'll take it," Mrs. Buckwalter announced eagerly.

"But we have staff to consider." Sylvia stood her ground. "We've got Melissa and Pat, but we'll need another one, maybe two counselors. I can't just move them to Montana at the drop of a hat."

Mrs. Buckwalter waved her hand, dismissing the objection. "There are people in Montana. We'll hire them." She pointed at Garth. "We could hire him. He could teach these boys what they need to know to be men."

Garth swallowed. He couldn't claim to be a role model for anyone. His relationship with his son wasn't one he'd brag about. And he wasn't proud of some of the things he'd done in his life. Now that Dry Creek had a pastor, he'd thought about going back to church, but he was a long way from role-model material. Still, he heard himself say it anyway. "I'll do it."

Sylvia looked at him skeptically. "But we can't just hire anyone. They need to be a licensed counselor. Besides, I'm sure it would be too much trouble for Mr. Elkton. He can't possibly want twenty or thirty teenagers around."

Garth didn't bother to think about that one. He might not want thirty teenagers around, but he wanted Sylvia around, and if he had to take thirty teenagers as part of the deal, he'd welcome them. After all, he'd had killer bulls in his corrals and free-range stallions in his fields. How much trouble could a few kids be?

"Besides, there's the matter of the rustling—" Sylvia remembered the fact gratefully. This was her trump card. No one would suggest putting down in the middle of a crime circle a camp to get kids out of crime.

"They've been quiet for a bit." Garth squeezed the

truth a little. He knew for a fact the rustlers were still there. He'd even been asked to help tip the Feds off on their whereabouts. He'd told the Feds he knew nothing. He didn't. But he knew instinctively the rustlers were still there. He suspected they were just regrouping their distribution efforts before swinging back into operation.

"These kids aren't interested in stealing cows," Mrs. Buckwalter interrupted impatiently. "Mr. Elkton's ranch is the place for them. Besides, if you wait to find the ideal camp, you'll be waiting three, maybe four years."

And in three years who knows who will run the Buckwalter Foundation, Sylvia thought to herself in resignation. It surely wouldn't be Mrs. Buckwalter. Sylvia doubted the older woman would be allowed very many of these eccentric fundings.

Sylvia steeled herself. She needed to put her own nervousness aside and at least consider the options. If the kids were going to have a camp anytime soon, they would have to do it Mrs. Buckwalter's way. And there were some pluses—the facilities were ready. She could take the kids away now. Especially John.

She knew the codes that the gangs lived by and, even though the Seattle gangs weren't as territorial as some, she knew that gangs lived and died by their reputations. Whoever was after John would want him even more now that they'd been stopped.

And it might not just be John. The kids in the center stood up for each other. They might all be in extra danger.

"Okay, I'll think about it." Sylvia said.

She didn't realize how intently the teenagers were listening until she heard a collective groan. "They ain't even got TV there," one of the older boys yelled out as though that automatically vetoed any decision. "Not in the middle of Montana."

Garth grinned. "Sure we do. Satellite. You can see educational programs from around the world." Garth grinned again. "Even get some old Lawrence Welk reruns."

An expression of alarm cross the boy's face.

"I'm not interested in educational TV or no Welk stuff. I want to know if you get *Baywatch*."

"You'll be too busy to watch TV," Sylvia interjected. She wasn't as optimistic as she sounded. Thirty teenagers and educational television. She wasn't ready for this. "We could have lessons in the various plants and animals around the area."

Another collective groan erupted.

"And maybe we can learn to—" Sylvia hesitated. What would they do in Montana in the winter? She couldn't see the kids taking up quilting. Or playing checkers.

"Skiing," Mrs. Buckwalter announced grandly. "In all that snow there should be good skiing."

The protest this time was halfhearted and the kids all looked at their shoes.

"That stuff's for rich kids," one of the girls finally muttered. "Skiing's expensive."

Sylvia hated it when she could see how some of her kids had been treated. The center served a mixture of races. Some Asian, some African-Americans and a handful of whites. All of the kids felt poor, like all of the good opportunities in life had gone to someone else. The fact that the kids were right made Sylvia determined to change things.

"We'll have enough to rent some skis," Sylvia

promised, resolving to make the budget stretch that far.

"Rent?" Mrs. Buckwalter snorted. "I'll personally buy a pair of skis for anyone who learns how to ski." She gestured grandly. "Of course, that only comes after they learn how to dance." The older woman's face softened with memories only she saw. "They'll need to learn to waltz for the formal dinner/dance."

Garth looked at Sylvia. He could tell from the resigned look on her face that she wasn't surprised.

"Mrs. Buckwalter wants the camp to teach them manners," Sylvia explained quietly to Garth.

"And you, of course, can help." Mrs. Buckwalter smiled at Garth. "A gentleman of your obvious refinement would be a good teacher for the boys. Opening doors, butter knives—that sort of thing."

"Me?" Garth choked out before he stopped himself. He already knew he'd do anything—even stand on his head in a snowdrift—if that's what it took to have Sylvia around long enough to know her. But gentleman! Butter knives! He was becoming as alarmed as the teenagers facing him.

"And, of course, you'll help with the dance lessons," Mrs. Buckwalter continued blithely.

"I don't—I—" Garth looked around for some escape. Butter knives were one thing. But dancing! He couldn't dance. He didn't know how. Still— He steeled himself. He'd flown fighter planes. He'd tiptoed around minefields. "I'd be delighted."

"Good," Mrs. Buckwalter said. The older woman's face was placid, but Garth caught a slight movement of the chin. The woman was laughing inside, he was sure of it.

Oh, well, he didn't care how she amused herself.

Rich society people probably had a strange sense of humor. He didn't care. He'd gotten what he wanted. Sylvia was coming to his ranch.

Maybe. He cautioned himself. He'd been watching the kids. He knew the battle wasn't over. As they'd listened to the older woman, their initial alarm had increased until they were speechless.

"Manners—" the smallest boy in the group finally croaked out the words. "We'll get beat up for sure when they find out we've been sent off to learn manners."

"We'll show them manners," John declared, standing defiantly. "We'll get them for what they've done."

"There'll be no payback," Sylvia said sternly. "We'll let the police handle it."

Meanwhile, at an early-evening meeting in Washington, D.C.

Five men, some of them balding, all of them drinking coffee from disposable cups, were sitting around a table. A stocky man chewing on an unlit cigar worried aloud. "Would he do it? The cattle rustling is only a small part of this operation, you know. He might not want to tackle a crime organization over a few head of beef."

"He would do it if he got mad enough," the youngest man said. He was on the shy side of thirty and was holding a manila folder. "His psychological profile shows he's strongly territorial, he protects his own, has a fierce sense of fairness—"

A third man snorted derisively. "That test was given twenty-some years ago before he got us out of that mess in Asia. What do we know about Garth Elkton today?''

There was a moment's silence.

The man with the folder set it down on the table. "Not much. He pays his ranch hands well. Health benefits even. That's unusual in a ranch community. He's widowed—he's got a grown son. His neighbors respect him. Closemouthed about him, though. Our agents couldn't get much from them. Oh, and he has a sister who's visiting him.''

"Sister?" one of the men asked hopefully. "Maybe we could get to him that way—if he likes the ladies.''

"No, the sister is really his sister,'' the young man verified.

"That's not much to go on.''

"He's our only hope,'' the young man said. "We have more leaks around there than Niagara Falls. They've picked off every agent we've put on the case. If we assign another agent, we might as well send along the coroner. If we want someone who isn't with the agency, he's it. Besides, he knows how to handle himself in a fight—he was in a special combat unit in the army. He missed the main action in Vietnam— too young—but he went deep into 'Nam with his unit, five, six years later to get some POWs. Top secret. Bit of a problem. The operation turned sour and he took the hit for the unit. He spent six months in a POW camp himself. Barely made it out alive. We've checked out all the ranchers in Montana—he's the only one who could pull it off.''

The third man sighed. "I guess you're right. We may as well offer again. Most likely he'll say no anyway.''

"I don't think so." A man who sat apart from them all spoke up for the first time.

The other four men looked at each other uneasily.

"What have you done?" one of them finally asked.

"Nothing yet," the man said as he rose. As if on cue, his cellular phone rang in his suit pocket. The rest of the men were silent. They knew a call on that phone was always important and always business.

"Yeah?" the man said into the phone. "Did you get it set up?"

The man started to grin as he listened. "What did I tell you? Some of these things go down easy." The man snapped his cell phone shut. Revenge was sweet. "I've taken care of it. If Garth Elkton's anything like his old man, he'll say yes."

"You know the family personally?" The stocky man removed his cigar.

"About as personal as it gets."

The stocky man grunted. "Well, see that it doesn't get in the way."

The man with the phone didn't answer. He couldn't stop grinning. Leave it to Mrs. Buckwalter to make the deal sweeter. He'd sure like to see Garth Elkton stumbling around a dance floor. Let him see how it felt to be clumsy in love with no hope in sight.

Chapter Three

Sylvia stood on the steps of the Seattle police station, as close to swearing as she was to weeping. She'd almost gotten them away. If she'd taken Mrs. Buckwalter at her word and gathered the kids under her wing yesterday and run off to Montana, she wouldn't be climbing these steps now on her way to try and bail them all out of jail.

The irony was she'd worked through her resistance to the idea of staying on Garth's ranch and decided she would do it. She had no other options for the kids.

She'd take the kids to Montana she decided—at least the ones for whom she could get parental consent. Likely, that would be all of them as long as she promised to only keep them for a month. A month wasn't long enough to interfere with any government support their parents were getting for them. And they'd get permission from the schools. Both of her staff were teachers as well as counselors and gave individual instruction to the kids.

Even a month would let the kids start to feel safe.

She'd learned early on that a month's commitment was about all the kids could make in the beginning. They couldn't see further into the future than those thirty days. So that's how she started. Once one month was down, she'd ask for another. Lives were being changed one month at a time.

But the kids getting arrested made everything so much more difficult. Some of the boys were on probation. A couple of the girls, too. The others had probably walked close enough to the edge of juvenile problems to be placed on probation with this latest episode. They might not have the freedom to decide what they wanted—not even for a month.

What, she thought to herself in exasperation, had possessed these kids to tackle a dangerous gang? But she knew—gang thinking was vicious. It made war zones out of school grounds and paranoid bush soldiers out of ordinary kids. She was lucky it was the police station she was visiting and not the morgue.

Sylvia swung open the heavy oak doors that led into the station's waiting area. There were no windows, but the ceilings were high and supported a dozen fans that slowly rotated in an attempt to ventilate the place. Even with the fan blades buzzing in the background, the cavelike room still smelled slightly on days that weren't wax days.

On Thursdays, when the janitors did an early-morning wax job on the brown linoleum floors, the room smelled of disinfectant. On other days the odor was people—too many, too close together and stuck there for too long.

Benches lined the room and there were two barred cashier cages on one side. The other side funneled into a long aisle that led into the main part of the police station. Sylvia's friend, Glory Beckett, worked as a police sketch artist and her workroom was down that hall and off the main desk area.

Sylvia started in that direction.

Glory might know a shortcut to get the kids out. The two of them had worked the system before. Sylvia said a quick prayer that Glory would be in her office. Yesterday morning Glory had called, worried about having dinner last night with Matthew Curtis, the minister who'd come to Seattle from Dry Creek to ask—Sylvia sincerely hoped—Glory to marry him. In Sylvia's opinion, it was about time. Glory hadn't been herself since they'd come back from Dry Creek after Christmas.

The door to Glory's workroom was closed and a note had been taped to the front of it. "She'll be in later today—try back again. The Captain."

Well, Sylvia thought, so much for some friendly help. She glanced at the police officer who was sitting at the desk in the open area across from Glory's workroom. She wondered how late Glory would be. It was almost ten o'clock now.

"Do you know—" she began.

"I don't know anything, lady," the officer said, clearly busy and exasperated. "All I got is what you see. I can't be answering questions every five minutes. You'll have to wait just like the other guy." He glared down the hallway.

"The other guy?" Sylvia's eyes followed his gaze.

The bench was at the end of the hall and a square of light shone in through a side window. That was the only natural light. In addition a row of ceiling lights burned weakly, leaving more shadows than anything. A man sat on the hall bench, staring at the brown wall across from him. Sylvia was too far away to see his face. But she didn't need to see it to know who he was. How many gray Stetson hats were there in Seattle in February?

The hall seemed far from the hub of the station and the noises that filled the rest of the building were muffled here. Sylvia was aware of the sharp snap of her heels as she marched down the hall.

Garth Elkton was the last person she wanted to face today. Correction. He was the second to the last. Mrs. Buckwalter was the absolute last, and as friendly as the two of them had been when they parted yesterday, she wasn't sure that what one discovered wouldn't be shared soon enough by both of them.

Ordinarily she wouldn't mind. She didn't have anything to hide. But this... She shook her head. She knew it would not look good to their potential sponsor to find all thirty-one kids from her center behind bars this morning.

As eccentric as Mrs. Buckwalter appeared, even she could hardly think this was a good beginning to their plans. Sylvia only hoped the woman wouldn't find out about the arrests. The older woman had made a verbal commitment yesterday. But nothing had been put in writing. Everything could change if Mrs. Buckwalter knew about the kids being in jail and had sent Garth to find out whether the arrests were justified.

Sylvia was halfway down the hall when the hat moved.

Garth didn't know why someone would put a stone bench in the hall of a police station. He'd perched on mountain rocks that were more comfortable. Not that anything about the building had been designed for comfort. Made a man feel as if he was locked up behind bars already. Guilty before he was even sent to trial.

The only good thing about the building was the hard linoleum floor. He loved the sounds of a high-heeled woman walking across a hard surface. Something about the tip-tap was thoroughly feminine. He hoped Sylvia would walk right up to him before she started to talk.

She didn't.

"What are you doing here?" Sylvia was a good five feet from him. The question could have been friendly. But it wasn't.

Garth eyeballed her cautiously. Sylvia had more quills than a porcupine and, unless he missed his guess, she'd just as soon bury them one by one in his hide. Slowly. He'd seen what tangling with a mad porcupine could do. He'd just as soon save his skin.

"Glory called me," Garth answered quietly. That much he could tell her. He wasn't sure her pride would want to know Glory had asked him to help keep Sylvia calm until she got there. "Asked me to meet her here."

Garth watched Sylvia's face. She might have porcupine quills, but her eyes were the tenderest blue he'd ever seen. And right now he wasn't sure whether they were snapping with anger or tears. Maybe both. Her cheeks were red and he noticed she hadn't pinned her hair back, instead sweeping her coal-black tresses back into a scarf.

"That's the only reason?" Sylvia eyed him doubtfully.

Garth smiled. "Well, she did tell me they had coffee here. I haven't seen any yet, but she said she'd get me a cup. Almond flavored."

Sylvia seemed to relax. "Glory does like her flavored coffee."

Garth decided disarming a porcupine wasn't such a difficult task. He moved over on the bench and Sylvia sank down beside him. He took a deep breath. How was it she always smelled of peaches? Made him think of a summer orchard even though it was raining outside and the humidity was so high that the concrete walls were sweating.

If it wasn't for the echo in the hallway, Garth would whistle a tune. He was that happy. Sylvia was sitting down beside him. She hadn't thrown any barbs at him. Life was good. Forget the echoes in the hallway, he thought. A good whistle would cheer everyone up. Garth drew his breath and then it came.

"I thought maybe Mrs. Buckwalter had sent you," Sylvia said quietly. "I thought she'd asked you to spy."

Garth choked on the whistle. "What?" His tongue was still tangled. How did she know about Mrs. Buckwalter? The older woman hadn't told him until he walked her to her car yesterday that she had a message for him from the FBI. She'd asked him again about infiltrating the rustling ring as a spy. He was going to dismiss the idea just as he'd done before—when she reminded him of the kids. The kids made him pause. Still, Sylvia could not know about the FBI's offer. He himself was sworn to secrecy. That was the way these things worked. Anyone who watched television knew that much.

"I don't know anything to spy about," Garth answered carefully. He wondered if Mrs. Buckwalter had told Sylvia. He always thought it was a mistake

for the FBI to use civilians. They never knew when
to keep quiet.

"So Mrs. Buckwalter doesn't know?" Sylvia said,
relief evident in her voice.

Garth eyed her. Sylvia had leaned against the
bench's stone back and actually appeared comfortable. Garth decided there was one advantage to the
stone. The pitted beige texture made Sylvia's hair
look silken in contrast. The black strands softly
caught in the roughness of the concrete and flew
around her head like a halo.

"About—?" Garth left the question to dangle.

Sylvia straightened up and looked at him critically.

Garth nervously tipped back his hat. He'd taken it
off earlier, but then put it back on.

"If I tell you, you have to promise not to tell,"
Sylvia said seriously.

Garth half smiled. She reminded him of a school-
child when she said that. He raised one hand in oath.
"Cross my heart and hope to die."

Sylvia smiled back faintly, so quick and slight
Garth would have thought he'd imagined it if her eyes
hadn't flashed, too.

Then she was solemn and worried. "The kids have
been arrested."

Garth wished he could take the worry off her face.
Taking care of some thirty kids was too much for
anyone, even Sylvia. "Glory told me there was trouble," Garth said. "Actually, Matthew told me—he
seemed in a hurry and didn't tell me much. He'd
called from the hotel lobby before he left this morning."

Sylvia nodded. "I'm waiting to see the kids. But

first I wanted to talk to Glory and see what chances
we have—maybe a kindhearted judge will help us.''

Quick footsteps came toward them and Garth heard
them before Sylvia. "Help is on the way.''

"We've got to hurry," Glory Beckett said as she
rushed down the hall and stood beside Sylvia. "I've
got ten minutes on Judge Mason's calendar—now.''

"Well, let's go." Sylvia stood. She and Glory had
been through this drill before.

Judge Mason sat behind the bench in his court-
room. On another day, Sylvia would have appreciated
the carved mahogany molding in the room. The court
reporter was present as well as a lawyer from the
D.A.'s office.

"Just so we're clear." Judge Mason looked over a
list he held in his hand and then looked directly at
Sylvia. "We've got an assortment of assault charges.
Aiding and abetting. You want to post bail for all
thirty-one of these juveniles?''

Sylvia nodded. "If I can. I have this." She held up
the watch Mrs. Buckwalter had given her yesterday.
"I'm hoping it'll be enough.''

"A watch?" The judge looked skeptical.

"Diamonds," Sylvia assured him as she twisted
the watchband so it would sparkle.

The judge grunted. "Doubt it'll be enough for all
thirty-one. But I tell you what. I'm going to keep it
low—ten thousand dollars apiece on the assault and
five thousand dollars on the rest. I'm going to over-
look the probation violations. You can bail half of
them out with the watch.''

"Half?" Sylvia's hopes sank. She couldn't take
half of the kids and leave the rest.

"I'll cover the other half," Garth said quietly.

Sylvia turned. She'd forgotten he'd followed her and Glory.

"You'll need collateral." The judge frowned slightly. "A few hundred thousand."

"I've got it," Garth said.

"But I can't repay you if—" Sylvia protested. She was used to risking everything on kids that might or might not come through. But she couldn't be responsible for someone else losing money. "The kids mean well, but there's no guarantee."

"I know," Garth said, and then grinned. "But since they're going to be on my ranch, I'll have a pretty good say in whether or not they show up for their court hearing."

"Which will be six weeks from now," the judge said. He peered over his glasses at Sylvia. "I know how you feel about these kids. We've covered that ground before. I don't need to tell you how important it is that they are back here for court."

"I know." Sylvia felt the rubber band inside of her relax.

"And get them out to that ranch in Montana as soon as you can," the judge said as he stood. He then turned and left the room.

"Thank you." Sylvia turned to Garth. "I can't thank you enough."

"Well, jail is no place for kids," Garth muttered.

"And you—" Sylvia turned to Glory.

Glory just smiled. "I'd best get back to work."

Sylvia looked more closely at her friend. Glory looked different. Her auburn hair was loose and flowing, instead of pulled back. But that wasn't everything. Then Sylvia realized what it was. Glory was happy. Beaming, in fact.

"Have a nice evening last night?" Sylvia asked cautiously. Yesterday, when she'd talked to Glory about her date with Matthew Curtis, Glory had been grim.

"Mmm-hmm," Glory said, lifting her hand to sweep back her hair.

"A diamond!" Sylvia saw what her friend was flaunting. "You're engaged!"

Glory laughed with glee and nodded.

"Oh, my!" Sylvia reached up and hugged her friend. "Congratulations!"

"Finally," Garth muttered. "Glad to see he had the nerve."

"Nerve?" Glory looked over at Garth, puzzled. "Why would he need nerve?"

Garth snorted. That's how much women knew about the whole business.

Chapter Four

The leather work gloves on Garth's hands were stiff from the cold. He was twisting a strand of barbed wire to see exactly where the cut had been made. Not that it made much difference. This time the rustlers had succeeded. His crew counted twenty cows missing.

"Might be they'll show up on the other side of the Big Sheep," Jess, one of his new hands, offered. Jess was nearing sixty, too old to be out riding the range in most outfits, but Garth had hired him five months ago, after all the other big outfits had turned the man down. In Garth's eyes, every man deserved the right to prove himself, and Garth assigned him to light duty in the calving barn. Jess had been pointedly grateful ever since.

"They must have hit last night and it's already late afternoon. I should have been paying more attention," Garth muttered as he pulled his Stetson down farther. The air around him was so cold it hung like smoke. A wet frost had hit last night and the barbed wire had stayed iced all day. Garth had thought he was safe from the rustlers in weather like this. The thieves must be desperate to get back into operation if they'd work in this cold.

"You can't check all your fences every day," Jess protested loyally. "Not with the land you have. No, you couldn't have known."

Garth grunted. He'd never know if he could have known or not. He wasn't concentrating like normal on business at hand. For the past two days he'd thought of little else but the camp he had promised to Sylvia. The bubble of euphoria—that Sylvia was coming to his ranch—had slowly deflated as he drove back to Montana.

No, he'd given almost no thought to his cattle. He had bigger worries. He had a three-day head start. What was he going to do with thirty teenagers? And, worse yet, what was he going to do with Sylvia?

He'd assigned every hand on his place something to clean and he'd put his sister Francis in charge of the inspections. He missed his son, but the boy had gone to Chicago to visit an old friend. Garth wished his son were here to help keep the men happy. Except for Jess, the men had all threatened to quit. They said they'd hired on to ride herd on cattle, not scrub walls. Even after Garth promised them a bonus, they still muttered. But they cleaned—cowboy-style—using a broom like a shovel and a rag like a whip.

Francis insisted they use ammonia and now the whole ranch smelled of it. Garth took a cautious whiff of his hand. Even through the glove he could still smell the stuff. The one good thing about it all was that Francis brightened considerably as she took to her task. She'd still not told Garth what was troubling her and he knew better than to push. But it was good to have his sister smiling again, and she'd promised to extend her visit until summer.

Sound traveled clearly on a crisp cold afternoon and Garth heard the rumble of a load-pulling engine before he saw the bus crawl over the hill that led to the main house.

"We best get back," Garth said as he walked over to the horses. Garth put his leg into the stirrup and lifted himself up. "We've got company."

Sylvia stood in the long wood-frame building. So this was the bunkhouse. Late-afternoon shadows filled the corners but she didn't turn on the overhead light. She could see what she needed to see. The plank floor was unpolished and smooth from years of wear. The small row of windows were half covered with frost and they lacked curtains. Eight cots were lined against each of the long sides of the building.

Puffs of heat came toward her, fighting the cold air. Metal grates along the wall indicated gas heating, but most of the heat seemed to be coming from a potbelly stove near the door. The stove door was closed but the bright glow of a steady fire shone through the door cracks. But as cozy as the inside of the bunkhouse was, the view out the windows of the afternoon sun reflecting off the snow-capped mountains was breathtaking. The girls would like it. They might not admit to it, but they would like it. She could hear the girls now, chattering as they walked to the ranch house from the rented bus.

Above the voices of the teenagers, she could hear Mrs. Buckwalter's deep laugh. Sylvia had to give the older woman credit. She hadn't just written a check. She'd spent hours shopping and packing for their camp. Finally, she had confidently asked if she could ride with them to camp. Sylvia would have refused, but she could use an extra adult on the trip, especially since Mrs. Buckwalter had a quelling influence on the rowdy teenagers. No one misbehaved around Mrs. Buckwalter; whether it was the promise of new skis or the fact that the older woman formally called each of the kids by their full name, Sylvia did not know.

Sylvia, herself, kept watching the woman cautiously, half expecting something to happen that would cause Mrs. Buckwalter's generous enthusiasm to disappear. Surely one of the woman's relatives would step up and say Mrs. Buckwalter wasn't competent to donate large sums of money. That was one reason Sylvia was glad to be away from Seattle. She doubted any of the accountants would bother with them when they were so far away.

Mrs. Buckwalter had made all the arrangements. The bus had been rented for a month even though the driver would fly back to Seattle once the suitcases were unloaded. The driver would return and drive them back when they were ready to go.

Sylvia looked around the bunkhouse again, reassuring herself that she had made the right decision. She had excused herself from the others, saying she needed to change her blouse. She had spilled coffee on it this morning, but the small spot wouldn't ordinarily stop her. No, she wanted a few minutes alone to gather her thoughts before she faced Garth again.

She remembered being in Garth's house that morning when he'd found her half-frozen and had brought her to his ranch. She could almost picture where he must be sitting now. He'd have his boots off and his feet propped up in front of the fireplace. Garth hadn't come to the door when the bus pulled up. It had been Francis who stood on the porch and called out, asking everyone to come up to the ranch house for a cup of hot cocoa and some cookies.

Sylvia had asked Mrs. Buckwalter to tell Francis that she'd be up soon. She had thought a five-hundred-mile bus ride would prepare her to meet anyone again. But it hadn't.

Now here she was—hiding out in the bunkhouse like a coward. She shook her head ruefully as she set her suitcase on one of the chairs near the stove. Even with the stove's heat, it was still a little chilly in the room. Sylvia took off her coat and opened her suitcase. She'd be quick. Maybe she'd put on her red blouse for courage.

Garth swore as he rode over the hill and looked down at his house. The bus was parked in the driveway and he could hear the sounds of voices coming from the living room. Knowing Francis, she had everyone inside thawing while she fed them cookies. Garth hoped she kept everyone there for a few minutes. He wasn't ready to meet Sylvia. She was a city woman and he didn't think she'd appreciate being greeted by a man whose hands smelled of ammonia and whose feet smelled of cattle. Fortunately he could slip into the bunkhouse and wash up before he headed up to the house.

Garth opened the door to the bunkhouse.

Mercy!

Since the time he was a small boy, Garth had been taught to close the door behind him in winter. It was a cardinal rule in these mountains. Heat was precious. But, so help him, he couldn't move.

Sylvia stood there. Her midnight-black hair was loose around her shoulders. Her turquoise eyes were opened in surprise. She was even more beautiful than he remembered. It wasn't until he noticed the red start to creep up her neck that he realized she wasn't wearing a blouse. And the lace contraption she wore for a bra made him warm even though it was cold enough inside the bunkhouse to frost the windows.

"Excuse me," Garth finally managed to say. His manners kicked in and he stepped inside. "I didn't mean to let the cold air in."

Once he was inside, Garth kicked himself again. He'd obviously stepped the wrong way. Sylvia looked embarrassed and he certainly didn't mean to embarrass her. "Don't mind me. I didn't know someone was in here. I can leave. I just came in to wash my hands."

Garth turned to go.

"It's all right. You can wash up here." Sylvia spoke. Garth had fished on creeks with thinner ice than Sylvia had in her voice. "The sink's in the back."

Sylvia wrapped her blouse around herself, waiting for Garth to pass.

What could a man do when he'd done everything wrong so far? Garth walked down the aisle between the beds to one of the sinks at the end of the bunkhouse.

He'd turned on the faucet before he looked up. Hallelujah! The mirror above the sink gave him a clear view of Sylvia. Her skin was golden in the light from the stove. Her hair shone like black coal. It took him a full minute to realize that Sylvia was half-frozen.

He'd seen that same stiffness in fawns caught in the headlights of a tractor.

He lowered his eyes and quickly washed his hands before turning off the faucet.

"There's lots of extra towels if you or the girls need them," Garth said as he turned around. Maybe Sylvia was shy. He pointed. "In the cabinet right here."

"We'll find them, I'm sure," Sylvia said.

Garth sighed. She had her blouse buttoned to her chin and her arms crossed.

"Anything you need, just ask." Garth wondered how mannerly he would need to be to make Sylvia smile at him. She certainly wasn't smiling now. She did nod.

"Well, okay, then," Garth said. He thought about removing his hat; but it seemed foolish since he hadn't taken if off when he'd first entered the bunkhouse. Instead, he nodded, too. "I guess the others are up at the house?"

Sylvia nodded.

Garth was defeated. He nodded again. This time he closed the door very carefully on the way out.

The sound of teenagers greeted Garth as he stepped on his front porch. He hoped they, at least, would talk to him.

Sylvia sat down. She was out of breath. She hadn't had an episode like that in years. She thought she had gotten a handle on her fears about men. And usually she was all right. Her days at the youth center had helped her deal with violence and fear. But sometimes something would happen that would take her by surprise and she wasn't in control. Like just now. With

Garth. He'd appeared so suddenly and she'd thought she was alone. She hadn't had time to steel herself, to hide her primitive reaction.

She wondered if he knew she had been paralyzed. She hoped not. It wasn't his fault she'd had bad experiences with men and violence. And she didn't want to hear his apology or, worse yet, the polite questions that invited her to tell her whole sorry story. Sylvia reached into her suitcase and brought out her Bible.

She sought the comfort of Psalm 91. The psalm had been with her for years and it always served to anchor her. "He is my refuge and my fortress: my God; in him will I trust." She repeated the verse. The familiar words soothed her. The psalmist was right. God was her fortress. She relied on that fact every day of her life. She hid herself in the folds of His love. He protected her. There was no other way she could have taken her fear of violence and used it to start erasing violence in the lives of the kids who came to the center.

But lately she had begun to wonder if she could continue living in that fortress. She was safe, but she was also alone. She knew God would not want her fear to be a prison. She closed her eyes in weariness. *Dear Lord, show me how not to be so afraid. Show me how to stop my fears.*

Tiny flakes of snow were falling by the time Sylvia stepped out of the bunkhouse to walk to the main house. She'd put several pieces of wood in the bunkhouse stove. It was almost dark outside even though it must not have been later than six o'clock.

Snowflakes settled on Sylvia's cheeks as she lifted her face in the early-night sky. She'd never seen darkness fall like this in Seattle—a blanket of thick gray covered the sky. No stars sparkled. No moon dipped in the sky. When night fell completely it would be deep black. She was glad the camp could start in the winter. It was a lovely time of year here.

Squares of golden light showed the windows of the main house. Sylvia heard the hum of voices before she climbed the steps to the house.

"Sylvia!" Francis opened the large, oak door before Sylvia had a chance to knock. The woman was wearing a denim skirt and tennis shoes. She had a dish towel draped over her shoulder and a plate of cookies in one hand. The smell of fresh-baked oatmeal cookies mixed with the soothing smell of real wood burning in the fireplace. "Come in. You must be frozen! I was just going to send Garth down to check on you. I just turned the gas heat on this afternoon. I wasn't sure you'd be here tonight. It's too cold—"

"There's a fire going," Sylvia protested as she shook the snow off her hair. She looked around the room. Francis looked as friendly as she remembered. The teenagers were grouped around something in the dining room. A few squeals from the girls told Sylvia she wouldn't get their attention soon. "It will be fine—"

"I don't want the girls to be uncomfortable," Francis said worriedly. She put the plate of cookies down on a small table near the door. "I know how girls like nice things."

"They like cookies even better," Sylvia said. She doubted the kids had had homemade cookies in years. Most of their mothers worked long hours. Cookies were a luxury.

"You'll have one?" Francis offered the plate. "I

haven't made any since Tavis—that's Garth's son— is away. I put in extra raisins. Kids generally like raisins."

"Thank you." Sylvia took a cookie. "And thank you for the warm welcome. You've gone to so much extra trouble."

"I've been looking forward to everyone coming since Garth first called."

"And you've been busy. I saw that all the cots were made up."

Francis smiled. "We worked on the girls' bunk-house first. I had Garth do some rewiring so they have more outlets for blow-drying their hair, and he even put in a telephone that goes between the bunkhouse and here."

"A telephone?" Sylvia said in surprise.

"I told Garth you might feel more comfortable that way." Francis looked more relaxed than she had in December when Sylvia had lain unconscious on the living room sofa. "That way, when you're in the house with us, you'll be able to call down and see that everything's all right. That is—" Francis looked shy "—I'm hoping you'll stay in the house with us. I told Garth he was to ask you. We have so much to plan—with Glory's wedding and all—"

"Wedding! The last I talked to Glory, they were going to go to a justice of the peace."

"Oh, not for our angel! Well, they are going to a justice for the wedding, but not for the reception. Not with Mrs. Hargrove around." Francis smiled. "When they said they didn't have patience for the details, Mrs. Hargrove told them she'd organize it all for them—this Saturday night. The whole town is in on it. I'm baking the wedding cake and you're to be the

maid of honor.'' Francis hesitated. ''I know you
haven't had a chance to talk to Glory since you've
been driving here, but she told Mrs. Hargrove you
were the one she wants to stand beside her when they
repeat their vows here. I'm to help make you a
dress—so you see, you need to stay in the house with
us. I told Garth he was to insist.''

''Oh, I couldn't—'' Sylvia bit off her words. Garth
hadn't mentioned anything to her earlier about staying
in the house. He might not want her there. They were
renters, after all. Not guests. ''I couldn't leave the
girls alone.''

''But with the phone you can call anytime,'' Francis protested, the disappointment evident in her voice.
''And later when you hire more camp counselors.''

''Oh, I decided not to hire any more camp counselors. I couldn't find any before I left Seattle, and
Pat and Melissa thought they could handle it if I pitch
in for the evening shift.''

''Nonsense.'' The booming voice came from the
side. Sylvia had not seen Mrs. Buckwalter walk up to
them. ''There's no reason for you to pitch in. Go
ahead and stay in the house. I daresay Francis would
like the company. Besides, I was talking to Jess
here—'' she jabbed an elbow in the direction of the
old cowboy who stood beside her with his hat in his
hands. ''Seems the young people in this town need
more jobs. A couple of them would do good crowd
control for you. If we don't have enough money to
cover it, I'll phone Seattle and ask for more.''

That was the one thing Sylvia didn't want Mrs.
Buckwalter to do. ''There's no need to bother the
foundation. I'm sure we can pay them with what we
have.''

Mrs. Buckwalter nodded. ''Robert's still in Europe anyway.''

Sylvia had a sinking feeling. She'd never heard Mrs. Buckwalter mention a name before and she'd wondered why. ''Is that Robert Buckwalter? Your son? The one who manages the foundation?''

Mrs. Buckwalter nodded.

Sylvia's feeling sank to the bottom. ''He's been in Europe for a while, hasn't he?''

Mrs. Buckwalter nodded. ''But don't worry. He'll approve your camp when he gets back. I keep telling him he needs to diversify. Him and his museums. All that old stuff. I told him before he went to Europe he needed to spread his wings. Invest in the future not the past, I said. I'm sure he'll love this camp of yours.''

Sylvia wished she was as optimistic.

''The Evans girl would make a good counselor,'' Jess interrupted nervously. ''She and Duane Edison have done all right with their restaurant in town— even if it is only spaghetti and hamburgers—but they need more if they're going to buy that farm.''

''Linda's perfect,'' Francis agreed. ''She's ridden herd on a couple of younger brothers ever since she was twelve. You wouldn't go wrong with her. She'll let the kids get away with just enough so they think they're having fun without getting into trouble.''

''We'd really only need someone nights,'' Sylvia said. ''She might not want that.''

Francis shrugged. ''Sounds perfect. Then she can keep the restaurant open days.''

''She'd have to meet the girls first,'' Sylvia said. The fourteen girls who had come with her all had good hearts. She'd swear to it. But they also had rough edges and even rougher tongues. If they didn't like a staff person, they could make the person's life miserable.

"I'll call her now and see when she can come over," Francis said as she headed for the telephone on the stand by the sofa.

A snort of half-suppressed laughter drew Sylvia's attention back to the knot of teenagers packed into the room off the living room. Sylvia remembered that room as being Garth's office, but she must be wrong.

"Yeah, Croc—yeah, Croc—" A simple yell grew in proportion along with some foot stomping and whistling.

"Garth must be ahead," Mrs. Buckwalter said complacently.

"But what—" Sylvia started to walk toward the room.

Mrs. Buckwalter followed. "They call him Croc after that Australian man."

"But Garth's not Australian." Sylvia paused at the threshold to the room and looked back at Mrs. Buckwalter.

"It's the whip," the older woman confided. "The boys are quite taken with it."

"Surely he doesn't have that whip in there!" Sylvia had to press her way through teenage bodies to get inside the room. If Garth was teaching those boys how to whip the hide off of something, she'd whip *his* hide. They didn't need to learn more violent ways to fight. They needed to learn—

"—sewing!" Sylvia was dumbfounded. Garth and Trong, an undersize Vietnamese boy who was the quietest of the bunch that had come with her, each sat on a straight-back chair. Each held a needle in one hand and a shirt in the other. She'd swear they were sewing buttons on the shirts. "Buttons?"

"Trong had a button missing," Mrs. Buckwalter quietly announced as though that explained everything.

Sylvia was speechless. A button missing! She'd go crazy if she worried about missing buttons on shirts. She was lucky to get the kids into neutral, nongang clothes. Buttons were the least of her worries.

"Garth bet Trong he could sew on a button faster than Trong could," one of the teenager boys standing nearby told Sylvia. "So we took bets."

"Not for money, I hope," Sylvia said sternly. She had a strict rule against betting for money.

"'Course not," the boy said indignantly. "We set it up boys against girls—losers do dishes for a week."

"Well, then—" Sylvia looked around. Every face was focused on the contest, except for… Some woman's intuition told her that several of the older girls weren't watching the buttons as closely as the boys were.

Sylvia looked again at the scene before her. She couldn't blame the girls. What grown man would take his shirt off in the presence of teenage girls and not expect them to notice the way the light shone on his chest, casting him in subtle shades of golden brown? How could he expect them not to notice the tiny ripple in his muscles as his fingers moved the needle furiously in and out? Or the way the strength in his back would remind any woman of those old sculptures of Native American warriors riding a stallion off to battle?

Sylvia was going to call a halt to the contest when she noticed Garth was watching Trong intently. The boy was biting his tongue in concentration as he worked to pull the needle through the shirt fabric and then dip down to poke the needle through again. Sylvia noted that Garth, without being obvious, was pacing his needle stabs to match Trong's.

Sylvia let the contest continue for Trong's sake. The boy had always been quiet at the center, as though he were still measuring the worth of the people there. He'd been pushed into a gang by older brothers, and the center had become a refuge for him.

Trong's parents had emigrated from Vietnam after the war and had moved to a Vietnamese neighborhood in Tacoma. Sylvia had often prayed for Trong, asking God to show her how to win his trust. She'd been surprised when his mother had signed the permission slip Sylvia had had to obtain from all the parents for this trip.

A cheer filled the little room as Garth and Trong brought the needle up for the last time. It took a moment for the boys and girls to look at each other suspiciously.

"We won." One of the girls claimed the moment. "Garth finished first."

"Did not," one of the boys declared defiantly. "Trong's our man and he pulled his needle out first."

"Trong. Trong." The boys started to chant. "He's our man. Trong."

The Vietnamese boy looked at the floor, but Sylvia could see a smile on his lips. Victory was sweet for the boy.

"But we won," one of the girls said, looking up at Garth for confirmation.

"I think I was just a little bit slower than Trong here," Garth said. But then he flashed a smile at the girls. "Don't worry, though. I'll help you with the dishes."

Sylvia could see the girls exchange hesitant glances. It was clear that the thought of Garth helping them with the dishes made the defeat more than bearable.

"Okay, then," several of the girls said, and one added, "But you do the pots and pans."

"Gladly," Garth agreed as he stood and slipped his arms into the sleeves of his shirt.

Sylvia almost groaned. She'd planned on struggling with finances on this trip. And quarreling teenagers. And cold weather. And plain food, if necessary. But she'd not come expecting the inevitable crushes it looked like Garth would inspire.

Lord have mercy on them all.

Chapter Five

It was only nine o'clock in the morning and Garth was tired. Bone-weary, butt-dragging tired. He hadn't been this tired after riding rodeo in Miles City last summer.

No, he thought to himself as he hid out in the barn, this kid-rearing stuff would wear a person out. No matter what he was doing, thirty pairs of eyes were watching him. No matter where he went, thirty teenagers came, too. He was beginning to wonder how mother ducks could stand it with all their ducklings following them and mimicking their actions. And the worst part was that he'd come to realize he wasn't a fit mother duck. He'd burned his finger on the stove this morning and—before he thought about it—he swore. Ten kids heard him. He knew these kids weren't choir boys. They could probably outcuss him. But what came out of their mouths and what came out of his mouth were two different things. He was determined to be a good role model if it killed him.

Right now he was thinking it just might do that.

And if it was going to kill him, it might as well do it now that breakfast was over.

He must have flipped ten dozen pancakes. All flipped to order—some deep dark for the guys who said they'd heard about bacteria in eggs. Others lightly seared for the group that didn't like them crusty. Half of them with bacon strips enfolded in the middle. He was thankful Sylvia had sense enough to put her foot down about eggs—the eggs were scrambled. Take them as you get them or not at all.

A slow grin spread over Garth's face as he leaned back into a bale of hay. It was almost worth it all to watch Sylvia's face during the whole production. She confided in him halfway through that she'd never fixed a meal for all the kids before. He nodded like he wouldn't have known if she hadn't told him. But it was obvious. Sylvia was as unprepared as he was. The kids ate more than the branding crew he fed each fall. He would have suspected they'd gotten up in the middle of the night for a game of football, but the snow was smooth on the ground. They must just eat this much. It was an alarming thought.

"It'll be macaroni and cheese for lunch," Sylvia whispered frantically as she stirred another pan of scrambled eggs. "Out of a box."

"Too many carbohydrates," Mrs. Buckwalter objected. The older woman had decided not to leave with the bus driver when he left late last night. This morning she'd tied a towel around her dress and was frying her seventh pan of bacon.

"We have a bag of apples," Garth offered. "Give them some raw carrots and an apple and they'll be set."

"Makes them sound like horses," Sylvia protested.

"They eat like horses!"

Mrs. Buckwalter grunted. "Maybe by dinner I can call my chef back home and get a big recipe for something stir-fried."

"Can't stir-fry for this many people," Sylvia said as she scooped the scrambled eggs into a bowl and handed it to a waiting teenager. "Not unless you've got a big wok."

Mrs. Buckwalter looked at Garth. He shook his head and shrugged. "Sorry."

"Well, surely people have something for crowds this big." Mrs. Buckwalter reached up to wipe a thin sheen of sweat off her forehead. She was beginning to look a little frantic herself. "I wonder if my chef could deliver something—you know like florists do—you order local and someone else delivers. Let your fingers do the cooking—that sort of thing."

"We'll think of something." Garth soothed the older woman. "I can always make hamburgers—" he flexed his hand and grimaced "—I'm just getting the flipping down."

"We vote for hamburgers," one of the girls said as a group of them held out their plates for more pancakes. "And paper plates so there'll be no cleanup."

Dishes. Garth groaned inside. The cooking was only the beginning. Then he needed to help with dishes. "Dishes will be fun." He tried to sound enthusiastic. "Lots of fun."

The girls giggled as they accepted their pancakes and walked back to the tables Francis had set up in the living room.

Garth was proud of himself for managing to be a good role model. He'd been giving some thought to what Matthew had told him about living the Christian life. Matthew insisted grace was the way to heaven. But Garth didn't trust grace or mercy. Not that mercy wasn't all right for some folks. Especially people that didn't have anything else going for them.

But Garth wasn't willing to bet his eternal happiness on something as uncontrollable as mercy. Not when he could beat most opponents by himself. No, he wasn't going to trust mercy. Not when he could pull up his shirtsleeves and work his way to redemption.

Yes, sir, he thought to himself in satisfaction. He could do it. Look at him. Not only was he flipping pancakes, he was spreading morning cheer. That had to rack up the points.

"Don't encourage them," Sylvia said stiffly.

"What—?" Garth protested.

"You know what I mean." Sylvia set the egg spoon down in the pan sharply. "I won't have their heads turned with—with—" She looked at him in exasperation. "With you."

"Me?"

Garth didn't get an explanation. Instead, Sylvia held her chin high, speared one of the remaining pancakes, tossed it on a plate and headed out to the tables in the living room.

"Me?" Garth asked again.

This time Mrs. Buckwalter answered him. Well, she didn't so much answer him as chuckle. "Ah, yes," the older woman said with what Garth could only describe as glee.

Then Mrs. Buckwalter took a pancake, too, and topping it off with three hot bacon strips, she followed Sylvia into the living room.

Garth decided to load a plate with the leftover pancakes, all three of them. One burnt, one broken and
one...well, one that wasn't bad. Then he headed out
to the barn. For generations the barn had been a refuge for misunderstood men. He'd eat his pancakes
there.

Sylvia squared her shoulders. She'd sat down to eat
her breakfast. But she couldn't. Something kept nagging at her and nagging at her. She'd driven a man
out of his home. He hadn't even bothered to put on
a heavy coat and it was cold outside. That Stetson he
wore wouldn't keep his ears warm, either. Sometimes,
she thought, treating others like yourself could be a
tiresome business. She owed him an apology. He did
seem unaware of the crushes he was inspiring. Perhaps he was innocent.

Never let it be said, she told herself as she stood,
that she had falsely accused someone and not had the
personal fortitude to apologize for it.

"I'm sorry." She said the words into the empty air
of the barn. She said them loudly and clearly so there
would be no need to tarry. A good clean apology and
she would be done with it and back to her breakfast.
Giving an apology, unlike firing a musket, did not
require one to see the white of an enemy's eyes.

She knew Garth was in the barn someplace. She'd
just seen him enter, carrying a plate. Still, she looked
into the shadows. The barn did not have windows.
The only light came from the huge, cut-out door that
swung up from the barn's side like a garage door.
Bales of straw were stacked in one corner of the barn,
next to a series of stalls. A trough of water, with a
faucet at one end, stood against the far side of the

barn. The sunlight filtered into the gray shadows. The straw was musty and made the air heavy, almost warm.

The only response Sylvia got to her apology was a grunt from somewhere in the bowels of the barn.

"I said I was sorry," she repeated. There, she'd said it twice. That should certainly be enough.

The grunt this time sounded closer.

"You shouldn't eat out here anyway. There could be rats."

"Rats!"

A form moved in the shadows and walked indignantly toward her, carrying a plate. "There's no rats in my barn! I keep a clean barn. Look around."

"All I meant was that you should eat inside—with people."

Garth stepped out of the shadows and smiled. "Are you inviting me to have breakfast with you?"

Garth had pushed his Stetson back and she could see his eyes. Warm brown eyes that teased. His cheeks were freshly shaved and the collar of his shirt was crisply ironed.

But it was the smile that held her gaze. Sylvia wasn't sure about that smile. Just this morning she'd seen a cat with that expression looking at a bowl of new cream after Francis brought the milk to the house.

"Well, no, not *me*—" Sylvia spread her hands. "You should have breakfast with us—the people here."

"Eating breakfast with thirty teenagers isn't my idea of the best way to start a day."

Sylvia decided she had done enough. She turned to leave. "Suit yourself. Be a hermit."

* * *

Unfortunately, Garth thought, even hermits have to do dishes. Especially when they'd promised fourteen young girls they'd help.

"I got soap in my eyes!" One of the girls tugged at Garth's arm. "Look at my eyes."

Garth looked down into the girl's eyes. They didn't look red, but maybe the soap hadn't had time to settle in yet. "Blink, and then we'll rinse them with cold water."

Garth was up to his elbows in hot water and suds. He was tackling the frying skillets from breakfast and the plates. The silverware was soaking in a tub and the girls were washing the cups and glasses.

He hadn't realized washing dishes was such a perilous task until everyone started getting soap in their eyes. He was beginning to wonder if they shouldn't do away with the soap and just sterilize the dishes in scalding water. Maybe he could rig up some kind of a hose and they could put the dishes outside while they sterilized them.

"I've got soap, too," another girl wailed just as Sylvia entered the kitchen.

Garth looked down at a pair of wide brown eyes. He took longer this time. He'd just as soon look at the girl's eyes as look at what his heart wanted him to see.

Sylvia had been outside, and when she entered the kitchen she unwrapped a red wool scarf from around her head. The static from the wool made her hair swirl around her in tender tiny strands. They softened her face until she looked young and vulnerable. The cold had made her cheeks—and her nose—pink. The pink in her cheeks made her blue eyes stand out even more. She was adorable.

And Garth knew he dared not look at her. If he did, his eyes might reveal the feelings churning inside him. He didn't know Sylvia well, but he knew her well enough to know he needed to go slow with her. She wasn't ready for the sledgehammer of emotions that were hitting at him.

"Your eyes look fine to me," Garth finally said instead to the girl. "Maybe it was just a little speck of soap."

"I think the girls have helped enough," Sylvia said as she took off her coat and hung it on a peg by the door. "Pat is waiting for them before he starts the math lessons."

The girls groaned, but they obediently folded their dish towels and filed out of the kitchen.

Garth took his hands out of the dishwater. He knew women liked sensitive men these days—men who weren't afraid of domestic chores—but he doubted dishpan hands were considered sexy.

Besides, he had better things to do than wash dishes. Sylvia might not be ready to know how he felt about her, but he could take one small step.

He figured his moments alone with Sylvia—with teenagers in the house—were going to be few and far between. He needed to make the most of them when he had them.

"I'll let everything soak for a minute," he said as he dried his hands on the towel wrapped around his waist. The towel! That was another thing that had to go. He almost wished he had a reason to bring out the leather chaps he used for roundup time. Women always seemed to like chaps. Even a man doing dishes would look good in chaps.

"That's good," Sylvia said as she walked over to

the kitchen table and sat down on a chair. "I wanted to talk to you about something anyway."

Garth congratulated himself. That had to be a good sign. Maybe Sylvia wasn't as indifferent to him as he thought. He walked over and sat down himself. "Talk away."

The clock in the kitchen quietly ticked in the background as Sylvia drew in a breath.

"You're doing more for us than you need to—" Sylvia's quiet voice began.

Garth didn't interrupt. He knew this wasn't the point Sylvia was talking toward. He knew because she didn't look him in the eye. She seemed to be talking to his chin. Something was bothering her.

"—and we appreciate it," Sylvia continued.

Garth nodded. "No problem."

Sylvia raised her eyes and looked at him directly. "But I'm worried—crushes can hurt people."

Garth tried to swallow. How had she known? He thought he was being subtle. He hadn't even taken one tiny first step yet and she knew where he was going.

"You don't need to worry about me," Garth finally said stiffly.

"You?" Sylvia said, surprise adding even more color to her face. "Why would I worry about you? It's the girls I'm worried about."

"The girls." Garth knew he was slow, but he didn't know what she was talking about. The only one around here with anything remotely resembling a crush was him. And he wasn't so sure it could be called a crush; it was more like an avalanche.

"All this business of soap in their eyes—" Sylvia

spread her hands and shook her head. "I know it's natural for girls their age to have crushes, but—"

"You think the girls have crushes on me." Garth was stunned and relieved at the same time. His secret was safe. "I don't think so. I'm old enough to be their father."

"Exactly. That's your attraction."

Sylvia studied Garth. He was old enough to be their father; that was obvious. He was even starting to act like one ever since he'd started cooking for the kids.

"The girls wish they had fathers like you," she continued softly. "They see you as someone safe."

"I am safe. I wouldn't hurt them."

Now that the cards were being laid out on the table, Garth found a slow, growing anger building in his gut. What kind of a man did she think he was? "I wouldn't let anyone else hurt them, either."

Sylvia smiled. "They know that. That's why they have crushes on you."

Garth felt his anger fade. "So what do you want me to do?"

"Be kind to them. But not too kind. And whatever you do, don't single someone out for special treatment. There'd be a fight for sure if you did that."

"I can do that," Garth said.

Garth finished the breakfast dishes and went out to check the calving barn. Jess had been up all night delivering twin calves. One of the calves needed to be bottle-fed and Garth snapped one of the agricultural nipples onto the bottle. While the calf sucked, Garth congratulated himself. He was beginning to think he had a handle on this camp stuff. Huge meals. He could do that. Mountains of dishes. He could do that. Treat all the girls the same. He could do that.

There was a time when warriors needed to fight each other for the hand of the fairest maiden. Garth figured he had it easy. All he needed to do was be Martha Stewart to thirty hungry teenagers. Well, that and learn to dance so Mrs. Buckwalter would be happy.

The calf sucked in the last of the milk supplement and butted its head against the empty bottle.

"Easy does it, fella," Garth said as he rubbed the calf along its back. The way the calf was eating, it would fill out in no time.

Garth sat back on his heels. Actually, he'd need to do more than just learn to dance to make the camp work as Mrs. Buckwalter saw it. He wasn't too sure what Mrs. Buckwalter meant by manners, but he was pretty sure she wasn't thinking of the country manners that said you just treated your neighbor like yourself and respected their boundaries and water rights.

He suspected, with all her money, Mrs. Buckwalter fancied manners of a different sort. He was pretty sure she'd let him slide on his share of the manners since he'd agreed to do what he could to help the FBI in their investigation. But she wouldn't let the kids slide, and since they looked to him for help, he'd need to make the correct motions himself.

Garth stood up and brushed the straw off his jeans. Now that he thought about it, he was beginning to wonder if warriors didn't have it easier after all. He'd rather face an opponent he could see. Manners were a completely different kind of target. He didn't even know whom to ask about manners. The closest thing to Mrs. Buckwalter they had around here was Mrs. Hargrove. Even though Mrs. Hargrove was plain speaking and plain dressing, she believed in style. The pageant she'd planned for the community over Christmas showed that. Maybe she could help him.

That same morning in a windowless room in Washington, D.C.

The "suits" had been called back together. The only clue that something was wrong was the silence in the room as they waited for the last man to sit down at the table.

"We've got trouble," the leader said. He tapped an unlit cigar on the table. "There's a leak somewhere—I'm afraid the rustlers might know about Elkton."

"They can't," the youngest man said confidently. He opened his manila folder as though it contained new information. "We just got the word back ourselves that he agreed to help. What makes you think they know anything?"

"Gut feeling," the leader said. "We were getting close to the inside man and then—all of a sudden—everything gets too easy. Like they want our attention diverted for a bit. I figure it's got to do with Elkton. They don't want us thinking about him."

None of the men disputed the older man's gut feeling. His gut was more reliable than their most sophisticated computers.

"Maybe we should send someone out to check," the younger man suggested.

"Can't. That would finger him for sure." The older man twisted his cigar again.

"We could send someone if they knew how to get in and out without being seen," the usually silent man offered. He'd expected another call on his cell phone from Mrs. Buckwalter saying everything was all right. But the call hadn't come. Not yet.

Just then the cell phone rang in the other man's pocket. "That'll be Mrs. Buckwalter."

The rest of the men were silent while he answered the phone. "Yes?"

The man's face went pale and he gripped the phone tighter. "Who are you?"

The men could hear the loud laughter on the other end of the phone.

"I'm not interested in your games," the man said. Nothing in his voice showed the strain he was under. "If you won't tell me who you are, I'm going to hang up."

The laughter on the other end of the phone stopped, and they could hear the mumble of conversation. Then there was silence.

"All right," the man said. "My name is Flint Russell. Now tell me yours."

The men exchanged looks of surprise. Flint was a veteran agent. He'd never give out his name unless something very serious was happening.

"Forget about the sister. She doesn't know anything." Sweat was forming on Flint's forehead, but he did not notice it. He knew he had to keep his voice calm. Why hadn't he thought about that? The rustlers were planning to sway Garth's sympathies by taking Francis. He only hoped they didn't know—

"That was a long time ago." Flint ground his teeth together so his voice would sound even. He supposed it wasn't a government secret that he had been married to Francis twenty years ago for two days. The ink hadn't even dried on their license before it was all over. After all that time he was surprised that anyone besides himself still cared enough to remember.

"Like I said, that was a long time ago. Don't waste your time taking her."

There was a sharp bark of laughter and the phone line went dead.

Chapter Six

"That's your salad fork," Sylvia reminded K.J. as the teenager grabbed his closest fork and speared a few macaroni covered with cheese sauce. "Remember, you use silverware from the outside in."

Lunch was underway. Sylvia had offered a brief prayer and then Garth had carried in one and then two more big roasting pans filled with macaroni and cheese. The ranch hands were sitting uneasily with the teenagers from the center. Everyone looked hungry. Sylvia hoped there was a recycler around for all the cardboard boxes they'd opened.

"Huh?" K.J. stopped with the fork halfway to his mouth.

Forty-three people were seated around three metal banquet tables that took up most of the living room. Francis had brought out some old linens to cover the tables and she'd called Linda to ask about borrowing fifty-odd settings of silverware from the café in Dry Creek. Linda had brought the silverware over earlier.

"Remember we talked about it after math? The

forks are placed in the order in which you use them. Salad first. Then the main meal. Remember, the first fork goes with the first food. Salad.'' Sylvia felt a throbbing behind her eyes. She'd already talked about forks for an hour today. She felt like eating her own meal with a wooden spoon. But Mrs. Buckwalter seemed happy with the progress the kids were making.

''But I'm eating macaroni and cheese first. First fork. First food. Ain't going to have no salad yet,'' K.J. explained. He looked around at the others for support and got a few confused nods, mostly from the ranch hands. The working men had mended fence somewhere this morning and so hadn't seen the training about forks.

''But the salad is supposed to come first,'' Sylvia explained again. She knew K.J. didn't like rules. He'd grown up without any and he chafed at the simplest ones. Sylvia knew teenagers needed structure and that kids like K.J. needed it more than most. She just wished all of the rules here could be important ones. She'd rather teach them ''Thou shalt not kill'' than which fork to use, but she'd given her word to Mrs. Buckwalter, and the camp would teach manners no matter how much patience it took. ''If it comes first, you use the first fork.''

''Gonna eat my salad last. For dessert like. Gonna use my salad fork then,'' K.J. offered, and looked a little mournfully at the two chocolate cakes Francis had baked. ''Can't have dessert. I'm not supposed to have sugar. Or chocolate. That stuff'll kill you.''

''But—'' Sylvia felt the throbbing in her head increase. She wondered what fork one used to eat an extrastrength aspirin.

"Maybe it'll help to remember that the big fork is for the big part of the meal," Garth suggested. He also had mended fences this morning, but it took little imagination to figure out what the fork talk had been all about. "The little ones just come before and after it."

K.J. set down his salad fork and shook his head. "Don't make no sense to me. Who cares what fork I use?"

"I care, Mr. Colton." Mrs. Buckwalter put her own fork on her plate and looked down the long banquet table at K.J. "And so will your employer someday when he takes you out to lunch to see if you've got the table manners to deal with important clients."

"I ain't got no job," K.J. mumbled as he looked down at his plate. "Ain't nobody gonna hire me anyway. Not for a real job. Not one like that where there's clients and all."

"Of course they will. You've got natural sales ability," Mrs. Buckwalter said briskly. "And when they do, you'll know you can dine anywhere and be comfortable."

Mrs. Buckwalter looked at Garth and added, "That reminds me, we need to have lobster one night."

Garth took the news like a man. He flinched but he didn't swear.

Sylvia panicked. "Lobster!" If it didn't come in a box, she couldn't cook it.

"We can't—" Sylvia looked at Garth for help. Mrs. Buckwalter hadn't been around for the lunch preparations. Maybe she'd forgotten they were all novices in the kitchen.

Garth smiled reassuringly at Sylvia before looking down the table at Mrs. Buckwalter. "You mean some casserole dish with that flaked lobster—or is it crab?—that they have in the grocery store in Baker?" We could probably use that in one of the recipes I had in the army. Tuna on a shingle—only, it'd be lobster on toast. Fancy like. I could make that. Might be good.

"Oh, no." Mrs. Buckwalter shuddered and waved the suggestion aside. "I mean lobster. Every businessman—" Mrs. Buckwalter looked at the boys and then the girls and added sternly "—and businesswoman needs to know how to eat a lobster. They're slippery little things, and anyone in business is bound to end up face-to-face with one of them at some dinner. They need to know how to crack them and how to dip them in butter delicately."

"Couldn't we have pizza instead?" one of the girls asked hopefully. Paula was a fourteen-year-old African-American who had come to the center last fall when her father had been killed. "We could make it anchovy if you're set on something fishy."

One of the boys groaned, but got an elbow in the ribs from his neighbor.

"I can order pizza," Garth agreed eagerly. "And it doesn't need to be anchovy. We could do sausage. Or pepperoni. They don't usually deliver out from Baker, but with an order this big—"

"No pizza. Not for the kind of job Miss Smith is going to have someday." Mrs. Buckwalter looked at the teenager assessingly. "And then again—maybe not. I see you as a teacher of some kind."

"Me?" Paula asked in surprise.

Mrs. Buckwalter nodded confidently. "Oh, yes, I've watched you helping the other kids with their math. You've got the knack for it."

Paula beamed. She picked up her dinner fork and speared a macaroni. "Well, I guess it wouldn't hurt to eat a lobster. Learn something new."

"So pizza is out?" Sylvia asked reluctantly. Maybe Mrs. Buckwalter had forgotten breakfast. She didn't seem to remember they needed to think boxes and cans when it came to menu preparation. They weren't even ready for steaks. And steaks were dead. No, they were definitely not ready for something that was alive.

"Really, it's no trouble to call for pizza." Garth tried again. "They even have those padded boxes that keep it warm until it gets here."

"Maybe we could have lobsters at the wedding reception on Saturday." Mrs. Buckwalter ignored Garth and continued to muse. "There'll, of course, be lots of dancing. And a nice sit-down dinner. Wouldn't that be just perfect?"

"At the wedding?" Sylvia gasped. They would need lobsters for at least eighty people! Everyone in Dry Creek was coming. They couldn't possibly cook that many lobsters. Someone needed to stop Mrs. Buckwalter. "Oh, but lobsters are…so big. I've always rather liked little finger sandwiches at weddings. You know you can make them with tuna or cream cheese and olives or smoked salmon. You can cut them into fancy shapes—hearts or squares. We could put them on doilies. Or if you didn't like that, we could bake those little quiches. Or wrap asparagus in ham."

Mrs. Buckwalter wasn't paying attention. She was surveying the teenagers like a general surveying her troops before she charged into battle.

"If everyone—" Mrs. Buckwalter waved her

hands at the kids "—is going to learn how to dance for the event, then I say let's make it special."

Dancing! Sylvia forgot about the lobsters. She had more immediate worries. She needed to turn these teens into dancers for the big event. The kids were all looking at Mrs. Buckwalter like it could happen. If the older woman said they could dance, they would. Sylvia wished she had as much blind faith. She knew dancing didn't just happen. Someone needed to teach them.

Sylvia was beginning to appreciate the difficulty of fairy-tale endings. Take Cinderella. It was obvious that the true hero in Cinderella wasn't the prince. All he had to do was look good and carry around a shoe. No, it was the fairy godmother who had to sweat. Sylvia wondered if the poor fairy felt like she did this very minute—like she'd promised the impossible and had no idea how to deliver it.

Then she remembered. She did not have to deliver anything. She had Garth. He could teach the kids to dance.

Sylvia put the last paper plate into the trash bag. They'd used large paper plates for the macaroni and cheese and small paper plates for the chocolate cake. If they hadn't needed the various sizes of forks, they would have used plastic silverware, too. Sylvia was glad. She'd rather burn the dirty dishes than have the girls wash them. She would have enough trouble with their crushes when Garth started teaching them to dance.

"You need to rest," Garth said as he put the last roasting pan into the sink and started to scrub it. Sylvia's shoulders were slumped and he didn't like it.

Thirty kids was a lot of responsibility. "The kids are having that English lesson with Pat. I can't believe they'd never heard the Cinderella story until you asked him to read it to them. Anyway, now's a good time to steal a nap. Even Cinderella rested after she scrubbed the fireplace."

"Cinderella never had a kitchen like this to rest in." Sylvia looked around. The midafternoon sun shone through the kitchen window. It was cold enough outside for frost to edge the window, but the hot dishwater made the air moist and warm inside.

She could see Francis's influence in Garth's kitchen. Everything was laid out square, the way a man would do it. But there were touches of red in the geraniums along one counter and in the cozy apple-shaped pot holders along another. These were from Francis.

Sylvia liked Garth's sister and was looking forward to getting to know her better. She might even find out what was making Francis so sad.

"Cinderella doesn't take too long to read. They'll be free in fifteen minutes." Sylvia squared her shoulders. She had more pressing things to do. She needed to start the fairy godmother task. Thankfully she did not have to do the actual work. "And I need to set up a place so you can start to teach them the waltz."

"Me?" Garth stiffened. He'd known this time was coming, but he'd hoped it wouldn't come until he could read the dance book he'd bought in Spokane. He hadn't even diagrammed the steps yet. He wasn't ready. He thought the dancing would come later. Much later. "I—well—I mean it's been a long time since I've waltzed. Since before the army. Did I mention I took a piece of shrapnel in the leg? Don't move as smooth as I used to—I'm sure someone else could teach the kids better.''

There. That was only stretching the truth a little, he thought. He had taken a small bit of shrapnel in the leg. And it had been a long, long time since he'd waltzed. Very close to never. And he'd wager his ranch that almost anyone else could teach it better than he could.

Sylvia stopped twisting the tags on the trash bag and set the bag down. She was quiet for a moment, just looking at him. It was going to be harder than she thought to be the fairy godmother. ''You don't know how, do you?''

''Well, I—'' Garth squirmed. She made it sound so final. ''It can't be that hard. I do have a book. I've read a few pages. Doesn't look too hard. Maybe if we put some music on, the kids will just pick it up. They're bright kids. Quick to learn.''

''I never learned how to dance much, either,'' Sylvia said as she sat down on one of the kitchen chairs. ''I left high school too young—went back when I was older.'' She didn't add that she'd married too young and counted her bruises for those ten years when other kids were out partying. ''I seemed to miss all of the dances and…things.''

''I only learned the shuffle,'' Garth admitted as he wiped his hands on the towel he had tied to his belt. He went over and sat down across from Sylvia. ''It was enough for what I needed—''

Sylvia arched an eyebrow in question.

Garth grinned. He liked to see the way Sylvia's eyes turned from deep blue to almost turquoise when she was happy or amused. ''It gave me an excuse to hold a girl in the dark.''

"I don't think that's what Mrs. Buckwalter has in mind." Sylvia smiled. She could almost see a young Garth doing the shuffle in some high school gym draped with purple crepe paper. She'd bet there had been a line of girls ready to snuggle in the dark with him.

"Well, how hard can it be to waltz?" Garth said as he stood up and bowed to Sylvia. "Can I have this dance?"

"Now?"

Garth shrugged. "We've got fifteen minutes to learn. It'd better be now."

Sylvia looked around the kitchen to be sure no one else was there. She wasn't sure why she didn't want to be seen dancing with Garth, but she didn't. "We don't have music."

Garth walked over to a counter and reached up to turn the radio on and then twist the dial. The sounds of a violin trickled into the kitchen. Garth turned the knob higher.

"Not so loud," Sylvia whispered as she looked over her shoulder to the doorway leading into the hall. "We don't want to attract an audience."

Garth felt his breath catch in his throat. Sylvia wanted to dance with him in private. Private was good. Maybe his feelings weren't as far out there as he feared. Maybe she shared some of them, at least.

"It'd destroy their confidence if they knew we don't know, either," Sylvia added.

"Oh."

"First rule of teaching," Sylvia continued. "Give the students confidence in you. First rule of fairy god-mothering, too. "

She was blabbering. She knew it. Garth had opened

his arms and she had no reason to hesitate about stepping into them. No reason at all except the fear she
knew would come when she felt a man touching her.
She needed to remind herself that they were only
dancing. Exercising really. Aerobics. She could do
this. She had to. The kids were counting on her. Mrs.
Buckwalter was counting on her. It was like holding
her breath under water. She could do it. It wouldn't
take long.

"You lead," Sylvia said as she stepped lightly into
Garth's arms.

Garth was home. He had his butterfly woman in
his arms again and, even if it felt as if she could fly
away at any moment, for now she was here and he
was home.

"One. Two. The waltz—" Sylvia was breathless.
It must be the counting that calmed her nerves. She
was actually feeling less trapped than she'd expected.
"Three. The waltz is meant to be danced apart."

Their feet slid across the linoleum. They were in
the middle of the floor. Garth led them in a square
without bumping into the refrigerator or the table.

"Just like the book says," he noted in surprise.
"Block formation. Kind of like football I suppose."

Sylvia stepped farther back from Garth. She had to
struggle to hear the sounds of the violin over the
thumping of her heart. "One. Two. Three."

Garth didn't care if Sylvia counted to a thousand.
He loved to hear the catch in her voice when she
talked. Besides, if she didn't count, he'd have to. He
had the one diagram in his mind, but even with it, he
was having a hard time remembering where they were
in the dance.

His attention kept being pulled to the shine of her

black hair and the smell of peaches that followed her. And her cheeks—they were lightly pink from the exercise, and he had to remind himself not to reach down and touch them. He didn't want to scare her away. Not now. Not when she was in his arms.

"One. Two." Sylvia made the mistake of looking up and into Garth's eyes. He must be remembering his high school days. His eyes were dark with longing. He was looking at her as if she was all he saw. And it was ridiculous, of course. He must be remembering someone else. The thought didn't comfort her like she thought it would. "Three."

Sylvia tripped.

Garth pulled her closer.

Sylvia would have tripped again if she hadn't been pinned against Garth's chest. She could feel the rhythm of his heart. The buttons on his shirt. The heat of his body. For a moment she wasn't afraid.

Garth held his breath. He could almost hear the emotions chasing themselves up and down Sylvia's spine. He felt the first tremble. That tremble he liked. It was the tremble of a woman in a man's arms when she's suddenly aware of where she is. But it was the second tremble that troubled him. The second tremble was pure fear.

Garth relaxed his hold slowly. He didn't want to startle her further.

"I'd never hurt you," he said simply as he backed even farther away until he was in respectable dance formation again. He looked into her eyes. Their turquoise color had darkened.

Sylvia blushed and looked away. "I know."

The sound of the violins on the radio scratched on

and they tried to make the next dance step work, but it didn't. They were out of sync.

"I'm sorry," Sylvia said stiffly. She hated the awkwardness of her problem. That's why she didn't date. Most men expected a woman to be able to tolerate simple things—a hug, an arm around the shoulders, a kiss. A dance. She could do none of those without fear. "It's got nothing to do with you—it's me."

Garth gave up the pretense of dancing. "If it's got to do with you, then it's got to do with me. We can talk about it."

"No point," Sylvia said, moving completely out of Garth's arms. She'd talked about her problems before. She'd had therapy. She'd made her peace with her past. She'd turned her fear of violence into a positive thing in her work with the kids. It was enough.

Sylvia walked over to the radio. They didn't need the violins anymore.

Garth stood still. He'd known someone was watching them for a bit now. He hadn't heard a sound. He'd sensed breathing—over by the living room door. It was a lifesaving sense he'd developed in the army.

Now the sense was merely inconvenient. Especially out in the barns. He'd get that tingling sensation every time a cow stared at him when his back was turned. He'd assumed the reason for his current prickles was one of the kids, and he hadn't wanted to look because it would break the spell with Sylvia.

"Aren't you even going to kiss her, man?" John's hissed whisper came from the doorway into the living room.

Garth turned around to see four of the teenage boys watching him with disgust on their faces.

''Man, you had her going and you didn't even kiss her!'' another one said, more loudly.

Sylvia whirled around. ''He did *not* have me going—'' She bit her lip. Too much anger would be a tip-off. The boys were bright. ''Besides, what are you doing sneaking around? You're supposed to be in class.''

''That Cinderella—'' one of the boys groaned as they all walked into the kitchen. ''The girls are all flapping about it—but it's sissy stuff. There ain't no magic pumpkins. No fairy godmothers, either.''

''Well, no, of course, there're no real fairy godmothers,'' Sylvia agreed as she sat down at the kitchen table and gestured for the boys to do the same. ''But that doesn't mean there's not people who help us in life. Like Mrs. Buckwalter—she's helping us.''

John thought a minute and nodded. ''Yeah, she ain't bad.''

''And Garth—he's helping us,'' one of the other boys said as Garth sat down to join them.

''Yes, he is,'' Sylvia forced herself to acknowledge calmly.

''And Mrs. Buckwalter's going on about this thing coming up like it was a royal ball,'' John added. ''Maybe we'll get to see some pumpkin action, after all.''

''Maybe that mean old cow out in the barn—the one with the black ears—maybe she'll turn into a pumpkin,'' one of the boys said, snickering. ''And the chickens can turn into footmen. And some old boot will be a shoe.''

''All I know is we'll have to be home by midnight,'' John grumbled. ''Mrs. Buckwalter already said no one can leave the party alone and go driving around. Don't seem fair when the girls are all going to get new dresses.''

''New dresses!'' Sylvia gasped. They didn't have money for new dresses. Then she remembered. The center wasn't as poor now as it had been last week. Maybe Mrs. Buckwalter was going to write a check. Still, it didn't seem right. Sylvia had no intention of spoiling these kids. They needed to know the value of money. ''If the girls are getting new dresses, they'll have to earn them. Chores or something.''

Sylvia congratulated herself. Nothing was getting by her. She would help the kids develop character through all of this. It was far too easy for Mrs. Buckwalter to write a check. There needed to be limits.

''Just out of curiosity,'' Garth began slowly, eyeing each of the teenage boys, ''what exactly did you expect to be driving around in?''

Sylvia gulped. She was wrong. Everything was getting by her. She hadn't even heard the slight reference to driving. ''And none of you even have driving licenses!''

The boys studied their knuckles.

Finally John cracked. ''We weren't planning to go far. Not actually for a drive or anything—''

''Do you realize the penalty for driving without a license?'' Sylvia started to lecture. ''Especially when you're already on probation! The judges here won't go so easy on you. We don't have Glory to run interference.''

''Don't see how anybody would know we'd even done it,'' John argued. ''Ain't no cops around here.''

''There might not be any police,'' Sylvia corrected

him firmly, "but believe me, there is a jail and a county sheriff who'd lock you up in a heartbeat."

John, along with the other three boys, went back to studying their knuckles.

"Of course," Garth said thoughtfully. His dark eyes had a twinkle in them. "A man does need to learn how to drive."

"But they're not—" Sylvia bit her tongue. They might not be men, but they were sensitive. She finished lamely. "They're not of age."

"One of the advantages of being on a farm is that kids can learn to drive earlier if they're driving…say, an old tractor. Out in the field."

Garth should have been a poker player, Sylvia decided. The twinkle in his eyes had hidden deeper until the only clue that he was enjoying himself was a slight smile.

"A tractor?" John looked up in dismay.

"An *old* tractor," Garth continued smoothly. "Goes fifteen miles per hour tops. But she corners good. I learned to drive on her myself. She's nothing fancy, but she moves."

"A tractor?" John asked again. "I was kind of hoping for a pickup."

"Master the tractor this summer," Garth offered, "and we'll talk about the pickup next summer."

Next summer! Sylvia expected the boys to protest that they'd only agreed to come this summer. They never made commitments into the future. She'd have thought they'd declare that next summer they'd be busy with their homeboys. But they didn't.

"Do we get to plough?" Trong, the Vietnamese boy, asked quietly from his corner of the table. "In my home we plough with an ox."

Trong didn't need to add that he missed the earth of his homeland. The longing in his voice said it all.

"The earth is a bit different here," Garth said. "More rock mixed in with it. Nothing like the deep richness of Vietnamese soil. But the smell is close. And when it's freshly turned behind a plough, there's nothing like it. If you want, I'll send you out with one of my hands when the snow clears off the ground. He's going to try tilling some land that we'll be putting into oats this spring. We've had trouble on that bit of land and he thinks a double tilling will do the trick. He'll let you ride with him in the cab."

Sylvia didn't protest that Trong would miss his school lessons. The boy's face lit up with a quiet joy as he eagerly nodded his agreement.

"The rest of you..." Garth looked at the boys sternly. "You can only drive the tractor when I'm around—and only after you've—" Garth had noticed that Sylvia wanted the kids to earn their rewards and he didn't want her to think he was too soft, so he tried to think of something they could do "—only after you've taught the girls to dance."

"Us?" The boys all looked up in startled unison.

"Sure." Garth decided he'd had a stroke of brilliance. "I've seen you guys play basketball. You're light on your feet. Dodging and going in for a setup. You move smooth. All you need is a little coaching and you'll know all the moves."

"Yeah." The boys looked at each other and agreed. "We are pretty good."

"Well, that's settled," Sylvia said as she stood up. She didn't care who taught the kids to dance just as long as she didn't have to spend any more time in Garth's arms. And Garth was right. The boys did have good coordination. "Garth will give you all the pointers you need. We've even cleared a place for you."

Sylvia waved around the kitchen. With the table moved to the corner, there was room for three or four couples to dance.

"No," Garth said as he stood and addressed the boys. "If we're going to do this, we're going to do it right. There's more room in the barn. We'll assemble the men there."

"Yes, sir!" John said.

Sylvia hid a smile. John was serious. She wondered if the boy even realized how much like a new recruit he sounded or if he was aware of the hero worship that shone on his face. Just because she wasn't always comfortable with Garth, she reminded herself to be thankful for him. He was giving the boys something they lacked—a man to look up to.

Now why had she said that, she thought to herself. She'd had men work with the boys before—kind, gentle men who showed them that a man didn't need to be violent to be worthwhile. But the boys had never bonded with those men like they already had with Garth. And she did not blame them. She'd been so worried about the girls being too attracted to Garth that she hadn't realized it was the boys who shadowed him most.

She wondered briefly if this attachment was good. Garth was, after all, not part of the program. Technically he was their landlord and nothing more. He could break all of their hearts and no one could even fault him. He had a ranch to run. He'd never promised to spend his summer with a bunch of kids.

"Someone else can teach them to dance," Sylvia offered to Garth's back as he and the boys were walking to the door. "I mean, if you have other things to do."

Garth turned and gave her an indignant look as he handed wool jackets to the four boys. "I can teach them."

"I didn't mean you couldn't," Sylvia protested softly. Garth had already pulled his Stetson off a rack by the kitchen door and jammed it on his head. He looked like a man who could do anything.

"Then it's settled." Garth nodded confidently as he opened the door for the boys. "We'll be back when we're done."

Chapter Seven

Sylvia felt the rush of cold air as the door opened and shut behind the boys. It wasn't snowing outside, but the layers from several days ago still covered the ground. She stepped close to the windows and she could see the low mountains in the distance out of the windowpanes. Even the edges of the windows were frosty.

It would be too cold to dance in the barn, she thought to herself, and almost went to the door to call the boys back to give them scarves to wrap around their necks. Then she stopped herself. Maybe suffering while you learned to dance was some kind of male thing. The boys certainly had sense enough to come back inside if they were too uncomfortable.

In the meantime she'd go check on the rest of the kids.

The other boys must have given up on Cinderella, too, because when Sylvia went into the family room where the class had been set up, only the girls were left.

"The closest thing I have to a ball gown is my bathrobe," one of the girls was complaining. Sylvia was surprised. Tara had never shown any inclination to wear any kind of a dress and certainly not something that could be called a gown. "And I sure ain't going to wear that old thing to a dance like the one we're planning."

"I promised we'd go shopping," Mrs. Buckwalter said, her eyes alive with enthusiasm. "I'm sure they have some lovely gowns in—" she looked over at Francis who sat in a nearby chair embroidering on a length of rose satin material "—what is the name of the town again, dear?"

"The closest town is Miles City, but we'd need to go to Billings to get dresses like the ones you're thinking of. There's a little shop, Claire's, that carries a few formals."

"Oh, we'd need more than a few," Mrs. Buckwalter said emphatically. "The girls will all need different dresses."

"Oh." Francis looked up from her sewing and blinked. "Well, I didn't think of that. Claire usually only has three or four styles. The proms aren't until May or so. This time of year she'll only have a few leftover holiday dresses and a basic black or two."

"Well, I'm not wearing my bathrobe," Tara repeated again. "It's all fuzzy."

"Maybe we could sew some simple gowns," Sylvia suggested dubiously. She didn't sew, but Francis made it look easy. "Simple sheaths shouldn't be too hard."

"We don't have time," Francis said as she knotted her thread and set down her sewing. "The reception is Saturday night. We only have two more days and we wouldn't be able to get any fabric until tomorrow. Besides, the girls won't have time for sewing. They'll need to decorate the old barn in town for the wedding dance.''

Francis looked at the girls assessingly. ''One of them could use my old prom dress if they wanted. Those old dresses are almost in style again.''

''I can call my son and have him send us some gowns from Europe. I think he's in Paris this week,'' Mrs. Buckwalter offered.

''No!'' Sylvia jumped into the conversation. Somehow she had a feeling that the less said to Mrs. Buckwalter's son, the better off they all were. He obviously didn't know what his mother was doing yet and Sylvia would like to keep it that way. ''There's no need to bother your son. I'm sure—I'm sure there's some other way....''

Sylvia's voice trailed off. She couldn't think of any other way. ''Maybe we could glitter up some T-shirts?''

''Absolutely not.'' Mrs. Buckwalter waved the suggestion aside. ''Even Scarlett O'Hara had sense enough to wear her curtains instead of her underwear.''

''Madonna wore her slip,'' one of the girls said brightly. ''Maybe we should—''

''Absolutely not!'' Mrs. Buckwalter huffed. ''This is a proper dance. I'll not have people in their underwear.''

''I have an idea,'' Francis interrupted quietly. Everyone looked at her. ''I think it'll work. I bet half of the women from my graduating class still have a prom dress or two boxed up in their closet. I'm sure they'd be happy to loan them to the girls. That is, if you want them." Francis looked directly at the girls.

"Are those the old fifties dresses?" Tara asked enthusiastically. "Those are so in now."

"Wait a minute, girls. We couldn't possibly ask Francis and her friends to do that," Sylvia protested. "I'm sure those prom dresses are special—they all have memories."

Francis got a faraway look in her eyes and smiled. "Seeing someone else wear the dresses again will only make the memories more real."

"I can pay a rental fee for the dresses," Mrs. Buckwalter offered. "We don't want to be in anyone's debt."

"Don't worry about it," Francis said as she stood up and headed toward the phone. "Send them out for a good dry cleaning and that's all anyone will want. People have talked about the kids coming ever since Garth first called and told us to start getting ready. The people of Dry Creek want to do what they can to help. They're just letting you settle in for a couple of days or they'd already be over with casseroles and homemade bread. Let me call Doris June and Margaret Ann. They'll start the ball rolling for everyone."

"Really? Casseroles?" Sylvia forgot all about the dresses. She supposed it was too much to hope for that the casseroles would be big enough to feed an army.

Sylvia sat down in an overstuffed chair. She could tell the girls were excited because they weren't talking. They were listening to the murmur of Francis's voice on the telephone.

"I wonder if they'll have one with net on it," one of the girls said dreamily. "I've always wanted to dance with net swirling around my legs. Looks so cool in the old movies when the men dip their partners.''

''I don't think the boys will be learning about dipping,'' Sylvia cautioned. She'd never seen so many stars in the eyes of these girls. Usually they showed their tough exterior and, she knew for certain, they were more comfortable in jeans than in lace. Who would have thought that inside they dreamed of being dipped?

After Francis came back and informed the girls that, yes, there would be dance dresses for them, Sylvia wrapped a heavy scarf around her head, put on a ski jacket and walked out to the barn. She knew it was asking too much for the boys to learn to dip, but the happy chatter of the girls made her want to come out and try anyway.

The barn wasn't far from the house, but her breath was coming out in white puffs by the time she arrived there. She didn't have snow boots so she followed in the footsteps the boys had made. The door to the barn was half-open and she stood in the doorway. The light was dim and it took a moment for her eyes to get accustomed.

Straw bales had been pushed back from the main floor of the barn and a couple of milk cows were contentedly corralled off to the side. The main floor had been swept clean—or, Sylvia corrected herself— was being swept clean as she watched.

The teen boys were twirling around the dance floor. Some of them held brooms as partners, with aprons tied around them. Others held shovels. One even held a fence post with a gunny sack tied on top for hair. They were all intently listening as Garth waved his arms like a conductor and called out the best. "One…two…three."

The boys danced stiffly, almost as if they were marching.

"And remember to talk. One…two…" Garth instructed. He was standing in the center of the floor holding a tape recorder with waltz music coming from it. "It's not enough to dance. Three. You need to talk as well."

"Ain't got nothing to say to a broom," one boy said glumly as he stared at his partner and shuffled his feet in formation.

"You ain't got nothing to say to a real girl, either," another shot back.

The other boy stopped dancing and swung his broom back like a club. "Says who?"

Garth moved over to the boys without losing the count. "One…two…three. There'll be no fighting at the dance. Besides, talk isn't hard. You can always tell a girl how pretty she looks. Girls like that."

The boys groaned.

"Or there's the weather," Garth continued as he punctuated the beat with the toe of his leather boots. "One…two…three. Nice night. Isn't it cold here? One…two…three. That kind of thing. You don't need to be Einstein. Just talk."

The boys obediently began to mumble at their partners.

Sylvia leaned against the doorjamb and watched Garth. His Stetson was pushed back off his forehead and he had a frown of concentration on his face as he counted out the steps. He almost looked as if he thought he could will the boys to dance through his own concentration. Watching him, Sylvia was half-convinced he'd be able to do just that.

"One...two—" Garth looked away from the boys and toward the doorway. His toe stopped tapping and his arms stopped conducting.

Garth blinked. Even with the snow the day was sunny and it took him a moment to realize that Sylvia was standing in the doorway. She had her hair wrapped up in a soft white knit scarf that was tucked under her chin. The sun streamed in behind her and gave her a halo. She looked adorable.

Garth realized he'd stopped counting when he no longer heard the brush of the brooms on the barn floor. The boys had stopped dancing and were looking at him in confusion.

"Three," Garth resumed. "One—"

The brushing resumed.

"Miss Sylvia, look at us," one of the boys called out as he moved with his broom. "We're dancing."

"I see," Sylvia agreed. "And you're doing fine."

"Dance with us," another boy invited. "Mr. Elkton has an extra shovel."

"Two—" Garth kept his mind focused. He didn't tell the boys, but in his opinion this was the problem with dancing. Being close to a woman made it difficult for a man to concentrate. And, if nothing else, dancing required concentration. "Three."

"One." Garth stopped even trying. Sylvia had taken the shovel and was twirling it around and laughing with the boys.

Another figure appeared in the doorway.

"Garth?" It was Francis. She'd thrown a coat over her shoulders and come out without a scarf. "Phone call for you."

"I'll call them back later."

"It's a strange call," Francis said quietly, walking closer to Garth until she could talk without the boys hearing her. "Some man insists he needs to talk to you right now but he won't tell me who he is or what it's about—just said you need to come."

"Probably just a salesman," Garth said, keeping his voice calm. He didn't want everyone upset. "You know how persistent they can be."

"We don't get many sales calls out here."

"Maybe it's someone from that new feed supplement company I'm trying. I sent in a form for more information." Garth set the tape recorder down on a straw bale and pulled his Stetson down farther before he started to walk toward the barn door.

Before he stepped outside, Garth turned and called, "Keep dancing. I'll expect you to be pros by the time I get back."

Some of the boys grunted. Others just bit their lips in concentration and began to count to their dance partners.

"Want a shovel?" Sylvia stopped twirling and offered her shovel to Francis. "It's kind of fun."

Francis pulled her wool coat more closely around her shoulders. Her face was pale and strained. She was clearly worried.

"It's probably just a salesman, like Garth said." Sylvia laid down the shovel and quietly walked over and put her arm around the other woman's shoulders.

Francis nodded slowly. "It's just that the voice was so intense...and it sounded like—like someone I used to know."

"Well, maybe that's it. Maybe it is someone you

know and they just want to talk to Garth about something.''

"No." Francis shook her head. "This man would never call here. I used to think so. But, no, he'd never call. Not after all those years. It's just that it made me remember—'' Francis pulled her coat tighter around herself and smiled. "But enough of that. Old memories are just that. Old.''

"Is there anything I can do to help?" Sylvia asked. Francis's smile didn't reach her eyes. Her lips moved, but it was clear the smile meant little. "I'm a pretty good listener."

"I wish there was something somebody could do," Francis said, her voice low and intense. "I thought by coming back here I could lay my ghosts to rest, but it hasn't worked that way—every place I look, I remember him."

"Ahh," Sylvia said sympathetically. "Old boyfriend?"

Francis tried to smile again. This time her lips only twisted. "We were married. Briefly. Or so I thought."

"Oh, I didn't know you'd been married."

"We weren't. The ceremony was fake," Francis said bitterly. "Turned out he wasn't the staying-around kind. Never even bothered to leave a note. Just left. Garth was in the army so he didn't even know about it. By the time he came back, there was no point in telling him."

"It must have been lonely."

"It was better when I moved to Denver. But I could never completely shake the memories so I decided to come back and face them. I thought they'd go away here."

Sylvia hugged her. "It's always best to face our past. Believe me, I know."

"You?" Francis looked up in surprise. "You look like you have it all together."

Sylvia laughed as the two of them started toward the barn door. "Believe me, I could tell you stories."

After walking back to the house in the crusted snow, Sylvia thought the inside of the kitchen felt stuffy warm. She slipped her tennis shoes off and sat down on a bench by the door. The thick wool socks she wore were wet and she pulled them off. She unwrapped her scarf and then stood to hang up her jacket. The kitchen floor was cold and her feet were still tingling as she started to walk farther into the house.

By then Francis was standing beside the kitchen counter. "I'm going to make us a cup of tea and we'll talk."

"Sounds good to me. I'm just going to go borrow some socks from one of the girls. I think they brought a few extra pairs over to the house this morning."

Sylvia could hear Garth's murmured phone conversation when she stepped into the hallway that connected the kitchen to both the living room and Garth's den. She couldn't hear the words, but his low tone coming from the den sounded cautious and reserved.

"Anyone have extra socks?" Sylvia asked as she stepped into the living room. The girls were sitting at the long table, doing what looked like homework. When she got closer, she saw they had spread out old dress patterns.

"We're learning about multiplication," Mrs. Buckwalter explained. "We're taking a twenty-five-inch-waist pattern and altering it to fit someone with a twenty-eight-inch waist. Then we're going to learn about doing some simple sewing—hems and turning up cuffs.''

"I always have trouble with jeans being too long," one of the shorter girls explained.

Sylvia had never realized the girls might want to learn these kind of homemaking skills. "I don't suppose anyone is dying to learn how to cook?" she asked hopefully.

"I can flip burgers," one girl said proudly.

"And eggs," another added.

"Want to help with breakfast tomorrow?"

The two girls shrugged. "Sure."

"Good. They can help with the lobsters, too," Mrs. Buckwalter looked up from the dress patterns and said matter-of-factly. "We'll need some cooks for that—"

"I've never cooked lobsters," one of the girls said hesitantly.

"Don't worry." Mrs. Buckwalter dismissed the concerns with a wave of her hand. "I've watched my chef do it, and it's easier than cooking burgers. Anyone who can boil up a big pot of hot water can cook a lobster."

"Oh." The girl brightened. "I can do that. Boiling water."

"Surely there's more to it than that," Sylvia said dubiously. "I mean I've never cooked one myself, but it just seems there'd be more to it."

"Sometimes things are easier than we think," Mrs. Buckwalter said airily. "I think our big challenge will be getting pots big enough for all the water. That, and finding a store in Miles City that will deliver live lobster."

"Have you asked Francis about stores yet?" Sylvia

almost fell to her knees. They were saved. Why didn't she think of that? There was no way a store in Miles City would have a hundred live lobsters just waiting around for a dinner party. They'd have to settle for finger sandwiches, after all. "There might not be any lobsters available."

"Well, surely no one else has bought them all," Mrs. Buckwalter stated blankly. "It's not Christmas."

"I'm not sure they routinely stock lobsters in the stores here," Sylvia said gently. "We're a long way from the coast and it's in the middle of cattle country."

"Why, I guess we are." Mrs. Buckwalter sounded surprised as she thought about it. "I'm just so used to Seattle. Don't know what I was thinking. But, of course, we're in cattle country. I've heard Garth mumble about those cattle rustlers ever since we got here."

"You have? I haven't heard him say a word about them. I thought they might not strike again."

"Oh, they're here all right," Mrs. Buckwalter said complacently. "That's another reason Garth didn't want the boys off driving by themselves. Don't know who they'll meet up with in these hills."

"That does it," Sylvia said as she took an extra pair of socks offered by one of the teenagers. "I'm sleeping with the girls in their bunkhouse again tonight instead of in the guest room here. I never thought about the rustlers still being active."

"Oh, they wouldn't come this close to the house," Mrs. Buckwalter assured her with a wink and a raised eyebrow, showing she knew all the girls were listening intently to her words. "I'm sure if everyone's tucked into bed by...say ten o'clock, we've got nothing to worry about.''

"Ten o'clock," one of the girls wailed. "That's barely even nighttime."

"Well, we all need our beauty rest anyway," Mrs. Buckwalter continued as she turned back to the dress patterns. "I asked Francis to call the hairdresser in town and she's coming out tomorrow for anyone who wants to have their hair done for the dance."

"I hope she can do a fifties look," another girl said as she shook her long hair. "If we have the dresses, I want to look the part. Maybe one of those braids."

"I'm sure she can do whatever you want with your hair," Mrs. Buckwalter said firmly.

Sylvia sat down in a chair and pulled the socks on her feet. "I can't wait to see everyone all dressed up."

"Bet we look better than the boys," one of the girls bragged.

"We better," another girl muttered. "It'll take us all day to get ready."

Sylvia started to walk to the kitchen in her warm socks. The socks were a little big, but cozy. Just the thing to wear when drinking a cup of tea with Francis and talking.

The wood floor in the hallway was slick and Sylvia slid in her socks. The door to the den was open and she could hear Garth's phone conversation. She realized he didn't know anyone was there because he heard no footsteps. She cleared her throat. She didn't want to eavesdrop even unintentionally. She heard Garth put down the receiver and mutter to himself. By the time she reached the door of the den he was coming out of the room.

"Oh, I didn't know anyone was there," Garth said as he ran his hands through his hair. Even with his tan, his face was pale and he had a frown on his forehead. "I don't suppose you heard the conversation?"

"Me? No. I just came into the hallway."

"Too bad. I could use a second opinion." Garth said, running his hands through his hair again. "Some crackpot who won't say his name calls up. Just tells me to watch Francis and not let her out of the house alone. I try to talk to him, but he won't say any more. Said the phones could be tapped."

"Did he sound rational?" Sylvia drew in her breath. She knew the drill. She was betting Francis did recognize that voice. Sylvia had seen enough violent confrontations between spouses to know that nothing was surprising—not even a boyfriend who waited twenty years to exact his revenge. "Did he sound like he was drinking or on drugs? Did he make any specific threat? Did he mention a knife or a gun?"

"Why no—" Garth sounded surprised. He looked at Sylvia. "Why would he? He can't even know Francis if he would want to hurt her. Francis makes friends with everyone. I don't think she has an enemy in the world."

Sylvia watched her words. She didn't want to betray Francis's confidence. "Maybe you should ask her. She might know of someone."

"I think we should do that," Garth said with authority as he started toward the kitchen. "Nobody's going to threaten my sister and get away with it."

Francis was just setting two mugs filled with hot

tea on the table when Garth walked into the kitchen, followed by Sylvia.

"We need to talk," Garth said as he pulled out a chair and gestured for Sylvia to sit down at the table.

"Well, let me make you a cup of coffee, then. I know you don't like tea," Francis said as she turned her back to walk to the cupboard.

"I don't need anything," Garth said as he pulled out another chair for Francis. "Sit down and talk with us."

"But you should have something hot. It's cold out and you never take a break." Francis turned and fussed at him but didn't sit down. "It'll only take a minute to make a pot of coffee. You need to take care of yourself. It won't hurt you to relax."

"Today all I've done is relax," Garth protested. "And you know I can get my own coffee if I want it. Nobody needs to wait on me."

"But it's the least I can do—and you never take time in the middle of the day to just sit and talk," Francis said as she walked back to the table and sat down. "I think it's a good sign. You're not so worried about everything with the rustlers and all."

Garth realized with a start that he hadn't thought about the rustlers all day. He'd gotten so involved with the kids and then this call about Francis. Getting that call reminded him that there were things in his life much more valuable to him than his cattle. He'd rather lose all his cattle than have someone hurt Francis.

"Rustlers aren't the only bad people in the world," Garth said slowly. He didn't just want to spring his question on Francis. But how did one ask it? "I don't suppose you've known many bad people."

"Bad people?" Francis asked blankly.

"You know, someone who threatened to hurt you. Or said they wanted something bad to happen to you?" Garth worked his way through the questions as best as he could.

"Me?"

Garth finally looked at Sylvia in appeal.

"He means someone who might hurt you," Sylvia said softly.

Francis looked at both of them in bewilderment. "Why would anyone hurt me?"

"Sometimes," Sylvia spoke carefully, "people who love us—or who say they love us—can decide to hurt us."

"But who—" Francis started, and then seemed to realize what Sylvia was implying. "Oh, no, he would never hurt me."

"He?" Garth asked.

Francis looked at Sylvia and then back at Garth. "My almost husband."

Surprise rocked Garth back in his chair. "Husband! When were you married?"

"Almost. When I was eighteen," Francis answered calmly.

"But," Garth sputtered, "you never said—"

"You were over in Asia," Francis said with a soft smile. "It all happened so fast. Dad had hired him to help with the branding that summer. He fired Flint quick enough when he realized Flint had asked me to the prom and then took me to Vegas, but it was too late."

"You could have written." Garth persisted. "I did get mail."

Francis smiled an apology to her brother. "Flint

left me after we got back from Vegas. The ceremony was fake. I haven't heard from him since. I didn't want you to know—I didn't want anyone to know. I was ashamed to be such a fool."

"Oh, no," Sylvia murmured as she put her hand over Francis's. "You were no fool. He was the fool to leave a woman like you."

Francis smiled wryly. "I like to think that's true. In any event, I haven't heard from him since, so you see it's not possible that he's thinking of harming me. I'm sure he hasn't even thought of me for years."

"But you said he reminded you of the voice on the telephone," Sylvia pressed. "Do you think it could have been him?"

Francis's face drained of color and her fingers gripped the handle of her mug filled with tea. "No, it's not possible."

Sylvia looked at Garth and saw her thoughts reflected in his eyes. Francis was wrong. It could be Flint.

"Just to be safe," Sylvia said casually, "you might stay by the house. No trips alone to Miles City or anything."

"I haven't planned to go anywhere," Francis said. She was still gripping the handle of her mug, but the color was returning to her face. "Oh, except with the kids tomorrow to help decorate the barn. We're stringing crepe paper banners. It's becoming quite a production. But then, I always love wedding receptions." Francis looked down at her fingers. "Never had one of my own. The closest I got to it was the prom. Flint took me and we—" Francis looked up and said briskly, "Well, enough of that. We went and had a good time. But it's over. And I can guarantee he's not waiting around to get his revenge for my bad dancing. That's all in the past. Goodness, it's been twenty years."

Francis pushed back her chair and stood up. "Besides, he has no reason to be angry with me. None at all."

"It doesn't always take a reason," Sylvia said quietly as she, too, cupped the warmth of her tea mug.

"Did the man on the phone actually threaten me?" Francis turned to Garth and asked.

"Well, no," Garth said reluctantly. "He said he was calling to warn me that someone else might try to kidnap or hurt my sister."

"Well, see then," Francis said decisively. "He wasn't threatening me at all. He was just worried."

"It doesn't always work that way," Sylvia offered. "Quite often men who are abusive in relationships don't think they mean to harm the person. They don't accept the responsibility for their actions. They always think the threat is someone else even if it's only another side of themselves."

"Well, it can't be Flint. It just can't be." Francis walked to the refrigerator and opened the door. "I say we just forget about it and have some chocolate cake with our tea."

Garth watched Sylvia as she moved her mug closer to herself. She wrapped her fingers around it like it was a heater. It wasn't cold in the house. If anything, it was too warm. But Sylvia looked like she was shivering.

"There's nothing to be afraid of," Garth said hesitantly while Francis took the cake out of the refrigerator. He wasn't sure it was physical fear that was making Sylvia tremble, but he offered her what he could. "I wouldn't let anything happen to anyone. And there's eight cowboys roaming around the place all day long. Believe me, if there's someone here who doesn't belong, they'll find him."

"I know." Sylvia looked up and smiled at Garth. "It's just reflex action. Too many memories."

"You can tell me about them."

"Sometime. Maybe." Sylvia wondered if she ever could. She'd only talked about the abuse in her marriage with her minister and with her therapist. She didn't usually discuss it. She'd told a few friends when it first happened, but she gradually realized that they'd begun looking at her as though she had done something to prompt the violence. She felt like telling them she wished she had caused it. Then she'd know how to make it stop.

"If someone's hurt you, I'll—" Garth began and stopped when he saw the startled look on Sylvia's face. He could tell she wasn't ready for the intensity of his protective emotion toward her.

"You'll do nothing," Sylvia said flatly. "I can't abide violence."

"It's not violence to protect someone you—" Garth stopped himself and stumbled over the words. "Someone who's—who's living in your house."

Sylvia started breathing again. For a moment she'd thought Garth was going to say "someone you love." But that was silly. He barely knew her. He was just the kind of man who would protect a stray cat if it was on his property.

"Okay, who wants cake?" Francis asked as she set some plates on the table.

"I'll have half a piece," Sylvia said. It was clear Francis was choosing to ignore the warning from the phone call. And maybe she was right. Sylvia wondered if she'd been around violence for so long in her life that she expected it even when it wasn't coming.

"I should get back to the boys," Garth exclaimed as though he'd just remembered them. "I have them out there twirling around to an old tape of Lawrence Welk and practicing their conversation."

"Do you think they could learn dipping while they're at it?" Sylvia asked. "The girls would like that."

"Dipping?" Garth shook his head incredulously as he stood up and walked toward the door. "I'm not sure I can teach them to keep time to the music—let alone dipping! I don't even know if that's diagrammed in my book!"

"You'll find a way," Francis said serenely. "And when you do, it'll be perfect."

Garth grunted as he pulled on his coat and walked out the door.

Francis smiled mischievously when Garth closed the door. "He hates it when I tease him about being perfect. But I tell him that's what sisters do. Besides, he usually does manage to pull it off—whatever he sets his mind to—"

"Well, it would be nice if he could teach them to dip," Sylvia said as she took a sip of the tea in her mug. Raspberry-flavored. "Mmm, good."

"But it's probably cold by now. We were talking so long." Francis fussed as she stood. "Let me get you another cup."

"No, this is just right," Sylvia protested, and waved Francis back to her seat. "Besides, I want you to tell me all about this secret boyfriend of yours."

Francis's face lit up and Sylvia's heart sank. Sylvia

hoped she was wrong about that phone call because it was clear that Francis still was starry-eyed and in love with her Flint.

Meanwhile, at the Billings airport

Flint gripped the receiver of the pay phone. He knew he'd been foolish to call and warn Garth Elkton. He'd tried to talk himself out of it all during the plane trip from Seattle. There were many reasons why he shouldn't call. He knew them all. The phone could be tapped. Even if the phone wasn't tapped, someone could be planted as a spy within the Elkton household and Garth would undoubtedly talk even if Flint told him not to.

And then there was the fact that Flint couldn't explain who he was. He knew Garth would wonder why a special agent was being assigned to the case when nothing had happened. People receive idle threats all the time. Special agents don't come to check them out. The truth was Garth wouldn't believe Flint was on his side no matter what he said on the telephone.

But even knowing all the reasons, Flint had headed for the pay phone the minute he'd walked off the plane. Even if nobody listened, he'd had to warn Garth that someone was going to kidnap Francis.

Chapter Eight

The early-morning chill made the walk from the bunkhouse to the main house a quick one for Sylvia. The gray morning light promised an overcast day and the snow-crusted ground still looked trampled from yesterday. Heavy clouds gathered around the Big Sheep Mountains and Sylvia rubbed her hands together to keep them warm. She could see her own breath—puffs of white that warmed her hands when she cupped them around her nose.

She hadn't looked in the mirror before she left the bunkhouse. She knew what she would see. She'd scrubbed her face with lukewarm water and twisted her hair up into a casual bun. The outside cold would have made her face tight and fragile looking. This weather was not kind to someone over forty.

But Sylvia wasn't in any beauty contest. She wore a man's flannel shirt with the sleeves rolled up and well-worn denim jeans with no designer labels in sight. They were the warmest clothes she'd brought with her, and she still buttoned the jacket Francis had loaned her all the way up to her chin. She must look a sight. Not that it mattered. She had more important things to worry about than beauty.

Still, when she started up the steps of the kitchen porch, she wondered if she shouldn't have turned a light on earlier in the bunkhouse so she could at least run a lipstick over her mouth. But turning on a light would have awakened the girls sleeping in their cots and she had decided they needed to rest.

The girls had fallen asleep late last night even though Sylvia had insisted they turn the lights out at eleven. Sylvia was amazed at how excited the girls were about the dance.

But then, Sylvia said to herself as she topped the stairs, she was getting excited herself. She could hardly wait to see the girls in their dresses. This dance was turning her kids into normal, not-a-care-in-the-world teenagers. Maybe Mrs. Buckwalter was right. A dress-up event did seem to bring out the best in everyone.

Sylvia twisted the kitchen door knob before she remembered Garth had locked all the doors and windows last night.

"Who's there?" someone called out softly, startling Sylvia until she recognized Garth's voice.

Sylvia looked again. The kitchen windows were covered with thick frost, but they were all dark.

"It's me, Sylvia."

The kitchen door swung open. The room was dark except for the illuminated hands on the clock above the stove. It was five-thirty. The smells of last night's hamburgers still lingered. The kitchen looked like it had before Sylvia left last night. Garth had washed the skillets and set them to dry by the sink. The table in the middle of the room had two big round boxes of oatmeal sitting in its center. She and Garth had announced at dinner that it would be oatmeal for breakfast. The teens had groaned until Garth had promised to put raisins and cinnamon in it.

And then Sylvia saw what was different in the kitchen. Garth had obviously pulled an armchair out of the living room and into the far corner of the room last night after everyone had left. A pillow and a rumpled blanket showed he had slept there. A sturdy baseball bat lay on the floor along with the telephone.

"You are worried, aren't you?" Sylvia shivered. She'd almost convinced herself that Francis was right and that the phone call was nothing more than a wrong number.

Garth stood and nodded. He rubbed one hand over his head. His chestnut hair was tousled and reminded Sylvia of the rich grains of a fine piece of mahogany. "The man on the phone just sounded so sure of himself. He didn't sound like a drunk at all."

"Is there someplace you could send Francis? Someplace away from here?"

Garth grunted. "Ever try talking sense to Francis? She wouldn't go. She doesn't look it, but she's one stubborn woman."

"Takes after her big brother, I bet." Sylvia smiled.

Garth had a shadow of dark whiskers across his face and his hair needed combing. He had on an old sweatshirt with a tear in the sleeve and he was wearing slippers instead of shoes, but Sylvia swore he looked every inch a knight in white armor. Francis was lucky to have an older brother like him.

"Maybe I am overly cautious," Garth said. "Stayed up all night and all I heard was the howl of the wind. Besides, I'd hear a car or truck before it came close. Not much chance someone could sneak up on us that way. A car engine has to work to make it up that rise.''

"And you know nobody's going to walk in this far from the main road," Sylvia agreed as she took off the jacket she'd borrowed from Francis last night. The kitchen was warmer than outside, but not much warmer. "I'll set the water to boiling. I don't know how big of a pot we'll need for all that oatmeal.''

Sylvia turned as she hung the jacket up on a hook and walked toward the table. "You'll have to show me where the raisins are.''

"Hmph," Garth grunted.

Now what was wrong with him, Sylvia thought to herself as she looked over at his scowl. "If you don't have raisins, we can use dried dates or just make do with the cinnamon.''

"We've got raisins," Garth said curtly.

"Well, then—" Sylvia prompted.

"Plenty of raisins." Garth walked back to his chair. "Use as many as you want. Raisins are good for the kids.''

"Well, yes, all right, if you're sure." Sylvia walked over to the table and picked up a large box of oatmeal. If he wasn't going to say what was bothering him, she wasn't going to dig it out of him.

"Nice shirt," Garth said, his back turned as he folded the blanket he'd used while sleeping in the chair. "Belong to a friend?''

"You like it? You can order one from the catalog if you want. I buy men's shirts sometimes for when I do repairs around the center. They're roomier in the shoulders so I can move better.''

"So there's no friend."

Sylvia paused, oatmeal box in midair. Oh, no, it's that time, Sylvia moaned to herself. She needed to pull out her speech about why she didn't date. She was collecting her words when Garth turned around.

"No, I don't suppose there's one," Garth said cheerfully.

It took a moment for Garth's words to sink in.

"What? Why not?" Even though Sylvia was ready to tell Garth that she didn't date, it was altogether different for him to assume she wouldn't have a boyfriend. She could have a boyfriend if she wanted. That was altogether different than choosing not to date.

"Well, if you were dating anyone," Garth said, "I would know by now. Those kids can't keep a secret."

"They can keep a secret if they don't know a secret," Sylvia said airily as she turned to the cupboard and opened the door to the shelves that held the pots and pans. Let him chew on that. She pulled out a soup pot. "I don't necessarily tell everyone about my personal life."

"Oh."

"Now where do you keep the cinnamon?" Sylvia asked as she turned on the faucet to fill the pot with water. "I suppose we wait until the oatmeal is done before we add the cinnamon, but I'd like to get it ready."

"We need to make toast, too," Garth offered sourly. "And I'll put on a fresh pot of coffee." He turned to her. "Would you really keep a secret from those kids?"

Sylvia smiled at him. "Would you keep a secret from Francis?"

"Not the kind she keeps from me." Garth grunted

and then looked at her fiercely. "I hope you're not going to tell me you have some husband hanging around, too, that you've conveniently forgotten to mention."

Sylvia chuckled. Even though she definitely wasn't interested in dating, it was nice to know someone cared whether or not she did. "No. No husband. Not anymore."

"Hmph. Well, that's good, anyway."

The oatmeal was lumpy. Sylvia didn't know why. She'd stirred oatmeal before and it had never turned lumpy on her like this. Of course, she admitted, she'd never made a six-quart pot of oatmeal before. She had hoped the kids would think the lumps were just extra raisins. It hadn't worked.

"They want more toast." Francis limped into the kitchen carrying an empty tray. It was her fifth trip in the past ten minutes. "And the jelly's running out."

"We don't have any more jelly," Mrs. Buckwalter said, bending down to the check the lower shelf in the cupboard. "We have jellied cranberry sauce—and pickle relish."

"We'll use the cranberry sauce," Garth said as he flipped the slices of bread he was grilling in the oven's broiler. He had given up on the toaster several platters earlier. "They might not notice the difference. It's red and they'll be able to spread it."

"I thought we bought a big jar of that grape jelly last week." Francis turned to Garth.

"Gone. The boys needed a snack yesterday after their dance lessons."

"Thank God we need to go to Dry Creek this afternoon to see about decorations for the reception,"

Mrs. Buckwalter said as she lifted two cans of cranberry sauce off the shelf.

"They'll still be hungry whether they're in Dry Creek or here," Francis said.

"But we can buy them lunch at that café I hear about," Mrs. Buckwalter said emphatically.

"But that'll be expensive," Francis worried. "They do tend to eat rather a lot. Linda's prices aren't high, but it would take a lot of food."

"I'd rather spend the money," Mrs. Buckwalter said as she picked up a can opener and sat down at the kitchen table. She twisted the handle of the opener around the first can of cranberry sauce. "My accountant will understand."

"You have a project accountant?" Sylvia laid out more bread slices to grill.

"More or less," Mrs. Buckwalter said grimly. "My son promoted him to Chief Financial Officer—now all the bills funnel through Robert himself. Remember my son?"

Sylvia dropped a slice of bread and then nodded. Of course, she remembered the woman's son, Robert. The one who was in Europe. The one who wanted to give all the foundation's money to museums. He was the last person she wanted to see their bills. Especially not a bill for thirty orders of hamburgers and fries from a small café in Dry Creek.

"Maybe we should try tuna sandwiches," Sylvia suggested brightly. She looked a little dubiously at the empty plastic wrappers that had come off the loaves of bread Garth had toasted. She wondered if there would be enough bread left for sandwiches. But they could make them open-faced if necessary. "That way we won't bother Robert."

"Oh, we won't bother him anyway." Mrs. Buck-walter fussed as she scooped the cranberry sauce out of the can and into several small bowls. "The bills will just sit on his desk until his secretary decides they need to be paid and sends them down to Accounting. Especially when he's in Europe. All he gets are print-outs. By e-mail at that. I've told him he needs to take more of an interest in the actual bills, but you know how boys are—they never listen to their mothers."

"Well, hamburgers it is, then," Sylvia said in re-lief. Garth had just removed the last bread crust from the last plastic bag and slipped it onto the broiler pan. They would have had to use crackers anyway.

"I'll call Linda and let her know we're coming," Francis offered as she started to walk toward the tele-phone. "We can't just spring this one on her—I don't know what she keeps around for supplies."

"You're going, too?" Garth asked Francis.

Francis turned around just before entering the hall-way. "Of course."

"Then tell her to figure on enough to feed me and the hands, too. I'm not taking any chances on that phone call. The farm chores can wait—besides, everyone enjoys a day in town now and again. Even Jess," Garth said.

"If Linda needs to go into Miles City for supplies, ask her if she can find a place to order the lobsters," Mrs. Buckwalter called out as she pulled another can of jellied cranberry sauce from the bottom cupboard.

"I don't think there will be any lobsters in Miles City, either," Francis said from the hallway. "But I'll ask. Maybe there's some kind of frozen ones."

"Frozen?" Mrs. Buckwalter stood up straight, a

horrified expression on her face. "Oh, no, that would never do."

Sylvia exchanged a quick glance with Garth and then looked at the older woman and offered softly, "No one expects more than maybe a sandwich and some potato salad. It's just being together as a community and celebrating the wedding that is the fun part."

"No," Mrs. Buckwalter squared her shoulders and said firmly. "I've said I'll give everyone lobsters and lobsters it will be. A Buckwalter does not go back on her word."

The café in Dry Creek had changed since Sylvia was there at Christmastime. Of course, the Christmas garlands had been taken down and all that remained of the hitman who had been hunting Glory Beckett was a picture on the cork bulletin board of him posing as Santa Claus.

Sylvia murmured a prayer of thanks remembering how close her friend Glory had come to being killed. They had all thought the boys were lying when they claimed another hit man had been sent. As it turned out, the boys had been going to Dry Creek to try and protect Glory instead of to kill her.

Sylvia glanced sideways at Garth. He had quickly looked inside the restaurant before stepping back to open the screen door for everyone. Sylvia could tell he was trying to be casual, but she saw him look over at that photo on the bulletin board, too. They had all miscalculated before and not listened to the boys' warning—*Please, Lord, don't let it happen again. Help us heed the warning and watch out for Francis. Keep her safe.*

"Oh, I love what you've done," Francis softly exclaimed as she entered the café and looked around.

Linda was walking toward the door and tying on a large white apron. Her long brown hair was pulled back into a ponytail and two hoop earrings hung from each ear. She beamed back at Francis. "Thank you."

"It *is* nice," Sylvia agreed.

The floor had been re-covered in checkered black and white tiles. The tables were topped with gray Formica, and each held an old-fashioned pair of glass salt and pepper shakers. Healthy geranium plants hung from several hooks in the ceiling, red blossoms peeking out from beneath abundant green leaves. White café curtains covered the bottom half of the windows. The photos on the bulletin board showed several birthday parties that had obviously been held at the café.

"Sort of a fifties diner look," Sylvia noted.

"You can tell?" Linda asked eagerly. "That's what we wanted it to look like, but we weren't sure. We wanted to order some stuff from a catalog but we couldn't afford it yet so we had to work with what we had. We laid the tile ourselves and my brothers helped us resurface the tables."

"It's lovely," Mrs. Buckwalter said emphatically, entering the diner behind the last of the kids. "You can tell it's the kind of place that takes the comfort of its customers seriously."

"Looks like the kind of place that has malted shakes," John said hopefully as he and several of the other kids arranged themselves around one of the tables. "The kind with real ice cream."

"That stuff'll kill you," K.J. said mournfully.

"Not today it won't," John retorted briefly while eyeing Linda. "You do have them, don't you?"

Linda nodded. "Any kind of shake you want—strawberry, chocolate, vanilla or mint—and bacon cheeseburgers with ranch fries, or chili dogs and onion rings…"

"Goodness, I couldn't have any of that." The older woman shook her head. "K.J. reminded me. My chef would scold me for sure if I even thought about it."

"You have a chef?" Jess, his hat pushed back, asked indignantly. "And you're going on about my diet. Anybody can watch their diet when they're spoon-fed by some sissy Frenchman."

"It's not some sissy Frenchman," Mrs. Buckwalter said complacently. "Jenny is Irish. Cute young thing. My son gave her to me for Christmas. He's worried about my health so I had to promise to eat right when I left Jenny in Seattle. She would have insisted on coming with me if I hadn't said I'd stick to my diet." Mrs. Buckwalter looked at Jess and added self-righteously, "Besides, it won't hurt either one of us to eat healthy. At our age."

Jess gave an indignant snort.

"Wait a minute." Sylvia hoped she was hearing right. "Your chef could have come with you? Here—to Dry Creek?"

"Well, it's a good thing she didn't," Mrs. Buckwalter said. "Then she wouldn't have been in Seattle to take my call and have all those lobsters shipped to us."

Sylvia's heart sank. "You asked her to ship us lobsters?"

"Of course. There are no lobsters here. Francis even called into Billings for me. Not a lobster in sight.

But they can be ordered. Jenny can order anything in the world.''

"I don't suppose she could order the lobsters to be cooked and then shipped."

"Of course not. Everyone knows lobsters have to be alive when they're cooked. We can worry about it after lunch." Mrs. Buckwalter turned to Linda. "Now, dear, what else do you have besides hamburgers?"

"We also have grilled turkey burgers—or veggie burgers—and a side of fresh vegetables," Linda continued proudly. "Mostly carrots and green pepper slices this time of year with a little bit of jicama."

"Perfect," Mrs. Buckwalter said as she lowered herself into a seat at one of the kids' tables. "Jess and I will have the veggie burgers with vegetables."

Jess grunted. "Make mine a double ch—" Mrs. Buckwalter frowned at him and he finished lamely, "A double on the vegetables. Extra green pepper if you have it."

The boys and Garth's ranch hands were having pie at the café still when Linda got a telephone call saying several women were delivering prom dresses to the hardware store.

"They have that big rack in back where Matthew hangs the horse bridles. It's high enough up so none of the hems will touch the floor," Linda reported as she slid the last pieces of pie into place on the table where the ranch hands were sitting. She looked at Jess. His was the only place at the ranch hands' table that didn't have a piece of apple pie at it. "I've got some extra apples in back. I could slice you some fruit and put a sprinkle of cinnamon on it. It'd be almost like pie.''

"No, thanks," Jess said mournfully. "It wouldn't be the same."

"Your arteries will thank you," Mrs. Buckwalter encouraged from across the room.

Jess grunted. "They better 'cause my stomach sure won't."

"Here, have a toothpick." One of the other hands held up a small jar of wrapped toothpicks. "That is—" the man looked over at Mrs. Buckwalter and grinned "—if it's allowed on your new diet."

"Mark my words, young man." Mrs. Buckwalter stood and walked toward Jess's table. "You'll be better off eating toothpicks than double cheeseburgers with fries."

"Who can think about food? How many of the dresses are here?" one of the girls asked eagerly as she started to rise from her table. "And where is the hardware store?"

"I'll show you," Francis said as she stood.

When Garth and the ranch hands stood, too, Francis glanced over at her brother. "Really, Garth, there's no need. We're in Dry Creek. I'm perfectly safe here. When was the last time a stranger even came to Dry Creek?"

Francis's indignant question hung in the air for a few moments before she realized what she had said, and then sat down. "But that was different. The hit man was after Glory Beckett because she'd seen that crime committed and she knew something. I've never seen a crime committed. I don't know any dangerous secrets. No one has any reason to put a contract out on me."

"Of course not," Sylvia agreed easily. "But you know what they say about an ounce of prevention—"

"I suppose you're right," Francis said as she folded her hands.

Sylvia hadn't noticed the kids looking at each other until one of the girls asked, "Is something wrong?"

"There's nothing to worry about," Sylvia said firmly. She didn't want the kids to have to worry about anything when they seemed so happy these days.

"Sylvia's right," Garth said, and then he looked at Sylvia. "There is no need to worry. But it is good for you to know that we got a threatening phone call yesterday. We're just making sure everyone stays safe."

"Was it a gang?" John asked indignantly.

"Oh, surely not." Sylvia was startled. She hadn't even thought of the rival gang. "They're back in Seattle. They wouldn't—" She looked over at Garth. Could they?

"It was only a telephone call," Garth said thoughtfully. "Now that you mention it, it didn't sound local. Lots of noise in the background, like it was coming from a pay phone. But how would they know about Francis?"

"Did the man on the phone actually say my name?" Francis asked.

"Well, no, I think he said 'your sister.' But how would some kids in Seattle know I have a sister?"

Sylvia shrugged. "Lucky guess?"

"Could be," Garth sounded doubtful.

"It makes more sense than anything else I've heard," Francis said decisively. "They're probably in

Seattle this very minute laughing their heads off, knowing they have us worried.''

''Sounds like the gang,'' John said darkly. ''When they say they'll get you, they find a way.''

''Well, that's a relief, then,'' Francis said as she started walking toward the door. ''No more need to watch out for the boogeyman.''

''Hey, wait for me,'' one of the girls called out to Francis. ''I want to go see those dresses, too.''

Sylvia hesitated on the porch of the hardware store. The air was cold, and even the wood beneath her feet felt brittle. Sunlight strained through the thin clouds and emerged more white than yellow. There was no softness to this winter day. Garth had pulled the bus into the first space beside the door and he left the engine running.

''It'll be too cold otherwise,'' he said as he opened the bus door and stepped down.

''Remember to keep it in Park.'' Garth turned and gave instructions through the open door. One of the boys sat in the driver's seat. The other boys were huddled in the back of the bus talking. ''If I see those wheels move an inch, you're out of there and standing with me out here in the cold.''

Garth put his hands in the pockets of his wool coat and stood with his back hunched against the side of the bus. He turned and closed the door to the bus. He wanted to make small talk with Sylvia and he didn't want the boys listening. He'd already told the boys all of his conversational openers during the dance lessons and they would start to snicker when they recognized his feeble words in action.

''They going to be long?'' Garth asked Sylvia as

he nodded his head toward the girls inside the hardware store.

"Probably," Sylvia said as she rubbed her gloved hands together. She could hear the excited squeals of the girls' voices. "But I'll see if I can hurry them up."

"No, don't. Won't hurt the boys to wait." Garth shrugged. "They're just anxious to start learning to drive that old tractor." Garth grinned at her. "I haven't told them yet that the wind will blow snow down their necks when they're sitting up that high and the rattle the old thing makes will leave them wishing they'd never made mention of driving."

Speaking of cold down the neck, Sylvia backed away from Garth slightly. If she looked up at him, the collar on her borrowed jacket bunched up and left a tunnel for cold air to race down her back. If she stepped back far enough, she could look up at him and still stay reasonably warm. Not that she had any need to look at him in the first place, she told herself. She hardly needed to worry about being polite. They were only waiting for the girls. They weren't even in a real conversation.

Garth grimaced when Sylvia stepped back. He was glad the boys weren't around to see him strike out on this conversation. The cold had turned Sylvia's lips pale and he could see her teeth start to chatter. But she looked beautiful to him. He wondered if the cold weather on the morning they had met had forever changed his definition of beauty. These days he was more likely to dream of women in a snowdrift than on a beach.

Sylvia knew Garth was looking at her. She didn't like it, but she refused to give in to vanity and wrap

the soft wool scarf around her cheeks. She knew her
face was pinched. Her nose was probably red and her
cheeks blotchy. He was looking at her so intently, he
must be remembering the day he'd found her half-
frozen and slumped over in her car. She'd looked a
fright then, too. He must be worried about her passing
out again like that morning.

"I'm all right," she lied half-defiantly. "It's not
really that cold."

She stepped even closer to the hardware store until
she could feel the heat from inside. She glanced
through the glass in the door and saw that the potbelly
stove was still where she remembered it, square in the
middle of the wooden floor. The two old men were
still sitting around it and a game of checkers sat half-
forgotten as the men turned to talk to the girls.

Garth glanced over his shoulder at the bus. Good.
The windows had fogged up so no young eyes were
watching him. He didn't need an audience for this.
His moves were not smooth. He'd already proved that
today. But as sure as a salmon swims north, he had
to try. He stepped a little closer to Sylvia. "But you
must be a little cold. I could—"

Sylvia looked up at him in alarm and stepped back.
"That's all right—I mean, we could always go in by
the fire if you're cold."

"No, I'm fine." Garth backed away from her
slightly. She was definitely prickly. He was only going to suggest that he stand in front of her so he would
block the wind. How was he ever going to get close
if she was afraid to get within ten inches of him? He
had his Stetson pulled down to cover the tops of his
ears and most of his forehead. His wool coat was
unbuttoned and he had leather gloves sticking out of

the pockets. "It's not bad. I've seen winter storms cold enough out to snap the phone lines."

Garth backed farther away and leaned against the bus. He hadn't broken that wild horse when he was seventeen without learning a trick or two. Give a wild animal room when you're making your move. "Besides, we haven't had a moment alone since morning."

"We don't need a moment alone."

"Of course we do. How else am I going to ask you to the dance?"

Garth stuck his hands in his pockets. He suddenly felt the chill in his bones, after all. What was it with women? He could feel the temperature drop another ten degrees in the air between them. Sylvia sure took her sweet time about answering his question.

Finally she spoke. "You don't have to ask me to the dance. I'm already going." She paused. "Everybody's going—even Jess."

"I know everybody's going," Garth said patiently. He might as well finish it up since he'd started this suicide mission. "But there's a difference between you just going because of course you're going, and you going with me."

Sylvia felt the cold air as she sucked in her breath. She had dreaded this moment. "I'm sorry, but I don't date."

Some men refuse to die. Today Garth decided he was one of them.

"But you already said you were going," Garth said smoothly. Patience wins in the end, he reminded himself. Don't take offense. Don't push. Don't let it die. "Technically you're probably going with me whether you agree to it or not, since I'm driving the bus."

"So we wouldn't be alone?" Sylvia asked in relief. She hated to point it out to him, but that didn't sound like a date at all. "All the kids will be there?"

"Well, they'll be sitting in the back of the bus," Garth agreed. "I was hoping you'd sit in the front with me."

"I guess I could do that." Sylvia shook her head slightly. It was, after all, little more than a seat assignment.

"Good. It's settled, then. It's a date." Garth pulled his Stetson down even farther on his head. "Oh, and Mrs. Buckwalter might want us to drive the pickup home. She's planning to have Jess drive it there with the lobster pots. But she won't want him to drive it home on account of his night vision being so poor."

"But then there'd just be the two of us." Sylvia frowned.

"Well, maybe there'll be a lobster or two still swimming around in the pots," Garth said cheerfully. "But they'll be in the back so you won't need to worry about them. That is, if we can find some pots to use—what with all the people in the county coming—" Garth left his worry dangling and, sure enough, Sylvia picked it up.

"Pots are the least of our problems," Sylvia said. "We don't even know what to do with lobsters! I can't believe she's just having them shipped here."

Garth congratulated himself. It appeared Sylvia was even more afraid of those lobsters than she was of him.

"We'll figure it out. I asked Mrs. Buckwalter— they send instructions with the lobsters."

"A recipe?"

"Something like that. I figure if we could make the

oatmeal from the directions on a box, we can do lobsters.''

''The oatmeal had lumps.''

''Well, the lobsters won't. They'll be perfect.''

The door to the hardware store opened and, along with the warmth, Sylvia could smell a richly brewed coffee.

''That's almond-flavored.'' Sylvia turned to Garth in surprise. ''Glory's favorite.''

''Figured that's why Matthew bought a case of the stuff. They have it every day now. Matthew says it brings in the business. I tell him nobody needs to drink flavored coffee while they look through the catalog for feed supplements.''

Two of the girls came out of the door carrying dresses covered with plastic bags.

''Mine's got gold sparkles on it,'' Paula announced proudly. ''I'll look like a queen.''

Francis came out the door, too, with two women behind her.

''Oh, Sylvia, meet Doris June and Margaret Ann. They're coordinating the dresses.''

''I can't thank you enough,'' Sylvia said as she shook hands with the two attractive women.

''Well, don't thank us yet. We forgot the shoes.''

''We might need to make a trip into Billings after all,'' Francis said.

''Let us see what we can do first,'' Doris June said. The blond-haired young woman looked comfortable in her denim jeans and a flannel shirt. ''I'll call around. We should have enough shoes here in Dry Creek. It's just a matter of finding them.''

The rest of the girls came out of the hardware store and rushed into the bus with their dresses. Garth stepped into the driver's seat and Sylvia found an empty seat midway back in the bus.

This really is going to be a Cinderella ball, Sylvia mused to herself as she looked around at the kids. Francis had called a hairstylist that worked in Miles City and the woman was going to come out tomorrow to help transform the girls into princesses. She looked at the boys. She wondered how Garth was coming along in his efforts to transform the boys into princes. After all, Cinderella could get to the ball with an old bus instead of a carriage, but it wouldn't be much fun if there wasn't a prince there to dance with her.

Meanwhile, nearby

Flint was careful to stay hidden until the bus drove away. There weren't many places to hide in Dry Creek, but he swore he knew them all. He'd been shocked last night to realize the little town had apparently not changed since he'd lived here twenty years ago.

Flint found he could still fit snugly into the crevice beside the chimney on the outside wall of Mrs. Owen's house. He'd leaned back against the cold brick wall and had watched as the slow-moving bus had pulled up to the hardware store. The bus worried him. It wouldn't make much of a getaway vehicle. If he needed to get Francis away from here fast, he'd be better off on the back of the horse he'd rented in Miles City.

He hadn't had to fret for long. He saw Francis— his Francis—and all breath left him. She followed a group of teenage girls off the bus. It was as close as he'd been to Francis since he'd ridden his horse up to the shrub-lined border of Garth's ranch yesterday. Someone less observant would say Francis hadn't changed over the past twenty years. Her face held the same sweetness. Her step had the same regal gait. But his memory of Francis had been frozen in his heart for twenty years and he could pick out the small differences. The sadness that slumped her shoulders. The hesitancy that slowed her step just a little.

Maybe because everything else seemed unchanged in this little town, Flint had to fight the urge to go to her and enfold her in his arms. She belonged in his arms. Or she had, twenty years ago.

Flint had closed his eyes and taken a deep breath. The twenty years hadn't been erased. If he knew anything about women, he knew Francis had forgotten him years ago. There was no turning back time, not even in Dry Creek. When he'd opened his eyes, Francis had gone into the store.

Only her brother Garth and the other woman had stood outside. Flint would not have known Garth except for the pictures Francis had shown him long ago. Flint could tell by the relaxed set of Garth's shoulders that the other man hadn't seen the tire marks that Flint had seen this morning while he rode his horse around the perimeter of Garth's ranch.

Flint knew that someone besides himself had been watching the ranch house from a distance last night. It looked as if it had been two men. They'd been amateurs. One had dropped a dozen cigarette butts and the cellophane wrappings of a candy bar. Flint had put everything in an evidence pack. Any professional would know not to leave trash lying around. The fact that the men were amateurs didn't comfort

Flint. In fact, it made him even more worried. At least
professionals knew what they were doing. Things had
a way of getting out of control in the hands of amateurs.

Chapter Nine

"It won't take more than another minute," Francis said as she pinned up the last turn of hem. Sylvia was wearing the dress, turning obediently so the hem would be even. The kids had willingly gone to bed early and Francis was doing the last-minute sewing on the dress Sylvia would be wearing tomorrow. Except for being too long, the dress fit well. "It's an old dress of mind. But it'll work for a maid-of-honor dress. Don't you think, Garth?"

Garth looked up from the magazine he'd been half reading. All evening he'd been fighting the urge to stare at Sylvia. He'd put a huge piece of wood in the fire earlier and the coals now gave off a yellow light that surrounded Sylvia where she stood. Sylvia had her black hair pinned back loosely, and the delicate arch of her exposed neck held a steady sweetness for Garth. Both women were concentrating on the hem and not paying any attention to him.

He was glad for the privacy. He wasn't sure his face could stand much scrutiny. He knew right where he wanted to kiss her. With a neck like that, she could be wearing a gunny sack instead of the soft pink dress and she'd be beautiful in his eyes. "It's perfect."

Francis nodded in satisfaction as she stuck the last pin into her pincushion and sat back to look up. "It was the dress I wore when I went to Vegas."

"Oh, but then—" Sylvia turned in surprise and looked at her new friend sitting at her feet with a tape measure looped around her arm "—are you sure you want me to wear it? Maybe you should keep it in the box. I could always wear one of the old prom dresses."

Francis shook her head. "I've lived with my ghost long enough. It's time to air the cobwebs out."

Francis fluffed the hem of Sylvia's dress one last time and then stood slowly. "In case you're wondering about doing the same thing, the ghost didn't bite."

Sylvia knew that was as close as Francis would come to asking about the past that haunted her own life. "Oh, but I've taken care of my ghost."

"Have you?" Francis asked softly as she put her pincushion back in her sewing box.

Sylvia didn't answer. Until recently she truly thought she had buried the ghost of her ex-husband. She could hardly remember anymore what his face looked like. She no longer had the urge to hide when she heard footsteps that sounded like his. The fear of violence remained, but she had used that to help others face the violence in their lives. She had thought it was enough. Now she was no longer sure.

"Sometimes it does help to talk," Garth said softly. He had long since laid down his magazine. The fire was dying down in the fireplace and Francis had turned off the overhead light before she started pinning on the dress. Garth hoped the shadows in the room would make Sylvia feel comfortable enough to talk.

"It doesn't always," Sylvia said as she turned so she faced both Garth and Francis. "Even friends don't always understand how it was."

"Friends would like to," Francis said softly. "Give us a chance."

Garth thought Sylvia wasn't going to answer. She turned to look into the fireplace. Only the coals were alive but the light they gave off was enough to silhouette Sylvia. She looked vulnerable as she stood with her back to him, but Garth knew he shouldn't go to her and hold her like he wanted to do. The battle within herself was one she needed to fight alone. He could not force her to feel safe with him.

Finally she spoke in low uneven words. "They called him Buck—his real name was Harry. I met him when I was sixteen. Ran off and married him at seventeen. I thought he was everything. It wasn't until we'd been married a year that his mean side came out. The first time he hit me I thought I'd done something wrong—I thought I wasn't doing it right—that if only I were a better housekeeper, a better wife—" She took a deep shaky breath. "If only I had a baby, I told myself it would make him happy. Then we could both be happy. I thought I'd never have a baby. Then one day it happened—I was pregnant."

Sylvia lost herself in the telling of her story and stared into the fireplace for a long minute or two. "I thought he'd finally be happy. That our lives would go back to the way they were when we had first married. I was two months along when he asked me for a beer one night. He'd been out and drinking but he wanted another one. We'd run out and I'd forgotten my ID earlier that day when I'd gone to the grocery store so they wouldn't sell me any. I told him we didn't have any and he started screaming. I tried to say I was sorry, but he started hitting me—'' Sylvia stopped and took a deep breath. Her voice came out flat. "He beat me so bad, I woke up in the hospital. I lost the baby."

Sylvia turned and looked at Francis and Garth. "When I got out of the hospital, I left him."

"I'm sorry," Garth murmured. He didn't know what else to say. All he wanted to do was protect her, and there was no way he could.

Sylvia watched Garth's face. His brown eyes darkened and she saw the pity in them. She'd seen the same kind of pity in the eyes of other friends. She lifted her chin. "There's no need to be sorry for me— I mother many children now."

"I'm not feeling sorry for you," Garth began. He knew he was walking through one of those minefields. He had to be careful. "I'm sorry this all happened to you, and if I ever met up with that worthless husband of yours I'd show him a thing or two about—" Garth stopped. Minefield. She had that little frown between her eyes. "But I'm assuming he was arrested—" Sylvia nodded and he continued gratefully. "And I believe in letting the law handle our problems." Her little frown went away. Unfortunately, the sweat that was gathering on Garth's forehead didn't. "What I mean to say is that I wish it had been different, and I would do anything if I could have been there to stop him."

"Thank you," Sylvia said softly as she stepped out of the circle of firelight.

Garth watched as Sylvia and Francis silently put away the sewing items. He wanted to stop Sylvia and talk to her, but the straightness of her back told him she didn't want to be comforted. For the time being, he had to be content that she had told him what happened.

Garth shifted in the chair he had dragged into the kitchen. He'd tried to go to sleep in his own bed, but with every creak in the old house, he was up and looking down the hallway. He finally decided he might as well come down to the kitchen and keep watch like his instincts were nudging him to do.

Everyone else might believe the Seattle gang was behind the telephone call, but the more he thought about it, the more he was convinced otherwise. It was the man's voice on the phone that made him uneasy. It hadn't been the voice of a teenager, or even that of a young man. It was the weary, stomped-on voice of a man who had been to hell and back and was only still talking through the sheer habit of it.

The voice belonged to a man that reminded Garth of the man he'd been himself when he first came back from Asia. And even as violent as gang kids were today, they couldn't have seen the lifetime of weariness that would produce such a voice. No, the voice was combat hardened.

Strange that the fighting had been over for over twenty years and it was still the reason that he was sitting up on a cold winter night unable to let his suspicions rest.

He'd given up years ago on his hope that the scars

would ever heal. He'd just accepted that he would always be lame inside. On that long drive over to Seattle, he and Matthew had shared life stories. They both had their scars, but Garth knew that, compared to his own, the scars haunting Matthew's soul were those of a choir boy. Garth doubted God would even want to look on his own scars, let alone heal them. That's why when Matthew had offered to pray for salvation in Garth's life, Garth had hedged.

Garth didn't trust mercy. And as for salvation, if he needed it, he'd have to find a way to earn it. That's always the way it had been for him. He'd learned that nothing came free in life. Of course, Matthew had argued with him on that. Ministers were big on hope. That was their job. Matthew had told him that it was no good patching up his own life. Only God could do it.

Garth didn't respond, but he knew at least part of what Matthew said was true. There was no escaping the mess Garth had made of his life. Patches wouldn't begin to cover it. All he had to do was remember what his wife had said. Until the day she died, his wife had complained bitterly about his failings.

Garth could only stand helpless by then. All that she said was true.

He'd come back from Vietnam a different man. He wasn't the man she'd dated in high school. The prisoner-of-war camp had almost killed him. He felt as if he knew things inside that no decent person should know and he had to walk very carefully or they'd all spill out. He hadn't wanted them to spill out on his wife so he had tread very carefully.

But bottling them up only made him seem cold. His wife couldn't see his distress and he couldn't explain it to her. She had accused him of turning into a hard-nosed old rancher just like his father, unwilling to bend in life for any reason. Garth had flinched at her words, but he hadn't cracked. It was true. He supposed that's why he couldn't believe in mercy. His father didn't believe in it, either.

"What you need," Matthew had said that day driving back from Seattle, "is a new skin—"

Garth couldn't argue with that. What was it Matthew had said again? Garth tried to remember, especially because he knew that if he couldn't call the words to mind he'd be awake all night. The partial words would be like a phrase of a song lodged in his brain. The only solution was to go to his office and look at the Bible Matthew had marked and then given to him.

Well, he never was a man to put off unpleasant things, Garth said to himself as he swept off the blankets and stood up. His feet were bare and the linoleum was cold on his feet. He quickly sat down again and pulled on a pair of wool socks.

On his way back into the kitchen with the Bible in his hand, he turned on the small lamp he'd placed by his chair. He opened the Bible to the marker Matthew had left. There it was—*Mark* 2:21, 22: "No one sews a piece of unshrunk cloth on an old garment. If he does, the patch tears away from it, the new from the old, and a worse tear is made. And no one puts new wine into old wineskins; if he does, the wine will burst the skins, and the wine is lost, and so are the skins; but new wine is for fresh skins."

Now what did that mean? Garth supposed Matthew was trying to tell him it would do no good to patch up his life—that he would only mess it up if he tried—and that what he needed was a whole new one instead. He supposed Matthew could get a few votes on that if he put it to the people around here. He couldn't help but wonder what Sylvia would think of him if he was a new man.

Likely it wouldn't make much difference, he told himself sternly, as he walked over to the frosted windows and peered out into the night darkness. She still wouldn't trust him enough to lean back into his touch. He felt his fist curl. He'd told Sylvia he would have let the police handle her ex-husband if he knew him, but it wasn't altogether true. He might let the police pick up the pieces, but he'd make sure the rotten excuse for a man knew someone had gut-punched him before he gave him over.

Garth opened the door to breathe in a gulp of icy air. He'd never be able to sleep if he thought of Sylvia's ex-husband. He stepped out onto the porch in his stocking feet. It was peaceful out here. He could almost hear the groaning of the ice forming in the water tanks out by the barn. They'd need to crack the ice in the morning so the cattle could drink.

He looked down the long dirt road that connected his house to the gravel country road. There was a thin layer of snow from earlier in the night that shone on the permanent ruts in the road. No tire marks disturbed the snow. No intruders were out there.

He looked down at the bunkhouse where the girls were staying. Sylvia had taken a flashlight and walked down there not more than an hour ago. All of the windows were dark in the girls' bunkhouse, and he glanced over at the boys' bunkhouse to check it. The lights were out there, as well. He felt a sudden wave of protective contentment as he looked at the two bunkhouses. There was no doubt about it. Those kids were growing on him.

He smiled to himself. He'd have to give another dance lesson to the boys in the morning. They wouldn't like it, but they would thank him when they were terror-stricken tomorrow night on the dance floor.

He looked down at his watch. There was barely enough light from the open door behind him to see the hands, but he could make out the time. It was two o'clock. He turned around. He'd better get some sleep if he expected to dance until midnight tomorrow.

A muffled kick against the outside kitchen door woke Garth. Startled, he grabbed the baseball bat he kept beside the chair and looked around. The morning light was gray but it streamed in through the windows strongly. Nothing looked out of place. The box of oatmeal stood in the middle of the table. The counters were swept clear except for the plastic canisters for flour, sugar and coffee that were supposed to be there.

He looked down at his watch. It was almost seven, but they'd planned a late breakfast. The alarms in the bunkhouse wouldn't be ringing for another half hour. And if it was Sylvia or one of the others at the door, he would see their form in the frosted windowpanes at the top of the door. They would have no reason to hide.

No, something was wrong. He had the sense that his ears had heard other scuffling sounds before the kick. Well, maybe not scuffling sounds, more like soft grunts and the scraping of soft-soled shoes.

He picked up the phone that he had pulled into the kitchen from his office last night before he settled himself in the chair. The dial tone was still active. That relieved his fears. Even an amateur would know to cut the phone lines if they were up to something. He wondered if he should dial down to the girls' bunkhouse and tell Sylvia to keep the girls inside or if that would just frighten them and make them want to run up to the house.

No, he was best to keep them out of it. Besides, they weren't in danger. It was Francis who had been threatened.

He tiptoed to the bottom of the stairs and called softly, "Fannie."

He didn't want to open that door until he knew Francis was all right. He knew about traps that baited the curious. "Fannie?" he called again. He didn't want to leave the kitchen door unguarded or he would climb the stairs and wake Francis himself.

"What?" A grumble came from Francis's room.

"Nothing," Garth called back up, relieved.

He hefted the baseball bat onto his shoulder and walked softly back into the kitchen. He adjusted the bat and then hesitated. He supposed it was possible the boys were playing a trick on him. They were that age. He didn't want to scare them spitless by coming at them with a bat. He lowered the bat to his side.

The lock snapped quietly open but the doorknob whined slightly as he twisted it. He needed to give it a squirt of WD-40.

He took a deep breath. Surprise was half of his ammunition in this operation. He swung the door open quickly and stepped into position with his bat. Well, he amended his actions. He tried to step into position, but something rolled against his legs.

"What the—?" He stared down at what looked

like a dirty ball of human arms and legs at his feet. "How the—?"

He counted heads. There were only two. With all of the arms and legs, he thought there would be more. But no, there were just the two. One was a pixie-faced young woman with very tousled short brown hair. The other was a man so indignant, Garth feared for the poor fellow's heart. Both of them were gagged with red bandannas and tied together with rope so new, it fairly squeaked. Garth suspected he'd find his new coil missing from the barn wall when he went out there later.

Garth doubted anyone could have tied them into the tangle of rope they now found themselves in. They must have twisted and turned their way into the ball of limbs at his feet.

"Who—?" Garth mumbled again in amazement until he saw the irritation blaze up in the man's eyes. Whoever was lying at his feet was obviously not used to finding himself unable to talk.

"In a second." Garth answered the man's demand as he bent down and briefly patted both of them for weapons. It didn't make the man any happier, but Garth wasn't taking any chances. The two had been rolling around in the snow and flakes of it came off in Garth's hand. Only then did he lift his eyes and look farther outside than the porch.

"What—?" He was speechless.

The day was overcast and the light was gray. But even in the half-light Garth would need to be totally blind not to see the small airplane that sat serenely between his house and his barn. He blinked and looked again. No, it definitely was a plane. A small two-seater plane to be sure, but a plane nonetheless.

He would have suspected it was a mirage, but he saw
Sylvia walking out of the bunkhouse and staring at
the plane, too.

Garth looked back down at the tangle at his feet.
And then he looked up again at the plane and noticed
the wide path in the snow that led from the plane to
the door. He looked down at his feet again. Would
you believe that? Those two had managed to form a
ball and roll their way to his doorstep. They'd even
hobbled up the steps somehow.

He needed to untie one of the bandanna gags before
he had any hope of getting his questions answered.
The only decision left to make was which bandanna
to loosen. The man looked like he'd as soon spit at
the world as talk to anyone so Garth decided to lean
down and untie the gag on the woman first.

"Oh, thank you," the woman said as he lifted the
gag out of her mouth. She took a deep breath and ran
her tongue around her lips. "Whoever washed that
bandanna last didn't get all of the soap out of it. Too
short of a rinse cycle I think."

The bound man grunted at her in annoyance.

"Well, they didn't," she turned to him and said
indignantly. "And I don't think you would have liked
it, either. Not that you probably even know what laundry soap smells like. I bet you've never done a load
of wash in your life."

The man glared at her.

Garth relaxed and smiled at the man. "Quarrel with
the wife?"

"Oh, no." The woman seemed genuinely alarmed.
"We're not married. I mean—no, we're not married.
I work for him, that's all."

The man grunted again.

"Well, I did work for him," the woman continued a little uncertainly. And then she added defiantly, "Actually, I work for his mother and I'm not even sure he can fire me."

The man grunted again.

Garth looked down at the man a little warily. He supposed he needed to untie the man's gag. He just wasn't sure he wanted to witness the argument that seemed in progress.

"Who are they?" Sylvia stepped onto the porch.

"That's what I'm going to find out," Garth said as he eyed the ropes on the man.

"I'm Jenny," the woman offered as she smiled up at Sylvia.

"And I'm Sylvia." She knelt down and pulled off her gloves to work at the knot behind Jenny's back. "Whoever managed a knot like this?"

Garth's fingers stopped. He looked down at the man's face. The man was boiling mad. Garth knew that once he untied the man's gag, Garth wouldn't get a word in edgewise with Sylvia this morning. And he wanted to reassure her that everyone was safe.

"Sorry. It won't be long," Garth said as he abandoned the man's gag and moved his hands over to help Sylvia's struggle with her knot. Sylvia's fingers were still warm from being inside her gloves. But she did not seem to mind the cold of Garth's fingers as their fingers worked together on the knot.

This is the way it should be, Garth told himself. He and Sylvia working together. When the rope unknotted, Garth gave Sylvia's hand a squeeze. The skin on her hands was chilly now, but still soft as a summer peach. He held her hand for a second or two longer.

"What are you doing?" Sylvia asked with a trace of panic in her voice.

"Congratulating you." Garth tried to be nonchalant. "Shaking your hand sort of. You did a good job untying that knot."

Sylvia relaxed. "Oh, well, thank you."

Garth looked down at the gagged man at his feet. For a man who was gagged and couldn't talk, this one sure had a cocky, knowing look in his eyes.

"Well, you're not doing any better, Casanova," Garth mumbled low in the man's ear as he bent behind him to untie the bandanna.

The hard footsteps on the floor behind him told Garth he had more company.

"What's going on here?" Mrs. Buckwalter demanded as she marched across the kitchen floor. She had a gray wool robe pulled securely around herself and several pink plastic curlers in her hair. Even in the robe, she'd taken time to put on her regular shoes.

Garth had a sudden wish he had so prepared. The snow that had shaken off his two guests was melting and it was making his socks wet.

"What is it?" A lighter voice came from the stairs as Francis came into view.

"We've got company" was all Garth could think of to say.

"Well, bless my heart," Mrs. Buckwalter exclaimed as she walked closer and peered at the woman. "It's Jenny!"

Then Mrs. Buckwalter got close enough to see around Garth as he knelt by the couple. Her face went white and then rosy. "And Robert!"

Garth's fingers stopped in midtwist. "You know them?"

"Well, of course, I know them," Mrs. Buckwalter said indignantly. "I've been telling you about them all week. That's Robert—" she pointed at the man as though that explained everything "—and my chef, Jenny."

Sylvia noticed the cold for the first time since she'd walked out of the bunkhouse this morning and saw the small plane sitting there so innocently. "R-Robert," she stammered. She stopped trying to unknot the rope behind Jenny's hands. "You don't mean—"

Sylvia looked in dread at Mrs. Buckwalter, but the older woman was beaming.

"That's right," Mrs. Buckwalter said proudly as she adjusted one of her curlers as if it were a royal crown. "Robert, my son."

"Robert Buckwalter," Sylvia repeated woodenly. *Dear Lord, we're doomed. He wasn't supposed to come. He was supposed to be traipsing about Europe someplace.*

Sylvia shook herself mentally. If she looked panic-stricken, he'd close them down for sure, thinking she was up to no good. She forced herself to smile. "Well, welcome."

Robert Buckwalter grunted. Sylvia's heart sank even more. He didn't look too happy.

"I know this isn't the way you're used to being greeted," Sylvia continued nervously. "Not that, of course, we had anything to do with this. We would never—"

Sylvia did a quick mental check wondering if any of the kids would tie up two strangers. No, she assured herself, of course not. She continued more emphatically. "We would never greet anyone this way.

And we'll be happy to show you around as soon as you're untied and have had breakfast—" Sylvia's voice faltered. She remembered they were having oatmeal. *Dear Lord, at least let me get this right. No lumps, please.*

"Now," Garth said as he sat back on his heels and watched as Robert rubbed his mouth. The gag was off. "Tell us what happened." He looked at Jenny. "Both of you."

"There was a man," Jenny began.

Robert snorted. "Not just any man. A man about five feet eleven inches tall. I'd say one hundred and seventy pounds. Wiry. Maybe forty years old. Had some karate skills, at least that's what it looked like to me. He never actually made those kind of moves on us—"

"He didn't have to," Jenny interrupted and glared at Robert. "You wanted to surrender right away. You wouldn't even fight for what is yours."

"The day I risk death for a planeload of lobsters is the day I—"

"Lobsters!" Sylvia gasped. Her nightmare had arrived.

"Well, just because you have more gold than King Midas doesn't mean you should just throw it away," Jenny scolded. "Lobsters aren't cheap. Some people don't have money to just throw them away like they were sardines."

"Back to the man," Garth reminded them patiently. Robert and Jenny looked at him blankly. He repeated. "The man who tied you up. Did he say why he did that?"

"Well, I assumed he was going to rob us," Robert said indignantly.

Sylvia went limp with relief. Someone had stolen the lobsters. Hallelujah!

"He didn't even ask for your wallet," Jenny countered. "You half threw it at him." She pointed over to the plane. "And it's still lying there in the snow."

Everyone turned to look at the black square on the snowy ground.

"Well, if it wasn't robbery, what was it?" Robert looked up at Garth blankly.

"I don't know," Garth said grimly. But as sure as he had breath in his body, he'd find out.

"He just seemed to come out of nowhere when we landed," Robert said. "At first I thought he was confused. Said something about getting—or was it not getting?—someone. Frank or something."

"Francis," Francis herself said softly. She looked at Garth bleakly. "There is someone out to get me."

"Well, maybe I have the name wrong." Robert looked up at Francis. "Or maybe it wasn't a name at all. Maybe it was something like frankly—maybe he said he was going to get us frankly."

"But he didn't," Francis pointed out softly. "He didn't get you at all."

"Well, he did tie us up," Robert protested weakly. "Maybe that's all he wanted."

Robert looked at Garth. Sylvia saw the look Garth gave him in return. Neither man believed anyone had said "frankly."

Chapter Ten

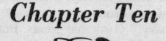

"Preserves?" Jenny asked as she lifted up one of Garth's juice glasses. She'd filled it earlier with some European apricot preserves that made Sylvia's mouth water even before she saw the fluffy biscuits that Jenny plucked from the oven.

Breakfast was later than usual because Garth and his hands had searched every building on the ranch looking for the man who had tied up Jenny and Robert last night. They spent two hours searching, but they didn't find anyone or any signs that anyone unusual had been around.

Jenny had made her first batch of baking-powder biscuits for the search party. She was taking the biscuits out of the oven just as they all came into the kitchen. The heat from the oven and the cold from the open door made a hazy steam.

"Whoever it is, he's gone," Garth had announced as he unwound the scarf from around his head.

Sylvia stared. That was the first time she'd seen Garth go outside without his Stetson. Instead of the hat, he'd wound that scarf around his head and neck and anchored it with a John Deere baseball cap.

"Must have been a—what do you call them here— one of your rustlers," Robert Buckwalter concluded. Robert had changed out of his snow-encrusted Armani suit and Francis had given him some of Garth's clothes—a red-and-gray flannel shirt and a pair of jeans. He'd worn a parka over them and joined the men in the search.

Garth only grunted at the theory and looked sideways at the women. "Doubt it."

"We don't need to be protected," Sylvia said indignantly. "You can tell us if there's trouble."

"When you're on my ranch, you're my responsibility, " Garth replied, tight-lipped. "You don't need to worry about trouble."

"I'm not a child," Sylvia snapped back. "I can take care of myself."

"Biscuits anyone?" Jenny interrupted and held a platter high. "I've got butter and apricot jam. If everyone finds a chair we'll eat."

"You're on my Christmas card list forever," Sylvia told Jenny as she bit into another apricot-topped biscuit. The two of them were sitting alone at the table after everyone else had finished breakfast. "You've saved us from lumpy oatmeal and half-burnt roast."

Jenny had come prepared with several boxes of food in addition to the lobsters.

Jenny laughed. "Well, I love to cook. And these kids—they're an easy audience to please. I promised to bring them pastrami sandwiches for lunch while they're decorating the barn and you'd think I'd offered them pure gold."

"They'd probably trade gold for some good food after my cooking," Sylvia said ruefully. "If there were any fast-food places around they'd be staging a mutiny already. I can't tell you how happy I am you're here to help."

"Well, it's good to have your cooking appreciated," Jenny said unhappily as she looked over at Robert.

Sylvia followed her gaze. Robert and his mother were standing in a corner of the kitchen and talking softly. Sylvia watched them closely, but it didn't look as if they were arguing. She was glad about that. So far, Robert hadn't said anything to her about the money his mother had donated to her center. But then maybe he was just letting her have her last meal in peace. She looked back at Jenny. "Well, if he doesn't appreciate your cooking, he must have had all his taste buds surgically removed."

Jenny smiled. "It's not that—it's just that he's eaten in some of the finest restaurants in Europe— from Paris to Rome. I've never even been to Europe. I can't compete with that."

Sylvia had been around enough teenagers to recognize the signs. "Why is it I have a feeling we're not only talking about food here?"

"We might as well only be talking about food for all the good it will ever do me," Jenny said forthrightly. "But I'm not one to sit around moping over what I can't have." She pushed her chair back from the table. "Especially not when I've got one hundred people coming for dinner."

"Well, I for one completely adore you—and your cooking," Sylvia said, and then added ruefully, "Besides, if you weren't here, I'd be trying to buy all the cream cheese in Miles City so I could make something resembling wedding appetizers on a stick.''

"Cream cheese rolled in those paper-thin ham slices with a toothpick stuck in them?'' Jenny guessed and grimaced.

"With chopped olives,'' Sylvia added, and then snuck another peek at the Buckwalters in the corner. "Oh, no.'' The Buckwalters were clearly in a heated discussion.

"Don't worry,'' Jenny said, giving her hand a pat as she stood. "He might not notice me, but he's a fair man. He won't just pull the rug out from under you without seeing you have someplace else to stand. And in the meantime, we have radishes to turn into roses,'' Jenny said as she gestured toward the kitchen counter.

"And don't forget the ice sculpture—'' Mrs. Buckwalter turned from her discussion with her son and beamed at the other women. "I want to do something special—'' The older woman stopped and then glanced out the window she was near. "Oh, dear, what's that?''

Sylvia heard a deep, rattling throttle and then the hard clicking sounds of boots walking across the porch. She saw Garth's silhouette through the door windowpanes before he opened the door and came into the kitchen.

Garth had his gray Stetson hat tilted back as though he had been concentrating on looking at something and then had forgotten to change the angle of his hat. He wore a wool jacket, but it was unbuttoned. His face had settled into lines of tiredness, but he was clean-shaven. At the moment, he looked exasperated. "Anybody see my ear muffs?''

"I think one of the girls borrowed them," Francis said as she walked into the kitchen from the living room. "I didn't think you ever used them so I thought it would be all right."

"It is," Garth said curtly. "I'm just looking for something to cut the noise. When these boys gun the motor on that old tractor, you can hear them in the next county."

It was a good two hours later before Sylvia had the kids loaded into the bus and delivered to Dry Creek so they could start decorating the barn. It was the same barn that Sylvia had seen decorated for the Christmas pageant a couple of months earlier. The wood inside had been scrubbed to a light pine shine before the pageant and even the rafters had been dusted. The barn would do justice to the dance to come.

"Throw me another roll of that rose paper," K.J. shouted from where he stood on a ladder underneath the hayloft at the back of the barn. They had three colors of crepe paper streamers—rose, light pink and white. They were draping them from the rafters in a crisscross pattern and were hanging big white wedding bells in the middle.

"When do we get to break out the sandwiches?" John asked for the second time in fifteen minutes. He was pushing a big, industrial broom.

"But it's only ten o'clock. Besides, we're not going to eat the sandwiches here," Sylvia explained again. "Matthew said we could go over to the hardware store for lunch. It's warmer there and he's going to heat us up some hot cocoa."

"Sure hope those heaters kick in before tonight," one of the girls said as she wrapped her sweater more closely around her. "Those dresses will be cold with-out heat."

"The heaters will work." Garth walked toward them. He had flecks of straw on his wool jacket and the headband of his Stetson. "I tried them out when Mrs. Hargrove first had her idea, and they warmed up the place nice—just took them a few hours."

"Hey, can somebody help with these tables?" one of the ranch hands called from the front of the barn.

Garth had offered the services of his ranch hands to help set up for the wedding dance tonight. He said it was a slow work week for them anyway. But Sylvia noticed that the hands took turns being stationed at the entrance to the barn, and from the way they kept looking outside it was clear their instructions were to be security guards.

"I've got the tablecloths for them," Francis said as she turned from where she was helping two of the girls twist the crepe paper. She looked to the front of the barn where two of the ranch hands were moving a long unfolded banquet table. "Just set it down and I'll snap the legs up on it. There's a trick to it."

"I'll come help you," Sylvia offered.

"No," Garth began and Sylvia turned to him again. "I mean—I was hoping you could help me."

"You?"

Garth nodded and then said in a low voice, "I need your help with something in this book—" He gestured to a small green book that was in his pocket. Sylvia looked but she didn't see a title. "I don't want the boys to see so I thought maybe you could help."

"Of course," Sylvia said. She always encouraged learning and if Garth needed something explained from a book she was honored he would ask her. "I applaud learning—"

"Well, it's not exactly that kind of learning—" Garth warned as he gestured for her to follow him and started to walk toward the back of the barn.

"It doesn't need to be highbrow," Sylvia said with a wave of her hand as she followed him. "All learning is important in the eyes of God."

Garth grunted. "Remember that."

Sylvia continued as though he hadn't interrupted her. She thought she was getting the hang of being around Garth. If she tried to picture him as one of the boys she tutored, she'd be all right. She had a full stock of learning platitudes. "We are what we learn. I'm sure I can help you with what you need. I may not understand it. I don't know much about farming. Or animals, really—unless they're cats, of course. But I can help with the words."

"Well, it's not so much the words—" Garth said as he stopped.

Sylvia looked up. They were standing at the foot of the ladder leading up to the hayloft. The steps up were steep, but that's not why Sylvia hesitated. The rest of the barn was brightly lit, but the light in the hayloft was dim.

"I can look at the book here," Sylvia offered.

"But the boys—" Garth nodded with his head to where the boys were standing.

Sylvia followed his gaze. Sure enough the boys were watching them. "Well, really, I don't see what it matters if they see—"

Garth looked mildly offended. "They need to think I know what I'm doing."

Men and their pride, Sylvia thought in exasperation. "Well, all right. We'll climb up there and read it. Although the light is much better down here."

"We won't need good light. It's mostly the pictures I need help with," Garth said as he stepped aside for her. "Ladies first."

Sylvia had one foot on the first step, but she turned around. "It's not geometry, is it? I'm afraid I'm not very good at geometry."

"Well, there is somewhat of a triangle involved. But go ahead—we'll work it out."

Sylvia stood in the center of the hayloft and looked down at the book Garth held open.

"That's not a triangle at all," she accused.

"Sure it is," Garth said as his finger traced the dance step in his book. "One. Two."

There were no windows in the hayloft and the only light filtered in from the opening at the front of the hayloft where a space was left for lowering bales down to the cattle below. The sweet smell of dried alfalfa surrounded them.

"But those are dance steps. And we already tried dancing. You don't need my help. You've been teaching the boys to dance already. I saw you."

"I haven't taught them dipping," Garth said as he took off his hat and laid it on one of the hay bales that lined the center of the hayloft.

"You don't need to take off your hat."

"A gentleman always takes off his hat when he dances with a lady."

Garth watched the emotions play across Sylvia's face. He was glad he hadn't just asked her straight out to dance with him again. The answer would have been no. But he knew she wanted the boys to learn dipping. He wondered if she wanted it enough to spend more time in his arms. "You'll need to dance with me anyway tonight. The kids will never rest until we've danced."

"I thought maybe I could dance with one of the boys—"

Garth shook his head. "As I remember it, at wedding parties the bride and groom dance and then the wedding party takes to the floor."

Sylvia looked at him blankly.

"That's us. Matthew asked me to be his best man. And you're Glory's maid of honor. We make up the wedding party."

"But we don't have any music."

Garth patted his other pocket and brought out a transistor radio. "It'll be scratchy, but it'll give us the beat."

Sylvia still hesitated.

"You don't need to be afraid of me," Garth said gently as he opened his arms. "I'd never hurt you."

"I'm not afraid of you," Sylvia protested stiffly as she stepped into his arms. "It's only a dance."

Garth didn't realize how tense he'd been until he felt Sylvia in his arms. Suddenly everything was all right again. His butterfly woman was in his arms. She floated with him. Their shoes brushed aside the wisps of straw as they danced.

"One. Two." Sylvia began to count.

Garth smiled. She could recite the dictionary for all he cared. The soft murmur of her voice warmed him. The sounds of a waltz scratched away on his radio. He was going to have to find out who ran the programming at that station and send them a thank-you ham. Maybe even a side of beef. Not that he needed the radio. His heart made its own music.

"Shouldn't we be dipping?"

Sylvia's question broke his reverie. Apparently his was the only heart that had been making music. Sylvia was looking at him suspiciously, as though she knew he'd used the dipping as an excuse to get her in his arms again.

"Just getting warmed up," Garth said defensively. Didn't the woman have any patience? "A guy can't just race around the dance floor and then dip—that's not very romantic. He has to wait for the moment when the music is just right and all."

"It's only for practice. We don't need a moment."

"Well, we do need the right rhythm."

"I'll count it out for us. One. Two. Three—" Sylvia drew out the last number expectantly and then paused. "You were supposed to dip on three."

"Nobody says I have to dip on three." Garth let go of Sylvia's hand and reached into his pocket that held the book. She slowed down and was going to pull away, but he pulled her back with his other arm. "Uh-uh, no need to stop. I'm just checking the directions."

Garth took his time looking at the diagram. "The woman in the picture is dancing a lot closer to the man than you're standing to me."

"A couple doesn't need to stand close to dance."

"Well, they need to at least be in the same vicinity," Garth said. His feet were still moving and Sylvia was still following him. He supposed he should be thankful for that much. He didn't know how much longer she'd take his lead. "Especially if they're going to—" Garth held his breath, took a firm hold on Sylvia's waist and dipped her.

Sweet Lord above! Garth felt his heart rise to his

throat. There'd been nothing in the diagram about the way Sylvia's eyes would look at him when he dipped her. Maybe it was only the surprise. But she looked at him like she was seeing him for the first time in a dream and liking every wrinkle on his sorry face. Her eyes only held him until she let out a soft kitten breath. Then he noticed her lips. They were slightly parted, as if she was going to say something but couldn't quite remember what it was.

Garth told himself he was only human. What choice did a man have? He bent his head slightly and kissed her. He knew he should keep the kiss light, but her lips were soft and he felt a jackhammer beating inside. A man had to take his chances in life. He deepened the kiss and tasted her sweetness. His last thought was that he could die a happy man.

It was Sylvia who pulled away. ''That's not in the directions.''

Garth pulled himself back to reality. ''Huh?''

''The kiss,'' Sylvia said distinctly. ''I'm sure that's not in the directions.''

Sylvia was still dipped but she was no longer looking up at him as if he was a dream. The fact is, she was looking at him more like he was an annoying nightmare that wouldn't go away no matter how much she frowned at him.

''It's implied,'' Garth said curtly as he straightened out his arm and brought Sylvia back to her dancing position.

''It better not be implied when you teach it to the boys,'' Sylvia scolded.

Garth didn't answer her. He usually knew what kind of ground he stood on, but with Sylvia he wasn't sure whether he was on granite or quicksand. Her cheeks were flushed and he could swear she'd kissed him back with all of the fervor he'd felt in his own hammering heart. But maybe he was mistaken. Maybe he'd been so moved by the kiss, he'd only convinced himself she was responding.

"We'd better get back downstairs." Sylvia drew away from him.

Garth let Sylvia float out of his arms and then he turned to pick up his hat. "You'll have to dance with me tonight, you know," he reminded her brusquely. "And I'll need to dip you to prove to the boys that I know how to do it."

"Well, you don't need to dip me. You could dance with someone else and dip them."

"You wouldn't want me to dip one of the girls."

"You're right on that," Sylvia said emphatically. "I don't even want you to dance with one of them unless you dance with all of them. But you're welcome to dip Mrs. Buckwalter."

Garth grunted. He doubted Mrs. Buckwalter would like that any better than he would.

Meanwhile, in the shadows of Dry Creek

Flint was cursing the cold. Why would anyone want to kidnap anyone in weather like this? He was wearing a beat-up brown parka and thermal underwear, but his bones were so cold he was afraid they'd start to rattle when he walked. The only saving grace, he ruefully admitted to himself, was that at least his legs were too cold to protest the bruising they'd taken last night on that horse. He'd been told her name was Honey. He'd hoped the name would sweeten her. It hadn't. Still, she got the job done.

He and Honey had been up all night guarding Garth's ranch. Flint knew the rustlers were out there. He'd even gotten close enough to two of them last night to hear them talking about orders to bring in the package soon. He'd hidden behind some low trees near Garth's west fence. He'd tied Honey up down the fence and lain on his belly on the freezing ground for a good half hour listening to the two men complain.

The two men hadn't mentioned whether the package they were going to ship was a certain woman or a truckload of cattle. It was annoying to wait so long and find out nothing but the kind of corn pads they used on their feet. He'd stopped listening when he heard the plane just before dawn. The two men scurried to their pickup like frightened toads in a thunderstorm when they heard the growing hum.

Flint thought the people in the plane must be involved, but the man and woman were more tourists than anything. They were deep in an argument when he pulled them from the plane. The only way he could stop the bickering was to put gags in their mouths.

Flint shook his head. Why would anyone fly into Montana in the middle of winter with a stack of live lobsters? It was the lobsters as much as the bickering that convinced him they were innocents.

Flint rubbed his gloved hands over his arms and shivered. Honey might be a pain, but he missed her all the same. She was the only breathing thing he'd talked to since he came to Montana.

By now she would be warm and cozy, content with her bale of hay. He'd bedded her down in an abandoned chicken coop that still stood on the farm just outside of town. He'd inherited the farm from his grandmother when she died twenty years ago. That property is what had brought him to Dry Creek long ago, and he'd never been able to sell it. The Montana winters managed to kill off the weeds each year or it would be overgrown by now. As far as he knew, no one but gophers ever visited the place anymore.

Chapter Eleven

The headlights on the bus showed up the ruts in the gravel road leading away from Garth's ranch. The lights weren't bright enough to dim the winter stars in the black night, however, and Sylvia looked out to admire them. She had to admit that Cinderella's coach couldn't have been more magical than this bus as it slowly ground its way to the ball.

Sylvia sat in the front seat, the one just behind Garth.

"I've saved this seat for you," Garth had said as Sylvia had stepped into the bus.

Sylvia was the last one to board the bus and she had assumed she'd need to squeeze in somewhere left over.

"Shouldn't you give that one to Francis?" Sylvia looked down the rows of seats. "She's carrying those bowls for lobster butter. They'll ride better in front."

The smell of Ivory soap was unmistakable inside the bus. The ranch hands were seated at the back of the bus with their hair slicked down and their hats in their hands. And the kids—she hardly recognized the kids. The girls were glamorous under their wraps. Upswirled hair and sparkling earrings peeked out from under serviceable parkas and thick jackets. Even the boys managed to look younger than they did in their street clothes.

"Francis and her bowls are fine next to Mrs. Buckwalter," Garth said patiently.

"But—" Sylvia looked at the front seat again. Someone had spread a fluffy white blanket open on the seat. And in the middle of the blanket lay a corsage of pink rosebuds laced about with baby's breath. Her eyes flew up to Garth's. "But—"

"A lady deserves a rose or two," Garth said softly.

Sylvia felt her breath catch. She hadn't stopped to take a good look at Garth this evening. She smelled the faint scent of a pine aftershave and noticed the boyish smile on his face. He was wearing a black tuxedo with cowboy boots and a wool hunter's jacket. The pressed white of his shirt made his tan look golden. He had on a different Stetson—this one a black so smooth, it looked like velvet.

"But where did you get it?" Sylvia knew there was no florist in Dry Creek. He would have needed to go to Miles City. That must have been where Garth went this afternoon. "I hope you were going for supplies, too."

Garth didn't answer directly. "Sometimes a special lady deserves something special no matter how much time it takes away from the chores." His voice poured over her spine and made it tingle. "And a gentleman makes it a point to see that those times come around."

"Oh." Sylvia snapped herself out of it. She was being a ninny. When Garth said the word *gentleman* she finally understood. He was showing the boys how to behave in a social situation. She felt herself relax. She was an object lesson in his role playing. She didn't need to worry. They were just team teaching. There was no need for the tingling in her spine. She was little more than a map on the wall in his class-room.

"Well, thank you. The corsage is quite lovely. Every lady—or girl—would be pleased with such a gift." Sylvia picked up the corsage and turned it so that the kids could see. She hadn't even lifted the roses up high before the boys started to stomp and applaud.

Sylvia turned back to Garth in satisfaction. "That worked very well. You're a natural teacher. Brilliant idea."

Garth opened his mouth and closed it again. What did she mean by "That worked very well?" By the sounds of it, it hadn't worked at all. He'd wanted to get a glimpse of the Sylvia he had dipped earlier. Instead, he got the congratulations of a schoolmarm.

Well, he assured himself, they hadn't begun to dance. She'd look at him with dreams in her eyes before the evening was over, or his name wasn't Garth Elkton.

It wasn't until he was parking the bus in front of the café in Dry Creek that Garth remembered his real name technically wasn't Garth Elkton. His birth certificate listed him as Gerald Elkton, in honor of a grandfather. He hoped that wasn't a bad omen.

Sylvia forced her eyes to look straight ahead. She was standing with her back to the entire population of Dry Creek, listening as the vows were read again to Glory and Matthew. It was a solemn moment. A holy moment before God. She had no business letting her mind, or her eyes, wander to the man standing just slightly behind Matthew. Just because the best man had the bad manners to let his eyes wander over to her instead of focusing on the couple reciting their vows was no reason for her to relax her attention or her spine. She'd count the buttons on the back of Glory's dress if she needed. Anything to keep her eyes in place.

"When it comes to better or worse," the pompous voice of deputy sheriff Carl Wall sounded forth. The deputy had an open Bible in his hand and an empty holster at his side. "I figure the two of you have already come to the bad part and waded through it pretty blamed good—so here's hoping that's all done and behind you. I wouldn't think there'd be more folks out to kill you."

Deputy Wall had offered to read the lines for Glory and Matthew as they re-affirmed their vows in the hearing of all of Dry Creek. When Mrs. Hargrove had protested that she'd not have an armed man read from the Bible, the deputy had pulled his gun out of his holster and set it on the counter at the hardware store. When she'd protested he wasn't a minister, he'd said that aside from Matthew, he was the only recognized official in the whole town of Dry Creek.

"And the minister can't marry himself," Deputy Wall had said emphatically.

"It wouldn't be right."

Mrs. Hargrove hadn't had an answer to that one.

"Besides, I have a uniform," Deputy Wall had continued. "I'll look good in the pictures. Hear they might send a photographer out from Billings. We'd want a good picture. Do Dry Creek proud.''

Mrs. Hargrove had given in and Deputy Wall had been at it for fifteen minutes now. Sylvia thought he sounded as if he was reading a prisoner his rights rather than reading parts of the most beautiful ceremony in the world, but Sylvia wasn't going to protest.

''I forgot the question about if anyone has any good reason why these two people should not be married they are to speak up—'' Deputy Wall looked out over the audience. '''Course it won't do any good since they were married last week and this is just an instant replay. But if you have anything to say, you might as well get it off your chest now.''

There was a minute of silence. Someone coughed in the audience and, at a chastising glance from Deputy Wall, muffled it quickly.

''I know some of you think I should be the one speaking out against this whole marriage,'' Deputy Wall finally said. ''And I'll have to admit that the angel—'' he glanced down at Glory fondly ''—and I have had our misunderstandings in the past, but that's all behind us. I'm here to say she's one of us now and I'd take a bullet for her. Just like I'd take a bullet for any other citizen of the fine community of Dry Creek, and I'd thank you to remember that come election time this fall. I'd also—''

Mrs. Hargrove cleared her throat in warning.

Sylvia looked over at the older woman. She sat with her arms crossed in the front pew of the church. Next to Mrs. Hargrove, grinning throughout the ceremony, were Matthew's twin boys, Joey and Josh. They had each carried a candle up to the altar earlier in the ceremony and both Glory and Matthew had bent down to kiss them before they began their vows.

"Anyway," Deputy Wall continued, "it's time for the exchange of the rings. And since the rings have already passed hands, so to speak, I want to present the happy couple with another circle to remind them of their meeting that took place right here in the fine community of Dry Creek just several months ago."

Deputy Wall reached behind his belt and pulled off the pair of handcuffs that were hooked there. He held them up dramatically, giving the Billings reporter a clear shot for a photograph. "These are the same cuffs that I put around that hit man's hands when I disarmed him right during our Christmas pageant—saving Glory here from being shot and killed. For their sentimental value, I'm giving them to Glory and Matthew to remind them that they have friends in Dry Creek—friends that would take a bullet for them. Not that," he hurried to add, "we expect any more bullets to be flying around—not with me on watch."

Deputy Wall gave the handcuffs to Glory with a flourish. Sylvia was close enough to see that the handcuffs had been engraved with both Glory's and Matthew's names and little hearts had been pressed into the metal. As she saw the reporter take his third photograph of the handcuffs, Sylvia had to admit that Deputy Wall knew how to stage publicity.

"And—for the record—no tax money was paid out for the cuffs."

Mrs. Hargrove cleared her throat again and, this time looked meaningfully at her watch.

"Well, it's getting time for dinner. And since the 'I do's' have already been said, and I expect put into practice—" Deputy Wall winked at Matthew "—I call this wedding official. I now pronounce you Mr. and Mrs. Curtis.''

Glory and Matthew turned around and faced the people of Dry Creek.

Sylvia had no trouble looking at Glory now. Her friend's face was pink with happiness. Glory looked up at Matthew, and the love shining in her eyes warmed Sylvia until she felt tears in her own eyes. *Thank you, Lord, for this blessing for my friend.*

''Oh, I forgot—'' Deputy Wall called out over the cheering. ''He's supposed to kiss the bride.''

Matthew wrapped his arm around Glory and drew her to him in a vigorous kiss that left no doubt of his affection. Sylvia felt more tears gather in her eyes. The love between Glory and Matthew was a beautiful thing to behold.

Garth patted his tuxedo, looking for a pocket. That was the trouble with fancy clothes—they never had any pockets, he thought to himself. And how was a gentleman to reach into his pocket and offer a lady a handkerchief, if he had no pocket? Garth was almost going to go looking for a handkerchief when Mrs. Hargrove stepped up to Sylvia.

''Here, dear,'' the older woman said, pulling a white lacy handkerchief out of her coat pocket and giving it to Sylvia. ''Weddings always make me cry, too.''

Garth grimaced. It was a sad day when he was outgentlemanned by Mrs. Hargrove.

Sylvia absentmindedly licked the butter off her fingertips and then remembered where she was and looked around quickly to see that none of the kids had seen her. Mrs. Buckwalter had given them a demonstration back in the kitchen on the correct way to eat a lobster, and it hadn't included any finger licking. Mrs. Buckwalter had been most emphatic about the use of the white linen napkins at each place setting.

Not that the people here would care who became impatient with napkins.

The whole town of Dry Creek had crowded into the café for the lobster dinner, and the quiet clatter of silverware could barely be heard over the laughing conversation of the people gathered. The café was so full that some of the ranch hands had taken their plates out to sit on the porch.

Mrs. Buckwalter had outdone herself. She'd had Jenny cook fresh asparagus and new potatoes to go with the lobster—although where she'd gotten the asparagus in February, Sylvia was afraid to ask.

"You know this isn't bad," one of the girls, Sarah, said quietly as she pulled some meat out of her cracked lobster. "I thought it'd taste funny, but it doesn't. It's all right."

"Just tastes like butter," Francis agreed as she dipped a chunk of lobster meat into a bowl of melted butter. "I haven't had lobster for years. I'd forgotten how nice it can be."

Sylvia noted that Garth had stationed two of the steadier ranch hands on either side of Francis at the table. They were quiet, muscular men who periodically checked the door. Garth wasn't taking any chances.

Francis, herself, seemed oblivious to the fuss. She was dressed in a long ruby-colored dress. The bottom floated around her like she was a Roman goddess while the top of her dress was covered with a practical, no-nonsense black wool jacket. It was a little chilly in the café.

"More lobster," Robert Buckwalter said as he pushed a utility cart close to the table where they sat. "It's freshly boiled. Ready for cracking."

Sylvia had to give Robert credit. For a rich man, he was a remarkably good sport. He had offered to help Jenny cook the lobsters and she'd said he'd make a better waiter than a cook so he'd gone to his plane and pulled out a tux. He looked every inch a sophisticated waiter.

"We don't usually eat lobster," Sylvia hastened to assure him. She didn't want him to think that the foundation's money was being used to feed her kids gourmet meals. "We've stuck more to the basics for meals."

Robert grimaced. "My mother told me. I wouldn't call macaroni and cheese a basic. I just hope the news media never hears about it. They'd love to tear apart the Buckwalter Foundation for taking a bunch of city kids out to the country and giving them a major case of malnutrition."

"We had carrots, too."

"Well, that's something," Robert said glumly as he sat down in a metal folding chair next to Sylvia. The chair was scratched and it creaked when he settled back into it, but he didn't seem to care.

All of a sudden Sylvia noticed that Robert, even in his tux, was looking a little wilted. "Tired?"

"I can't be," Robert said stiffly. "I work out an hour every day in the gym. I do power exercises. Strength training. I'm in top physical shape. I could run a marathon. Pushing a few lobster around on a cart is nothing for me."

"Good."

Robert was silent for a moment. "She doesn't like me, you know."

Sylvia wiped the butter off her fingers and patted Robert's arm. "Your mother?"

"My mother? Why would you think my mother doesn't like me?" Robert turned and looked at Sylvia indignantly. "Of course my mother likes me. It's her." Robert jerked his head toward the kitchen. "She doesn't like me."

"Ahh," Sylvia said in what she hoped conveyed sympathy. "Jenny."

"I offered to buy her an evening gown for tonight. Something special. I could have had a designer original here in three hours, maybe two," he boasted, snapping his fingers. Then he looked back down at the table. "She didn't want it. Wouldn't even talk about it. Said if I brought it here, she'd give it away to one of the girls."

"Maybe she had something else she wanted to wear," Sylvia offered.

Robert snorted. "She's wearing her chef's apron. Lobster stains and all. I think she's even going to wear that ridiculous hair net." Robert looked directly at Sylvia. "You're a woman. Tell me why any woman would turn down an evening gown—a designer original evening gown—in favor of an old chef's apron?"

Sylvia shrugged. "Why don't you ask her?"

"Maybe I will." Robert stood and started to push his cart back toward the kitchen.

"And ask her to dance while you're at it," Sylvia called after him.

Robert turned and nodded curtly. "I think I will."

Sylvia smiled to herself. The dance coming up was going to prove interesting.

Garth was watching Sylvia smile. She was standing in the middle of the barn and looking around at the decorations the kids had made this afternoon. There were long streamers of pink crepe paper and wedding bells from every rafter. The kids had actually made the old barn glitter. As Sylvia completed turning around and studying the decorations from every angle, her smile deepened until she glowed.

Now this, Garth said to himself, this is the Sylvia he wanted to dip on the dance floor. He looked around. Where was the music? The sooner he got to dancing, the sooner he could get to dipping.

Garth looked over Sylvia's shoulder. Good, Francis was sitting down with some of the older women in the town. He needed to keep her in sight. Not that there was much to worry about tonight as long as Francis stayed with the crowd of townspeople.

The quiet sound of music grew in volume until the rich sounds of a slow-dancing song filled the barn. Garth looked over—the sound system he had bought for the town when they hosted the Christmas pageant was being put to good use. He hoped they had a whole stack of slow cassettes. He didn't want to be moving too fast when he dipped Sylvia.

Sylvia needed to clear her throat. No, she needed to swallow. She wasn't sure what she needed to do. All she knew was that her throat had turned to cotton about two minutes into the dance with Garth. She felt as if she was thirteen again. She didn't even know

where to put her hands. What she did know was that
he was too close.

"Remember you're the leader," Sylvia finally
mumbled into his shoulder.

Garth blinked. He was so caught up in the soft
sway of the music and the smell of Sylvia's hair that
he hadn't been paying attention.

"I'm sorry. Did I miss a step?"

Sylvia lifted her head and whispered distinctly, "I
didn't say you're leading. I said you're the leader—
the boys will be watching you."

Garth looked around. It didn't appear that the boys
were watching much except the girls they had in their
arms. He looked back at Sylvia. "Why would they
watch me?"

"They'll want to know how close they can dance
with the girls."

Garth noticed that Sylvia had bright red spots on
her cheeks. Her arms were braced against him,
whether to hold him away from her or hold herself
away from him he wasn't sure. "Isn't that up to the
girls?"

"Of course not," Sylvia said shortly. "Teenagers
need to know the limits and it's up to the adults to
set them."

Garth looked around at the dancers again. "I don't
see anyone who's dancing so close as to make it a
problem."

"Well, they will be," Sylvia retorted softly. She
half stumbled and Garth steadied her. "We need to
be a good example."

Garth opened up his arms and gave Sylvia more
room. "If you need more space, you can tell me. It
doesn't need to be about the kids. It can be for you."

"I don't—I—" Sylvia sputtered and then took a breath and said simply, "Thank you."

"It's all right," Garth murmured as he slowed his step.

"I'm sorry." Sylvia removed her arms from Garth's shoulders and wrapped them around herself. "Maybe you want to dance with someone else. I—"

Sylvia looked up at him and Garth would have traded his ranch for the chance to pull her into his arms and comfort her. But it was clear she wouldn't be comforted by that gesture. She looked thoroughly miserable and nervous at the same time.

"I'm sorry," Sylvia repeated, and stared over Garth's shoulder. "I think maybe I'll go sit with the women. If you want to ask someone else to finish the dance, I'd understand."

"I don't need to finish the dance. I'm happy to sit out the rest of the night with you if that's what you want."

"But you won't get to show off your dip," Sylvia protested halfheartedly. "That's what you came for."

"I came to be with you," Garth corrected her softly. "I don't care about the dip."

"I'm sorry I'm not very entertaining tonight," Sylvia said as she started to walk toward the knot of older women who were sitting beside the door.

"You don't need to entertain me." Garth followed her. "I'm your friend. Friends sit with friends when they need them."

"I don't need anyone," Sylvia protested stiffly as she nodded a greeting to Mrs. Hargrove and sat down on a metal folding chair near the older woman. "I do just fine alone."

"Well, maybe *I* don't do so good when you're

alone,'' Garth said in exasperation as he turned an empty metal chair around so that he could straddle it and sit facing Sylvia. "Maybe this is all selfish on my part."

"You're just being kind," Sylvia said woodenly as she rubbed her arms to warm them.

"No, I'm not being kind." Garth looked over at Mrs. Hargrove. "Those heaters are working, aren't they? Sylvia's cold."

"You don't need to—"

"See that the heaters are working?" Garth finished for her in astonishment. "Can't a man do anything to help you without you pretending you're all right?"

"I am all right." Sylvia stopped rubbing her arms and smiled up at him brightly. "There, see. I'm fine."

Garth looked at Sylvia skeptically. The gown she wore was cut so low off her shoulders that he knew the skin of her back was pressed against the cold metal of the folding chair she was sitting in. Her arms were covered with goose bumps. Granted, the sight of her in that dress made his blood boil, but it didn't keep her warm. "I'll check the heaters."

"But—"

"If you're cold, other people will be, too," Garth insisted as he stood.

It was then that he noticed Mrs. Hargrove had stopped talking with Doris June who was sitting on her left side and was now looking to her right side and studying him and Sylvia with frank approval.

"Excuse me," Mrs. Hargrove said when she saw that she'd gained Garth's attention. "I couldn't help overhear. If Sylvia is cold, she's welcome to borrow Francis's jacket. Francis got up to dance and left it here. I'm sure she won't mind."

Mrs. Hargrove held up the black jacket that Francis had worn earlier. "Those old varsity school jackets— I see more of them around Dry Creek than you'd think. Before the old high school closed." She turned the jacket so Sylvia could see the emblem of the tiger on the back of it. "They were the fighting tigers. They were a small school, but they had pride."

"Who was Francis dancing with?" Garth asked, his eyes skimming the couples on the dance floor.

"Jess asked her."

Garth searched the dance floor again. "I don't see them." He looked at the people lining the walls of the barn, talking. "Are you sure she's not with someone else?"

"Why, no, it was Jess. Why, there he is himself— ask him."

Garth turned to the older man. "Is Francis with you?"

The older man flushed. "That's what I came to tell you. I excused myself to visit the men's room and when I came back, one of the kids said Francis went to the bus to get some cassette she'd brought. She said she'd be right back, but I looked and I didn't see her."

"She can't be gone." Garth said the words without thinking. He scarcely noticed that Sylvia had stood and put her hand on his arm.

"We'll find her." Sylvia comforted him. "She's probably just gone to the rest room. Or maybe she stopped to talk to someone. There's so many people here. She can't be far."

"I'll just go to the bus and check if the cassette is still there." Garth felt the emotion drain from him.

He couldn't afford to feel anything. He needed to think. "Did she say what the song was?"

"'Blue Velvet.'" Jess shuffled his feet and looked miserable. "I can ask around inside and see if she's talked to anyone."

Garth nodded. "I'd appreciate that."

"And I'll go with you," Sylvia offered decisively.

"You can't—we don't know who's out there."

"Whoever they are, they're not looking for me," Sylvia protested reasonably. "Besides, four eyes are better than two."

"Okay." Garth nodded. "She's probably just out looking at the stars anyway. She always did like the night sky."

Sylvia nodded and started to the door. "We'll find her."

"Wait," Mrs. Hargrove called. She held out the jacket to Sylvia. "You'll catch your death of a cold out there. Take this."

Sylvia walked back and took the jacket.

"Thanks," she said as she slipped her arms into the jacket sleeves and took the red knit scarf out of the pocket and wound it around her neck. "We'll be back soon."

Meanwhile, outside in the dark of night

Flint swore. No wonder being a hero had gone out of style. His leg still stung where Francis had kicked him in her glittery high-heel shoes, and one of his toes could well be broken where she had stomped on it. Next time he'd let the kidnappers have her. She was more than a match for most of the hired toughs he'd seen in his time.

And thinking of his toes, what was she doing with shoes like that anyway? Women only wore shoes like that to please a man. She must have a boyfriend inside that old barn.

Flint's only consolation was that his horse seemed to know he needed her and was behaving for once.

"Now I know why I call you Honey," Flint murmured encouragingly as he nudged his horse down the dark road.

"Haaargh," the angry growl came from the bundle behind him, but Flint didn't even look back. Except for being temporarily gagged, Francis was doing better than he was. He'd even put his jacket around her. Not that she had thanked him for it.

"Yes, sir, you're a sweetie, all right." Flint continued quietly guiding his horse. Honey knew the way back to her home even if it was only a humble abandoned shed. That horse could teach some people the meaning of gratitude.

Or, if not gratitude, at least cooperation, Flint fumed.

If it wasn't for his years of training as an agent, Flint would have turned around and told Francis a thing or two. What did she think?

There was no time for the niceties after he heard those two hired thugs repeating their instructions about kidnapping Garth's sister in her black lion jacket. They planned to wait for her by the bus parked right next to that old cattle truck they'd come in. And they mentioned a third man would be coming to help. Flint had already identified the truck and disabled it as best he could by dumping some of the sand from the café's large ash can into the gas tank while the men were eating lobsters with everyone else. He'd cringed at having to do it, but the men had chained the hood shut so he couldn't get to the spark plugs. He would have disabled the three men, too, but Francis didn't have sense enough to stay inside long enough for him to do it.

He was halfway to the bus when he recognized her silhouette in the door as she opened it briefly. There was no time for fancy plans. The only way to protect Francis was to grab her first and worry about the men later.

He knew the men would be a problem, but he hadn't counted on Francis's resistance. He thought once she knew it was him she'd come quietly. Perhaps even gratefully. But the moment he saw recognition dawn, she fought him like he was out to kill her. He hadn't planned on gagging her until she made it clear she was going to scream.

And all the while she was kicking and spitting, he'd been doing her a great service.

Yes, he sighed, he could see why being a hero had gone completely out of style. It wasn't easy being the knight on the shining white horse. Not with women today. Come to think of it, it wasn't even easy with the horses of today. Honey made it clear she'd rather be eating oats than rescuing a damsel in distress.

"Tired. That's what you are," Flint said softly as he leaned over the horse's neck. Honey sighed and he gave the horse another encouraging nudge. "We're both tired, aren't we? But don't worry. We're almost there. Then I'll have something sweet for you."

The bundle behind him gave an indignant gasp and then another angry growl.

"I was talking to the horse." Flint smiled in spite of himself.

Chapter Twelve

Sylvia put her hands in the pockets of Francis's jacket. The ground in front of the barn was frozen and crusted with patches of old snow. The snow and dead grass crunched beneath her feet as she walked beside Garth. It must have been about ten o'clock and the night darkness was just turning deep. If it wasn't for the light streaming out of the barn doorway behind them, there would be no light except the distant stars in the sky.

"She has to be still here," Sylvia finally realized. "It's so dark we would see taillights from a car for miles. No one could have kidnapped her and already gotten away."

Garth grunted. "Unless he turned off his lights."

"In terrain like this?" Sylvia asked incredulously. "There are snowdrifts all along the road. And ditches on the side that you can barely see with lights. No one is that foolish."

"We can hope not," Garth said grimly. He privately thought that someone foolish enough to kidnap

Francis wouldn't have sense enough to avoid getting stuck in a snowdrift.

"There's the bus." Sylvia saw the dark form of the bus emerge from the black night. It was still parked where they'd left it, next to the café. There were a few scattered pickups and one cattle truck next to it that must have been left by ranchers who had come in for the wedding reception. "All these outfits— that's probably why Jess couldn't see Francis. She's probably in the bus now looking for her cassette. Maybe it fell down beneath a seat."

"I don't see anyone in the bus." Garth worried as they walked closer.

Sylvia looked carefully. If Francis had gone inside the bus, wouldn't the door be half-open? And there were no dark shadows that looked like someone was inside walking down the bus aisle looking for something.

"You stay here," Garth ordered as he opened the bus door.

Sylvia hunched her shoulders. The jacket she'd borrowed was a little large and it left a gap that allowed air to funnel down her back. If she hunched her shoulders, she could close the gap. She could see a dark shadow of Garth as he walked down the bus aisle, checking in each of the seats. Maybe Francis was inside the barn still, Sylvia thought. Maybe she was having a good time and had just forgotten Garth would be worried if he didn't know where she was. *Please, Lord, protect her wherever she is.*

Sylvia could see the shadow of Garth as he turned and was now walking back down the aisle. She then suddenly smelled something. Her first thought was that it was an old rag that someone had left outside.

It smelled of old garlic and sweat. Then she realized with a start that a rag left outside in the cold for any length of time would freeze and not smell at all. She didn't even have time to turn around before the rag was being passed over her eyes and down to her mouth.

"Aaarrrgh." Sylvia's scream was muffled as the rag settled into her mouth.

"Zahat taaa mugft." Sylvia tried to ask what had happened, but the words never left her mouth. She jabbed her elbows back, hoping to stop her attacker. But all she managed to jab was air. She was being captured by bulky shadows. She'd swear the men had not been there two seconds ago, and now they hovered over her. She couldn't see any faces, but she could smell the men. They smelled like old socks that had been worn hard and then tossed inside a gym locker to ripen.

"That's the jacket," one of the men said confidently to the other as he held Sylvia's hands behind her back. "It was easier than I thought. She didn't even give us much of a fight."

Sylvia tried to move at that one. She tried to tell them that the only reason she hadn't given them more of a fight was because she hadn't known they were coming. If they had fought fair, she would have gotten her licks in.

"Hmph," the other man said as he twisted a rope around Sylvia's hands until she was securely bound. "Maybe she's just smart. Knows we wouldn't mind plugging her if she gave us any trouble."

Sylvia stilled herself. She needed to focus—and to see. She could barely see the detail in the men's clothing, but she knew she needed to locate the bulges that would tell her if the men were just trying to scare her or if they really had guns. If they were armed, she had to act fast. Garth was inside the bus and would be an easy target when he opened the bus door and stepped down.

Sylvia looked down. She wished there was something to kick. A bucket would make a big enough noise to alert Garth. But there was no bucket. The dirt ground was covered with patches of snow. There weren't even any rocks she could kick up against the side of the bus.

The only thing on the ground in front of her eyes were the four feet of the men holding her. Sometimes God calls us to be resourceful, she reminded herself, as she did what she had to do. She lifted her foot and stomped down hard on the toe nearest her.

"Hey, watch what you're doing!" the man protested loudly as he danced his feet back out of her reach.

"Shhh." The larger of the two men turned to the other and shushed him with a whisper. "Stop your caterwauling."

The man defended himself. "She pounded my toes."

"Forget about your toes. You can buy new toes with what we'll get off this deal," the larger man ordered.

"Just make sure you tie her feet together before we take her to the boss," the injured man said. "He won't like something like that—might even decide it's our fault for not teaching her better manners while she was with us."

The injured man turned to Sylvia and smiled. Or, at least, she thought he smiled. She saw the white of his teeth as he bared them. And then she smelled the sour garlic. She'd seen friendlier smiles on the faces of the cougars at the Seattle zoo just before feeding time.

"Bet I could teach her some pretty manners," the man continued. "Pretty little thing like that. Would be a pleasure."

His voice was greasy with what Sylvia supposed served him as charm. It made her want to spray the air around her with disinfectant.

"We haven't got time for that nonsense," the larger man whispered wearily, and jerked his head to the barn. "You're forgetting we have an army over there who could come tramping out here. We need to get her out of here. The boss will know what to do with her."

Sylvia felt her blood turn cold. She didn't want to meet this boss. She wished they'd take the gag off so she could tell them they had made a mistake. The boss didn't want her. Then she realized her dilemma. They must want Francis, and if she told them that she wasn't Francis, they would go out and find the other woman instead. *Dear Lord, what do I do?*

Garth shifted his legs. He'd crouched down in the stairwell of the bus. The frost covered most of the window, but it had left a thin strip at the top. It was this strip that allowed Garth to see outside.

He'd counted two men, but he knew there was at least one more. He could tell from their murmured voices that they were only hired help. That meant there would be another man around. Hired help never worked without a lookout. That's part of what made them so successful. They didn't care enough to take unnecessary risks.

Garth felt around on the rubber mat behind him. When the bus driver had flown back to Seattle, he had left a long flashlight there. It was the closest thing to a weapon Garth could find. At first he picked it up and hefted it like a club. It wasn't heavy enough to do much damage. Then he had an idea and shifted the flashlight to its regular position.

Garth took a deep breath and pushed on the bus doors so they opened with a decisive swish. He counted on the sound of the doors opening to get the men's attention. It worked. The men both turned and looked straight at him. Then Garth raised the flashlight and clicked the button to the on position.

Good, thought Garth, the batteries were strong. The brightness spotlighted the two men and they froze, caught like deer in the headlights of an oncoming truck.

The light stopped the two men as no amount of hammering would have done. They had been out in the dark so long that night that the burst of light had to hurt their eyes.

"What the—?" one of the men said as he raised his hands to cover his eyes.

Garth didn't wait for a formal invitation. He tackled the man in his midsection while taking care to push the man he was aiming for into the other man. Garth had been up against two men a time or two in his life and he knew how to fight them. The key was to keep the action fast and always be a moving target. Most men, who were fighting more than one man, made the mistake of focusing. In a brawl one couldn't focus and win. One had to spin more than aim. And always remember the domino effect. A man pushed into another man makes both men fall.

Garth had the situation under control. He had one man in a hammerlock, the man's head in an elbow vise, while the other man lie moaning on the ground. Sylvia, a gag in her mouth and her hands tied behind her back, was squirming around and obviously trying to yell. Garth supposed she was doing what she could to help him by cheering him on, and the thought warmed him. Dancing wasn't the only way to win a lady's heart.

Garth was almost going to smile a victory smile at Sylvia when he felt it—a cold, little round circle pressed into the middle of his back.

"That's enough," the man's voice behind him said. "Be a pity to put a bullet hole in that fancy suit you're wearing. Rented, I expect. Still, they'd make your kin pay for it."

Garth carefully released his hold on the man in the hammerlock and the man fell to his knees. Garth thought carefully. He didn't want them to think he was poor just in case it made a difference. "The suit's mine." At least for tonight. He'd borrowed it from Robert Buckwalter. "From Italy."

The man with the gun whistled in respect.

Garth turned around slowly and checked on Sylvia. He couldn't read her eyes in the darkness, but he supposed she was frustrated with him. He hadn't gotten her message. Sylvia hadn't been cheering him on at all. She'd been trying to warn him.

"Italy, huh? You must get around more than most folks in this forsaken place." The man with the gun looked casual. Even in the darkness Garth could see a gun in one of the man's hands and a length of rope in the other. "Don't figure there's much call for suits when you spend your days slopping the hogs."

"This is cattle country," Garth said mildly as he looked away from Sylvia and focused on the man with the gun. The fact that the man was willing to talk was a good sign. It was always harder to shoot a man after a civil conversation with him. "Though we do have a few chickens. You ever raise a chicken?"

The armed man grunted and dipped his gun slightly to point at the man who was stirring at Garth's feet. "Lenny there used to have a dog. When we lived in Kansas. But that's the only animal we ever had. It died."

"Oh, you must be brothers, then?" Garth hoped the man would dip his gun again, this time farther down. A dip like that could be the only chance he'd get to disarm the man. "Never had a brother myself, but always thought it'd be good. Someone to get into scrapes with you."

Garth kept his stance friendly. A hired killer would sense a tensed up body before Garth would get a chance to make his move. Garth willed his heart to slow down.

The man grunted and nodded his head toward Sylvia. "Got yourself a sister, though. Bet you think a lot of her?"

Garth followed the man's eyes. So that was why they had Sylvia.

"Sometimes sisters can be a pain," Garth said casually. Before he claimed Sylvia as his sister, he needed to know if that fact would help her or harm her. He guessed it all depended on who was trying to take his sister. "Once, mine up and ran off to Vegas and never even told me about it."

The man with the gun looked completely indifferent.

Well, that eliminated Sylvia's ex-boyfriend as the gunman at least, Garth said to himself.

"Don't suppose the boss cares about that." Garth tried again. This illusive boss might be the ex-boyfriend, after all.

The gunman didn't answer that question. He seemed more interested in the other man behind Garth who was starting to stand. Garth knew that when the other man stood, his chances of getting the gun would be much less. Not that Garth needed to get the gun away from the man right away. If Garth could tease the man into firing the gun, the men inside the barn would know something was wrong.

"Come get the rope," the gunman ordered the man who was beginning to stand.

So that was why the man was so willing to chat, Garth thought. The man needed to wait for one of his buddies to recover enough to be able to tie the rope.

"Here." Garth turned slightly and spoke to the man behind him. "Let me give you a hand. It's Lenny, right?"

Garth held his breath while he began to pivot. Hopefully the man holding the gun would believe Garth was the old-fashioned, gentlemanly kind of man who would help his enemies, even when they were going to tie him up. Apparently the gunman did.

Garth was halfway turned when he made his move. He spun and fell to a crouch. The inevitable bullet from the man's gun buzzed quietly over his head. Garth's hopes fell. He hadn't seen the gun clearly, but he'd hoped it was just a plain unadorned gun. He'd counted on the sound of a gun shot to alert his men inside the barn that something was wrong. But the gun had a silencer on it. The quiet snapping sound it made wouldn't alert a gopher in a hole next to them.

Garth would have to do this the hard way. He rolled toward the gunman and, sensing more than seeing the man aim, quickly dodged to the side. The bullet slammed harmlessly into the frozen ground where Garth had been. Then Garth half rose and dove toward the man, tackling him at his knees. The man grunted in surprise. Garth rose up farther, knocking the gun out of the man's hand as he was struggling to aim it again.

The gun fell to the ground and Garth tried to kick it under the bus. Instead it fell into a rut the tire tracks had made in the snow.

Sylvia tried to scream. She'd tried to scream ever since Garth had stepped out of that bus, but the gag choked back her screams and made her sound more like a cat in heat than a strong woman calling for help. Where was that deputy sheriff when they needed him?

It was unlikely anyone inside the barn would hear her scream or the scuffle by the bus. She wouldn't have even known bullets were being fired if she didn't hear the click of the gun and see the groove in the ground where the bullet buried itself.

Sylvia kept her eyes on Garth. He should have stayed in the bus. The other men hadn't known that anyone was inside the vehicle. She doubted very much they would have staged a search. There was nothing to be gained if both she and Garth were shot.

Sylvia strained to scream again.

Garth was breathing hard. He knew he should have

kept up his army training exercises. He'd been able to do a hundred push-ups back then. These days he was lucky to squeeze out thirty. The three men were circling him like vultures waiting patiently for the final breath to leave their prey. Garth was obliging them by stepping around. Fancy dancing like a boxer did. Garth was hoping they wouldn't see the direction to his shuffling.

That gun was only four more feet away from him. Once he got close enough, he'd make a dive for it. He was beginning to hope it was the only gun in the game plan. None of the men had pulled out another weapon. They must be amateurs if they didn't come more prepared than that, but Garth didn't have time to waste worrying about whether they were hardened criminals or fools down on their luck enough to take a job like this.

Garth was only two feet from the gun now. Easy reaching distance. The men had closed in until they were about three feet from him. They still looked hesitant.

"He ain't all that much," Lenny finally muttered. "Don't know what the boss was so fussy about. Them Purple Hearts don't mean much when a man's old."

The man closest to Garth grunted. "He's no older than you are. Not so sure he couldn't take you and Buck both if you were here alone."

Garth took his breath silently. He was finally convinced Francis's ex-boyfriend wasn't behind this. Garth didn't get the Purple Hearts until he was back home, and Francis's boyfriend was gone by then. Garth had clung to the hope that it was this Flint. The alternative was chilling. Somehow that crime syndicate who was doing the rustling had found out he'd promised to help the FBI. They may have even found out that he'd already given the FBI one important clue and was soon to deliver another.

But what would they want with Francis?

Now, Garth muttered in his mind as he dove for the gun. The night was still dark and he was grateful for the black handle of the gun. Even in the shadows it stood out clearly from the white snow surrounding it.

Garth had guessed wrong. He realized that as he heard the angry grunts of the men above him and then the click of a trigger behind him. Just because the other two men hadn't pulled their guns earlier didn't mean they didn't have them.

The palm of Garth's hand pressed flat onto the frozen ground where the gun had been before one of the men kicked it away.

Garth had missed his chance. He quickly rolled away from the gun. He knew what was coming. The bullet slammed into the ground just inches from his side.

"What're you doing?" The man who had the silencer earlier hissed at someone over Garth's head.

Garth thought the man was talking to him until he heard the whine of the other man answering him. He rolled over and faced them.

"He was goin' for the gun," Lenny mumbled, jerking his gun at Garth again. "I ain't going to let him take a shot at me. Silencer or no silencer. Have to shoot him.."

"The boss still won't like it. Neither will the men inside that barn," the other man said. "They could've heard the bullet. I told you to get a silencer for that gun before we came out here."

Garth listened hopefully. The shot had not been loud since the ground had muffled it some. Lord knows he could still hear the shot ringing in his ear. But apparently no one inside the barn had heard it. If they had, he would be hearing the door on the barn open up and the people inside shouting, wondering what was wrong.

The night was silent as a tomb. The men had been lucky.

Apparently one of the men thought the same thing. "Get them into the back of the truck. We're getting out of here."

The man walked over to the back of the cattle truck that stood to the right of the bus.

Garth saw his chance. He could roll left under the bus and be into the café before the men could reach him. They likely wouldn't even be able to shoot him under the bus as the shadows were so deep. The only problem was Sylvia. He couldn't take her with him—not with her being so far away and having her hands tied. And he couldn't leave her.

Lenny grunted at Garth. "Don't try anything. I shot at you once. I'll do it again. Don't care what the boss says."

"Well, you better care." The other man scolded him impatiently as he hoisted himself up into the back of the truck to pull up the gate. "Don't be dim-witted. I explained how this job was different. Nobody messes with this kind of boss."

Garth's heart sank. It was the crime syndicate. They were in big trouble. He looked over at Sylvia. Even in the darkness he could see the tension in her body. She was frozen. She knew what the men were saying, too. And given her fear of violence, it must be painfully hard for her.

"Leave her here." Garth jerked his head toward Sylvia. "Take me if you have to, but leave her here. She doesn't know anything your boss wants to know anyway." Garth felt the sweat break out on his forehead. He needed to convince them. "She doesn't know a cow from a heifer. Or a Guernsey from a Holstein." He saw the two men on the ground exchange worried glances. It was clear they didn't know, either. "She'd only waste your boss's time. She wouldn't know a rustler if she met up with one in a dark alley. She'll only slow you down."

"Just get your sorry face up there," the man with the gun finally ordered defiantly as he pointed to the back of the truck. "We'll let the boss decide who knows what and who doesn't. Holstein, Guernsey or pure horse manure. We only deliver. It's up to him to sort it out."

"Well, it's your funeral." Garth forced himself to be nonchalant as he drew his knees up and then stood. He casually brushed the snow off his suit. Anything to stall. Maybe someone had heard something and would think to check in a minute or two.

"Get in the truck," the gunman repeated impatiently.

"In a minute," Garth said as he continued brushing. "The snow will ruin this suit if I don't get it off before it melts."

Lenny snorted. "Who cares? You ain't gonna need it where you're going."

"Cost me six hundred dollars," Garth said with mock indignation as he continued brushing. "Imported from Italy."

"What's the holdup?" the man inside the cattle truck called down to them.

"He needs to clean his suit," Lenny yelled back.

"What the—?" The man inside the cattle truck stuck his head out of the back opening.

Lenny looked up and whined, "I might want that suit."

"You've never worn a suit in your life." The man inside the truck snorted. "No reason to start now. Just get them up here and make it snappy."

"I'll go a lot quicker if you leave her here." Garth stopped brushing his suit and laid his cards out on the table.

"Worried about your sister, huh?" The man standing inside the truck asked with a sneer. "Well, if you're really worried about her, you'll get your sorry butt up here or I'll—"

Garth felt his heart squeeze. The man standing on the truck had pointed the gun with the silencer straight at Sylvia.

Garth didn't take any chances. It took him five long strides to reach Sylvia. He didn't care if they shot him on the way there. He didn't breathe until he was standing in front of her. "There's no need to talk about shooting anyone. I'm cooperating."

"Good." The man on the truck bed grunted. "'Cause the boss didn't say nothing about keeping her alive. Now, you he's a little fussy about. But her—she's nobody, if you get my meaning."

Garth got his meaning. That was the reason they wanted his sister. They wanted some way to convince him to do whatever it was they wanted. "You tell that boss of yours that if he harms one hair on her head, he's bought himself more trouble than he can handle. He won't just answer to me—he'll answer to an even bigger boss.''

''Who's that?'' Lenny asked nervously.

''Someone who could grind your boss into chicken feed if he wanted.'' Garth hoped God didn't mind being referred to in those terms. And he hoped Sylvia was praying. He wasn't too sure God would answer his prayers. He and God had an understanding that Garth could look out for himself. But if Sylvia was praying, it'd be all right. The Almighty couldn't say no to Sylvia.

''You're sure we should—'' Lenny asked his brother on the truck bed.

''Just get them up here,'' the man inside the truck ordered. ''Don't you know a bluff when you hear one? I swear you're the dumbest of all us kids. You take after Uncle Joe.''

''I do not—'' Lenny protested indignantly, but he turned his attention to Garth and Sylvia. ''Get on up.'' He gestured with his gun toward the truck bed.

Chapter Thirteen

Sylvia tried to concentrate on the openings between the wooden slats that made up the frame of the truck bed. She could barely see them. It was like seeing a black slat against the even deeper black of the night. She could feel where the slats were, easier than she could see them. The openings between the slats provided the only fresh air coming into the back of the truck and it came in small frigid streams. She lifted her head to align it with one of the slats. She needed the fresh air so she wouldn't pass out.

She'd never been so scared in her life.

She was frozen with fear and couldn't stop the trembling. She wondered what Garth thought. She was scooped inside of him and felt the tension all along his body. He was coiled and ready to spring. The men had tied them up together when they finally pushed them up into the back of the truck. Ordinarily, being tied up spoon-style with a man would make her heart race with fear. Maybe it still was—she couldn't tell. The other fear was so overwhelming, she couldn't separate which trembling came from which fear.

"I'd never hurt you," Garth pleaded softly in her ear. "You don't need to be afraid of being close to me. I'd never hurt you."

Sylvia realized Garth must have been whispering those words over and over into her ears. He was saying them like a chant.

Lord, he must think I'm a ninny. I'm not afraid of him.

It took a moment for the realization to sink even farther into her mind. She checked the nerves in her stomach. She shifted slightly to pull at the rope that tied her to Garth. Yes, she thought to herself in quiet jubilation, she was not scared of Garth. They were sitting here, thigh to thigh, torso to torso—tied up like two circus clowns in a barrel—and she, Sylvia Bannister, was not afraid.

Not that, she hesitated to assure herself, it had much to do with Garth himself. No, it must be that she had just never been forced to live with her fears long enough to conquer them before. She'd never had to sit inside a man's lap until the trembling stopped. That must be it.

It must be. Because the alternative—that she had special feelings for Garth that made her fears disappear, that maybe she was even a little bit in love with the man—was starting up a trembling all of its own. And this trembling rocked her to her foundations.

Dear Lord, I'm in a mess. What do I feel for him?

Garth wished he'd paid more attention when Matthew had explained prayer to him. On the long drive over to Seattle, they'd talked about everything. Even

Matthew's ability—and at times, lack of ability—
to pray.

Garth had never been fond of prayer. It always
seemed somewhat sissy to him to have to ask anyone
for help, even God. Not that Garth was opposed to
other people praying. It seemed all right for them. In
fact, he wholeheartedly supported it for some folks.
But Garth had been raised to take care of himself, and
prayer had never been part of his life.

His father had taught him that help was to be accepted warily as it always came with strings. A man
didn't accept help unless he could pay it back in good
measure and soon.

When he was alive, Garth's father was the king of
bargainers. He figured everything was a deal made
between two people and that the number-one rule was
that only fools believe in free lunches. Everything had
a price and the price needed to be checked out before
the favor was accepted. If Garth's father had been
around, the Trojan horse would still be rotting outside
the village walls.

In short, the Elktons didn't trust the help of anyone,
not even God.

What his father had never taught Garth was what
to do when he needed help. Like now. His heart was
breaking with love for this woman sitting here trembling in his lap and there was nothing he could do to
make her trust him. He couldn't fight her ghosts. He
hadn't been there in her past to protect her. He
couldn't go back in time and change things.

He was helpless in the face of her fear. She was
shaking like a leaf in his arms and he could do nothing. He couldn't even cuddle her as that would only
make her more afraid.

No, Garth's father had never told him what to do when there was no one who could help him but God alone—not even when Garth needed that help more than he needed life itself.

Garth didn't even know how to talk to God. He just knew he needed to try.

Well, You know I'm not very good at this. Garth started to fumble a prayer. *Should have talked to You long before now. Wouldn't blame You if You decided not to help me. But if You have any mercy with my name on it, use it to get Sylvia out of here. She didn't ask for this. They can have my sorry hide. But not her. I refuse to let them have her.*

Garth stopped. He knew God had no reason to listen to him. Garth had never even pretended to listen to God. He had no way to pay God back. He knew of no way to prove his sincerity. No way to show how important this was to him. Unless—the thought came to him with the force of a sledgehammer. He didn't even stop to consider whether or not his father's rules would apply in this situation. He only hoped they did for he had one small thing he could offer God.

Lord, Garth continued. He felt the pain slice through him. *If you do this for me—get Sylvia out of here alive—I'll give up any claim to her. Not that I have one. I've never been good enough for her. But I'll lay down any hopes I have.*

There, Garth thought to himself, if God knew anything about him, He would have to know Garth was sincere. He'd just offered all he could to repay the favor. Not even God could ask for more.

Sylvia shifted. She was suddenly too warm. She knew the temperature was freezing. But the direction her thoughts were taking was heating her up like an oven. She'd been tied in Garth's arms ever since one of the three brothers had coaxed the sputtering engine to life. The truck had run fine for a couple of miles, but then the engine had started hammering away at itself, making so much noise, Sylvia half hoped the men in the barn could hear them if they stepped outside.

She was obviously not the only one who had noticed the engine.

"Thought you got that thing tuned up." Two of the brothers—Buck and Lenny—were squatting down in opposite corners at the front of the truck bed and they were arguing quietly. Sylvia wondered if it was any warmer closer to the cab. In the darkness she could not see their faces, but she could see their shapes. "We ain't even making five miles an hour. For pity sakes, you was supposed to see to the tuneup when we were in Miles City."

"I did."

"Does that sound like you got the truck tuned up?" Buck demanded impatiently.

There was silence while the brothers listened to the heavy chugging of the engine.

"But I did take it to that shop—remember the place was painted blue? Cost me eighty bucks."

Buck grunted again. "You got taken then. They might have took your money. But they didn't do nothing to that engine."

"I could go back—get my money back," the younger man offered softly.

"Why don't you just put in a complaint with the Better Business Bureau while you're at it?" Buck suggested sarcastically. "I swear, sometimes I think you're even stupider than Uncle Joe. You can't go back there. We've just kidnapped these two and who knows where that'll lead…."

Buck let his voice trail off and then he turned his attention to Sylvia and Garth. "You two been mighty quiet."

Sylvia blinked. In the darkness it was almost possible to pretend that the two men were just voices in the air. They were not real in the dark in the same way that Garth was. She felt his muscle around her. His warm breath on the top of her head. When the truck hit a bump in the road, it was Garth's legs that held her in place.

"Didn't know you required our conversation," Garth said quietly to the two men. "Sounded like you're doing pretty good on your own. You know, if it was me, I'd think some about that getting your money back on that tune-up. You can tell something's wrong. The truck acting up like this might be a sign."

One of the brothers grunted. "A sign of what?"

Garth kept his voice pitched low. He didn't want them to know how desperate he was for them to listen to him. He took a deep breath. The faint scent of peaches came to him along with the old scent of cattle. The peaches were from Sylvia. She had miraculously stopped trembling a little bit ago and had settled farther into his contours. He couldn't help himself. He used his forearms to try and cuddle her closer. If he didn't know better, he'd swear she'd snuggled into him.

"Could be a sign of trouble." Garth forced his mind back to the brothers. "Sometimes when something goes wrong right off in a mission, it's best to scrub the whole thing. Learned that with my buddies in the army. Once one thing goes wrong, it's downhill from there. Some good men died because they didn't listen to the signs.''

"Do you think maybe—" Lenny began to whisper.

"I swear you have oatmeal for brains," the older brother scolded impatiently. "Don't you see what he's trying to do? He wants to psyche us out."

"Suit yourself," Garth said casually. He was glad the brothers couldn't see him in the darkness. He shifted his shoulder. He'd trade his left arm if he could move his right one to enclose Sylvia properly. What kind of demon had tied their hands together in front like this with his arms loped over Sylvia's shoulders? The most he could do was hug her neck.

"But what if—" Lenny whispered again, this time more quietly.

"We wouldn't even need to tell the boss you changed your mind," Garth offered. A strand of Sylvia's hair was flying free and ticking his cheek. He'd never felt anything softer. "Just take us back to the dance and we can pretend this never happened. I'll even take your truck back to my ranch and fix it properly so you can go home—wherever that is. The boss won't even know what happened."

Buck grunted. "The boss would know."

"Well, then we can talk to the deputy sheriff. Maybe he could arrest you—"

"What?" Buck protested indignantly.

"Hear me out," Garth continued. "If you take us back now, you won't do much time at all. Maybe just some probation or something. And if the boss is real big—" Garth already had a strong suspicion about who the boss was, and if Garth was right, the men were wise not to sell out too soon. "Well, if he's real big, you can turn state's evidence. Get put in the witness protection program. Get a whole new life somewhere—maybe Florida or someplace where it's real warm. They set you up with a cozy house. Three solid meals a day. A big-screen TV. Laying in the sun, sipping lemonade. Maybe get a dog for Lenny. Could be a great life.''

"It *is* cold up here," Lenny dreamed quietly.

"We ain't turning no state's evidence," Buck said emphatically. "The Gaults aren't tattlers."

"But—'' Lenny protested softly.

"No. Mama raised us better,'' Buck repeated firmly. "We took on the job and we'll finish it. No matter what we need to do when we get these two delivered to the boss.''

Garth didn't argue further. Talk of what the brothers thought they might need to do stopped him. He'd known all along that the boss wouldn't want witnesses when he'd finished interviewing them. Still, he didn't want Sylvia to hear the words spoken.

The dark inside the back of the truck was so final that even the air smelled empty. The cattle truck had been built to keep cattle warm on cold winter drives. Its roof kept the stars from opening up the blackness of the night. On a summer night a deep darkness like this felt like velvet. But not in the biting cold of winter. The dark of this night reminded Garth of the suffocating lack of light found in deep caves that went so far down in the earth, there was no surface light left. Garth had been in a cave like that once. That kind of darkness chilled a man.

In the darkness of the truck bed, all was quiet except for the coughing of the truck engine and the distant rumble of— Garth listened closer. He'd swear that was the rumble of that Seattle bus pulling a load and pulling it hard.

Garth shifted his arm to try and communicate his excitement to Sylvia before he realized he needn't. Sylvia was clearly nervous and trying to communicate something to him through her gag. It sounded like boos, woos—no, boys.

Garth followed her thinking and felt a sinking feeling. Suddenly he hoped that it wasn't the bus he heard. Because if it was the bus, it meant that it must be the boys who were coming to their rescue. Jess was the only one of his hired hands who would drive the bus and he couldn't see well enough at night to take the wheel. Besides, adults would surely have had sense enough to send Deputy Wall and his siren instead.

Sylvia started to pray that the truck would go faster. She didn't want the boys to catch them. But the old truck was sputtering worse than ever. At this rate, the bus would catch them in seconds. And here she was, not even able to talk. Maybe if she could talk, she could explain about the boys. Lenny and Buck didn't seem such bad men. Not really. Maybe they'd let the boys off with a warning.

Garth felt Sylvia's neck move. She must be chewing at the gag in her mouth, trying to work it down. He knew from the angle that she didn't have much of a chance at it. She needed help. Garth could not see in the dark, so he moved his chin closer to the back of her head. Her hair was soft and smelled faintly of peaches. If they got out of this alive, he'd buy her a case of that shampoo she used. He'd never eat a fresh peach again without thinking of Sylvia.

Garth could feel Sylvia stiffen as he nuzzled her hair, trying to locate the knot.

"Easy," he soothed her, not daring to explain what he was trying to do in case Buck and Lenny were listening. He felt the rag tangled in her shoulder-length hair. Garth had never noticed the texture of hair as closely as now. He couldn't see her hair clearly. It was more shadows than anything. But the texture—it wasn't soft like a baby's hair. No, he could tell it belonged to a grown woman. Full-bodied and strong. He rubbed his chin more deeply into the waves of her hair and found the knot holding her gag in place.

Garth positioned his chin above the knot and tried to push downward on the rag. By now Sylvia must have figured out what he was doing because she'd become still. The rag was tight and didn't move.

Garth wasn't sure how much of this he could take. Nuzzling Sylvia's hair was reminding him too much of what he'd like to do if he was alone in the dark with her. He didn't suppose she'd notice if he— Garth brushed his lips lightly against the back of Sylvia's neck and held his breath. Good, she hadn't noticed. He knew because she hadn't pulled away from him or even tensed up.

His relief quickly turned to a dry taste in his mouth. A stolen kiss wasn't as sweet as he imagined it would be. It only reminded him of what a full-blown, real one would taste like—one that Sylvia didn't return, as well.

It was time for teeth, Garth decided. It was the only way he knew to get Sylvia's gag worked down far enough so that she could talk.

"Something's coming," Buck announced from the

truck bed as he pounded on the back of the cab and shouted to the brother who was driving. "Get this thing moving."

Garth heard the truck driver trying to shift gears. Instead of shifting, the truck gave a belch and then a few feeble rumbles as it slowed to a crawl.

"I said, get it moving," Buck called frantically to his brother. "We got company."

The truck took a final cough and stalled completely.

There was a moment's silence in the dark truck bed.

Then Lenny whispered, "What're we gonna do now?"

"Get your gun ready," Buck said wearily. "If we can't outrun them, we have to outshoot them."

"But they're only children," Sylvia protested.

Garth congratulated himself. He'd moved the gag down enough for Sylvia to talk.

"Can't be helped," Buck said. Garth could hear the man stand to his feet. The scrape of his boot heels along the wood of the truck bed announced he had pulled himself up to a kneeling position and then a standing one.

"No need to shoot anyone," Garth reasoned calmly. "They can't stop you anyway. They're only kids. You still have the one your boss wants—me. I'm not planning on going anywhere, so just let Sylvia talk to the kids and order them back to the dance and—"

"How stupid do you think we are?" Lenny whined triumphantly. "Even I can see that's a trap. They go back and call the law, and before you know it we have more cops around here than flies."

"There are no flies in February around here," Garth continued, his voice pitched low and soothing. "And that's just how many cops you'd have to worry about. No, the smart thing is to let us tell the kids to go back home—let them take Sylvia with them. She knows you're serious. She'll be sure they do what you ask."

"I'm not leaving you here," Sylvia protested quietly.

"You'll do it for the kids." Garth felt prickles of cold sweat on his shoulder blades. What did she mean, she wouldn't go? "We'll both do it for the kids. The boss only wants to talk to me. I can take care of myself."

For the first time in his life he said those words and followed them with a prayer. *Remember our deal. I'm counting on You. Keep Sylvia and the kids safe and You can have me.* He kept talking to be sure he sounded convincing to Sylvia. Everything depended on her being willing to leave. "No need to worry. I've been in tight places before and come out all right. Right now we need to think of the kids."

"But—" Sylvia began to protest when they heard the bus pull to a stop behind the truck.

Buck and Lenny had moved to the back of the truck and they were peering out between the slats.

"See anything?" Buck whispered to Lenny.

Garth could see the two black shadows at the end of the truck bed. He could also see the guns in their hands.

"Don't you know what hostages are for?" Garth finally demanded. He could hear the bus door opening slowly. That and what sounded like the muffled hoofbeats of a horse in the distance. "You take me and threaten to shoot me if anyone comes closer."

Garth didn't know how else to keep those kids in the bus. For all he knew, the kids didn't even know what they were up against. For all he knew they were out here to ride horseback in the moonlight and thought there were cows in this truck.

Garth saw the two shadows turn around.

"Think they'd do it?" Lenny whispered to Buck. "Might be the kids don't like him all that well. He's kind of mouthy."

"The kids like me," Garth assured them. "The boys especially."

"I don't know—" Lenny wavered.

"For Pete's sake, they let me teach them to dance!"

"Did, huh?" Lenny said in surprise. "Guess they must, then."

"Hold it right there," Buck shouted from the truck. "We've got hostages and we'll start shooting them if you don't back off."

Buck shot a hole in the roof of the cattle truck for emphasis.

Garth squeezed his arms tight around Sylvia. She'd stopped trembling some time ago. He figured the shock had frozen her by now.

"No need to go shooting." Garth forced himself to continue to speak calmly. He firmly believed no one ever shot a man while they were talking. It was human nature to at least wait for the final sentence to be said.

"Yeah, we'll have to pay for that when we take the truck back," Lenny whined.

The sound of the hoofbeats came closer. Garth listened to see if the beat matched any of his horses. It didn't. Strange. Who else would have a horse out tonight?

"Everyone get back in the bus," Garth shouted. He decided to do the talking for the brothers. "Turn the bus around and go back to the dance."

The hoofbeats stopped. Whoever had been riding up had reached the bus. Garth only hoped the horse was being ridden by someone with sense—which, come to think of it, didn't seem likely. Only a fool would be out riding a horse on a night as cold as this.

The hushed sound of Lenny and Buck whispering together made Garth uneasy before he heard the words from Buck. "I suppose it could be the boss out there. He must ride. And we are late in getting Elkton to him."

"No." Sylvia twisted in Garth's arm.

Garth felt the worry coil through her.

"Best not be shooting out there, if the boss is there," Garth said, as much for Sylvia's benefit as he did for the brothers'. "Wouldn't want to make any mistakes in the dark. 'Course, don't suppose it'd be so bad if you shot the man dead—but I wouldn't want to be in your shoes if you only wounded him."

Garth hoped the brothers were wrong. The rhythm of the hoofbeats suggested the horse was well past its prime. Maybe it wasn't the boss out there with those kids.

Lenny and Buck looked at each other. Garth could almost hear them thinking.

"Boss? That you?" Buck finally called out.

There was silence. Garth was almost ready to feel relief.

"The boss sent me," a man's deep voice finally

answered. "Told me to tell you to call it off. He's changed his mind."

Lenny and Buck whispered together.

"How do we know the boss sent you?" Buck called back. "He'll have our hides if we don't—"

"Shhh—" Lenny's frantic whisper interrupted Buck and led to another huddled conversation.

"I was just up the canyon," the man's voice continued smoothly. "The boss was sitting out there in his Ford pickup chomping on some chewing tobacco. You know how he likes his chewing tobacco. Now, what was the brand name he uses…?"

Buck and Lenny had stopped whispering midway through the man's words.

"Black Medicine," Lenny said quietly to Buck. "He chews Black Medicine. I saw the can when we were up there talking. He reached into his pocket and pulled it out—"

Garth let out his breath. He didn't know he'd even been holding it until he felt his whole body relax.

"The boss must have changed his mind," Garth repeated for the brother's benefit.

Garth decided he'd seen a miracle. Only God could have pulled this one off.

The relief that flooded Garth was followed by a gut punch. If God had done what Garth had asked, that meant Garth had to do what he promised. Just let Sylvia sit in my lap a little longer, he bargained—just a little longer. Forever will be a long time without her.

Sylvia rubbed her wrists. The brothers had taken the bait whole. They'd stepped down from the truck and into the arms of first one and then two lawmen.

The weak lights from the bus showed the three brothers bound and gagged in the middle of the frozen road. The kids had had the presence of mind to bring along Deputy Wall, and then there was a federal agent. Who would have thought a federal agent would be out riding horseback just when they needed one? Granted, he didn't look too happy to be there. Sylvia would guess he hadn't slept in three or four days and he kept muttering something about women, but she didn't care. He was a miracle.

Yes, she thought to herself in satisfaction, tonight was a night for miracles. She could hardly wait to show Garth that she was no longer afraid of him. He might assume from her lack of fear that she'd fallen in love with him, but she decided to tell him anyway. Maybe she was a little in love with him. Her friend Glory had been telling her all along that Garth was just waiting for her to come around. Well, tonight was a night for miracles.

"I'm glad you were with me in there," Sylvia said shyly, walking over to where Garth stood. She hadn't made a move on a man in years. If it wasn't Garth that she was talking to, she wouldn't have had the nerve. "I felt safe with you there."

Now if that isn't a road map to my feelings, nothing is, Sylvia thought to herself in quiet satisfaction.

"No problem," Garth said quietly, and then moved over to where the boys were standing by the open bus door.

Sylvia couldn't move. She didn't know what she had expected. But she hadn't expected him to treat her announcement so coldly. He hadn't even looked at her, let alone smiled. He'd been smiling at her like a model in a toothpaste ad ever since he showed up in Seattle, and now, when she wanted nothing more than to see a smile, he just turned away.

It's too late, she thought to herself bleakly. Or maybe I was wrong. He sure didn't look the least bit interested. Maybe I misread his friendliness. She looked at him again, standing over by the boys. She'd forgotten about the boys. His friendliness must have only been a tool to guide the boys in the art of being gentlemen.

She lifted her chin in pride. Well, she could get along without him in her life. She could get along just fine without him.

Chapter Fourteen

Garth was chopping wood.

He'd been chopping wood for three days now and had just sent a couple of his hired hands over to Augusta to bring back another truckload of the waste timber the forestry service had for sale. He had steadfastly refused to use the electric saw even though he had blisters on both of his hands from the heft of the ax. Jess had carefully placed the saw within easy reaching distance two days ago and then had hung around watching him, shaking his head and muttering that they had gas heat anyway so who needed all that wood.

Garth didn't stop to explain that he wasn't chopping the wood because he needed wood. He was chopping the wood because he needed to chop. He needed the satisfying crack as he buried the ax blade deep into the wood.

"Want some coffee?"

Garth was prepared to scowl at whoever was interrupting him until he looked up and saw that it was

Matthew. Matthew was standing beside the mountain of wood Garth had chopped and was holding two mugs of coffee in his hands.

"As I remember, you take it black," Matthew said as he held out one of the mugs toward Garth. "You didn't answer my call so thought I'd come in person."

Garth took one last swing and drove the ax blade into the trunk of what had been a diseased tree. "Been busy."

The only call Garth had taken in the past three days was one from his contact at the FBI telling him that the crime syndicate behind the beef rustling was falling apart. The Gault brothers had known enough to finger "the boss" and he was on the run to Mexico. The FBI didn't think there would be any further trouble in Montana.

"Mrs. Hargrove tells me that agent that showed up is Francis's old boyfriend," Matthew said as he settled himself on top of a pile of kindling. "Thought it might be worrying you."

Garth looked over at the man he'd come to know as his friend on their long drive over to Seattle several weeks ago. "Not a bit. Francis told me it was none of my business and I believe her. She's a grown woman. If they want to let the past stay the past, who am I to question it? It was a bit of a shock, but I'm fine with it."

"So that's not what's worrying you?" Matthew repeated thoughtfully.

"What makes you so certain something's worrying me?" Garth asked indignantly.

Matthew cocked his head at the stack of chopped wood.

"Can't a man chop a little wood without somebody thinking something's wrong?"

"Well, it's not exactly a little wood," Matthew said ruefully. "And you do heat with gas. According to Jess, you'll both be long gone before you use up all that wood."

"Tell Jess to speak for himself. I intend to—to build some fires in my fireplace," Garth said staunchly and then winced. Watching a fire all alone sure sounded like a desolate way to spend a winter evening. He supposed, though, he might as well get used to it. His whole life stretched before him—more empty and barren than he would have ever imagined possible before he met Sylvia.

"I see." Matthew took a sip of his coffee and settled more comfortably into the woodpile. "I didn't figure there was anything wrong. After all, if I've ever seen a man who had it all made, it'd have to be you."

Garth grunted. "Yeah."

"You've got a good piece of property."

"The best."

"And a sister who thinks a lot of you."

Garth grunted again. Matthew was right. He did have a lot to be thankful for.

"Yes, sir, God has blessed you big-time."

"God can mind his own blasted business from now on." Garth put down his mug of coffee and started to rise.

"Ahhh." Matthew took another sip of his hot coffee. "So it's God you're mad at?"

"I'm not mad at anyone," Garth said as he walked toward the ax and hefted it. He raised it and aimed it square at the heart of a twisted tree limb. "Got no reason to be mad. God and I understand each other."

"That so?"

"Yes," Garth said as he swung the ax and hit the tree limb, shattering it in two. "We've got an understanding."

"Just out of curiosity, what would that understanding be?"

Garth eyed the other man warily. "You asking as my minister?"

"Didn't know you've been going to church enough lately to see me as your minister."

"I've thought about going. Been thinking about it for months. Almost drove down for a service last month."

"Ahhh." Matthew nodded and set his coffee down. "Well, then I guess I could answer as your minister if that's what you want."

"Don't have much use for ministers." Garth twisted the ax handle, breaking another piece off the tree limb.

"Yeah, we can be a frustrating lot," Matthew agreed mildly as he lifted his coffee cup and took a sip.

"No offense."

"None taken."

"It's just all this deal making," Garth finally said as he took the pieces of tree he'd cut and threw them on top of the huge woodpile. "Something's not right when God holds all the cards."

"God doesn't hold all the cards. We have free will."

"Some free will—it doesn't help us much in tight situations."

"Like when you were kidnapped? But God got you out of there. John had gone outside and just happened to see them putting you in the back of the truck. I have to believe God had a hand in the timing of that.''

Garth looked over at the other man. Confusion was stamped on Matthew's face.

''I know God got us out of there—believe me, I know. I prayed for Him to do it and He answered my prayer.''

''Well, that's good, isn't it?''

''Yeah.'' Garth sighed, dug his ax blade into another tree limb, then sat down next to Matthew. ''I'm glad He answered my prayer— He kept the kids and Sylvia safe. I owe Him everything for that. And that's what I promised to give Him so I've got no complaints. I aim to pay up on my debt. We Elktons stand by our word.''

''I don't suppose there's any chance that what you promised to give God was your love, devotion and a life of service to Him?''

Garth looked at the minister as if the man had gone balmy. ''What would He want with me? No, I gave Him the only thing I figured He'd want—I promised to stay away from a certain woman whom I know He regards very highly.''

Matthew chuckled as though he finally understood. ''Sylvia.''

''I'm not naming any names.''

''You don't have to name names.'' Matthew smiled widely. ''You're forgetting I drove to Seattle with you. I had to listen to you rehearse your 'I'm in the neighborhood, thought I'd drop in' speech. So have you told Sylvia how you feel?''

Garth shook his head in exasperation. ''Have you gone deaf? I promised God I wouldn't have anything to do with her.''

"And you think that's what He wants?" Matthew asked incredulously. "God doesn't make those kind of deals."

"Well, He made one with me. I had nothing else to offer."

"You didn't need to offer anything. God gives mercy, grace, forgiveness—they're free. You can't make deals for those kind of things."

"I can't?"

Matthew shook his head. "Let me explain how it works."

"This better be good."

Sylvia couldn't take it anymore. She had enough of her grandmother's Italian blood in her that she needed to cook when she was upset. The fact that she'd never learned to cook—never even learned when pasta was officially done—had stopped her for two days; but she woke up this morning and decided to make lasagna. After all, she reasoned, it was topped with mounds of mozzarella and anything topped with that much cheese had to taste good.

Besides, she remembered her grandmother not only chopping garlic and onions but also squeezing red Roma tomatoes to make the sauce. Sylvia suddenly wanted very much to chop something or squeeze something until it bled—even if it was only a vegetable.

What had ever possessed her to be such a fool as to actually believe she and that—that cold, insufferable man had anything between them? If he hadn't been so eager to fall in with Mrs. Buckwalter's scheme to teach the kids manners, he wouldn't have even paid any attention to her. He just needed a Ginger Rogers to play opposite his Fred Astaire. Some gentleman he turned out to be. He'd certainly gotten over the idea of courting her now that the dance was over. Just thinking about him made her want to get her hands on a ripe tomato and start to squeeze.

Garth paused outside the kitchen door and took off his Stetson. He slicked back his hair and bent his head in prayer. *Lord, Matthew better be right about your mercy. 'Cause I haven't got a chance without it.*

Garth looked at his reflection in the small square of half-frozen window to the side of the door. He looked a little scruffy. He wondered if he should go change before he went inside and made a fool of himself. Then he reasoned there was little point. Sylvia was always so much neater and composed than him that she wasn't likely to be impressed by his attire no matter what he wore. She hadn't even commented on the suit he'd borrowed from that Buckwalter fellow for the dance. And it was Italian.

Garth opened the kitchen door and his heart stopped.

It was dark inside the kitchen, but he could see clearly enough. Sylvia stood at the kitchen counter with tears running down her cheek and red splotches all over her clothes.

My God, she's bleeding!

"Where's the cut?" Garth demanded as he covered the space between the open door and the counter. Maybe the FBI was wrong. Maybe "the boss" wasn't headed to Mexico after all. "Who did this?"

Garth grabbed Sylvia's shoulders to steady her. She was looking at him as if she was disoriented, and he took action. The first thing they needed to guard against was fainting from loss of blood.

Sylvia knew what the girls meant when they said they could die from embarrassment. He was the last person she wanted to witness her humiliation. She'd taken on the vegetables and they had won. If she had her way, she'd turn and flee the kitchen, but she couldn't. He had her shoulders in a grip that didn't promise to let up anytime soon.

"Let's get you up on the counter," Garth said urgently. "That'll stop the blood flow."

"Oh, no, it's not—" Sylvia started to explain softly but it was too late. Garth's hands had found her waist and he hoisted her up on the counter and tipped her back until she was lying down in a bed of garlic peels and tomato pulp.

"Where does it hurt?" Garth demanded as he ran his hands over her stomach.

Sylvia drew in her breath involuntarily. She knew the kitchen was still cold. She could feel the ridges of cold pressed Formica against the back of her shoulders as she lay on the counter. But, even more keenly, she could feel the heat of Garth's hands through the cotton blouse she wore as he searched for a cut.

"It doesn't hurt—I didn't—"

"Don't be brave. I know it hurts."

"No." Sylvia took a deep breath. Why did she always seem short of breath when she was around him? "I'm not hurt. It's the tomatoes."

Garth smelled the tomato pulp at the same time as Sylvia spoke. Now he knew what the kids meant when they said they could die from embarrassment. "Sorry," he mumbled. "Reflex reaction, I guess."

Garth reluctantly took his hands away. Well, he'd

certainly done it this time. Still, he looked a little closer—he rather liked Sylvia lying on her back looking up at him with a slightly dazed expression on her face. "You're sure it's only tomatoes?"

"I know it's a mess," Sylvia said stiffly. "I had no idea tomatoes could be so full of juice. But don't worry. I intend to clean the kitchen."

"I'm not worried about the kitchen."

"I was making lasagna."

"Lasagna sounds good." Garth reached down and pulled a paper towel off the roll inside the cabinet door. He couldn't help himself. He dabbed at the tomato on Sylvia's cheek.

"Well, there's not going to be lasagna now." Sylvia looked at him as if he was dense. "I never even got the sauce together."

"Something I can do to help?"

Sylvia looked at him as if he'd gotten even denser. "You?"

"I can cook," Garth protested. And then, to be more truthful, added "Well, we can cook."

His reward was a beautiful smile. Upside down and slightly out of focus. With tomato juice to one side. But it was the most beautiful smile he'd ever seen.

"Just like we can dance?" Sylvia teased.

"Hey, we made it around the floor." Garth arched out his arm like a gentleman so Sylvia could use it to pull herself upright. "I'm sure we can put together a lasagna."

Garth looked at the recipe in the cookbook. It talked about the preparation stage, the sauce stage, the assembly stage, the cooking stage and even the cooling stage. The only thing it didn't offer an opinion on was when in the whole process it was best to ask a very important, very personal question. He supposed it was the gentlemanly thing to do to wait until the cooking stage.

"It looks ready for the oven to me," Garth said as he eyed the two pans of lasagna they'd prepared.

"I'm just adding a little extra cheese."

Garth opened the oven door and grabbed a pot holder. "Just tell me when you're ready to move them."

Garth took a deep breath. He was close to the cooking stage and he needed a springboard before he took his dive. "Moving them," he continued. "That's the kind of heavy lifting thing that women like husbands around for—"

"Why?" Sylvia looked up, puzzled. "They're not that heavy."

"I didn't mean these in particular." Garth started to sweat. "I just meant in general. Husbands are good for lifting things. Heavy things."

"I have a dolly."

Lord, that mercy thing you have—maybe you could kick some in now. At least let me get the question out. "Well, of course, that's not the only thing husbands are good for—"

"I should hope not." Sylvia put the last of the cheese on the lasagnas and nodded toward the oven. "These are ready."

Garth took the reprieve and lifted the lasagnas into the oven before closing the door.

"It's set at three hundred and fifty degrees. That should be hot enough," Sylvia said as she reached behind herself to untie her apron. "I think I'll go change before I tackle this kitchen."

"Before you do, why don't you sit down a minute and answer my question?"

"What question?"

Garth decided he needed to sit down even if Sylvia didn't. "Well, I'm getting to that. Continuing our conversation and all."

"You have a question about lasagnas?" Sylvia asked as she sank down into a chair across the table from Garth. "You're more likely to find the answer in the recipe book."

"No, it's not about lasagnas. It's about husbands."

Garth watched Sylvia stiffen. His hopes plummeted.

"I know some people think every woman needs a husband to be complete, but I don't." Sylvia said the words succinctly.

"Well, of course, you don't need a husband." Garth was starting to sweat in earnest now. "My question was more along the lines of whether you wanted one."

"I can get a date if I need one." Sylvia's lips were pursed. "You don't need to set me up with anyone."

"I'm not trying to set you up." Garth ran his fingers through his hair.

"Well, then, what exactly is your question?"

Sylvia looked at him in a way that made him feel sympathy for an insect pinned to the pasteboard of some third grader's science project. Garth looked at the wall to his right. He looked to the wall to his left. He even looked up at the ceiling. He hadn't timed this right. There were no flowers. No violin music. Not even a smiling woman sitting across from him. He was dead.

"My question is 'Will you marry me?'" he said softly.

Sylvia looked at him in shock. "Marry you?"

The color drained from Sylvia's face and then rushed back in a flush as she looked behind her shoulder. "And who's listening to the lesson this time?"

"What?"

"Your lessons on how to charm women," Sylvia said sharply as she stood up. "I'm tired of being part of an object lesson that you use to try and teach these boys manners."

"You think I'd want them to propose to someone just to show that they have the manners to pull it off?" Garth was astonished. "What kind of a fool do you think I am?"

Garth fumed about that question long after Sylvia left him sitting at the kitchen table. He hadn't really expected her to throw her arms around him and say yes when he asked her, but he'd certainly expected to be taken seriously. Instead, she'd stood up and run from the kitchen as if he had the plague.

Maybe I do have the plague, he thought to himself glumly as he cleaned the kitchen. Even God's mercy didn't help him get a respectable answer. He wondered what Matthew would have to say about that. Ah well, there was cleaning to do. He took his sponge and wiped off the back of the stove. There was even tomato pulp on the salt shaker. He didn't know Sylvia was standing in the doorway until he heard a little surprised squeak.

"I didn't think you'd still be here," Sylvia said. She'd obviously taken a shower and washed the tomato pulp out of her hair. "It's my mess. You don't have to clean it up."

"I don't mind."

Sylvia took a deep breath. She'd changed into a clean peach-colored blouse. She'd put on light peach lipstick and curled her hair. But she still didn't feel as poised as she'd like. Garth had rattled her and she'd reacted badly.

"I need to apologize," she began stiffly.

"No, you don't."

"It's just—I was a mess."

"There's no need to apologize. I'm sorry if I took you by surprise."

Sylvia bit her lip. She felt suddenly very lost. "It's just—whatever gave you that idea to propose?"

Garth looked at her and smiled, warm and lazy like a long summer afternoon. For the first time since she'd started squeezing tomatoes, Sylvia felt her soul lighten.

"I've had that particular idea for some time now. Maybe since that day I pulled you out of that snow-drift."

"You mean, you're serious?" Sylvia watched his eyes.

"Of course I'm serious," Garth said as he stepped closer. She'd forgotten how his eyes darkened and his lips turned up in a private half smile. "I wouldn't have asked you to marry me if I wasn't serious about it."

"But why?"

Garth stepped even closer and this time he cuddled a hand under her chin. "You're the love of my life. I'd like nothing better than spending the rest of my life with you."

"But I have all these kids—" Sylvia stalled. She needed to think. *Dear Lord, was he serious?*

Garth shrugged. "I've got plenty of room for kids."

"You're serious?" Sylvia repeated. The squeezing inside of her stomach was being replaced by a warm glowing heat. Garth wanted to marry her.

"I've never been more serious about anything in my life."

Sylvia looked at him. She'd become an excellent judge of the twitches that gave away kids who were lying. All she saw in Garth's eyes was a steady, unflinching sincerity.

"Are you going to ask me again?"

Garth smiled. "Try and stop me."

Sylvia smiled, too. Then Garth dipped his head and kissed her. Garth's kiss ran through her like a kick and ended up like bells in her ears. No, wait a minute, that was—

"—lasagna," Sylvia muttered as she pulled away from Garth. "The lasagna's done."

The kitchen timer was impatiently ringing.

"Mmm, it can cook a minute or two longer," Garth murmured as he nuzzled her ear. "First, I want to hear your answer to my proposal."

"You haven't even said if you love me yet."

"I love you more than life," Garth said simply. "I'm not perfect and I know you deserve a man who is more devout than me even though Matthew says all men start out from the same place with God—"

"He's right on that one," Sylvia said.

"I do promise you," Garth continued, "that as long as God gives me breath, you can always count on the fact that I'll do my best to love Him and love you."

Sylvia watched his face. The face of her beloved. She could spend a lifetime learning to know his face.

"Then the answer is yes," she whispered. "Yes, yes, yes!"

Epilogue

A month or so later

Sylvia and Garth had thirty flower bearers for their wedding—each one of the kids wanted to carry a bouquet of roses and Mrs. Buckwalter promised Robert would personally fly in dozens of roses from the flower marts in Denver. Mrs. Buckwalter gave Robert special directions on how to pick out the best of the pink roses and the freshest of the white roses and the most perfectly shaped of the ivory ones. Finally she offered to go with him to see that he did it right.

Robert assured his mother that he ran two Fortune 500 companies; he could see to some roses. Mrs. Buckwalter didn't listen. She sent Jenny with him.

As for Sylvia, she blanched when she realized how many roses were being planned. She pointed out that the money could provide for another teenager or two. Mrs. Buckwalter paid her no attention.

''It's your wedding day, my dear,'' the older woman said as though that explained everything.

And maybe it did, Sylvia thought.

As for Garth, he had only one request for the wedding. He wanted to surprise Sylvia with fresh preaches. He had Jenny help him place an order for a truckload of fresh spring peaches. Their odor filled the barn with summer and Sylvia smiled as she walked down the aisle.

*   *   *   *   *

Dear Reader,

I hope you enjoyed the story of Sylvia and Garth. I wanted to show a woman who—like most of us—has struggled with fear in her relationships. It would have been easy for Sylvia to listen only to those fears. But, in doing so, she'd have missed out on the gift of love Garth was offering.

If you have similar fears in your life, I pray you will not let them stop you from accepting the love of others, whether it be the love of a friend, a family member, or the love of that special man. In the beginning of the book, I chose the words of Isaiah 14:3 to remind us that God can give us rest from our fears. Once our fears have been put to rest, we can accept the gift of love and friendship others have for us.

May we all love well and fearlessly.

Janet Tronstad

REQUEST YOUR FREE BOOKS!

2 FREE INSPIRATIONAL NOVELS
PLUS 2
FREE
MYSTERY GIFTS

YES! Please send me 2 FREE Love Inspired® novels and my 2 FREE mystery gifts. After receiving them, if I don't wish to receive any more books, I can return the shipping statement marked "cancel." If I don't cancel, I will receive 4 brand-new novels every month and be billed just $3.99 per book in the U.S., or $4.74 per book in Canada, plus 25¢ shipping and handling per book and applicable taxes, if any*. That's a savings of at least 20% off the cover price! I understand that accepting the 2 free books and gifts places me under no obligation to buy anything. I can always return a shipment and cancel at any time. Even if I never buy another book from Steeple Hill, the two free books and gifts are mine to keep forever.

113 IDN EF26   313 IDN EF27

Name _____ (PLEASE PRINT) _____

Address _____ Apt. _____

City _____ State/Prov. _____ Zip/Postal Code _____

Signature (if under 18, a parent or guardian must sign)

Order online at www.LoveInspiredBooks.com

Or mail to Steeple Hill Reader Service™:

IN U.S.A.	IN CANADA
P.O. Box 1867	P.O. Box 609
Buffalo, NY	Fort Erie, Ontario
14240-1867	L2A 5X3

Not valid to current Love Inspired subscribers.

Want to try two free books from another series?
Call 1-800-873-8635 or visit www.morefreebooks.com

* Terms and prices subject to change without notice. NY residents add applicable sales tax. Canadian residents will be charged applicable provincial taxes and GST. This offer is limited to one order per household. All orders subject to approval. Credit or debit balances in a customer's account(s) may be offset by any other outstanding balance owed by or to the customer. Please allow 4 to 6 weeks for delivery.

LIREG06

CLASSICS

TITLES AVAILABLE NEXT MONTH

Don't miss these stories in January

SECOND CHANCES
AND
LOVE ONE ANOTHER
by Valerie Hansen

Love blossoms during an Arkansas summer
for two Southern couples.

NEVER ALONE
AND
NEW MAN IN TOWN
by Lyn Cote

Children help two women find the men
they've been waiting for.